Jacky Gillott was born in 1939 and began her writing career on the *Sheffield Telegraph* in Yorkshire. She worked in arts, news and current affairs divisions of the BBC, was the first woman reporter on ITN's News at Ten programme, contributed to *The Sunday Times, Punch, The Listener, Nova* and *Cosmopolitan,* and regularly reviewed novels for *The Times*. Until her recent death in September, 1980, Jacky Gillott was well known for her involvement with the BBC Radio 4 programme, *Kaleidoscope*. One of this country's finest writers, Jacky Gillott was the author of four other novels, including the highly acclaimed *The Head Case*.

Also by Jacky Gillott

Salvage
A True Romance
War Baby
The Head Case

Non-Fiction
Providence Place
For Better, for Worse

Jacky Gillott

Crying Out Loud

A PANTHER BOOK

GRANADA

London Toronto Sydney New York

Published by Granada Publishing Limited in 1981

ISBN 0 586 05389 1

First published in Great Britain by
Hodder and Stoughton Limited 1976
Copyright © Jacky Gillott 1976

The extract from 'I am vertical' is from *Crossing the Water*
by Sylvia Plath, published by Faber and Faber Ltd,
copyright Ted Hughes 1971.

Granada Publishing Limited
Frogmore, St Albans, Herts AL2 2NF
and
36 Golden Square, London W1R 4AH
866 United Nations Plaza, New York, NY 10017, USA
117 York Street, Sydney, NSW 2000, Australia
100 Skyway Avenue, Rexdale, Ontario, M9W 3A6, Canada
61 Beach Road, Auckland, New Zealand

Made and printed in Great Britain by
Cox & Wyman Ltd, Reading
Set in Baskerville

Granada ®
Granada Publishing ®

Part One

The sombre fact is that we are the cruellest and most ruthless species that has ever walked the earth . . . In general however it seems to be true that aggression in the female is only fully aroused in response to threat, especially if the young are involved: whereas male aggression operates more spontaneously in rivalry, territoriality and display.

Human Aggression by Anthony Storr

It is more natural to me, lying down
Then the sky and I are in open conversation
And I shall be useful when I lie down
         finally:
Then the trees may touch me for once and
    the flowers have time for me.

From 'I am Vertical' by Sylvia Plath

I

"ANSWER ME!"

Peter turned his gaze away from Fu Manchu and saw his mother wearing the red, screwed-up expression that made his ribs go cold and hard. He stared at her blankly for a second.

"Well?" she demanded.

"What?"

"Poached or *boiled*?" she cried, her eyes shooting upwards with exasperation.

Hypnotised by her, he hesitated. "Poached or boiled?" he repeated.

"Oh, come on!" And then, "Rod?" she asked of his younger brother, lying on his stomach before the television, unmoved by the exchange.

"Poached," said Rod. "*Please*," and he rolled over lazily to smile at his mother.

"Boiled," decided Peter.

"Oh, for crying out loud!" Maggie's face went rigid. Her lower teeth showed for a second as she clenched both jaws together. Then, making an effort to control herself, she swung towards the door.

"You shouldn't *ask*," remarked Kit from behind his newspaper. "*Tell* them. Save yourself the sweat."

"Don't you start," said Maggie rudely and went out. She came back. "What about you?" she asked.

"Me?" Kit put his paper down.

"Poached or boiled?"

"Me? Oh, I don't feel like anything just yet. Later."

The door slammed and the three males of the Makin household returned to the sources of their absorption. "I'll make my own," yelled Kit from (as the family joke had it) behind *The Times.*

An Oriental gentleman swung at his victim with a sword. Something resembling a hairy football rolled across the palace floor and came to rest against the clawed leg of a chair with gilt, carved wings.

"Yuk," exclaimed Rod, and making an imaginary cut across his throat rolled over gurgling, then rearranged himself comfortably, stomach downwards, on the enormous velvet patchwork cushion.

"I'm sure it's bad for you," Kit mused, shaking the pages straight to search the lower columns for a letter on the origins of well-dressing. Nobody moved.

When the programme ended, Rod, without getting up, reached his arm as far as he could and punched up another channel. As his hand returned to its cupping position beneath his chin, Maggie appeared simultaneously on the screen and in the room.

"Here you are!" she sighed loudly, kicking the door wider open to allow for the tray. She banged it tinnily down on the table and caught sight of herself on the box. She laughed.

Maggie on the box was trim and fresh. Morning sunlight fell across her smooth, dark hair and made her blouse opaquely pearly. She smiled at (next shot) two blond children seated the far side of a scrubbed pine table. They were waving their spoons in delight as she poured Wheatinuts into their bowls.

"Little toads," observed Maggie, of the children.

"They just *love* it!" smiled Maggie, to the camera.

"If they're paid to eat it." Maggie struck at the top of a boiled egg.

"They *know* what's good for them!" cried the whole of the Makin family in silly voices and turned away from the rest of the commercial.

"Poached, boiled." Maggie moved the plates around the low table. "Three poached for you," she said, handing Kit his. "I'm not cooking twice. I hate cleaning out the poacher."

"I'd've done it."

"Like hell."

She sat down beside him on the sofa and took a cigarette from his packet. Lighting it, she drew a lungful of smoke and slumped back. "That's better. I'll be nice again in two seconds. Turn the telly off, Rod."

"Oh, but it's . . ."

8

"Turn it *off*."

He made a groaning noise and did as she said. "Can we watch Z Cars later?"

"No."

"You said you'd be nice again in two seconds."

"I meant ten."

"It is ten."

"I meant twenty then."

"Oh . . . *you* . . .!"

"I don't know why you can't go outside and play." With one hand Kit dusted his eggs with salt, with the other he removed his glasses and rubbed his eyes against the back of his knuckles.

"Head?" Maggie asked gently.

"Oh not too bad."

"There's no-one to play with," said Rod.

"There's one another," said Maggie.

Peter nearly said something, but silently stuck a teaspoon into his egg instead.

"Yes, for heaven's sake, you've got one another to play with." Laboriously, Kit began cutting at the plate in his lap, keeping his knees together.

"This egg's full of slime," Peter observed.

"It *would be*."

Not knowing what his mother meant but feeling the cold breath of her sarcasm, Peter avoided the transparent, slippery stuff and pierced the yolk which was still unpleasantly whole. Something flipped in his stomach and landed flatly. He looked up and saw his mother was speaking to him.

"What?" he paused, sick.

"What *do* you like?"

"Oh, lots of things." He couldn't think of anything.

"Do you eat everything at school?"

"What?"

"*Do* you eat everything at school?"

"You've got to."

"You've got to at home as well." Kit explored his eggs.

"What?" Peter turned to his father. Actually, he'd heard him, but he needed a space.

"You must wear your hearing aid, darling."

"I do."

"At home, I mean, darling," explained Maggie.

"He forgets to bring it home," Rod pointed out.

9

"Oh shut up." Peter aimed a knee at his brother under the table.

"Oh well," yawned Maggie, "I'd rather he forgot to bring it home than forget to take it to school."

"Shepherd's pie, chips, fish fingers . . ." Peter listed things, trying to remember.

"You don't like *my* shepherd's pie."

"Well," Peter shrugged and stirred up his egg a little. "It's got *things* in it."

"*Things?*" echoed Maggie dully.

"If he eats every bit of his egg can we watch Z Cars?" tried Rod.

"The sun is *shining* outside." Kit sounded resolute. Rod looked at his father and grinned. "O.K.," he said; "you come and play with us."

"Sorry, Rod, I've got a head."

"Daddy's head hurts," said Maggie, expelling smoke over their supper. "Poor Dad."

"Is it the bullet?" asked Rod eagerly. Rod, the smaller and younger (by one year and one week) of the two boys, loved to hear about the bullet. They both did, but he asked more often.

"Either that or Fu Manchu," smiled Kit, ducking his head to catch a glistening streak of yellow.

"You shouldn't let them have the volume on so loud," Maggie said.

"We can't hear if we don't," Rod replied, mouth full.

"*I can.*" Peter aimed another blow at his brother.

"Oh, don't fight."

"Tell us about the bullet."

"Not again, darling, leave Daddy in peace."

(What a nice word peace is, thought Peter. But he wanted to hear the story.)

"It was when you were in Vietnam, wasn't it?" urged Rod.

"You *know* it was."

"When you were covering the advance down Highway One, wasn't it?"

"No, when I was dancing with the Bolshoi ballet."

"And you got caught in an ambush, didn't you?"

"Or was it in the three-legged race on the sands at Burnham-on-Crouch?"

"Oh, come *on*, Daddy!"

"Not now, darling." Maggie reached for Rod's plate. "Daddy doesn't enjoy going over it all again. He was *hurt*, you know." She emphasised the word — meaninglessly, to Rod, who had never in all his nine years ever hurt himself badly. He fell out of trees and bounced.

"Was your leg shot up at the same time?" asked Peter. "Or was that later?"

He knew it was the same time, or fractionally before, since the shell had gone off first and his father, attempting to escape, had given his position away and been shot at by a panic-stricken A.R.V.N. But he wanted to know all the same. He wanted the details absolutely right to tell the other boys. They were a guarantee of friendship. The other boys would give him sweets and let him in their gang if he told them about his father. One boy, whose father had been killed in Belfast, was even more popular. But he was a boarder and boarders had all the luck.

"Yo—ou make me feel so ol—ld!" sang Kit, handing his plate to Maggie, who stood up. "War experiences," he mused, "the lifeblood of old men."

Maggie gave him a quick look, pressed her lips together as if to prevent an invalid's smile, then bent for the other plates. "Outside now, darlings, *please*."

"Don't we get any pudding?"

"You can take a banana out with you."

"I hate this garden," said Peter.

"*Please!*" He glanced up and saw the imploring look. He thought his mother might cry and he couldn't bear that. She'd cried quite a lot since they'd moved here.

"All right . . ." he grumbled, walking out of the room as slowly as he possibly could. "C'mon, Rod."

"Shall we take our guns?"

"O.K."

And they clattered up, over the uncarpeted stair boards, to find their guns, one of the few precious things they hadn't entrusted to the bottom of packing cases and trunks.

"You be a V.C. and I'll be a Yank."

"No," argued Peter, uncertainly though, for he wasn't completely sure that the Yanks *were* heroes in this particular case. Heroes were getting muddled. He preferred the clear alliances of World War II. "Let's be Germans and English," he suggested. That was easier.

The garden was a peculiar, but not interesting shape . . . like a triangle with its top sliced off. In fact, the entire plot on which the house and garden stood was a perfect triangle, with the pavement outside the front gate forming an apex. Behind the wrought-iron gate lay a short path flanked by small areas of what Maggie had called crazy paving. Then the house, and behind it, surrounded by high red brick walls, the dull rhomboid of garden. A stretch of grass, then a stretch of dry, pale brown soil with a sprout of pampas grass in the corner. That was all. In spite of the height of the red brick walls, they were not sufficiently high to prevent anyone on the first floor of the houses either side overlooking the Makins' patch because their house, number 43, Wellington Gardens, lay right in a fork of the road, its two branches passing either side of the stranded triangle. Their house seemed to have been left like a beached ship in the middle of the road which continued on, down to the river. You couldn't see the river from number 43 (except from the window of one bedroom too dilapidated to use as yet), because, although it was only thirty yards or so away, their view was obscured by a large solid block of grey pebble-dash, which rose above their back wall and formed the rear, windowless elevation of another house that *did* face the river with a complacent air of ugly grandeur.

Maggie didn't yet like the boys to go down to the river on their own to play so they mooched around their unfeatured patch, kicking at the plantain-strewn turf and morosely clicking their guns at one another. The flat leaves of the plane trees (which lined Wellington Gardens and gave this suburban, Edwardian street a cool, green, luxuriance it wholly lacked in winter time) dipped over their red brick wall and sighed mutedly in the evening breeze.

Bored, they began to wrestle with one another, trying to work up a little feeling fury. Their breath came in noisy, smothered bursts but they were otherwise quite silent in their battle. A jet, on its flight path to London Airport, roared overhead.

They no longer bothered to stop and look up, or put their hands over their ears, although, on their first night at number 43, Rod had fallen out of bed screaming when the roof had shuddered through his dreams.

For the past three years, they'd been accustomed to the night-clamour of the countryside, cows bemoaning lost calves and a confused cockerel, crowing. Understandable noises. Even the squeals of creatures carried off by the owl or the vixen's scream hadn't seemed as threatening as the turbulent sound which had shaken their first evening here.

Aware of the rumble, though not looking up, Peter thought everything here was much closer . . . the people, the houses, the traffic.

And yet, in another sense (he managed to hold Rod, face down, arms pinned behind his back), they were all much further away. They carried on in their own fashion. Nobody smiled at you in the street. Nobody waved from their cars. ("Leggo!" shrieked Rod.) Everything just whizzed past. "*Leggo!*" Rod yelled again, his face smothered.

The distance that Peter's poor hearing placed between him and other people could be infinitely lengthened by an effort of will. He sat astride his brother's back, ignoring his shouts. He didn't find it at all difficult just to sit there thinking his thoughts.

More by accident than design (perhaps Peter's concentration wavered) Rod wriggled himself free from the hold, swung over and struck his brother hard in the mouth. Both yelled, Peter at the higher and more sustained pitch, for when he took his hand away from his mouth he saw, streaked across his palm, rich slugs of saliva and blood.

"*Well!*" asserted Rod nervously as he watched the blackish stuff ooze from his brother's swelling upper lip, "You asked for it."

2

To PREVENT ANY further outbreak of violence, Maggie suggested the home movies.

"Oh Lord," Kit cried, "it's half past bloody eight already."

"Never mind," Maggie said quietly, and she heaved Peter on to her lap. He didn't resist. Sometimes she felt warm and soft.

Rod, asked to help find and erect the screen, managed to drop it so many times that Kit, cursing gently, limped over to fix it himself. He propped it up on the back of the sofa against the wall and returned to the projector, lowering himself with small grunts, on to the floor.

Eventually, the oblong of light was focussed sharply and centrally on to the screen. The projector roared.

"This machine's going to pack up soon." Kit knocked it experimentally.

"You bought it with my first maternity grant."

"So I did. Well, there you are then: ten years old. Ready, everybody?"

Because they possessed no curtains and it was still palely light outside, it was impossible to see the pictures very clearly, but they were so familiar it barely mattered.

Most of the films had been taken when the boys were tiny. Kit had been very enthusiastic about keeping a complete record, making Maggie push the pram up and down the same stretch of road or street market or past a flowering shrub until he'd composed his background properly.

The first pictures were of Peter, small and blind looking, in Maggie's arms.

"Ah-h, isn't he sweet?" tittered Rod, jealous that it wasn't his turn yet.

The baby blinked and tried to push the sun away, but failing, shook both fists, silently squalled and turned his head into a green cotton chest.

Peter again. Lying on the floor, waving and struggling as if stranded, then suddenly ejecting a spout of vomit. Rod laughed.

"You were always being sick. You smelt awful," mused Maggie, kissing Peter's head. (In the dusk, he let her, pretending he hadn't noticed.)

"This is the one *I* like." Kit sat back on his haunches with enjoyment.

A shot, looking down into a dark, basement area. An open door, half glass, and — facing it — two dustbins. Nothing else for a moment and then, unexpectedly placed, a dab of movement from behind the door, low down. Nothing recognisable. Then a further bolder movement. Peter's (then curly) head, peering out, weaving, gazing crossly upwards, his head wobbling at the end of a plump, naked body which was suddenly propelled out into the narrow grimy yard.

"Our slum period," laughed Kit.

"The Royal Borough of South Kensington."

"When am *I* coming on?" enquired Rod peevishly.

"Soon."

"Hurry up then. Gosh, don't you look funny?"

Peter. Trussed up in a baby bouncer, he sprang helplessly up and down in the frame, his face red and blotchy. He slowed with his back to the camera after a lengthy spiralling twist and hung there, his sealed, pyjama-ed feet dangling two inches above the ground.

"You loved that," said Maggie. Peter thought it looked horrible. He had no real memory of it.

"Crumbs, you are heavy," Maggie shifted.

"Here I am! Here I am!"

Rod lay against the green cotton chest, still and sleeping. A much more peaceful baby he looked.

"What an ugly mug," jeered Peter.

"Look who's talking, *Dracula*."

The smiling, downturned faces of grown-ups, suspended over the baby. The cot. The baby in the cot. Two small hands gripped the side and Peter's furious face looked over. The cot tipped towards him. A large, blurred hand came down in front of the camera, balanced the cot and withdrew. A single small hand reappeared on the far side, waving a floppy yellow bear aggressively.

"Making friends," said Kit in the sort of voice that left Peter wondering.

"When's the newspaper bit?" he asked, to get rid of the feeling.

"Soon."

"I was easier, wasn't I?" enquired Rod with exaggerated gravity. "To have."

"Second babies always are. It's only natural," his mother answered.

"Mm."

Peter. He sat upright on the floor holding the arms of a clown doll in both hands and loosely bounced the creature up and down just slightly out of the crawling baby's reach. Rod made a grab and tipped over on his face.

"Ha! Ha!"

"Shut up — here's the newspaper bit."

Everybody laughed. There, sitting on the old sofa, just like Kit, Peter sat behind *The Times*, his feet sticking out from beneath it, his arms too short to hold it fully open. From the bottom right of the frame a dark head appeared. The subsequent body was hauled unsteadily up against the sofa and Rod made a lunge for the newspaper. There was a lot of soundless flapping and snatching. Eventually, Rod tore off a whole sliver of newspaper and, stuffing it in his mouth, turning towards the camera, he began eating it. He staggered forward, losing edge. A furry, pink, chomping mouth filled the screen.

"I walked jolly early, didn't I?" he remarked.

"At ten months."

"When did Peter walk?"

"Oh, I don't know, about fourteen months. But then he didn't have anyone to copy as you did." Maggie tried to deflect Rod's sense of competition.

"Did I talk earlier than him?"

"Oh, belt up!" Peter made a pushing gesture and felt his mother's grip tighten.

"Did I?"

"Well, yes, I suppose you did. But you always *were* a gas bag. Anyway," Maggie added, "he couldn't speak properly because he couldn't hear properly, but we didn't realise that then." And again she kissed him lightly on the top of his head. Peter wriggled.

"I get sick of you talking," he said to his brother. "You never stop. And you say such stupid things."

"Oh yeah?"

"Yeah."

"Oh, look!" intervened Maggie brightly. "Cowboys."

The pair of them sat in a sandpit wearing huge cowboy hats over their noses and nothing else at all.

"I can see your willy!" Rod rolled himself up in a ball on the floor and giggled.

"What's so funny about *that*?"

"Nothing," snorted Rod, giggling.

"The picture's improving. It's getting darker outside." Kit adjusted the focus a little.

"Nearly bedtime," said Maggie.

"Oh, not yet! Not yet!"

"A bit more then." Kit turned, "How's the mouth?"

Peter remembered his sore lips. "It hurts like hell," he said.

"Like what?"

"Like hell."

"Don't . . . oh, well, *I* do it." Kit tried to sort out some of the film unspooling on the floor.

"Where were we living then?"

"I can't recall. Highbury, I think. Mags?"

"Highbury, yes. No, Stoke Newington."

"There's the park."

"Yes, I loved the park."

"I can remember the park," said Peter.

"Can you?"

"Yes, there was a zoo."

"A little one. It was nice."

"How many places?"

"How many places, what, Rod?"

"'Ve we lived in?"

"God knows," said Kit.

"How old was I then?"

"You, Peter, oh, about four."

"I can remember it."

"Yes, you have a good memory."

"I can remember it too," claimed Rod.

"You can't."

"I can."

"What can you remember?" demanded Peter.

"I remember that zoo. I remember that playground." (Seeing swings on the screen).

"Only 'cos *I* said."

"No, I *do*."

17

"What was in it then?"

"Oh, lions, tigers, that sort of thing."

"No there wasn't. There wasn't anything like that."

"Pack it in," said Kit wearily.

"We've lived in ten different places. Haven't we?"

"Oh, I don't know, Rod. I've lost count."

"Why've we lived in so many?"

"Oh, heavens, I remember *that* . . ." Maggie laughed as she saw a piece of film she'd taken — Kit and the boys having a race on Hampstead Heath. The images were interspersed with black-outs and eliminating flashes of sun. Kit was puffing and panting, and waggling his elbows in an extravagant display of effort, pretending he couldn't keep up with his sons.

"You were *pretending!*" observed Peter, aware of it for the first time.

"I was *then*," Kit replied. Peter looked at his father quickly. The light of the projector etched his profile. It was sort of stiff as though Kit was looking at the screen but *not* looking at the same time.

The film ran out with a clattering sound and the unimpeded light of the projector bloomed forth, enlarging all their outlines.

"Oh-h-h!" moaned both boys. "Isn't there any more?"

"No."

"What, honestly?"

"Bedtime."

"Nothing of Sigvales?"

"Not on this reel."

"On another reel?"

"I haven't joined it up. There isn't much."

"Oh, go on."

"Yes, go on," urged Maggie, "I'd like to see something of Sigvales."

Six valleys. The clustered meeting place of Dorset hills and streams they'd so recently left.

"As long as you don't mope about it. There isn't much, I warn you."

"It won't take long then," cracked Rod, pleased with his sharpness.

"You can help me spool this up first," said Kit.

"Hadn't we better go and get changed into our pyjamas?"

"You idle little bastard. All right, then."

"It's so beautiful," breathed Rod mournfully, a few minutes later, as they once more looked out from the hill behind their house. Smoothed knobs of green, peculiar, piled-up shapes dotted with sheep and beyond them, bluer hills, paler valleys, never coming to any conclusion, simply folding away one after another until their blueness was that of the sky itself.

"I wish we were still there."

"How can you wish that?" Maggie sounded almost cross.

"I miss it," said Rod dolefully as the lens travelled through steep, sandy-banked lanes, pitted with badger setts, and then panned upwards over ivied tree-roots to the delicate tent of leaves overhead. They moved, overlapping greens, vainly nudging out winks of sunlight.

"That's a good shot, though I say it myself. I don't know why I didn't keep it up." Kit's profile eased into pleasure.

"How *can* you miss it," Peter heard his mother say hotly, "when you never really explored it properly. All *you* ever looked at was the telly."

There was no reply. It was an old, tired issue.

They saw Maggie alone, digging. Maggie driving the smokey-faced cow through a deep meadow of buttercup-grass. Maggie pursued by geese.

"*There* we are!" Rod pointed.

"*Loving* it," said Maggie sarcastically.

They were making feeble pokes with a broom and a pitch-fork at a pile of dirty bedding. Then Peter was trying to sweep up his brother instead. When Rod raised his pitchfork, the picture was suddenly cut off.

"You hit me," complained Rod.

"I certainly did," his father replied mildly.

"Any more?"

"No."

"*Is* that all?" Maggie was disappointed. "Truthfully?"

"Yes."

"Oh."

Peter could feel her sadness as though her heart expressed it right through her jumper.

"Ah well," she breathed out briskly, and he felt her about to rise, about to push him off her lap.

"I'm sorry," he said quickly, meaning sorry for her.

"Don't *you* start trying to pretend you care. Let's face it, you hated ever going there. City lads, the pair of you."

He wanted to protest against her unfairness, but she'd

19

dumped him off her lap and was brushing the creases out of her skirt. He lost the sweet smell of her. Not a put-on smell, a fragrance that seemed to come from inside. At Sigvales she'd smelt of milk and animals. He'd hated that.

"Bed."

"Oh!" Rod had to make the statutory wail.

"*Bed.*"

"I wish Aunt Carrie hadn't ever died," attempted Rod again with an air of resentment he didn't quite feel, but it was a way of stretching time a little further.

"BED!" screamed Kit suddenly, from the floor. "Why do you always have to wait until you've made us angry? Why do you want us to shout?"

"Mummy isn't shouting."

"I shall soon. Now go on."

"I still wish she hadn't died."

Maggie ignored him. She knew his tricks. "Upstairs." One hand on his bottom she steered him out of the room and upstairs, Peter dawdling, leaden-footed behind.

"Why didn't you just *sell* this horrible house of hers?" Rod trailed one hand over the faded brown print of the wallpaper. Everything was brown, thought Peter. The sticky-looking woodwork, the bare boards, the cupboards in the kitchen, even the light that seeped through the ginger-coloured stained glass in the front door first thing in the morning. It flowed through the house like the kind of soup you had in hotels. He heard his mother explaining something.

"What?" he said.

"I said it all worked out very well for us."

"*Why*, though?"

"Because we couldn't afford to stay where we were."

"But *why*?" Peter wasn't convinced his mother had told them all the reasons. He thought she'd given them a special, simply constructed account that left out a lot of tangles. Now she was repeating it, saying there had been more work than she could manage on her own since Daddy was ill, and when he replied that Daddy wasn't there that often anyway, she said that was another reason: the travelling had become too expensive.

"How can we afford to stay here then?" Rod chipped in as they reached the bathroom, its huge, four-legged bath standing like a monument on brown lino, patterned to resemble parquet flooring but fooling nobody. A buyer had not been found for the cottage in Sigvales yet, so where, he wanted to know, was the money coming from?

"It's easier to find work here," Maggie repeated quietly and reached out for the blind. She'd put it up to stop the neighbours peering in. At Sigvales, the leaves outside formed a screen beyond the window and when, in the autumn, they fell off, leaving a lattice of twigs, it didn't matter since there was nobody nearby to look in. "And if they did, I shouldn't care," Maggie had laughed once.

She turned on the great harsh taps and a rumbling began to stir throughout the house.

"What?" said Peter.

"I said she always wanted children here."

"Why didn't she invite us then?" Rod was peeling off his clothes and dropping them on the floor as if undressing was still a race between them — as it had been when they shared a bath and someone had to sit with their back to the taps. Now they were too big; they made the water slop on the floor so they took first and second turns.

Maggie shrugged, and stood, hands on hips, watching the iron-tinted water splash in the bath. "She was a bit screwy towards the end."

"*Really* screwy? What did she do? Did she look like this?" Rod crossed his eyes and let his tongue loll out.

"Stupid," sniffed Peter.

"No, of course she didn't . . . She . . ." Her voice was drowned.

"What?"

"Was just a very old lady."

"Do you think she'll come back to haunt us?"

The house had an attic floor, riddled with curious small rooms all opening one into the other, some with doors only boy height as though the servants had been dwarfs, once. Rod and Peter had been promised it for themselves but they found it creepy after dark.

"I should think she'll be too glad of the rest she's getting to bother."

"But just *suppose*," pressed Rod who extended all conversation to its furthest possible length even when he frightened himself doing so.

"No, I won't suppose," answered Maggie firmly and felt the water. "Oh, hurry up Peter, would you — you haven't started yet and it's nearly ten o'clock."

"Come on, come on, come on." Kit limped in. "Everybody's tired."

"It *is* a shame." Maggie bent to look at Peter's damaged lip. "You are a little pig, Rod."

"He was asking for it. I didn't mean to."

"If't'd been you, you'd've yelled your head off." Peter was suddenly aware from Maggie's face, that his own was spoiled by the injury. He wanted to hit out.

"Always Peter who suffers." Maggie was bent, picking up strewn clothes. Kit, noticing, said, "You might learn to tidy up for yourselves. Can't you see your mother's exhausted." He stood impatiently, hands in pockets. "Come along, I want to watch the news."

"So do *I*," said Maggie, "want to."

"Don't start quarrelling," checked Rod, sensing a dull spark. He stuck a toe in the bath.

The grown ups laughed and looked at one another. Peter, struggling with a shirt sleeve he had left unbuttoned, felt relief open up a gap in his throat (though he'd been quite unaware of the restriction until it was removed). Sometimes he wished he could just move moods around like his brother did. Rod seemed able to arrange people's moods to suit himself, or adapt until the atmosphere was congenial. *Manipulate* people was the expression his father used to describe this gift. Rod wasn't frightened of speaking to anyone though he was often frightened of *doing* things. More frightened than me, thought Peter who'd once accepted a dare to walk alone down a twisting, branch-encircled lane at night. Rod wouldn't do it. At least, he'd gone outside and pretended he had, but they'd watched him from an upstairs window and seen that he'd simply hung about in the open, milky-looking meadow for five minutes before running back into the house. Recalling it gave Peter a satisfaction that spread through him like a warm drink on a cold day.

"Tell us a story!" tried Rod. Maggie enjoyed telling stories.

"Not *now*."

"What?" Peter said.

"*Hurry up!*"

People always shouted at him. He could pull a blind down between himself and their shouting; just cut it off. Dull the anger of it. They'd always shouted at him. He was accustomed to hostile faces split with frustration thrusting suddenly into his — he could make his eyes go out of focus so that all he saw was an undefined quivering. They had always shouted because he rarely heard the first time. They'd thought he was a dreamer. They hadn't realised he was deaf.

His mouth hurt the moment he lay in the dark with Rod twitchily asleep in the next bed and the television muffled downstairs. He got up and opened the door a crack so that a little light came up from the naked bulb in the hall and then clambered back into bed. He still couldn't adapt himself to the unfamiliar angles of the house and its abnormal noises. It smelt odd, too. It smelt of a particular kind of lavatory, like one he'd once, in desperation, been forced to use in Quiberon on their single foreign holiday. The crude Breton lavatory, a dank hole in the ground, seemed to be drilled down to the sea bed — out of it came a gust of excrement mixed with rotting fish and the salts of the sea. It was here, in this house too, very faintly and not just in the Edwardian willow pattern lavatory that his mother thought so splendid. (It possessed a dangling, rusty chain that he hadn't mastered. You had to pull it down and release it very, very slowly if it was to work at all and sometimes it failed to flush, even then.)

The whole house was a jumble with dark rooms and darker fireplaces all facing nonsensical ways, threaded unevenly together like a many-beaded necklace made with clumsy fingers and too thick a string for the beads to lie easily alongside one another. He thought about that, and liked it. It was a good way to describe the arrangement of rooms — the kitchen particularly. There were three kitchens really, the main one, a yellow square that connected to another, bare of everything but a green enamel stove, and the third, the smallest of the succession, a narrow tiled place with a useless and ancient black boiler in it. From there a back door opened on to the dustbins. The house was not a perfect square although it had all the solidity of a cube. Peter thought that from one of the many planes that flew overhead, it might appear to be a fat and irregular triangle, shaped to fit its eccentric island site in the fork of the road. Inside it was always dark, as other houses were when it rained outside.

Sharp, unexpected pains shot through his lip and kept him from sleep and comfortable dreaming.

A dreamer . . .

(That's what they all used to call him.)

"Just one of nature's dreamers . . ." Granny had always sighed kindly whenever anyone showed signs of being cross over something they took to be a blunder or piece of absent-mindedness. Just a *dreamer*. And then she'd say that Maggie was a dreamer, Kit was a dreamer . . . and so . . . And she'd smile as though the logic was obvious.

He'd come to resent the description. Pressing both hands to his mouth to smother the ache, Peter thought with annoyance of the way grown ups had always tried to pretend (since he *was* a dreamer) that his dreaming was of a fine, high order. "What are you dreaming about?" they'd say with fond and silly expressions and if he told them . . . I'm thinking of rockets. Or Daleks. Or (sometimes) nothing in particular . . . they would look terribly disappointed. So he didn't bother telling them anything at all usually.

They'd gone on and on, he thought, pulling the blankets up around his throbbing face, about his *imagination*, seizing his paintings and drawings, overpraising them, buying expensive paints and French crayons which looked very nice but didn't interest him terribly. Well (he corrected himself as he lay in the dark) he'd stopped being interested once Rod had stopped drawing rotten matchstick men and started copying his own drawings — pages full of soldiers in proper uniforms and hand grenades that exploded if you drew a ragged star shape round them.

And there was the piano.

He'd hoped it would be left behind in the move, but no, it was grimly trundled in through the front door of number 43, swathed and roped like a corpse. His mother had once told anyone who asked that she thought Peter was musical. But what she didn't know (and he smiled to himself) was that the decayed mouth of keys couldn't be made to play in tune.

But that was before they'd found out what was wrong. It had taken years to find out. Peter hadn't known he was partially deaf of course, but certain incidents, things that happened before the deafness was properly established, stood out in his memory. Thinking of them now, with the wisdom of awareness, he realised they'd been clear enough signs. *Why* had no one guessed?

When he was . . . (and he calculated in his head, counting back the moves they'd made) . . . about four, he'd started to cross a road without Maggie's hand gripping his. He'd heard her scream but he hadn't heard the lorry until its brakes hissed and wailed and the whole thing had seemed to jolt over itself on its thick front tyres.

The driver had flung himself out of the cab swearing at Maggie, waving his arms, pointing. And the anger of the man, so *wrong* somehow, so streaked and raw and wrong, had made him sob into his mother's skirts.

("If you'd been *much* deafer," she'd once explained, "there'd never have been the confusion . . . But everyone said, oh, he's a dreamer. Or, first children often *are* late talkers . . .")

Some time after the lorry incident (the interval was vague even though he thought about it hard to try and shut off the mumble of television that seeped up from downstairs), he'd had his adenoids and tonsils out. And there, Maggie, who had shouted at the lorry driver, shouted all over again, pushing her way through the ghostly white nuns who surrounded him, pecking round him like phantom geese. She'd pushed through and sat beside him ignoring the subdued flapping and hissing of the flock.

At least my ears have never hurt me, he thought miserably, his mouth feeling as large and loose as an uncooked sausage. It was very tempting to go downstairs and whimper to his parents, but they'd only send him upstairs again, so he thought about the time his tonsils were taken out and the peculiar man who'd taken them out. He'd worn a mirror fixed to his forehead and he wasn't English. He was very small and bald and he wore sparkling glasses that glittered so much you couldn't tell if he was looking at you or not. And when he spoke all the words were unfamiliar.

He'd made Peter stand in a corner and then he'd walked away to the further opposite corner, turned his back and started whispering things.

"Can you hear vat I say?" he'd demanded, turning. "Repeat vat I say." And he'd gone on whispering things . . . numbers, words, only a few of which Peter could recognise, but because he'd understood the man wanted him to say something, he'd mumbled some shapeless responses.

After that, everything had gone on the same as before. They'd watched and waited for the improvement, but everything was much as it had always been. When they'd gone back to see the man with the foreign voice, he told Maggie severely that everything was all right and Peter had just let it "become a habit".

Rod made little whimpering noises in his sleep. Peter scowled at him in the darkness but couldn't be bothered to go and hit him. Anyway, he'd now become quite interested in remembering things. He was remembering Miss Clements who'd first taught him at primary school.

Miss Clements hadn't liked little boys. Miss Clements had had pale sandy hair which she drew back from her face in a knot too complicated to contain it all. Behind her glasses — which had no frames and looked as though they cut into her nose and the little swell of cheek beneath the rim — had bristled two rows of perfectly white eyelashes. She'd always dressed in sandy colours which gave her the appearance of a meek plump animal — a hamster or a guinea pig perhaps — but she'd had a predator's swooping temper.

He could feel her now, descending on him . . . feel her at his shoulder blades. He could hear himself crying "What?" (the word came from him like the habitual silent tic of somebody else, a spasm of eyelid or nostril). *"What?"*

"You're so slow!" she'd shouted. "You haven't been listening!" And her biro had come slashing through his book like a knife, leaving a fine gash of scarlet across the page.

She'd kept him in and sent a letter to Maggie which she had read with trembling anger. The following day Maggie had come to fetch him from school, looking quite unrecognisable in a friend's borrowed clothes . . . a black fur hat and a long, fitted black coat which looked as though it had been made of tiny moleskins all stitched together. She had worn her own very high, laced black boots. And she'd stood in the doorway, a fine black eagle, more than a match for Miss Clements' tawny owl. (He smiled to himself as he recalled her stepping into the classroom on her high, proud heels. The door had closed behind her and after that, Miss Clements had tried to be as nice as pi to him. She'd moved him to the front of the class where she'd petrified him with her attentive smiles.)

Why don't you listen . . . ! (It was actually Maggie, more than anyone, who shouted.)

Downstairs, there was a religious ooze of music on the television, like something squeezed out of a barrel organ. He tested his upper lip with his tongue to see if the swelling had subsided at all. He half-hoped it hadn't. He remembered once hitting Rod in the mouth when they lived in Sigvales. He'd been very envious of the mulberry protrusion which had attracted such a lot of sympathy.

Sigvales . . . When his mother had tearfully said they would have to leave the cottage, he'd been rather excited at the idea of going back to a town.

26

(Still, it was there they'd discovered what was wrong. Things were better after that.)

When they'd first moved to Sigvales, Maggie had dragged him round a whole new range of specialists. For the fifth time he'd sat in front of an audiometric machine with earphones on, nodding Yes every time he heard the signal. But it had been different. He'd only said Yes when he really *could* hear the signal and not when he thought they wanted him to say Yes. In that hospital, nobody had seemed cross with him at all and they hadn't made an excessive show of being pleased only when he'd answered Yes. They'd even said Good when he'd answered No.

Like the others, the new specialist had worn a mirror on his head, but he spoke English in a slow and gentle voice. He spoke to *me*, thought Peter. Not Mummy. He explained to *me* what they were going to do.

He'd been given an anaesthetic while they explored. That was good, in hospital. The nurses had been nice and didn't say he had to stay in bed all the time even if he didn't feel ill. They'd had ice cream every day if they wanted it, in hospital. And he hadn't minded when the doctor had said there was nothing they could do except give him a hearing aid. He hadn't even minded having a hearing aid. It was a rather nice little machine with a black box to keep it in and a special place for the batteries and spare lead. It didn't show under his long hair.

But something hadn't been quite so agreeable. The stain of it lay in his mind still and after thinking hard for a few moments, it came back to him quite distinctly . . . A very odd conversation between Mr. Stephens the specialist and his mother.

"You say you're rhesus negative, Mrs. Makin?"

(That's why he remembered it so clearly. He'd been alerted and surprised by the word rhesus. He'd thought rhesus was something to do with monkeys.)

"Yes," she'd said.

"And you say Peter is your first child?"

And then there'd been a pause during which Maggie had snapped her bag open and shut. "Yes," she had repeated eventually.

He had seen that she was looking very tense as though her teeth were crushed together.

And then Mr. Stephens had said something about this kind of thing being caused by "antibodies" which rhesus mothers had in their bloodstream after their first babies. And his mother had gone on repeating that he, Peter, *was* her first child until she'd

27

abruptly turned to him and asked if he would wait outside for her.

(Funny, Peter reflected, how much trouble grown ups took to prevent his hearing things he wasn't supposed to be able to hear anyway.)

He'd sat outside in the corridor, swinging his legs, feeling the pleasant weight of his new lace-up shoes and wondering how serious it was to have a rhesus-negative mother.

When Maggie emerged, he had decided from her expression that it was very serious indeed. But the high throb of anxiety had receded when she'd taken him down into the centre of the town and bought him the model Colt he most wanted and a pair of Star Trek pyjamas. The only annoying thing had been her saying, to be fair, Rod had better have a model Colt as well or they would scrap over his. She was always very scrupulous about fair shares.

All the way home, they'd talked about monkeys.

As he thought about it, he realised that the little pip of discomfort which had lodged in him that day, was still there — forgotten, but there, a small, nagging presence.

I don't know what it was all about really, he thought, and lay on his back, puzzling.

Downstairs, the anthem began warningly and was switched off. Instead of the normal thumps and bumps that signified a dilatory tidying, Peter heard a muffled sobbing. Soothing moos from his father.

They must have been watching a feature film, lucky pigs, thought enviously. He wished that he had gone downstairs after all.

The sitting room door clicked open and they came out into the tiled hall knocking against the coat rack thing of Aunt Carrie's (an umbrella, or maybe it was a putting iron, clattered to the floor). He imagined them bulkily together as the sobbing rose more distinctly. He wished their old dog Hymie was here. Hymie stopped people clutching one another and crying.

Rod stirred and moved his mouth stickily in sleep.

"You go up. I'll bring some coffee," he heard his father say.

One foot was placed on the wooden stairs.

"He breaks my heart," cried Maggie softly, as if into a sleeve or a cheek.

Peter supposed it must have been a very sad film. And reaching further down his bed for the quilt, pulled it right over his head to block out the curiously plangent note.

3

"WE SHOULDN'T HAVE let you stay up so late! We'll *never* make it! See if the milk's arrived, Peter . . ."

Maggie flung two burnt pieces of toast on to their plates and consulted her watch at the same time. "Crikey! Five to eight! *Hurry up!*"

Peter opened the front door and peered out, one hand holding up his pyjama trousers which were too long and wrinkled over his toes. Four pints of milk stood in the tiled porch. He tried to carry all four. One under each arm. One in each . . . but it didn't work. He swapped them round. One under his arm, two clasped against his chest, one . . .

"*Hurry up* for God's sake!" Behind him, cutlery rattled like rifle fire in the kitchen drawers.

Two under his upper arm, one gripped between forearm and chest. . . .

"What the hell are you doing?" Maggie flared at his back. Starting, he half-turned and dropped a bottle on to the complicated brown and yellow tiles. Milk exploded everywhere.

"Oh, you *idiot*! Just look at me!" Her navy velvet trouser suit was speckled all over. A hand seized the back of his collar and propelled him over the broken glass; miraculously, without injury. "Get in there, get on with your breakfast and then get into your school clothes. *Fast*. Or you'll miss the bus. *Kit!*" she shrieked, rubbing at herself fruitlessly and muttering oaths. "Kit! ACTION!"

"Thank goodness we get our milk in bottles now," remarked Rod, ignoring the commotion. Taking the remaining bottle his brother brought to the table, he stuck his thumb through the tinfoil and poured the milk on his Wheatinuts. "Instead of in a bucket," he added, "full of straw and cowshit." He was already dressed.

"You've taken all the top of the milk." Peter was indignant. His mouth still felt sore.

"Sorry. It was an accident." Rod smiled. "I *say*, you're *still* in your *pyjamas*."

"KIT!"

"All right. All right. Batman is here."

"About bloody time." Maggie shoved a floorcloth into his hands. "You may have noticed," she snapped. "In the *hall*." Then: "Get the boys on the bus would you — I *must* go."

"Are you taking the car?" He sounded aggrieved.

"How the hell else do I get there?"

Kit shrugged and beamed round trying to adjust the atmosphere. "Any more coffee?"

"Did you bring your mug down?"

"Er, no. Thank you for bringing it up by the way. The coffee."

"We'd never have you on your feet at all if I didn't. You'll get it intravenously tomorrow." Maggie switched the radio on with one hand (only to hear the eight o'clock pips which drew forth a groan) while, with the other, she brushed her hair, looking in a handbag mirror she'd propped up on the shelf.

"You shouldn't brush your hair in the kitchen," announced Rod with his mouth full. "You are revolting."

"*Darling*," hissed Maggie through teeth full of hair grips.

"Any special jobs need doing?" Kit, wrapping his dressing gown more firmly round himself (the cord was lost) determined to meet the morning sunshine on its own bright terms.

"Oh!" Peter suddenly went scarlet. "I forgot to do my homework."

"Oh-h-h!" A yelp from Maggie, her lips drawn back from teeth with grips positioned like broadside guns.

"*Now* . . ." Kit raised a restraining hand and his dressing gown fell open revealing a worn pair of lilac underpants and a hairy bulge of stomach. "Give it to me while you eat your breakfast. Go on, fetch it."

Maggie began bundling things into her handbag. "Ever noticed how we all speak to one another in imperatives," she observed, pausing to spray something inaccurately behind her ears.

"Pooh," chimed Rod.

"Shopping? Housework?" Kit was trying. "We just don't have the *time* to complete a sentence . . ." He peered inside the now empty cereal packet and sighed.

"Oh, use your imagination, would you? I'll try and ring later."

"What about supper?"

"Supper? Supper? Oh God, I don't know. I'm going to stink of milk all day."

"You never used to mind that." Pointedly, Rod began scraping the charcoal off his toast. Peter, still in his pyjamas, returned with his exercise books. "I've got to draw a centurion," he said.

"Oh *Lord*." Kit took a pencil from the case and licked it. Peter sat down, examined the empty packet and began to say something accusatory.

"Go and get *dressed*!" screamed Maggie.

"What?"

"You heard."

"But I haven't . . ."

"Do as I say!"

"If they're late, they're late," soothed Kit, outlining a helmet.

"I don't want to be late. I'll get a black mark if I'm late," Rod intervened.

"So?"

"Goodbye darling! Have a lovely day!" With a gust of scent, Maggie backfired from the kitchen. Peter crept out after her.

"By-ee!" the other two called, unmindful of anything but what each was immediately doing.

"Liver or something!" came a cry from the front door, then a crash. All the stained glass lozenges shivered and cringed as if they'd never before been treated in this fashion.

"I'm not very good at it." Kit studied his centurion. "Didn't they wear pleated skirts or something?" he asked of his younger son.

"Leather thong things."

"Oh, of course, yes."

"You're going to make an awful mess of it. Peter hates messy drawings."

"Too bad," breathed Kit, using a pellet of bread to erase the wrong lines.

"What're you doing with that?"

"It's what *I* used to do."

"Well it doesn't work, does it?"

Kit looked down. "The quality of the bread must have deteriorated," he concluded. "Damn."

"Have you got my garters on?" Peter came in, prosecuting.

"No."

"Let me look."

"They're mine."

"Let me *look*!" And Peter grabbed his brother's leg while Kit continued drawing.

"Hey."

"Gerr-off!"

"Shove off, you!"

"You *have* got mine on!"

"Well?"

"They *are* mine!"

One was. One wasn't.

"Use some string," suggested Kit.

"Look at the time! The bus!"

"Christ!" exclaimed Kit. Then, "Hell, I'm not suitably dressed for a bus stop. Can you manage without me?"

"Yes," they chorused, uncaring.

Normally Maggie walked the length of Wellington Gardens with them and saw them across the main road at the top end. For the first week they'd attended Hill House School they were glad to have her there. The traffic seemed to use them for target practice, never stopping or slowing. They'd dived and dithered and been stranded on the island in the middle of the road hanging on to Maggie's hands in a way they'd normally be ashamed to do. Maggie mouthed obscenities at the drivers, advancing a little, retreating a little and they had to tell her to shush.

Today as they hovered in the middle of the road, traffic fleeing either side of them, the big red bus trundled to a halt at the stop: about twenty yards down the road to their left.

"Wave," urged Peter. And Rod waved.

But the bus pulled away, making a car, about to overtake it, hoot ferociously. Inexorably it gasped past them, the driver staring straight ahead.

"Oh rats," wailed Peter and he stood there crimson with humiliation because he always believed that everybody was watching him.

"C'mon!" Rod suddenly plunged across the road and left him alone. "There's another one coming!" He reached the safety of the far pavement and began to run towards the stop. Peter was left, stranded.

A dull panic gushed into his chest. He hesitated, lunged forward, then hung back. Another car sounded its horn angrily. He was going to miss it. It was going to go without him. The bus halted and Rod disappeared out of sight behind its bulk.

An old Morris stopped and flashed its headlights at Peter. He could just see a low dome of white hair behind the wheel. Too overwrought to shout his thanks he ran, certain that the bus would leave before he could reach it. His sandals slapped the pavement and then he saw Rod swinging from the rail, one arm and leg outstretched like a starfish, his head turned in cheerful conversation with the conductor.

"Here he is!" he announced as Peter puffed alongside. "I asked him to wait for you," he said and performed a single leap into the central aisle of the lower deck. "Thanks," he grinned to the conductor who winked and rang his bell.

The ordeal wasn't over. "Oh crumbs!" Rod's hand flew to his mouth. "Dad forgot to give us the fare."

Peter hung his burning head and stared at the shoes he'd forgotten to clean. Another black mark.

"You *are* in trouble, aren't you?" The conductor hung on to the overhead rail and swayed. "What are we going to do with you?"

"We could pay you tomorrow."

"Shan't be on tomorrow."

"Well we could pay the other man double."

"What's all this? Your brother crying?"

Peter shook his head fiercely and watched one ungartered sock slide down his leg.

"How much do you need?" A young girl with false, model eyes burrowed in the pocket of her long cardigan. "Ten pee O.K.?"

"Thank you *very* much." Rod gave her his charming smile and wobbled over to take it.

"In luck this morning, eh? Wish I could get the girls to do that for me." To Peter, "Cheer up son, panic over."

But his face was swollen with heat and he didn't want to raise it. He didn't want to smile at anybody in case they noticed the loser's swelling of his mouth. He mumbled and wished the bus was for schoolchildren only as it had been at Sigvales where it waited outside the church until everyone had arrived and then wound round the lanes to the low, white schoolhouse in Chewton Caunale. And it hadn't mattered if you forgot your money because Mr. Atkins drove the bus every day and he just wrote it down in a little book that had a cover like blue marble. Peter hated London Transport and he hated 43, Wellington Gardens and he hated Hill House School.

The uniform was all right, though.

They'd never worn uniform at any of their previous schools and were delighted with every item they'd tried on in the shop. Maggie had protested at the price of each separate article.

The regulations stated that they had to have rugger shorts, cricket sweaters, track suits . . . all sorts of wonderful things as well as socks with navy tops and Chairman Mao hats which Maggie had said were most inappropriate. There was a school crest (a hand clasping a sword) and a motto (*Semper Fortis Semper Paratus*) and a different pair of shoes for each sport. They felt very superior in their uniform. They felt even more superior attending a school that was just for boys — the exclusion of girls confirmed a feeling they had that girls lowered standards. The girls at their old school had gossiped and tittered together like old women and tried to spoil all the playground fights.

The feeling of blue-capped and badged superiority ebbed as they climbed uphill towards the substantial doorway of Hill House School, built rather like a portcullis to blend with the grey stucco Gothic fortress, a bizarre medley of crenellations, turrets and lancet windows. It stood oddly among the Georgian dwellings that chiefly graced the steep slope up to Hammond Park gazing disdainfully down over green undulations of beech and oak and horse chestnut which billowed low to the river's edge.

Unobtrusively, they joined a stream of boys in dark blazers and pullovers identical to their own — except that theirs were newer looking.

Maggie had bought them with room to grow in and since she wasn't very skilful at turning things up had left the hems exactly where they were — encroaching on knees and fingertips. "You'll soon fill them out," she'd said, pulling Rod's shorts up above his waist. But they'd slipped down again. And then she'd stitched on forty-six name tapes with black, spidery stitches that made the tapes look as though they were crawling inside their clothes. Kit had done the last dozen or so with meticulous neatness, remarking that the Army hadn't been entirely wasted on him, which made the boys feel that sewing wasn't cissy at all.

34

A bell rang and they hung their clothes up in a frenzy, merging in the general rush for Prayers, presided over by the headmaster Mr. Carberry who wore an impressive black gown.

They *could* have gone to the primary school which was only walking distance from Wellington Gardens, but Maggie had said Peter must remain in a small class, and if the only means of having one was paying for one then she'd damn well do it. So that there should be no unfairness, Rod was sent too. "As long as we can afford it anyway," Kit had warned, adding mildly, "Daft, the way we bust a gut to treat you two equally when all you do all the time is fight for supremacy. You make a pig's arsehole of politics." And Maggie had sighed "*Boys*," as she often did, seeming to include Kit in her plural noun.

They split and went to their separate classrooms. Each had been entrusted to an older boy to supervise them through their first weeks. Patel, Peter's guide, was an Indian boy with an accent as chiselled as the Prime Minister's, which was only one of the puzzling things about Patel who said his family came from Africa — Kenya — though as far as Peter was concerned, he was an Indian. Patel called Peter 'Makin One' and Rod, 'Makin Two'. It was a rather pleasing form of address although, for a few days, another boy, Cotley-Smith, tried to call him 'Whoopee' (short for Makin Whoopee) and that was less pleasant. Nobody much took it up though and the joke faded away.

It was maths first. Maths was taken by their form master, Mr. Oliver, a youngish man with the kind of sandy hair that went white at the edges and a rather girlish curve to his nose and mouth. Maths, which had been Peter's strong subject, the thing he knew so much more about than either his mother or father, was a different matter at Hill House. The textbooks were smaller and more densely printed and didn't have pictures of children doing things. The sums they tackled had letters as well as numbers in them and Mr. Oliver spent a long time bending over Peter's shoulder explaining.

"Got your aid on, have you?" he enquired kindly.

"What? Pardon, I mean."

"Got your aid on?"

"Yes, sir."

He began to understand. It was simple, really.

"What happened to your lip, Makin?" Patel asked at break.

"Oh. It was a fight."

"Hurts a bit, I should think."

"I won."

Patel considered the lip gravely and pursed his own round a straw, sucking milk out of a bottle. He had very thick, dark lashes which seemed somehow to prolong his gaze. "Mm," he concluded, mysteriously. "You can be in my team for cricket, Makin. Until," he qualified, warily, "we see how you shape up."

"We played rounders at my other school," said Peter, pleased.

"Played what?"

"Rounders. You know."

"Mm."

There was a pause. Patel sucked until the straw gurgled.

"I'm quite good at swimming." Peter was learning the proper modesty.

"*Are* you? That's excellent. We need some decent swimmers in our House."

Peter had quickly become proud of his House. He and Rod (and Patel) were in Wavell. Each House was named after a General . . . Haig, Gordon, Auchinleck (which thought itself the best) and Percival which nobody wanted to belong to because Percival had lost Singapore in the last war by having his guns pointing the wrong way. Being a Percy was shaming.

"We're going to lam Auchinleck in the Sports this year," Patel promised. "Trounce the Auks." And Peter giggled loyally at the prospect.

They played games — or *had* games, as the expression seemed to be — every afternoon at Hill House School. At least, the school itself had only a relatively small area of turf behind it, enough for some nets, a long jump which Peter had imagined was a sand pit and a single tennis court on which the senior boys played a laconic game. For cricket and running they went to Hammond Park a little further up the hill where a special area was marked out for them — beautiful white lines circled and crossed the grass like toothpaste. Swimming didn't start until after half term which was a pity as both Peter and Rod were much better at swimming than all this running and jumping now expected of them.

The serious regard in which sports were held came as a shock to them. Games were not quite games any longer but something in which a determined physical ardour was expressed, a competitiveness which Rod quite relished and Peter grimly pretended to enjoy. He was relieved to find that lots of boys were far worse than he was. Even Patel, who spoke so keenly of games, was, he noticed that afternoon as they thudded cross-country, something of a rabbit when it came to running.

Threading through the rhododendron bushes, their glossy darkness splashed with the first exotic pink and purple of the year, Peter saw that Patel's face was contorted. His feet flopped out sideways in an ugly, feeble fashion. He spurted ahead of Patel a little to the stile and sprang over, glancing again at the lank, pink tongue that dangled out of the sallow mouth. He remembered his father telling him that dark people sweated more than whites. "We're all different," he'd said, "in so many ways. It's a pity we have to pretend we're not sometimes!"

And as he ran, legs aching, across the tussocky grass of the park, he pretended he was racing in a desperate bid to be free of pursuing rhinos or, as the moment altered, Arabs, armed to the teeth, or, finally (as the road came into view) American police. All things his father had once done. Kit had done some fabulous things before he was hurt.

From the pavement outside Hill House School you could look down over the cascading trees, some, the horse chestnuts, thick with blossom as though topped with good cream, down, down, to the still sheet of river which curved away towards Popesvale and that part of the river where Wellington Gardens ran down to the water. But you couldn't, from this high point of the hill, see any solid brick or chimneys, no flowerbeds or gates or parked cars. It was as though an eighteenth-century lord had landscaped the entire vista for his personal pleasure. The river slipped through wooded parkland, a serene curve of muted silk, a little golden embroidery of willow at its edges here and there. Far to the east, the haze of London hung, obscuring its own high towers and stacks.

A tiny boat stole along the river below the boys as they looked, its movement barely breaking the surface.

"Come on," urged Peter, hot and untidy. "Dad'll be at home."

Rod hung back, gazing wistfully down. Around his feet were scattered a few fallen petals from the red may tree. "I wish we could sail to school. D'you think he'd let us?"

"He might. Let's ask him."

It was such a good idea, it kept them happy all the way home. It was the sort of idea that Kit would like.

(It was nice to go home and find him there, like other fathers. While he'd travelled, there had been long weeks when the house was empty of him. And when he came back from his months abroad, tanned, unfamiliar, his baggage labelled and labelled again, Peter had felt fury mingle with his welcome. He had clung to his father until he could be sure he was hurting him. Or, as he'd grown older, had simply refused to run and greet him, keeping his face firmly towards the television when he heard the front door open and the cases bang to the ground. He had kept his eyes coldly indifferent, his heart alone decked out with flags.)

Kit sat at the kitchen table, wearing a flowered apron, photographs spread out in front of him.

"What was it today?" he cried cheerfully. "Mud-slinging? You're filthy."

"It was clay!" Rod wrapped smeary arms round his father's neck. "I forgot to take my potting shirt." He smelt the comfortable fragrance of fathers, skin and scorching and a remnant of beer.

"How does Peter keep so clean?" Kit adjusted his glasses, knocked awry by Rod's embrace.

"I don't do it any more."

"What? Pottery?"

"No, I don't do it any more."

"Why?" Peter had been good at modelling in clay. They'd tried to encourage him.

"Don't want to."

"We've got a smashing plan!" Rod burst in, anxious to be first.

"A boat!" shouted Peter, above him.

"Let me! Let me!"

Together, in a torrent, they told him.

Kit thought it a splendid idea, save for one thing. "We can't afford a boat," he said, but he said it slowly as though it were a problem to be considered, not a reason for dismissing the notion altogether.

"Think of all the bus fares we'd save!"

"That's very sharp of you, Peter. True."

"We could put our pocket money in a box with a hole in it."

"I think you might have something . . ." mused Kit, but he made them put their scheme away until Maggie came home. "Don't get *too* excited."

Maggie would raise objections. Silently, they all knew that.

38

But, and their spirits refused to be lowered, they had a strength of numbers. Even the five black marks they'd harvested between them — for dirty shoes, missing garters, a forgotten potting shirt — lost some of their weight. They managed to laugh about them a bit when they told their father.

"Anyway," said Rod to whom the better side of things continually presented itself, "I got two red marks as well."

"You liar!"

"I did."

"What for?"

"Art and English."

"I bet."

"Why do you always accuse him of lying?" Kit intervened. He was clumsily pouring squash from a gallon flagon into two mugs.

"Because he does."

"He *exaggerates*," corrected Kit. "Just like his mother." He handed them their drinks.

"Mine's got less in than his," complained Rod.

"He *lies*."

The quarrel remained unpursued. It was one of a number of themes, regularly aired. Just a way, Kit often said, of releasing stress. "They make you work pretty hard, don't they?" he said.

"Like stink. At the other school it was baby stuff. What's for tea?"

"Tea? . . . Eggs?"

"Not *again*!" they cried in unison.

"Why don't you just have a wedge of bread for now and eat supper with us later?"

"What's for supper?" Peter asked suspiciously.

"Well now . . ." Kit paused uncomfortably and glanced at his watch. "I wonder if the shops are still open. . . . Tell you what, you run round to the shops with a list I've made and I'll take you to the pub when it opens. You can play outside and have a Coke."

"O.K." They agreed happily. Rod, going to look for a basket under the stairs, stopped to gaze at the photographs.

"What's all these?"

"Some I brought back with me, some I got Bill to send." Bill was the photographer who'd worked with him.

They looked.

Figures in a flat landscape, conical hats and tattered clothes, bearing small burdens; a mattress, pans, the wrapped body of a child. A woman, lying, breasts exposed, indecently bleeding from the mouth and nose. A young soldier, helped by others, staring into the camera as though it were the hell he was now regardless of entering, one leg missing from the knee. A baby, lying in the foreground of the street, its body black with spattered blood while blurred figures in the background ran in both directions, heads down.

"That's war," said Kit. "That's what it's really like."

4

"You *what*?" Maggie bounded upright from her slumped position in the chair.

"I asked them round for a drink."

"You are a sod."

"Rubbish. We need to know our neighbours."

"But *now*! . . . I'm pooped." And she fell back again.

"It'll do you good."

Liver and onions sizzled in the pan.

"Here, have a drink now, Mags. Set yourself up."

"Gird me loins," she said sardonically. Shadows furrowed the skin beneath her eyes. She'd kicked her shoes on the floor. "I'll have to start clearing up."

"Whatever for? They know we're not sorted out yet. Nobody minds."

"I mind."

"How suburban of you."

"We *are* suburban. Suburban to our sawdust souls."

"Christ, you have had a bad day."

"There's something deeply and irreducibly unsatisfying about demonstrating non-stick pans."

"*Irreducibly*, eh? Mmm."

"Don't start twitting me about my language or I'll find something far more choice. Something . . . *pithy*."

"I bet you will, my lady. Here, have a gin."

"Have you told her?" Rod came in, swinging his home-made machine gun. He'd nailed it together out of bits of wood.

"Told her?"

"About our *plan*?"

"Oh. Yes, no — no, I thought I'd let you."

"You forgot to feed those rotten rabbits again last night and this morning," said Maggie, sipping.

"You forgot to feed your rabbits," said Rod to Peter, who trailed after him looking crumpled. He gasped guiltily and looked at his mother.

"They're alive," she remarked. "Just."

Quickly, he left the room.

"They're yours as well, Rod."

"No, they're not. Anyway, I've got this *thing* to tell you." And he explained about the boat.

"But you can't row."

"We can learn."

"What when it rains?"

"We can wear capes. Or go on the bus," he added doubtfully.

"I don't suppose you can just moor anywhere."

"Well . . ."

"Anyway, we can't afford it at the moment." She drained her gin thirstily.

"We'll ask the ferryman . . ."

She heard his voice fade and looked up at him. "What started all this?" she said and smiled.

And he told her about the bus that morning, aware that his mother's expression was fastening stonily on Kit. "Oh, *well*," she said. "If it's a matter of being either drowned or run over . . ."

"We were *all* behind ourselves this morning. Arse over elbow, the lot of us." Kit sat down on the narrow window seat and looked at the surly brick houses across the road. "*I* don't think it's a bad notion at all."

"No. It's very Jock of the Bush Veldt. I don't know why we don't have a camp fire in the middle of the lawn and roast all those miserable grey squirrels that abound around here. I could stitch all their little skins together to make a canoe."

"You can't sew for toffee," said Rod.

When Peter came back he smelt bitterness, like an odour in the room.

"I know you miss it," his father was saying softly.

"What really bugs me, is that when we had the space, *had* streams, *had* the fields and trees, nobody gave a damn about it."

"All they want to do is get to school," said Kit gently.

There was a silence.

"You're right," she said suddenly. "That liver's burning." And she got to her feet.

"Can we then?" Peter, furious that Rod had told before him, was now anxious to know the outcome. He was used to his mother ploughing through objections before capitulating, as though she *needed* to fight. You just had to wait.

"We'll see," she flung over her shoulder.

The boys skipped soundlessly behind her back.

Maggie turned, and, catching them, gave a fleeting grin. "Have we got time to eat before the Who-is-its arrive?"

"I should think."

"*Who* is it coming?" Rod picked it up.

"The Fergusons. From over the way."

"Not that *girl*?"

"Girl? What girl?"

"That *girl*."

"Probably," said Kit, following Maggie into the kitchen.

"I expect Peter fancies her," Rod said airily.

"I don't."

Jostling, they all trooped in Maggie's wake.

"You said hello to her yesterday."

"Well?"

"Well."

"I *don't* fancy her."

"Hoo-hoo," warbled Rod, ducking.

"Did you put any salt in the potatoes?" asked Maggie.

"Oh, *hell* . . ." Kit snapped his fingers in self-reproach.

"Never mind," said Maggie wearily. And she put the apron on.

"We should have brought Belinda." Sally Ferguson fingered the lapel of her lurex thread shirt and realised that the drinks were to be brief and the party very small. "She would have loved to play with you."

Rod gave Mrs. Ferguson a sickly smile that was intended to be seen as false though he thought she was probably too stupid to notice. Sally Ferguson manufactured a little laugh high up in her nose and turned attentively towards her husband, a man as blond as she was herself, but big and sloping — a little carelessly put together whereas *she* (and Rod considered it for a moment as he picked furtively at a scab on his elbow), *she* looked as though she were packaged like something off the top shelf of a sweet shop.

"I'm sure you'll love it here. The *river*'s so lovely, isn't it?"

Maggie grinned ferociously. Peter saw that Mrs. Ferguson

bored his mother. He hoped she wouldn't let it show too much. She could be fierce and impatient but very funny. (When the Fergusons have gone, he thought, she'll do an impersonation of them.) He could see his mother drinking up the feeble blondeness, the tiny chiming of the woman.

The men were chatting away quite happily. Keith Ferguson, Peter overheard with interest, was in electronics. The central finger of his left hand was missing.

"It must have been an awful worry for you . . ." (Sally Ferguson's bleating voice again. She sat on the edge of the threadbare armchair.)

"No more worrying than his absence used to be really. Then I simply imagined what was going wrong all the time. But," Maggie shrugged, "you get kind of used to it."

"*Used* to it!" There was a horrified tinkling. "I'm sure I shouldn't get used to that kind of thing . . ."

The tinkling, Peter noted, had a metallic quality.

"Ah, well, I'd rather worry about him at home than worry about him away. At least, I think I would." Maggie was beginning to burble, her attention shifting from Mrs. Ferguson. Peter adjusted his Action Man's commando uniform.

"Yes, I can see that." Mrs. Ferguson made a twittering movement as if looking for somewhere to put her glass, but finding nowhere, remarked, "I can't think how you manage a full-time job."

Maggie followed the course Sally Ferguson's gaze had taken round the wreckage of furniture, the dog-stained rugs that covered only small areas of wooden flooring, the stacks of books with string round them. "Well," she said, a little defensively, "until Kit gets fixed up."

"Oh. You *mean* . . . Oh, I see. I thought he was, well, *recuperating*."

"He was."

"But . . ."

"He's resting, to use a phrase from the profession of which I failed ever to become a full member."

Rod took the peanuts Maggie had found and offered them round. They were rather old.

"It's not recent then, his accident?"

"It happened over a year ago," supplied Rod.

"Oh, *really*." Delicately she took a peanut and cast a surreptitious glance at Kit. "How *did* it happen exactly," she half-mouthed.

"He fell into an ambush." Rod put down the saucer of peanuts to demonstrate more effectively. "The V.C. were supposed to be a mile up the road. Then —"

"Shut up," said Kit, "would you?" He pushed his glasses back up his nose.

"I'm only telling."

"Well, don't," said Kit, "I'm sick of hearing about it."

"I'm *sure* you must be . . ." Sally gave him a tilted, nurse's smile and resumed concealed work on a lodged fragment of peanut. "We really *should* have brought Belinda," she said again, a little desperately.

"Yes," Maggie agreed, and yawned. "Oh, help! I *am* sorry."

"You must be tired."

"It's just standing all day."

"Your husband said. When he met Keith earlier. In The Swan."

"That's where they met?"

"Yes," she smiled lengthily, unable to think of anything further. Then: "Have you discovered the park yet?"

"Yes, I have."

"It's lovely. It's so nice for the children to have somewhere close by to play. You don't have to worry about them."

"She didn't have to worry before," said Peter.

"No. No, I suppose you didn't. In the country. Silly of me. How you must miss it. I've always said I should love to live in the country."

Maggie gave Mrs. Ferguson a withering smile which implied (Peter thought) that Mrs. Ferguson would last two seconds in the country.

"It's very hard work," said Maggie. "*Was.*"

"Oh, not harder than you've done today, I'm sure."

"Much. But better. Sensible work. You can't call selling non-stick pans *work.*"

"I think they're awfully good myself. Well worth the extra."

Maggie rose very quickly. "Let me repair your drink," she said, her face turned away to the scant bottles on the dresser which had somehow ended up in the sitting room.

"*Peter* is it?" Mrs. Ferguson held out her glass. "Would you be so . . ."

"Rod."

"Pardon?"

"I'm Rod. He's Peter."

"Oh dear, I don't seem to get anything right."

45

"It's all right," said Rod and took her glass.

There was a pale flush on her neck and the exposed V of her chest. "Just a small one! And then we really *must* go. *Keith!*"

"Yes."

"I'm worried about Belinda."

She worries an awful lot, thought Peter, hoping they *would* go, so he could put the television on.

"Oh she'll be fine. She knows where we are."

"All the *same*."

Maggie crossed the room for Keith's glass. He smiled at her approvingly. "So Kit here is writing a *book!*"

There was a pause as small as a breath. "Yes," she replied, evenly.

"Well, *planning* it," said Kit.

"Yes," repeated Maggie, turning.

"Certainly got plenty to write about!" Keith Ferguson swung his large torso towards his wife and made a reassuring gesture in her direction. "Perhaps Maggie here would be interested in one of your Tupperware parties."

"I don't know," wavered Sally.

"I would not," said Maggie, loosing a laugh at them all.

"You'll get used to her," Kit explained comfortably. "She's frightfully rude. Badly brought up, but harmless."

"Oh, that's perfectly all right!" Pinker than ever, Sally Ferguson addressed herself to Kit as if discussing an awkward child with him. "*Perhaps*," she dared, once more attempting to draw Maggie, "you'd be more interested in the Conservative Women . . .?" Sally Ferguson had the innocence to imagine that anyone whose life bore a physical resemblance to her own, voted as she did. Seeing a rejecting amusement rise again in Maggie's face she pressed wildly on. "It's our fiftieth this year. We've persuaded the Prime Minister to come and speak to us!"

"Can I watch Dad's Army?" pleaded Peter from his corner. Nobody answered him and he bent his Action Man into a running position.

"Really must go!" gasped Sally Ferguson, gulping her drink in discomfiture. But her husband was leaning in Maggie's direction.

"So you're an actress, eh?"

"Brought out of retirement. If you can call the odd commercial and dressing up as a chicken, acting."

"A *chicken!*" Kit put his glasses back on to look at her.

"You're no chicken!" he remarked solemnly. "Completely unsuitable."

"It's an egg promotion. It's what I was offered today. I was very fortunate not to be given the part of the egg."

Peter saw the way Mrs. Ferguson looked at Maggie; her face was narrowed with a mixture of suspicion and envy. As though she thinks my mother is dangerous, he thought inwardly and smiled to himself. My mother is prettier than Mrs. Ferguson he decided. More interesting looking.

Her eyes were often deep with amusement even when the rest of her narrow, hair-draped face was still. Sometimes her lack of open expression was puzzling. Then, suddenly, she would laugh, as she had just now, a shouting, absolute laugh. Gleeful. People could forgive her a lot for that laugh. It just came, a gust of mirth and wind, and blew objection away. A whole room could be altered by her. Its whole feeling. It wasn't that she tried to change things to her way of wishing. It was just the way she was.

And then Peter noticed that Mrs. Ferguson was only half-won. She was patting her blonde hair in that assertively non-assertive way women have. Men don't pat or wind their hair, he thought. They don't put their hand under their hair and lift it, letting it fall back against the neck as if it was a soothing thing to do. As if such a gesture said, me. I'm here. My father doesn't do that. Nor, he thought with a small lift of surprise, does my mother.

"You're not *accepting* the part of a chicken!"

"A chicken can earn just as much as Hedda Gabler."

"And it *lays* better," Kit weighed seriously.

"You *are* coarse!"

Keith Ferguson had slapped his thigh quite painfully at what Peter took to be a joking exchange between his parents. Even Mrs. Ferguson was making a hurt little noise. Peter looked slowly from one face to the other and considered their laughter warily. He felt that somebody was being laughed *at*.

One summer morning, two years ago, they had gone to visit the most haunted house in England. A deserted weekday. Stepping through a wicket gate into the walled garden of the old stone house, they'd glimpsed a solitary figure in the distance, an elderly man wearing shorts and tennis shoes with a stomach like a sling. He'd been trimming a hen-shaped hedge on the far side of the garden. He'd lumbered over the grass, waving his shears. As he approached, the family had become

47

aware of a faint, but high-pitched whine which seemed to accompany him.

"Eh? Eh?" he'd bellowed, lashing the shears about.

And Peter's father had asked if they might visit the house. "Follow me! Follow me! Eh!" And they'd followed him into the cool, dark, stone-flagged hall of the house where he'd asked for their 'two bobses' and thrown the money on a pewter plate with a terrific clatter. The whine had become very loud.

Then he had stumped briskly through the house using his shears to point at objects of interest, describing them with great rapidity and completely ignoring all the polite and interested questions Kit and Maggie had asked. The whine was like a whistling kettle.

The only part the old man had seemed to enjoy was describing his ghosts and then he'd pushed his sandy, glistening face into theirs, rolling his eyes in a fearful fashion.

Not until they were safely outside the gate had everyone but Peter collapsed with laughter. "What a marvellous man!" Kit had gasped weakly. And Peter had asked him why such a peculiar old man was marvellous.

"He'd found the perfect solution to the hoi-polloi."

"What?" Peter had asked, urgently. "What was the solution?"

"Howlback!" Kit had cried, clutching his sides. "What a clever and delightful creature!"

And they had all rolled about except Peter who had thought the old man with the hearing aid rude and alarming. He had wished they would stop laughing. After that he had only worn his hearing aid when the teacher reminded him.

". . . simply *must* go . . ." Mrs. Ferguson was saying again. She stood up. "If there's anything I can *do* . . ."

"Do?" Maggie looked bewildered.

"While you're out. Shopping, cooking — lunch for your husband perhaps, the children . . ."

"Kit can look after himself," said Maggie, mystified. "But thanks for the offer."

"She likes to see men suffer." Kit arranged Mrs. Ferguson's lacy, white stole. "It's her revenge for being raped at an early age."

The stole tightened round Sally Ferguson's shoulders and the spare fold was swung high across her blazing V.

"Ignore him," said Maggie, leading the way.

"Why not?" countered Kit, amiably. "*She* does. Nice of you to come round."

"We must ask you back some time."

Peter leapt across the room and switched on the television.

"Sunday morning?" Keith Ferguson fixed his wife's polite response more exactly.

"Sunday, yes," she echoed.

"Lovely," said Kit.

The studio audience's laughter billowed out of an imageless screen.

"What did you have to say that for?"

"What? Rape? Or yes to Sunday?"

"Both. Rape."

"Shut up!" Rod turned up the volume. "We've missed most of it already."

"It gives them something to talk about. It's our contribution to community life."

"What a marvellous example you set."

"Human beings adore stories! I promise you, we shall be the most popular couple in Popesvale in no time at all. Anyway, looking at Stuart Pidgeon I'd say it *had* to be rape."

Peter crawled closer to the screen so that he could hear above the giggling but the end titles rolled up. "Blast it!" he cried. "It's the news now!"

"Shush then," said Maggie, "Daddy'll want to watch it."

"I want to know what that tit of a Prime Minister had to say in Bournemouth today. I hope you get yourself an invitation to the Conservative Ladies Jubilee, Mags."

"*I* wanted to watch Dad's Army," Rod pointed out.

"We had visitors, didn't we?"

"Why did we have to stay around while they were here? Why couldn't you have gone and sat somewhere else, jabbering?" Rod punched the cushion he was lying on.

"So you can learn the art of civil conversation. When you're grown up you don't ask people round and then watch television. Not if you're middle aged and middle class anyway," added Maggie.

"I shall."

"Call that civil conversation?" sulked Peter.

Maggie bent down and seized him round the waist. "No," she laughed, "it was bloody."

"*He's* not too bad." Kit searched round for glasses.

"He's got a finger missing."

"Has he?" Maggie gawped at Peter, then giving her glass to

49

Kit said, "It was probably bitten off in a rugger match. If he hadn't known you had a bad leg he'd have asked you to play rugger or soccer or some other nasty rough game with him. I can tell that sort a mile off. I wonder why," she mused, tipping stubs into one ash tray, "why women don't play things together. Except golf I suppose and that's hardly a game, just a walk with pauses."

"They utterly lack the sporting spirit of course." Kit dumped the glasses and threw himself down with a small yelp of pain. "Anyway, shut up, darling heart, I want to hear the news."

"Oh!" squeaked Peter in the middle of the news, one hand to his mouth.

"What is it?" Maggie opened her eyes. She hadn't been watching.

"I haven't done my homework!"

"Not again! What have you got to do?"

"Write a story," he said.

"Well you'd better get your stuff and do it. Do it on the kitchen table. I knew I'd regret ever having a television."

"What?" said Peter.

"I knew it was a mistake. You watch too much."

He didn't bother to point out that they'd spent most of the evening listening to her boring friends. He couldn't bear the television argument — more of a nag than an argument. All the same, when they hadn't had a television, when they'd lived in the cottage, Maggie had told them stories every night. Wonderful stories with different voices and gestures. Sometimes she became so carried away by her own creations she couldn't sit down to tell the story but had to get up and act the whole thing out. He missed those evenings.

Silently he went to fetch his briefcase and unpacked his books on the kitchen table. It was a Scripture prep. They were doing the Bible from the very beginning this term. Easter and Christmas terms were all New Testament stuff, Patel had told him. Patel didn't believe in Jesus but listened (so he informed Peter) with critical interest. He liked the Old Testament stories better.

Peter carefully uncapped his fountain pen (biros weren't allowed at this school), and wrote *The Story of Adam and Eve* at the top of the page. Then he underlined it with his ruler, removing it cautiously so as not to smudge the ink. The writing glistened in a satisfactory way. He could hear the signature tune of the Morecambe and Wise show starting up in the sitting room then the door opened and Rod, protesting, was told to go upstairs to get changed. As his brother's feet stamped slowly up the stairs Peter wrote, "Once upon a time . . ."

Later, after he'd finished and got changed himself, he came downstairs to fetch a glass of milk and found Maggie reading his story.

"Hey!" he said.

"You don't mind, do you?" She looked up and smiled.

"Not really." He liked sharing things with her. Having her to himself.

"Poor old Eve," she murmured. "You've spelt 'innocence' wrong, by the way." And she altered the word herself. When she'd finished (it didn't take long as he'd written exactly one page) she looked up and said, "It's only a *story*, you know."

"What do you mean?" he asked, sipping the icy milk carefully. The cold made his lip ache.

"You mustn't think it's *true*. That it was all Eve's fault."

"But it *was* her fault. She stole the apple when she'd been told not to."

"Yes, but what I mean is, the beginning of things wasn't like that. Life began in a different way . . . perhaps we came up out of the sea. Perhaps we developed from single-cell life."

"I thought," he said gravely, "that we were monkeys." And the word 'rhesus' flashed across his mind again recalling his mother's guilty tension. (At the time of that discussion with the specialist he remembered wondering with horror whether his mother had had a monkey first, before him, and was terribly ashamed of it.)

"Apes. Well, yes . . ." She ruminated a moment. "I hate that story," she said at length, " 'in sorrow thou shalt bring forth thy children'. Horrible, really. Spiteful. Anyway," she went on, "the point is, it isn't even the first of the Bible stories to be written. It was just made up to help people explain their own beginning in a simple way. Nobody *knew* exactly."

"But that's why *you* say stories are important . . ."

"Yes, well, so it is. We need stories to explain things we only sense in our bones. That doesn't make them *true* necessarily. Not in a factual sense anyway. But they tell truth about ourselves, the truths we can't or won't hear in any other form. The things about ourselves we refuse to listen to most of the time."

He didn't quite follow her. But her attention was anyway turned back to his own prep. "You've written it very nicely," she said. "A bit on the brief side, eh?" And they grinned at one another.

There was a roaring the other side of the door which Peter had allowed to close behind him. Now Kit couldn't get in because the knob had dropped off the door again on the hall side.

"All right!" called Maggie. "I'm coming. What a ruin this place is!" she laughed, opening the door. "The wiring's lethal and the drains don't work. Bed, Peter darling."

"Is that why it smells?" he asked, gulping down his milk and putting the glass in the sink.

"Does it smell?"

"Does it *smell*?" echoed Kit, limping over to the fridge for the ice-cube container.

"You're not having another drink?" queried Maggie.

"If we've got it we might as well drink it and we've got it because I brought those nice people round to see you. What about you?"

"No thanks," she said.

"Can't *you* smell it?" Peter persisted and wasn't satisfied until she'd had a good sniff. "It's age, mostly," she concluded. "And neglect. It'll be all right one day."

Then she hustled him along kindly, clasping him to her. "It *will* be all right, Peter, I promise you. It's an *interesting* house. Once it's painted, you'll see."

As if determined that he should, she collected the bucket and stripping knife Kit had left in the hall. "I'll do a bit tonight," she said.

And he heard her, long after he'd gone to bed, scrape, scrape, puff, puff, puff at the staircase wall.

"I *am* a bloody good actress," she averred faintly at one point. (His father must be standing in the hall too.) "So why does nobody employ me as one?"

He heard Kit laugh, a slow, rich sound. "Too intelligent," he said, "too intelligent and too bloody argumentative."

"That's my problem, is it?"

"And ignorant of course. All that intelligence roaring around an almost empty head. Lethal combination."

"So *that*'s my problem." Scrape, scrape.

"The female firecracker."

He hoped they weren't going to argue. At Sigvales, no

argument ever came to anything. If real, hot argument, threatened then Hymie, their dog, would start barking and trying to bite Kit and that put a stop to it. Hymie worried about people kissing too. He became just as agitated if Kit put his arms around Maggie; he saw both forms of embrace as a collision of kinds. A collision that called for his intervention. The similar shapes of love and war confused him.

Hymie was called Hymie because the man they'd got him from had said: "You know why a dog is a man's best friend? Ever tried spelling dog backwards?"

And Maggie had said (out of hearing) that if *that* were the case the dog had better have a Jewish name.

Peter thought about Hymie wistfully. Hymie was the only one of their animals he'd really deeply loved. Hymie was a blond, hairy mongrel with eyes so expressively naked in their feeling, it was sometimes hard to look him straight in the face. He played with the boys as if he believed he was a boy himself, sharing their ball games, trying frustratedly to climb the same trees and sleeping on the mat outside their bedroom door, paws just touching.

I wonder if my mother misses Hymie as much as I do, he thought. Maggie had said no dog of hers was going to live in a city and had given him to Sam, the neighbouring farmer. How could she have done that, he thought. I wish he was here. I wish he was lying outside my bedroom door.

Thinking of Hymie made him dream of the dog. Hymie was running down the main road, searching the fumey air with his nose, his tail half-wagging unhappily as he tried to find Wellington Gardens. And then, darting among the traffic, Peter (who was now stranded on the central island though apparently invisible to Hymie) saw the once-friendly farmer carrying a gun and he knew that unless Hymie could be attracted and called into number 43 he would be shot, or worse — as he swerved away from the bus, tail shrinking between his legs — be crushed by the traffic which drove in both directions on the same side of the road.

He whistled and whistled, mouth frantically pursed, but the weak sound he blew forth was drowned by engines and wheels.

He woke, not screaming, but aware that his mouth was screwed in a silent whistle. Sweat lay on him like a cold and heavy dew.

Past the unfamilar angles of the dark house, he stumbled his way to Maggie's bedroom and found she had locked the door. He shook it and shook it, but quietly, as though he didn't truly, in his heart of hearts, want to wake her. The effort of shaking aroused him sufficiently from the anguish of his dream. As he stood there, grasping the smooth, round handle of the door, the panicky feeling slipped away from him.

But when he curled back into bed, warm and calmer now, he knew that his mother missed the dog as much as he did. She must do. She had locked her door.

5

"IT'S YOUR HITLER YOUTH night tonight," said Maggie on Friday when they came home from school.

She had tried, but failed, to come home a little earlier herself that evening, to avoid the weekend traffic. But from four o'clock onwards the west-bound routes out of London were jammed like railway sidings, black and slowly jolting. The seven-mile journey had taken over an hour to complete — though, as she admitted, while struggling to unscrew the top of a jar, a little of the delay was caused by a man smashing her offside wing mirror as he'd tried to outmanoeuvre her at the lights near the cemetery, and then having the nerve to get out and shout.

Maggie (who couldn't care less about the wing mirror) had let him shout, staring at him balefully.

"Keep your hair on cock," she'd answered calmly when he'd finished. "What's been getting up your nose today in the office?"

He'd paused, disbelieving, almost bursting with the desire to say more, but the lights had changed to green, other cars were snarling and he'd dashed back to his car. Maggie had driven on his tail all the way to the Hammond turn-off where their paths separated. She had given him a big smile and two fingers.

"What do you mean, Hitler Youth?" said Rod, diving into the Cub jumper Kit had ironed for him. But Maggie just laughed shortly and spread peanut butter on his slice of bread.

"What about you?" she asked of Peter, who sat at the kitchen table, reading his *Valiant*.

"What?"

"What about you? Peanut butter or chocolate spread?"

"Er . . .?"

"Come on!" She stood, knife poised.

"Is there any Marmite?"

"I never mentioned Marmite. Peanut butter or chocolate spread?"

"Er . . .?"

"Nothing," said Maggie, and screwed the tops back on the jars.

"Chocolate spread," he decided. Unscrewing the top, she changed the subject.

"And what about Cubs?"

"What about them?"

"Are you going?"

"Um . . .?" He bent his head over the comic and pressing his hands to his ears, drummed the fingers on the back of his neck.

"Your mother," Kit, who sat beside him, reading the *Dandy*, intervened, "your mother asked you a question."

"I don't know."

"Don't know?"

"He doesn't want to miss Tom and Jerry," said Rod helpfully.

"It isn't Tom and Jerry tonight," Peter argued.

"Well, whatever it is, you don't want to miss it. Do you think my badges look nice?" Rod, one hand holding a bitten-out chunk of bread, looked down his other arm admiringly. "Which do you like best?"

"They're all splendid." Kit looked up briefly from the escapades of Dirty Dick, then glanced across to see what absorbed Peter.

"I like the yellow one," declared Maggie. "What's it for?"

"Athletics."

"*Athletics!*" Peter didn't even look up from The Rough Tough Boyhood of Alf Tupper as he made scornful echo of his brother.

"Isn't it funny the way all the parents are made out to be monsters?" Kit observed, flicking through.

"Skipping, that's all you can do," said Peter. "That's all they ever did at Sigvales. Skipping and leapfrog."

"Don't you ever read them?" Kit demanded of his wife who had begun the day's washing up and was slamming crockery violently in the sink.

"I'm too busy to read them."

56

"You should," he urged. "These are the cultural influences of your children."

"Do they still have Desperate Dan?"

"Oh, yes, he's here somewhere." Kit turned back through the limp pages.

"Good Lord, still crashing his stupid head through brick walls . . .?"

"Ah, yes, but here we are, here's the more modern touch . . . Young Foo, Curly's Commandos . . ." He went on searching. "Sergeant Strong . . . Vee-ee-um-sh-sh! . . . Scrunch! . . . Kraak! Yaah! . . ."

"Very cultural."

"Here's a boy after your heart," Kit nudged Peter. "Scrapper, the boy whose villainous parents stop him watching telly and order him to take up tropical fish instead and here he is keeping his Siamese fighting fish inside the telly so he can watch them swimming round. And . . ."

But everybody was laughing. Maggie swished the water around to make the soap lather.

"And Dennis the Menace!" cried Rod, leaping aboard the waggon of laughter.

"And his friendly pooch, Gnasher!" Peter joined in.

"And his neighbours," said Kit. "The Basher Street Kids."

"Stop!" cried Maggie. "No more!"

"Hey," Rod suddenly remembered a joke he had to tell, "do you know the one . . ."

"Made your mind up?" Maggie, addressing herself to Peter, interrupted. "You haven't started your bread yet, by the way."

"I don't want to go."

"You *are* going."

"Why?"

"Because you are."

"Why?"

"Because you slide out of too many things."

"I'd go if Rod didn't."

"Why?"

"Because he's such a show-off. He embarrasses me."

"*Let* me tell you! It's about the Englishman, the Scottishman and the Irishman . . ." Rod was not to be put off.

"Must you?" groaned Kit.

"Get your things on," ordered Maggie.

"And they were all going to be gassed in the gas chambers."

"I'm counting to ten."

"And they were all told they could take one last thing with them by the S.S. officer . . ."

"I'll walk down there with you when I've finished this WASHING UP." Loudly, with a look at Kit. She threw a tea towel over his head. Kit didn't move but pretended to carry on reading.

". . . The Scottishman took a bottle of whisky . . ."

"Hurray!" From under the tea towel.

". . . And the Irishman took a piece of peat to sit on . . ."

"Well, marginally less Irishly stupid than taking it to eat."

". . . And the Englishman took a piano . . ."

"A *piano*?"

"*Talking* of pianos . . ."

"And when they unlocked the gas chamber door afterwards, the Englishman was still sitting there singing and playing and the others were all gassed and dead and the officer said, 'How ees eet you are shtill alife?' . . . And the Englishman sang . . ." Rod folded up with mirth, his Cub cap tipping over his nose.

"Well, go on . . ."

"And the Englishman sang . . ." Rod took a deep breath to sing himself, "Tunes help you breathe eas-ier!" He collapsed, jelly-boned.

"That's a ghastly joke," said Maggie.

"It's an *exceedingly* tasteless joke." Kit removed the tea towel and glared benignly over his fallen glasses.

The boys were both giggling helplessly.

"If you don't go to Cubs, you could always play the piano," Maggie suggested.

Peter leapt to his feet.

"Anyway," remarked Kit, rising painfully and picking up a soapy glass, "it's very good for you, Cubs. It teaches you not to smoke."

"It what?"

"Baden-Powell said a chap should never smoke. It once interfered with his fellow-officers' sense of smell so severely he was the only one able to scent the approach of the fuzzie-wuzzies."

"*Kit!*"

"*He* called them fuzzie-wuzzies."

"That just goes to show you what a dreadful old man he was."

"Why do you want me to go to cubs then?" Peter saw his opportunity.

"TEN!" shouted Maggie and flapped a dishcloth at Peter's retreating figure.

"You know *why* he doesn't want to go?"

"Why, Rod?"

"Because I've got more badges than him."

"Have you?"

"You know I have."

"No I don't. Daddy sewed them on."

"Well, *look*!" And he twisted his emblazoned arm proudly.

"I ought to cut your hair," said Maggie. "It sticks out in a funny way." And she touched his smoky-dark curls with a damp hand.

"I've got to clean my shoes," he squeaked, ducking.

"Well, that's *something*," she acceded.

"They adore the uniform. They adore parade. And it makes them keen to clean their shoes. It *must* be good for them." Kit blew on a glass and rubbed it more thoroughly. When he wiped up he liked the glass to sparkle.

"*Boys* . . ." sighed Maggie. "*Boys* . . . I used to think," she went on, fishing for things in the water, "before I had sons, that the only differences between boys and girls, apart from the *absolutely* obvious, that is, were conditioned differences. What rot." She peered, grimacing, into a pan Kit had used for burning soup in. "They're different from the womb on. They're different all the way down to their toe-nails. It's not just a matter of boobs and balls. It's *brain*."

"Ha!" Kit nudged his glasses up his nose with a free wrist. "Took you a long time to get on to that."

"I don't mean brains, quantity. *Quality*, I'm talking about."

"*Brains*," Kit repeated with satisfaction.

"Do you want to hear another joke?" asked Rod hopefully.

"No thanks."

"How can you tell there's an elephant in the fridge?"

"You can't close the door."

"No, the footprints in the butter, stupid."

"*Brains*," Kit sighed sonorously. "You can't compete in that department. "Ouch!" As she kicked him. That's my bad leg."

"No it isn't."

"Well, it could easily have been."

"Come on Desperate Dan," she said, "all bulk and paranoia?"

"What's that meant to mean?"

"It's a definition of the male of the species."

59

"It could equally well have described Queen Victoria."

"Actually," Maggie paused, "it wasn't just having boys. It was Sigvales."

"Go and chase Peter, would you, Rod, the feminist philosophy class has just started."

"I'm reading."

"It was being with the animals so much."

"*Go on*," Kit urged Rod.

"Seeing the difference, how plainly, how purposefully defined it was."

"I thought you *liked* me to read," said Rod.

"That's why you had everything in sight gelded and castrated I suppose," Kit remarked to his wife.

"The males were a menace."

"I admit that old Sam's billy goat was disgusting, but we're not all like that."

"The cockerel. Don't you remember how it used to pin me in a corner?"

"It didn't attack *me*," said Rod.

"It didn't have a chance," replied Kit. "Your mother ate it."

"Who killed it?" Maggie demanded to know.

"Me of course, you were too wet to do it. You just gave the orders."

"And the gander."

"You ate that too. The moment anything looked nasty, you ate it if you couldn't have its balls off. Including me."

"That was ages before."

"Did you have Daddy's balls off?"

"He means the vasectomy," said Maggie.

"Oh," said Rod and lost interest.

"Anyway," Maggie put in, "that was your idea."

"No it wasn't. I was all for *you* having the operation."

Maggie laughed. "Not really," she grinned.

"*Really!*"

"You fool."

"Could you help me with my necker?" Peter came in holding his green neckerchief. "Have you got my woggle?" he demanded of Rod.

"Here's your woggle." Maggie took it off the shelf where the coffee, tea and sugar were kept and holding it between her teeth, dried her hands and helped Peter fold his necker correctly.

"*Very* smart." Kit looked approvingly.

"Hurry up," agitated Rod, "or we'll be late."

"Hark at him . . . '*hurry up*' . . . The snail speaks," cried Maggie mockingly.

"We're putting up a tent tonight," said Rod.

"Oh, great." Peter moved more quickly.

"I'll walk along with you." Maggie peeled off her apron. "Kit?"

"My feet," he said, "are killing me."

It was a pleasant evening.

Lazily, the sun had begun to lower itself in the sky, throwing an idle warmth through the trees that overhung the narrow road running alongside the river. It was six-thirty and people were drifting towards The Swan, the white-painted pub whose balconies and bow windows rose above the road and gazed across the water, making the building look as if it were a lovely old ship about to put to sea. In the garden beside it, a fine magnolia flowered, its waxy violet-veined petals scattering the pavement.

"This bit's nice." Maggie stopped and gazed across the slow brown width of water. "I'll have this bit. No," she then said, on second thoughts, "I'll have the other side," and she pointed to the far bank, the Sweetings side of the river where the rough grassland frothed with cow parsley. Beyond the bank, some fifty yards further back was a line of trees, the elm and beech bright with a tender newness of green that would subside in another month. The may was coming, late, into blossom.

"*That's* my side," she repeated.

"Why's it yours?"

"Because I like it better."

No houses were visible on the Sweetings' side although, behind the trees, stood one great Jacobean house which, later in the season, would be open to visitors. They would be able to take tea in the rose garden. But it couldn't be seen. So close to London, the place had a rare wildness.

"I like *this* side best," said Rod. "The playground's this side." The playground lay behind them, in the opposite direction to the one they now took. Peter preferred this side too. Beyond the playground was a skating rink. Nearby were swimming pools and cinemas. It seemed to him to have a lot to recommend it. If it weren't for the smelly house they had to live in, he would have been delighted with the move to Popesvale. His father had said it was one of the best suburbs you could possibly live in. It had everything. Well, almost.

"Why *can't* Hymie come here?" he asked his mother as they ambled below the balcony of The Swan.

"It wouldn't be fair."

"We could take him for walks in the park."

"*We?*" she grinned, eyebrows ironically raised. "No, it's not the same."

"*I'd* take him . . ."

She said nothing and Peter knew she didn't believe him.

"*Honestly.*"

"In the winter, it'd be dark by the time you got home. And Daddy can't walk very far."

"Well, *you'll* be home most of the time when he goes back to work."

"It's not the same," she murmured and then, as if to assure him, "I miss Hymie too."

The pavement ended and they walked in a further silence along the road, hastening to catch up with Rod who was now running up one of the walls that here obscured private gardens and hid the river from sight. He ran up a pace and bounced back again, missing people. It was like a promenade in this part. People dawdled between the old brick walls which were bluish and pitted with age. They were draped with the weeping branches of ash and willow and beech.

"*Did* you take Hymie's balls off?" asked Peter suddenly.

"Yes, actually," she said as if in apology. "We had to. He was making a nuisance of himself."

"Oh . . ." he answered slowly, understanding better. "The bitches, you mean?"

"Yes. And the postman."

He frowned.

"What?" he said.

"He attacked Mr. Clark, the postman. Well, pretended to."

It still didn't quite make sense. Mr. Clark was a man. He tried to fix a picture of Hymie in his mind, attacking, to see if it yielded any connection. But all he saw was Hymie, bouncing, wagging, barking with delight, joining in all their games.

"It's the same instinct really," she offered, by way of explanation, looking down and seeing his scowling bewilderment. "The same drive. As someone said . . ." and she racked her brains for the words, ". . . you can sometimes only tell whether it's sex or aggression in animals if two males are doing it, or one male and one female are doing it. Or," she added, pulling his ear gently, "sometimes it's just play between young animals. Experimenting, practising."

"Like puppies?" he asked.

"Like puppies. Like you played with Hymie."

"Rod didn't play. He *teased*."

They were approaching that part of the road arched by a little bridge overhead, a small, concrete Rialto. On the wall to their left, dribbled in white paint, someone had slapped the words *Up The Sheds* and *Cunt*.

"Same things," said Maggie. "Puppies, all of you. Rod just behaved towards him without the inhibitions, the restraint an adult has. Any adult animal, however many legs. That's why Hymie bit him. It was play for him too."

"Play? *Biting?*" He ran a little to keep up with her.

"Yes, Rod invited it. But both of you were pretty rough with him you know, when you were smaller. If he weren't such a sweet-tempered dog he'd be ruined."

"*I* didn't tease him."

"Not as much," she acknowledged. Rod hopped back to them.

"*You* teased him," said Peter.

"Who? What?"

"Hymie."

"Rats," said Rod and hopped off again because one of the few things that burned his heart in a way that turned and lingered, was the knowledge that he'd once kicked Hymie and broken a small bone at the base of his tail. The dog had screamed and screamed, a sound they'd thought no dog could make, and then come crawling back towards them on his stomach as though wanting to be forgiven. Rod couldn't endure the feeling in his heart. He jumped up, as high as he could, to touch the white clusters of lilac. Their scent was so heavy, it made the air droop.

"What badge are you trying for tonight?"

Peter heard his mother but didn't reply. He was fed up with badges. "Mm?" she pressed.

He left her and ran after his brother because Rod had reached the entrance to the embankment garden which ran back along the river as far as the bridge they'd passed under and then opened up into the broader, formal lawns of Lion House Gardens on the other side of the road. They liked the Embankment Gardens. They were raised up above the level of the road and inside were three, murky, rectangular pools you could jump over. They went and jumped. Swifts were diving from the concrete balustrade on to the exposed river mud below.

This neat concrete area where elderly people sat on the benches staring into their past and the disgrace of the boatyard opposite, led into a more bosky area of the gardens where a massy monument rose up among the trees.

It made them laugh. They hung over the wall to see how far off their mother still was and ran to peep at the naked ladies.

At the top, high above them, was the queen of the women, her stone hair flying, her arms lifted as if about to rise in a gesture of leadership or victory, but momentarily held in a modest attempt to shield her breasts. She stood on the back of two winged horses, half-rearing above a gentle flow of water, which slipped down into two vast oyster shells, trickling thence, in turn, over their roughened edges. Between them, back towards the boys, knelt another woman, arms unrestrainedly upheld towards the queen and all around her, posed on other rocks, some to one side, some below, divided from the onlooker by a brackish pool in which lilies managed to grow, were other women, broad-backed, muscular, hurling themselves with various degrees of grace towards the topmost woman. One seemed to have fallen and sprawled awkwardly over her rock as though she'd dropped something in the water.

It was a peculiar arrangement of forms. Maggie had laughed with them when they first saw it and said the one piece of statuary missing, the thing that would make sense of their sporty movement, was the stone netball they were clearly flinging to one another.

They peered and giggled at the robust group before running off to catch Maggie up.

She left them at the Scout Hut in River Lane, next to the church which looked like two churches badly stuck together, half Norman and half Georgian, red brick and pale stone wedged complainingly into one another.

Their energy lessened as they joined the other boys in their green and gold-piped caps.

"It's all right," said Maggie, "you won't be shy for long. Games stop that." And she stood thoughtfully until they'd disappeared.

After she'd left them she turned and walked back, right past the bottom of Wellington Gardens, on as far as Queen's Lodge Park where the ferry that crossed to the Sweetings bank was moored.

6

"DID YOU BUILD your tent?" she asked eagerly, all the brittle control gone from her face. "Tell me what happened while I make you something proper to eat."

"We couldn't put one up," said Rod disgustedly, "on wooden boards."

"They just showed us diagrams." Peter pulled off his cap disconsolately.

"Perhaps we could put ours up on the Sweetings bank one day," she said, "if you like."

"Oh yes!" they chorused, clapping their hands, "yes, *please*!"

And as she turned away to busy herself at the stove she said, "I went over there this evening. In the boat."

"You went over there? Without us?" complained Rod.

"It's nice over there," she said.

Noticing the new movement in his mother's face, the tranquil smoothing of her skin, Peter asked later, "Would you tell us a story tonight, Mum, *please* would you?"

She looked at her watch. "All right," she conceded. "Let me think . . ."

While she thought, Peter ran and turned off the overhead light so that only the small lamp on the table between the beds burned a little pinkish circle of light. Then he leapt into bed and both boys wriggled and burrowed about under the clothes, making everything as comfortable as possible.

Maggie sat on Peter's bed, on the far side from the door so that her knees touched Rod's bed. It was lovely to feel the weight of her anchoring the blankets, Peter thought, and he wondered what she would choose tonight . . . phantoms or battles or fabulous beasts. Something witchy took over when she told her tales. All that was Celtic in her swam to the surface, altering the register of her voice. Some mothers, some teachers, when they told stories, lowered their heads and waggled them, peering into the faces of their audience one by one, but Maggie didn't look at anybody. Once, long ago, he'd seen her in a play, alone in a single spotlight, and her eyes had made him shiver. They'd looked like underwater gateways to another world. They didn't look like that in the commercial she did.

The two boys peered out from under the rumpled hood of their eiderdowns and waited.

"In a clearing," she began, softly, "the two creatures faced one another. They made low, growling noises. Sounds that ended in little yelps. Briefly, they bared their teeth. All the whines, the half swallowed rumbling sounds held many meanings for each creature.

"They held their ground, each creature searching out the features of the other. Neither animal moved its head at all. All around them though, there was movement. The jungle stirred, lifting and subsiding as though it breathed. But it was the small hidden movements of birds and other loping creatures that made the leaves lift like tongues.

"The sunlight fell in streamers on the upturned heads of yellow, white and scarlet-spotted flowers. Scent was burned out of them. Bees were drawn deep into their throats. The insects dipped and sucked and zithered, undisturbed by the circling movements the two creatures now performed . . ."

"What sort of creatures are they?" Rod asked.

"Wait," whispered Maggie, "and I'll describe them to you." And she continued.

"Their hides were the colours of shadow and sunlight, gold-striped where they passed through the poles of light, and dusky — the same soft brown as tree bark, or the mould on the ground that they stirred up as they moved.

"They moved smoothly, gracefully — even when a forelimb was quite violently raised or one of them swung, cringing — as though their bodies conformed to a silent music they carried in their heads.

"The attention that each had for the other was total. Neither the lengthy slinking of patterns along a branch, nor the screeching swoop of a bird, thirty-five separate shades of green, disturbed them at all.

"Suddenly . . . !"

"Oh!" Peter's breath ran backwards into his chest. His mother was poised, hands raised, level with her throat. "*Suddenly*, the larger of the two creatures sprang forward, seized the neck of the other between its teeth and clung there, growling. Together, they swayed, holding the posture, until, by a swift shifting of his balance, the larger animal was able to bring its body into a parallel alignment, driving the neck of its victim lower towards the ground . . .!"

The boys jumped as Kit crept into the room. He held a finger to his lips and sat down in the corner on a tiny chair.

"The chatter of birds, the song of the insects, even the hidden tumbling of water, ceased. For a while, they held still." And Maggie paused a moment.

"Then the pinioned creature broke free, darting behind the trees, uttering cries that made the birds hurtle upwards from their branches, making a yellow monkey leap into a darker thicket of leaves.

"In and out of the trees they raced, skins glinting like lamps. But it was a brief escape . . ." Maggie's voice fell again. "As the range of their circle again decreased bringing them back into the clearing — empty except for a single tree whose thorny, speckled boughs drooped under the succulent weight of purple fruit — so, the distance between them also decreased until the larger animal was able to bound on to the back of the smaller, dragging it down again."

"Ah-h-h," wailed Rod into his sheets.

It's a fight, thought Peter. I bet Mummy makes the smaller one win.

"It was dragged down. There was a flurry. A yelping. Muted sounds though, as if the captured creature was ready to surrender. Certainly that's what the larger animal seemed to understand by it. It eased a little, then lowering its head licked that part of the neck it had earlier pierced with its teeth. Slowly, it licked along the ridged length of the smaller creature's spine. The growling became a mumble — only rising to threatening pitch when the creature beneath it attempted to move. But she — for plainly, it *was* a she-creature — remained so still most of the time that flies settled in radiant clusters on the silk of her back."

"Is she dead?" asked Rod.

"Shut up," hissed Peter.

"Above them, the monkey, clutching a leaking peachy fruit to its chest, returned. It settled to eat and to watch. A small yellow bird alighted between the animals, pecking at the dust before flying off with a lustre-plated beetle in its beak.

"The two creatures mated.

"A white tigress with chocolate stripes stretched herself lazily on a bleached bough that swallowed her magnificence. And when the he-creature raised his head and uttered a long cry to the burning scrap of blue visible overhead, the tigress yawned and jungle fowl scurried through the foliage."

"Are you quite sure . . . ?" Kit began, ". . . has this got a U certificate?"

Both children shushed him. Here was an element that tightened their attention.

"Now it was the she-creature who bounded and licked. Vigorously, she attended to her smooth pelt before settling beside her drowsing mate. But, like the flies that spooled in his crevices, she was restless. She scratched herself, shook herself and, rising, stretched each limb in turn before padding swiftly away in search of water.

"She drank heavily from the concealed stream and then, returning, nibbled at whatever fruits and berries hung within reach. Now, in the thin rods of sunlight, the purple fruits of the spiky tree glistened.

"Their fragrance clung to the delicate inner membrane of her nostrils. Hesitantly, she drew within reach of the difficult clusters, each one ringed by thorns.

"The powerful instinct to eat, an involuntary yearning of the jaws, brought the she-creature to the low-hanging, aromatic fruit. But something . . . an underlying hint of bitterness in the odours . . . the spotted bark of the tree, flecked to conceal whatever scaly creature cared to coil itself upon the branches, made her wary. She prowled, paused, scented again. The smells were good. The skin of the fruits were swollen to splitting with inner ripeness. Another hour and they would burst upon the ground, spoilt. Raising herself waveringly on her hind legs, she took the fruit between her teeth and pierced the swollen, royal skin.

"A tremor passed through the forest. A pale sigh that stained the consciousness of the sleeping he-beast. The skin that lay in glossy ridges across his ribs tightened as he sprang fearfully to his feet. A warning cry escaped him but the she-creature, unperturbed, turned her head, her jaws streaming with juices, and smiled.

"It was an alien expression, uncustomary in her species but

not unfamiliar to the he-creature. He had seen it on the face of his Master and knew it signified good things. It conveyed pleasure.

"Again she rose on her hind legs, more steadily now. He shrank from her steadiness, baffled, apprehensive. She stood higher than he and he drew back a pace as she advanced towards him cradling the offered fruit. With one hand she fed him. With the other she caressed the long, coarse hair of his head just as his Master caressed it. Her touch was not comforting to him. The glad instinct to submit that such a touch normally aroused in him, was no longer there. He cringed beneath it, lifting the skin of his lips warningly as he bared his teeth. The desire to bite, truly to bite, to bite through his repugnance of blood was so strong, his skin trembled convulsively. Again she uttered a cry that had no place in their throats. It was the sound of laughter.

"A new instinct seized hold of him, a terrible, driving desire to kill. Never had he felt anything grip him so strongly. Never before had he been aware of the cruel inhibition that prevented him. The two impulses raged in his body as humbly he fed from her hand.

" 'Eat!' she commanded in her strange tongue.

"New patterns of sound formed themselves in him. Raising his head, he heard himself cry, 'Why do you laugh in this way?' and the sound of his own voice troubled him.

" 'Look at yourself,' she said.

"And he did so. He found he was able to gaze at his own body as if it were a separate thing. As if his head, his eyes, had been removed and set on a branch to stare at the thing that remained. In order to study himself fully, he stood and found he stood higher than she. Now it was *her* body he gazed upon. She carried his odours and he was ashamed by the comical, graceless spectacle they presented, neither animal nor Master but a parody of both. 'Hide yourself!' he cried, and ran to seize broad fig leaves from a fallen tree."

"Oh, I know what it's all about!" Peter sighed, smiling. But his mother didn't pause from her trance-like telling of the tale. Her sing-song voice went on.

"He could hear no crackling of predators in the forest. He could smell no dangerous animal odour — other than his own. But his own alarmed him as though he were his own enemy. He tingled with fear as if the dark shapes of the forest dwelt in him. In the new separate dimension of himself. And when, as he urgently entwined the stems of the leaves, he looked upon his mate, the fear intensified as though the threat lay in her too. She, who was his, she who padded after him, she who hung back from feeding till his belly was filled, now stood, her underside exposed, facing him with herself, teeth bared in smile. He was afraid.

"Fashioning a girdle of leaves, he placed it around her hips. Then he made another for himself.

"'Why?' she demanded, laughing, 'why do you do that?'

"He saw that she was not afraid of herself. She had no sense of being separated from herself. She gazed lovingly and proudly at her own body, touching it with delight. She made as if to pluck the girdle from herself, but, hearing an urgent calling, she halted. They turned their heads, alerted by the note.

"Except for the stream which sang, not *to* them now, but about them — about their exclusion from forest things — all else fell quiet. Confused, they shrank into the darkest foliage as their Master drew near.

"Entering the clearing, he looked about for them, his expression sad.

"Now they saw themselves in his image as clearly as they had once seen themselves in the stream and thought themselves a part of the cool, clear water they had drunk. But the resemblance they knew, was not exact. They were as separate from him as they were from themselves, as they were from one another. All the bonds of the forest life which bound them to its inseparable centre were broken.

"Dejectedly, as he called, they crept towards him, stooping to conceal their uprightness.

"'What have you done?' he asked sorrowfully. 'What have you done?'"

They were without answer.

"'You cannot,' he said in a heavy voice, 'remain here any longer. You are not part of the forest now. You cannot live off the innocent air and water shared by my flowers and lions and okapi. The web of the forest cannot hold you now.'

"Anger welled in the he-creature. 'It was she!' he cried. 'It is all her doing!' And he swore aloud in his anger that if he could not be a part of the forest he would destroy it. He would visit his own curse upon it. He would destroy its bees and streams and birds and build his own jungle, a finer place than this and then, tormented by the wretchedness and fury that beset him he turned on the she-creature who drew back alarmed, her gaze flickering swiftly from him to the Master and back again.

"Raising his hand, the Master stepped between them. The he-creature's vengeful lament ceased. He hung his head in shame.

" 'You will know sorrow,' said the Master to the she-creature as she stood, facing her mate. 'He will bring you sorrow and suffering. He will punish you always. Even though you love him. Even,' he said, in a slow and heavy voice, 'even as he will love you.'

"Puzzled, she took a further step backwards. She wanted her mate near her, but she feared him. Like him, she perceived herself as an object of her own vision, as distinct as the thorny fruit-laden tree whose rank sweetness filled the clearing. But she loved what she saw and could not comprehend why it was her mate rolled his head and gnashed his teeth in anguish.

" 'Now,' said the Master softly, taking her hand and drawing her near, 'now you are the mother of all living things.' And he looked at her with such pity, she wondered at the strange, unhappy honour he had bestowed on her.

"Lifting his throat to the sky, the he-creature gave forth a long and dreadful moan.

" 'And now,' urged the Master, 'you must go from my garden or you will break its peace for ever.'

"And he led them eastwards out, through the trees and trailing blossoms, out of the dappled sunshine and darkness, to a gate that opened on to a flat, wide, yellow world where sky and sand were as sharply divided from themselves, as inimical to one another as the two creatures now knew themselves to be.

" 'Cleave together,' commanded the Master gently as he bade them farewell. But they stepped beyond the gate without looking at one another and walked slowly away in silence.

"As they went, on clumsy, stumbling feet, the Master stood by the gate watching them and only when he saw the woman reach out and take the man's hand did he sigh and draw back.

"Where he had stood, a flame broke out of the ground winding upwards into the air. The heat of it was so intense it made all surrounding objects shimmer as if their foundations had become uncertain.

"Behind the sword of flame, the gate quietly closed."

"Is that it?" asked Rod after a short silence.
Maggie nodded, her eyes dreamy.

"It's a pretty funny story," concluded Rod. "Where did they go?"

"It's about Adam and Eve, isn't it?" Peter asked, pleased that he had guessed right. "But you've messed it about a bit."

"It's blatant propaganda," grinned Kit, creaking up from his low, painful chair. "You missed out all sorts of things. Still, I don't know where you get it all from. You're a funny old thing, Mags. Where does it come from I wonder?"

She stretched, the spell broken. "I don't know." She shook her head vigorously from side to side, hair flying in sheaves. "It's the same thing as acting does for me. I get a charge."

Rod was still thinking crossly. "You left the snake out," he said.

"Not *really*."

"Yes you did."

"You made out that it wasn't really Eve's fault," complained Peter.

"Ah, you noticed that," observed Kit, tickling him.

"Well," Maggie defended herself, "Perhaps if Eve alone had possessed the gift of knowledge, we shouldn't all be tied up in such knots. Perhaps the world wouldn't be a violent place."

"You've really got a thing about the aggressive male haven't you, dolly drop?" Kit stopped tickling Peter who was bunched up like a grub and seized Maggie instead.

She shrieked.

"Well, it's true. You can't deny it. Your little Y chromosome is fixed forever. Final. *Ouch!* You can't escape it. It's not your — *don't* do that — not your fault. It's your — ahh! — *fate*."

"Tickle me!" begged Rod.

Kit did so.

"I'll grant you this," he shouted, trying to get his fingers into Rod's armpits and prevented by Rod's perverse clamping of his arms to his sides, "that before the Jews decided they'd like to have a male god to get on with things more efficiently, they were ruled by a goddess. I think she was even called Eve — or some Yiddish equivalent."

"So they had to make up that miserable little story?" Maggie looked pleased. "It all makes sense. Heavens," she said, throwing Peter's furry toy koala bear up in the air and catching it, "I don't know why you lot, you chaps, don't admit how much you like scrapping and bashing and doing one another down." She ducked Peter's attempt to grab her and his bear. "You

72

always pretend you're squabbling for some peaceful purpose, putting a nice gloss on your nasty nature — look at the bomb."

"What bomb?" demanded Peter.

"*The* bomb. We'll be up to our ears in plutonium before you lot own up to the defect in your natural composition. Ruined by a chromosome!"

"But what about the *snake*?" demanded Rod, red in the face and refusing to be settled down.

"Oh, it's *all* about the snake," smiled Maggie mysteriously. "In a way. That's precisely what it's all about. But I'll explain that bit to you when you're fifteen."

"Oh-oh!" wailed Rod. "Why not now?"

"We're much nicer than you make out," alleged Kit, straightening Rod's bedclothes. "You're fast becoming a chauvinist sow. What's freaking you?"

"You."

"Me?" He looked astonished and a little hurt, standing up to adjust his glasses. "*Me?*" he repeated. "How can you say that when I'm such a classic case of the liberated male. Look what a beautiful job I make of the washing up! Look how eager I am for you to go out and earn our living! What more do you want?"

"You're marvellous," she conceded, kissing his ear. "In that respect."

"What do you mean, *me*, then?" He rubbed his aching leg and waited for an answer.

"Are you a Woman's Libber?" Peter intervened suspiciously. He'd seen shots on the news of women shouting and waving banners. The sight bothered him rather.

"Come on, come on . . ." urged Kit impatiently, waiting. Then, to Peter, "Women haven't given *up* apple scrumping. They're still at it. Still trying to assert themselves."

"You don't *mind* that!" Maggie stated.

"Of course not. I'm just pointing something out, that's all. All the more reason why I want to know what I've done to bring out your animosity."

Maggie sat down again on the edge of the bed, swinging the bear from one hand. "It's not what you've done so much," she said, "but what was done to you."

"You're blaming my mother now?"

"No," she laughed and pointed her toes so that they touched one another while she searched for words. "The war," she said. "What that did to you. Nearly killed you. Damaged you."

"I didn't start the bloody war," he said.

"No." She left a long pause. Without looking at him she said, "But you wanted to go. Wanted to be involved. The idea excited you. You thought it was someone else's war. An assignment, that's all, just something you could go and have a look at then come home as easily as if you'd been covering a horse show. But nobody can just go and look and walk away. You didn't even walk away. You were carried away. And you're scarred by it. Not just here . . ." And she touched his thigh gently.

"I wish I could have gone," said Rod wistfully.

"Scarred?" repeated Kit irritably. "I just learnt my lesson, that's all. I learnt what a filthy business it was."

"But you wanted to be there."

"Of course I wanted to be there. I'm a journalist. I'm in the business of informing people. *Was*. Someone has to do it."

"It satisfied something else in you as well."

"Rubbish," denied Kit, and he leant past her to sort out the muddle of Peter's bedclothes.

"*Are* you?" repeated Peter. "One of those women?"

Maggie stooped to turn out the light and paused with her hand on the switch. "Not the fighting kind," she said reassuringly. "That just makes enemies. I want us all to be friends. All right?"

He *thought* it was all right. It sounded all right. "Yes," he murmured, thinking of the angry women he'd seen. Why were they so angry? He couldn't imagine any of the mothers he knew in Sigvales doing things like that. They hardly ever got cross. But his own mother . . . he glanced up at her as she watched him musingly. Since they'd come here, he'd seen her angrier than he'd ever seen her. "You do get cross sometimes," he said.

Her face changed. Saddened. "Do I?" she said. "I'm sorry, my darling. I don't mean to. I don't want to."

He relaxed inside. "It's all right," he said forgivingly and he hugged her, before she switched the light off and tiptoed, with his father, outside the bedroom door.

He heard them laughing gently as they went downstairs. "Do you understand about the snake?" asked Rod in the darkness.

Peter considered for a moment. "Not really," he said.

7

"I KNOW WHAT it is about this house," said Maggie at breakfast next morning (it was Saturday and she had the time to sit down over her own coffee and toast instead of throwing it angrily at someone else). "I can't think why it didn't strike me before." And she gave a small, deprecating snort, as she pulled the morning's post towards her.

"I'm all agog," said Kit, poring over the Employment Opportunities.

"It's not *just* that we can't see the river from our windows, the whole aspect of this house is the wrong way round. It's turned its *back* on the river," she laughed. "Had you realised, it's the only house in the whole of Wellington Gardens that faces towards the main road, towards London?"

"Of course I had."

"Of *course* you had . . .!"

"Yes, of course."

"Oh," she said, crushed. "Oh, well."

And they all ate peacefully for a while.

"Can we go out somewhere nice?" said Rod, noting his mother's good mood.

"There's the house . . ." she began jovially, "the work . . ."

"Why not?" Kit looked up. "Where would you *like* to go?"

"Swimming," said both boys together. They'd discussed it in bed that morning.

"Swimming, eh? All right, Mags?"

She looked at Kit levelly for a second. "All right," she said and lowered her head towards the wide, shallow coffee cup, using one hand to hold back a curtain of hair behind her ear.

"*Mags . . .?*" He pressed her, looking over the rim of his glasses.

"All *right*," she repeated irritably.

"*I'll* take them . . ." he said.

"I know."

"You *do* sound grateful."

Her lips parted as if eager to say something and then were meekly lowered again to the bowl of the cup.

"You going to swim, Dad?"

"I might, yes."

"I can show you my dive."

The door bell rang.

It was Belinda. She wore a trim pair of bell-bottom jeans and a white smock affair over her striped T-shirt. Her long, fair hair was tied, Alice-fashion, with a pale blue bow high on the back of her head. Around her neck was a string of pink plastic beads that looked as though they'd come out of a Lucky Dip.

"I've come to play," she announced to Maggie who stood, unselfconsciously, in her nightdress. It was not quite nine o'clock.

"The boys will be delighted," lied Maggie and stepped back to let Belinda in.

"Are you still having your breakfast!" Belinda followed Maggie into the kitchen. "*Heavens!* . . . I've come to play," she said to the boys.

They looked at her, their mouths moving in slow and dismal judgment of the situation.

"We're going out swimming later," said Rod.

"*I'd* like to go swimming."

"*Can* you swim?"

"Of course I can, silly." She giggled at Maggie conspiratorially, betraying her mother's absurd reliance on female togetherness. "Are you *all* going?" Again it was to Maggie she addressed herself. The men stared gloomily at her, then gloomily amongst themselves.

"I'm not," said Maggie. "I can't. There's work to do."

"Oh, I see." Belinda looked coldly at Rod, Peter and Kit, sizing them up with her large, hard blue eyes, then twitched her sharply uptilted nose and decided that it would be all right. "I'm surprised *you're* going," she said to Kit, "I thought you were disabled."

"Oh, you'd be surprised what I can do."

"You would indeed," sniffed Maggie, as though a further

female presence, however minimal, freed her to speak out. "*I* am. Yesterday he couldn't walk to the shops. Today he can go swimming."

"It's good for me. The doctor said so."

Maggie jumped up and clasped Kit's head to her stomach. "I know, I know," she cried, "I'm sorry." She hugged him. "Bitch," she said of herself, "I must try harder."

"Try what harder?" Belinda demanded to know.

"Never you mind, miss," Maggie grinned at her. "Go and ask your mother what she thinks. You'll have to manage in the changing rooms on your own."

"I've done that thousands of times," claimed Belinda, doing something swan-like with her neck. "O.K." And she let herself out of the back door.

"Gnash it!" growled Peter. "What'd you have to say anything about swimming for?"

"It's all right. We can duck her," suggested Rod.

"I'm *sorry* . . ." Maggie caught at Kit again, took his hand. "Why *am* I so awful?"

"You're not. You've just got too much to do."

She laughed a little at his contradictions. "All the same . . ." she murmured and lowered her head on his shoulder.

"Urr-rrk! There they go!" cried Rod of his parents' embrace. "I say, there's a horrible smell in here."

"We need a holiday." Kit was smoothing his wife's hair gently.

"A holiday!" It was a smothered, equivocal sound, a cry that signified the idea's absurdity. "Where do you suggest?" she said with mock seriousness. "Nassau? Nairobi? Guadeloupe?"

Kit buried his head in Maggie's breast and snuggled there for a moment.

"Oh crumbs," groaned Peter. He wished his mother wouldn't wander around in her nightie. Belinda could easily have seen the shadowy triangle . . . quickly, he poured himself a glass of milk.

"Anyway," said Maggie cheerfully, "I've gone off holidays."

"Why?" Kit smiled, bewildered.

"After the last time."

"Last time?" Kit searched his memory.

"Nearly four years ago."

"*Four* years . . ."

"Italy."

77

"Italy? Oh God, yes." Kit looked thoughtful.

"Tell us what happened in Italy!" chorused the boys.

"Another time," their mother promised, tracing her finger the length of Kit's nose.

"My God yes . . ." Kit repeated. "Italy. I'd forgotten that."

Belinda appeared at the back door.

"I'm ready," she announced.

"We're not," said Rod.

But it wasn't long before they left Maggie to her dishes and her recollections.

Kit had been due home from Calcutta after three weeks away. The plane was to touch down in Rome, and Maggie, excited by the plan, had said she would meet him there. They would spend a few days together, alone. She had never been to Rome before.

They had just settled themselves into their hotel when the phone rang. It was Kit's news editor. There had, he said, been rioting in a village near Naples . . . how about . . .?

"It'll all be over by the time we get there," Kit had laughed, knowing the Italian temperament. "But it means a couple of extra days on expenses. Why not?" And Maggie, who'd been looking forward to her first glimpse of Rome, agreed, why not.

The drive had been uninteresting, a long, flat yellow pursuit of the motorway. To find the village, which was called Casel di Principe, they'd eventually turned into narrower roads, asking directions in ludicrous Italian of peasants unwilling or unable to answer. They never had found a signpost. Just suddenly arrived in the place they had sought. They had known it was the right place immediately. More of a small town than a village, it possessed a considerable market square, a large exposed area flanked on all four sides by substantial buildings whose windows had, in the main, been smashed. The square had been ringed (on all four sides it seemed in retrospect, but in fact, on two sides only, the two sides that angled their entry) by silent men.

Across the square, two green buses, overturned on their sides, had smouldered gently. The men — there were no women in sight at all — had stood patiently waiting, it seemed, for them. But when Kit had parked the white hired car near by, nobody had moved towards them. Not even the solitary, uniformed police figure who had, if anything, been even more dreadfully fixed in his place than the others. His gaze had gone over the roof

78

of their car as if they were not there and when Kit had clambered out, and gone, with the persistent innocence of the British abroad, however well travelled, to ask for information, the man had raised his eyes to a thick spiral of smoke which twisted above the damaged roofs opposite. Broken glass had littered the ground.

All Kit had then known was that this was a strongly Communist area, that the Government had delayed in compensating the peasants for damage to their crops after the Volturno had flooded the previous year. He had known the bare facts. But he needed to know the history and nature of their resentments and he needed the time to discover them. To judge from the dark stance of the men in the square, the troubles were far from over and, seeing a telephone sign over a café on the far, southerly side of the square, he had gone to book a call to London, to warn his office a story would be filed later.

Maggie had watched him from the car, his figure growing unreasonably small as he'd crossed the wide, dusty square and disappeared inside the café.

Because the car had been parked in the full glare of the afternoon sun, it was breathlessly hot inside it and Maggie had let herself out, walking a little towards the shade cast by the buildings on the nearest side of the square where the watchful villagers were most thickly gathered. She had stood, not close to them, not facing them, but some ten feet away, her back towards them, her face towards the café, staring at it with the same fixity the villagers displayed in their scrutiny of her.

Nothing had moved for a while — save for a few charred scraps of paper, a sheet of polythene which had blown against a wall and there subsided. Then she had become aware of light footsteps and turned to find small boys, their heads as brown and smooth as nuts, their eyes darkly shining, creeping up on her.

She had met their smiles, as one does the smiles of children, and her response had widened theirs. Their numbers had grown as each child detached himself from between the unmoving figures of older men and had run forth to join his friends, encircling Maggie slowly as if they were about to break into an old, traditional dance.

They had started to utter little cries, quietly at first, inquiringly, and she had gestured with the air of a fool's apology, that she did not understand. "Inglesa," she had said. But the cries had swelled — unevenly at first — a childish harmony, part

79

curiosity part delight it had seemed to her. And then: "Fucky! Fucky!" one, bolder than the rest, had called, retiring a little to test the impact of his impudence. And the others, giggling, had taken up the refrain, "Fucky! Fucky! . . . Fucky! Fucky! . . ." And they had pressed closer both to her and together as their numbers grew, some squeezed backwards by the shoulders of bigger boys. Two rings they had formed, then three, then they had begun to pluck at her arm, to touch her, lightly, swiftly, darting back momentarily as if a small electric charge had passed from her clothing along their fingers. A fourth ring of older boys had formed. A chorus, urging on their younger brothers. And their delight enlarged and gathered, making them fearless as if they had been either drunk or drugged by the ecstasy of their mutual company and they had plucked at the skirt of her dress, a small orange awning, lifting a little, dropping, lifting further, dropping, laughing, lifting higher, more wildly, as her hands had begun to fly out at them, nervous birds, afraid to strike, and she had been spinning, a silly top, from one playful pair of hands to the next, "Fucky! Fucky! . . . Fucky! Fucky! . . ."

Somehow (even now she couldn't recall how) she had fought her way through their hot and slippery ring, struggled back into the car and slammed the door, her heart forced up to her throat with fear. And they had squeezed their fingertips through the tiny gap between the glass and the metal, forcing the windows down, reaching in, pulling her hair, her breasts, the chain around her neck which had broken and dropped in her lap. They had stretched after it, or after the place in her lap where it had fallen, tweaking at her, so that even through the material of her dress she could feel the mean tug of rooted hair.

Faces, faces. Boys' faces pressed against all the glass, blackening the interior of the car. Laughing and screeching they had clambered on to the roof, on to the bonnet and begun to rock it to and fro, the arc of movement increasing a little with each swing. In panic she had pressed her hand to the horn and the sound, her response, the arrival of Kit, something, all these things together had made them fall briefly away, just sufficiently for Kit to force a small passage through. She had glimpsed his arm wrestling with the locked handle.

Pushing her roughly over to the other side of the car he had fallen in, slammed the door and started the engine. But the boys had recovered, were jumping back on the bonnet, rocking, rocking their slow passage across the square.

"Go faster!" she had screamed. "*Faster!*"

But he had not accelerated. Could not. Had he knocked against one of the boys, injuring him, however slightly, he knew with a certainty that was quite cold, that held quite steady in the centre of their panic, that they would both have been killed.

"But why did they do it?" she had cried, her voice high-pitched with fear, as his foot was at last pressed down harder and the village drew away in their rear window. "Why? Why?"

"Number plates," he'd answered tersely. "Rome number plates."

"But why, why, why?" she'd repeated, meaning why should that have mattered so, but he had answered her differently, mistaking her persistence.

"Because you're a woman," he had said.

But when they had stopped some miles away and she had looked at him, and she had seen, coating his face, the same oily sweat as coated her own, she had been shocked to discover he could be so frightened by his own kind.

"Watch me! Watch me!"

Rod hopped up and down on the blue-tiled edge of the pool, fighting for attention in the throng. Between him and his father, who sat against the wall on a wooden bench, head dodging backwards as spray flew up from the water, were all the Saturday people. All the children, all the fathers. "I'm going to do my dive! Watch me!" Rod waved through the white limbs, the draggled hair, the gouts of water and seeing a space, avoiding a small girl with inflated yellow arm bands whose head was thrust out of the water as fanatically as a dog's, he dived in, slightly bent.

Down he went, hair streaming, pushing aside legs that looked like pale green roots weaving around him. He groped underwater, thinking he was near the place where his father waited, but when he surfaced, he found he was facing round the wrong way and had to flip his hair sharply out of his eyes to see where Kit was. The bottom was just a toe's length below him and he had to keep bobbing.

"Dad! Dad! Did you see me?"

Kit (a little blindly, without his glasses) was smiling, his head turned away towards two older girls in bikinis who were trying to drag a younger, protesting girl into the water. Their shrieks became part of the general, hollowing howl that rose and boomed against the glass roof of the indoor pool.

"*Dad!*"

Now Kit heard. His head turned vaguely this way and that, still smiling as the pleasurable image remained with him, searching out the one sound that was meant for him amid the squeals and the wingeing thump of the springboard.

Rod had to bob and tiptoe into the shallower water to grip the edge directly below his father.

"*Dad!*"

Now he saw him. "Hi, Rod! Super!"

"Why don't you come in?"

A prancing group came between them, flicking water from their fingertips. One thin girl in a black woollen swimsuit wiped a long streamer of catarrh from her nose.

". . . like a sardine tin."

"Not down the other end. You could take me down the other end. I could go in the deep end if you came in."

"You could go in now."

"It says no-one under ten without an adult."

"Oh, they wouldn't . . ." Kit began, then realising his raised voice might be overheard by one of the effete young men in T-shirts and trunks who were supposed to save lives, called instead, "When am I going to see this terrific dive of yours then?" And glimpsing the sudden slide of expression on Rod's face, added, "There was somebody in the way last time."

Peter and Belinda, being ten, fairly tall (she, taller than he) and both competent swimmers, were in the deep end which remained fairly empty until about lunchtime. The only other people — apart from those who swam doggedly up and down, faces either under the water or raised and blinded by it — were a group of teenage boys whose voices had a raw, ragged depth used at full volume as though their owners were not, as yet, accustomed to the new sound in their mouths. Blaring like immature cattle, they dared one another on the top board.

Her hair scraped back in a rubber band from which it fell in a thin, wet streamer, Belinda swam a careful breast stroke across the width of the bath. It was a very exact and neat performance, as if done by numbers. Sitting on the side, his feet in the water, Peter watched her approach him, her eyes secured to the point where her outstretched fingertips would meet at the conclusion of her stroke.

She reached the edge beneath him. They did not speak. After a short rest, she turned, and once more set out on her meticulous journey across the pool. He let her get a third of the way across and then he dived in, surfacing into the first stroke of a rapid, splashing crawl that made her wince away as he passed her. At the far side he waited for her to catch up.

They hung together side by side for a moment recovering their breath and watching the confused wrestling above them on the top board. "Can you dive?" asked Peter, casually.

"Yes, of course."

"Let's dive then."

Wearily almost, she turned and swam to the steps in the corner, clambered up and waited for him. He didn't look at her or hang about but dived straight off the edge, feeling his knees bend as he entered the water. Thrusting the hair from his eyes, he saw her dive, a cautious tidy plunge that barely raised a splash.

They repeated the performance. Then again. And again. Peter's ears were beginning to hurt.

Intently, they continued the pattern of their diving, until Belinda tired of it and called (giving herself a start), "Race you to the other side!" and she began a crawl that would have matched his own for speed had he responded to the challenge. When she came running indignantly round to his side of the pool, he pushed her in, in a friendly way, and she burst up, above the transparent turquoise skin laughing and shaking her fist at him. "You wait!" she cried, spitting water and tossing her lank pony tail. But he didn't wait. He jumped in and clutched at her white, underwater feet. She kicked. He clasped her more tightly, then lurched away before she could catch him, all her neatness gone now as she laughed and swallowed and squealed.

She caught him round the neck with her arms, then wound her legs round him as though making him carry her piggyback. He felt the slithering warmth of her legs sliding over his hips, lowering his trunks a little, her thighs crossing over his thighs. Breaking away from the oddly warm grip, he ducked, slipped below the surface and turned lithely — all of a piece, like a fish — and caught her in the same position, hoisting himself on to her hips, wrapping his legs around hers. Clinging, chest to back, he felt a deep and tingling sensation flood his lower body as though he might pee in the water but wouldn't really. He held her very tight round the neck, assuring himself of the brief pleasure, then sensing from her struggle that he was hurting her, he let go: but not immediately. He let himself feel her struggle.

"Pig! Pig!" she squeaked, turning over on her back and

batting her arms away from him until she lay full length, toes upturned a few inches away from his face. Because it seemed to him an invitation to be tickled, he did so. The effect was electric. She roared, or howled, with uncontrollable pleasure, and disappeared in a massive flurry of spray.

"I'm *terribly* ticklish," she said, re-appearing beside him.

They tickled and splashed some more. In between he told her that they were going to get a boat and she could have a ride in it if she liked. And then, quite suddenly, just as she was squirming and yelping particularly vigorously, she stopped. The arm that had been clamped to her side to control a lovely spasm, flew up, armpit exposed, in a salute of some kind. He followed her gaze, treading water exhaustedly.

"Kathy!" she was yelling, "Ka-athy! Hi! It's me!"

Another girl, importantly tucking her curls into a pink bathing cap with a cluster of rubber flowers over one ear, broke off from her task and waved back.

Belinda swam strongly towards her. They began calling out to one another in a conversational way long before they actually met. Once together, out of the water, their faces came extremely close as if they had only secrets to discuss.

Slowly, Peter swam after them.

"Oh, Kathy! This is Peter." Casually, Belinda flung out an arm. "He's just moved into our road. C'mon in. It's lovely!"

Already the warmth of their bodily contact was fading. The water felt quite cold.

"We're going to go off the board, Peter! Coming?"

He didn't believe they could dive, only jump. He was anxious to go first, and raced out of the water ahead of them. He walked along the springboard which reached out some six feet above the water and tried to avoid looking at the painted lines waving on the tiled bottom.

As he'd been taught, he raised his arms straight over his ears, then slowly leaned forward, keeping his arms taut. Then, trying to straighten his legs as he went, he fell in. It wasn't too bad. He didn't hurt himself.

Belinda ran and jumped, holding her nose. Kathy followed. They scrambled out and ran before he could get there, back on to the springboard, Kathy ahead, running fast, springing and — wonderful — completing a somersault which ended in a rather harsh entry into the water.

I bet she stings, he thought.

But she and Belinda (whose performance he'd missed) were

up and out again, racing for the board. They jumped higher, twisting this time.

Peter took his turn.

"Hurry up! Go on!" they giggled behind him as he flexed his toes and raised his arms carefully. "*Hurry up!*"

He realised he was slowing them down, withdrawing a little excitement from their pace, but he dived in his own time and perfectly.

They took no notice.

"*Après vous!*"

"*Non, non mam'zelle, après vous!*"

Thereafter they bounded along the board in a quick succession of running dives.

Peter saw his father appear at the side of the pool. "Ve-ry good!" he mouthed at them. Rod, shivering and lilac-tinged, hung beside him. "Enough?" Kit yelled. Or that's what it looked like.

Peter's ears *and* lip were aching now.

But while Kit waited, the girls did their running dives again, their complete, smooth bodies flying almost carelessly through the air.

Peter crawled showily over to his father. "Come on," said Rod, "I'm freezing."

"O.K." Peter swam to the steps and Kit's face fell open with surprise at the lack of argument. He helped haul Peter out but Peter pulled his hand free.

"Come on!" he shouted at Belinda, walking away. "We've got to go."

"See you! *Au revoir!*" Belinda raised one arm and flapped her hand from its wrist to her friend, a gesture immaculately copied from her mother.

"Thank you *very* much for bringing me," she gasped up at Kit, her head (goofily, Rod thought) to one side.

The boys scrambled into their clothes. Because they hadn't dried themselves properly their vests and pants stuck clammily to them. They began to enjoy that after-swim sensation of warmth and cold, mixed.

Rod wanted to have a go with the hot-air machine but Peter pulled at him. "Move," he said rudely, stretching Rod's jumper.

As they gathered their belongings and went out to meet the others, he noticed that as well as the pain in his ears and the pain in his lip, a wincing ache seemed to have developed deep in his chest.

8

THE HANDLE OF the kitchen door had dropped off again, but the force of three bodies hurled at it, shoulders leading, made it fly open all right. A steamy warmth of bubbling vegetables wrapped itself around them instantly.

"What the . . .!" Kit cried out. And they all stood, rooted to the spot, in varying states of disbelief, laughter and bewilderment as a large but composed chicken held a saucepan to the lid of a pan and drained boiling water into the sink.

"Dear God . . .!"

The chicken, whose uptilted yellow satin bottom was awkwardly balanced on two wrinkly orange legs, turned its head. Beneath the matching orange visor of its beak, Maggie's face peered out. She had tied her flowered apron around her neck, like a bib.

"Oh, good," she said, "lunch is nearly ready." And she tipped the potatoes into a bowl.

Kit sat down weakly. The boys continued to stare.

"Enjoy your swim?" she asked.

Then they began to giggle. Uncertainly, at first: there was something grotesque to be overcome before the comedy could be enjoyed.

"Meat balls," she said calmly. And reached for the peas.

"Cock-a-doo-dle-doo-oo!"

Kit threw back his head and, arms bent from the elbows, he flapped them vigorously, advancing with a gleam upon the barnyard object. Clapping his wings over hers, he pinned her from behind and clucked gently. A trilling warble. Then, at length . . . "How do you get into this thing?" Maggie continued working at the sink and the boys laid their heads on the table, gasping amidst the cutlery.

"No egg jokes? . . . No laying jokes?"

"Promise."

She turned and, with her one free hand, lifted the apron. "Concealed zip," she said.

"How very wonderful." Kit turned gravely to the boys. "Look," he said, "a convenience-packed, ready-to-stuff bird." And snuggling his face into her neck, he searched for the tab of the zip with his teeth.

"You're being silly," said Maggie, and returned to draining the peas. "Your hair's not wet," she added crossly.

"You should have seen the water! Well . . . that's the point, you couldn't see the water. As thick as turds in the Aegean they were. The people."

"It would have done you good."

"Another time," he mused, tweaking her tail.

"It wasn't full in the deep end . . ." Rod began, but silenced by a look from his father, asked, "What's for after . . .?"

"Rhubarb."

"Blerr-rk."

"What's it *for*?" Peter stared at his mother as she set glasses on the table.

"What's what for?"

"*That* . . . that costume."

"Costume?" She looked blank. "Costume? This is my natural plumage. This is what I'm like underneath my clothes."

"You're *not* . . ." He sniggered uncomfortably.

"It's her working clothes."

"You're not going to work like *that*!"

"Are you going to drive the car like that?" Rod enjoyed the idea. "You'd cause a crash."

"How are you going to sit down?" asked Peter faintly.

"Easy." Maggie dragged a stool out from under the table and demonstrated. "Would you fetch me a large spoon out of the drawer, Rod?"

Barely able to take his eyes off her, he did as she asked. "It's the legs *I* like." Kit sat down himself and leaned back to judge the whole effect. Maggie's legs were not her strong point. They were rather thin, rather widely set apart at the thighs which gave them a childish and bandy appearance. "I've never seen a chicken with its legs falling down before."

"I'll have to buy a smaller pair." Maggie began serving the food. "Of tights, I mean."

"Oh, I don't know, depending on the difference in price of course, it might be worth spending a bit extra and getting the legs."

"How many can you eat?" Maggie dipped a spoon in the casserole and waited.

"Pardon?" said Peter.

"How many?"

"Oh, two," he answered weakly, a terrified feeling that his mother was going to wander about like this in public, beginning to rise in his chest. Maggie's large hazel eyes were quite expressionless. "I hope Belinda doesn't come back after lunch," he said.

"Don't you like her?"

"What? Oh, she's all right."

"They've got *onion* in!" Rod sniffed accusingly, his face screwed up beneath its damp cap of curls.

"No they haven't."

"Yes they have. I can smell it."

"There's nothing *wrong* with onion," Kit insisted, concluding the ritual of protest. They all hung back waiting for Maggie, to see how she would eat.

"No problem," she remarked, aware of their interest, and manoeuvred a meat ball under her beak.

"I think it's very fetching." Kit began cutting his food. "I hope you'll wear it for the Fergusons tomorrow."

"Oh you *won't*!" Peter was aghast.

"I thought I might."

"You *won't*!" he repeated, fork poised in horror two inches away from his mouth. He didn't really believe her, but sometimes his mother did peculiar things. Once, she'd collected him from school wearing a Nell Gwynn outfit, but that wasn't anything like so bad. A sticky ball of apprehension lodged in his chest.

"Pass the grinder would you?" was all she said for the moment and throughout lunch the blockage prevented his swallowing properly.

His parents began to talk of other things, ignoring the dreadful possibility they'd raised while Rod gobbled and edged things out of his mouth.

Please, thought Peter, please don't let Belinda come round. Then: "What?" he said.

"Are you going to leave all that?"

"I'm not very hungry." Disconsolately, he gazed down at the

mash he had subtly spread all over his plate. But she didn't start wondering why she ever bothered or even insist on his swallowing one last mouthful for once. She didn't even seem to notice that Rod had picked out a few incriminating slivers of onion. She just said "O.K." and began collecting the plates together.

"I love you," Kit said suddenly as she bent down to the oven, presenting an impertinent peak.

And when she returned to the table carrying a rhubarb pie, he slipped an arm around the funny, Disney waist. "*I* couldn't do it," he said (rather seriously, Peter thought, and he tried to imagine his father dressed up as a chicken, but couldn't). "Are you sure *you* want to?"

"It pays quite well." She set the pie down and, pushing up her beak, leaned quickly down to kiss Kit's forehead. "Anyway," she said, "it doesn't matter to me so much."

"What?"

"Looking idiotic. It doesn't mean anything to me."

"Meaning?"

Peter watched his father's eyes follow Maggie as she went to the fridge for a tiny carton of cream. As she straightened she saw her husband's anxious, tender face and smiled. "I don't mind," she repeated softly.

Kit took her hand as she sat down.

"Small one for me!" Rod put in swiftly, but they ignored him. They were looking at one another in a private way.

"You were *right* . . ." she was saying, "not to take that *Ask Uncle* page. It's cretinous. You were *right*. But for me, this sort of thing . . ." and she looked down at herself with resigned mockery, ". . . it's not important." She seemed to shake Kit's hand off and attended briskly to the division of pudding.

"A very, *very* small one for me," Rod said again.

"Peter?"

"Small, please."

"Women dress up all the time anyway," observed Rod, grasping at a little of the substance.

"Exactly." Maggie smiled beneath her orange cap.

"I *could* have done *Ask Uncle* . . ." Kit demurred.

"No," she replied firmly. "I know you couldn't. It was insulting of them to ask you after all you've done."

Doubt creased Kit's eyes. "Do you really believe that?"

"You know I do."

"Honestly?"

"Do you mean that letters page?" nosed Rod, feeling left out.

"Yes." Maggie answered both questions at once without either looking at or satisfying the two questioners. Kit expressed his dissatisfaction silently, taking his plate and poking at the greenish lump of pie with his spoon.

"What's wrong with a letters page?" Rod persisted, feeling he hadn't quite parted the skirts of secrecy adults cast about them, that inadequate patchwork of decent fragments.

Spoons tapped decorously against the china.

"*What's* wrong with it?"

"Oh, shut up." Peter could tell his brother was leaning on something for which there was no proper explanation — something, which even explained, they wouldn't understand. But Rod went on. "I liked *Ask Uncle*," he said.

"Precisely," his father answered. But Rod could see nothing precise about it at all. They ate without speaking while the kettle began, windily, to boil.

"All the same . . ." Kit started again eventually.

"*No.*"

". . . you wouldn't have to scratch around like this . . . like something hatched from an elephant's egg."

"You don't have to worry about my sense of pride," Maggie replied, quite sharply. As if, Peter thought, she meant there was something else, something quite different, his father should be worrying about.

To his intense relief, Maggie removed her chicken costume after lunch. She'd only been trying it on, she said . . . it had arrived that morning and she'd thought it would make them laugh. And Peter wondered why, if she'd thought it would make them laugh, she'd worn it with such solemnity. He was thankful to see it hang emptily on its hanger, a slippery, shiny carcase. So intense was his relief to see her back in ordinary clothes he agreed quite eagerly to go for a walk in the park with her, although normally he loathed walks with her. She was inclined to say boring things like "Oh, look at that lovely flower!" all the time. Unless she was in a playing mood. Then she could be good fun. She *really* played. Not like other mothers, who merely made a gesture of it. She would hide behind bushes and jump out with ear-splitting squawks when she felt like it.

"You come too, Dad," he pleaded. And reluctantly Kit agreed to come some of the way.

His leg, Peter reflected, seemed to be troubling him more now than it had during those long months of recuperation at

Sigvales. Then, he recalled silently, his father had spent quite a lot of time cutting hedges or digging in the vegetable garden. But now, unless Maggie was there, he seemed to retreat indoors. Perhaps, he decided cheerfully to himself, his father was just being brave about the pain while Maggie was around.

Before they went out, Peter fed his rabbits, hoping his mother wouldn't notice and ask why they hadn't been fed first thing that morning. But, as she went to close the door of the small conservatory that opened off the sitting room, she glimpsed the cow parsley trailing through the wire of the hutch. "Humph," she murmured and quickly he closed the pores of his skin to stop anything she might say from stinging. But all she said, thoughtfully, was, "They need a run, a proper one. They're getting too large for the hutch."

And she raised the matter again as they walked along the leaf-roofed road to Queen's Lodge Park, asking Kit if he couldn't build a run perhaps.

"They could have our run," he suggested airily.

"*Our* run?"

"The back garden. It's just a nice size for two rabbits." He made Maggie laugh.

Under the avenue of horse chestnuts, their tapering white candles invisible from beneath, it was deliciously cool. On their right, lay the river, pewtered by sunlight. On the left was a shaven expanse of grass. The playground lay at the far end of it and here the boys now ran, racing for the one vacant swing.

Peter reached it first and refused to budge off the seat in spite of Rod's violent shaking of the chains. "Me first," he said, "you go on something else." But Rod wouldn't. He just stood there, furiously.

Peter worked himself, slowly at first, then higher on the long, squeaking chains, higher than the girl next to him, higher than the little boy whose mother nervously pushed with a piping cry of "Whee-eee!" . . . So high, the chains jerked at the peak of his arc, so high, he made himself feel delightfully sick as he swept down and up again, above the grey asphalt. He could see Rod glaring up at him, standing with his arms folded, his face an upturned daisy. He could see right into the tree tops where clumsy pigeons wobbled. He could see his parents walking on, beyond the playground, disappearing through the clustered trunks of the horse chestnuts.

He slowed, swinging on a decreasing pendulum until his

sandals scraped the ground at each passing sweep, and then, before the movement had fully ceased, he jumped off leaving the seat bucking and clunking behind him. He ran in the direction he had seen his parents go. Rod, he ignored.

He caught up with them by the ferry.

It was more than just a ferry. There was a boat like a Noah's Ark, permanently moored. The ferryman seemed to live inside it. Moored alongside the swaying bridge of planks were many other boats, some of them, the rowing boats, for hire. Others, a few with outboard engines, were privately owned. They bobbed quickly in the detritus of the water's edge.

Kit and Maggie, arms linked, were deep in talk. An overheard fragment, something about the newspaper, told him they were still pursuing the things they'd discussed at lunchtime. But whatever it was, it ended abruptly, as he boo-ed them and made them whip round.

Kit clasped his heart and collapsed on a nearby bench. "Err-rrgh!" he groaned.

"You shouldn't make him jump like that!" Maggie went over to Kit.

But it was all right. His father wasn't really suffering. Peter looked carefully into Kit's face and saw all the little signals of exaggeration . . . the one closed eyelid, the downdrawn mouth. All the same . . . (he thought vaguely) . . . how would I be absolutely sure if . . . But the wondering went.

"Wake up!" he said, and punched his father hard in the firm ooze of flesh that escaped the division of his rib cage. Kit responded with a healthy gurgle.

Peter laughed and hit him again. Harder.

"Stop it," rebuked Maggie mildly.

Harder. With his left fist this time, the shock of it travelling up his knuckles and into his shoulder.

"Hey! Hey! That's enough."

But his fists acquired a volition all their own.

Kit caved inwards, arms crossed coweringly over his chest, the left arm slightly higher than the other as if to ward off a blow that might land on his chin.

"What're you doing, you bully? Mind my specs!" He was half-laughing.

A couple, walking past, nudged one another and commented amusedly.

Dimly, Peter heard them, conscious that he was not being

taken seriously. Seeing a gap open between Kit's arms, he plunged in hard.

"Ouf!"

Maggie seized his right forearm. "*Stop* it!" she repeated, more forcefully.

"What are you trying to do!" Kit recovered and sat up. Safe now that Maggie held a wriggling Peter, he adjusted his glasses.

Fighting back a blurred and boiling feeling that made his arms go on working at the air, Peter fought for words and burst out, "I was . . . I was *testing* you!"

"*Testing* him? What for?" Maggie sounded amused. "Testing what?"

He didn't know. Not knowing, he ceased to struggle, the fire dying down in him.

"Mm?" Kit's eyes were screwed up in the sunshine.

Peter shook his head brusquely and looked away to see if Rod was coming.

"A challenge," said Maggie. "Challenge-my-leader." And she hugged him cheerfully.

"Another couple of years and he'll bloody well win," grinned Kit ruefully, and stretching his arms out along the back of the bench, he tilted his head backwards, revealing the sharp protuberance of his Adam's apple.

"Here's Rod," said Peter in an off-hand voice, relieved to see his brother. He was puzzled by himself.

"You stinking pig," said Rod. "Going off. Hey! Can we have an ice lolly? The refreshments place has opened." The little tea bar was beside the playground.

"Got any money on you?" Kit asked his wife.

She found a 50 pence piece.

"Let *them* go," he said. "We'll wait here."

When, ten minutes later, they returned, their lollies half eaten, their tongues scarlet, Kit and Maggie were slumped against one another on the bench, faces turned up to the early summer sun, eyelids closed. They'd slipped into the general indolence of the afternoon, sharing it with people who idly trundled pushchairs along the path or paused, waiting for heavy, padding dogs that stopped to sniff each tree-trunk and bench leg. On the river in front of them, a silent line of moored motor launches, some gracefully peeling, rose and fell in a leisurely way whenever a powered boat, however small, chugged by, pushing the beginnings of a wave up in front of it.

Behind their parents ran the railings of Queen's Lodge Park, the Lodge itself, a visible white cube beyond the elms and oak trees. The pressed turf of the park was scattered with lolling couples, their peace only a little broken by the occasional stumbling run of a small child. Beyond them all, the faint rumble of traffic. Lethargy threatened.

"Come on! Let's go!" The boys skipped and hopped impatiently.

Reluctantly, Kit stirred, one eye unwelcoming. Maggie, more dutifully, offered to take them over to what she called "my side" on the ferry, but even she had to be pulled, one boy on each arm.

"I'll wait for you," called Kit, producing his newspaper.

The ferryman was very tall, thin and stooped with a receding rush of snowy white hair. The pale, almost milky, blueness of his eyes was made all the more startling by the smudged brown skin of their sockets. He seemed to look out at them from another world altogether. He spoke so very softly in his cultivated voice, that Maggie had to repeat her query about half-fares.

Something about his distance, the isolation that his whole body expressed as he handled the tiller, made all the passengers fall silent until they reached the other side. Rod leaned over, trailing his hand in the water.

"You should have asked him whether we could moor our boat at his place," he said, as they negotiated the steps on the Sweetings bank.

"What boat?" retorted Maggie crossly, then smiled, as though making a special effort for Saturday.

"*Our* boat, stupid."

"Don't build up hopes," she sighed warningly, and headed westwards away from Hammond across Sweetings common where the may flowered and the grass was thick with dandelion and meadowsweet.

Picking up a stick, Rod swished at nettleheads as they walked. "I wish Hymie was here," he said.

Peter, searching for a stick himself amidst the deep grass, found a thick, bent piece of wood. Handling it to feel its nice balance, he pointed it at his brother and made a firing noise. Rod dropped into a crouching position, stick raised beneath his chin and panned it across a landscape in which Peter formed the central point, with a rat-atat-ata-ata-atata.

"That's no good as a gun. It's too thin."

"Tat-a-tat-a-tat-a-tat-a-tat-a!"

"Huh."

"There must be some nests up there . . ." murmured Maggie. But the boys weren't interested in nests. They raced ahead, taking occasional cover behind a tree or a litter bin, stopping only to watch the spruce progress of river police in a white boat that moved with such speed it made the waves slap and the ducks bob.

"What are they looking for?" Peter wondered out loud.

"Bodies," said Maggie.

"In the river?"

"Probably." -

"Smugglers I expect," decided Rod.

"Are there *really* bodies in the river?" Maggie's imaginings could make Peter nervous.

"Of course," said Maggie. "All swollen and white."

Was she about to start one of her stories? Peter looked at her half in hope half in fear but Maggie seemed to be drawing in the smells of crushed herbs with the sensory desperation of an addict. She was very, very good on ghosts and murderers. He waited.

"That's the sort of boat I'd like," said Rod, spoiling it and pointing to a large white motor cruiser with a polished, blonde deck. It poured pop music overboard. Its chrome parts flashed in the sun. A girl in shorts and sunglasses lay on the front of it, propped up on her elbow while a plump man, bursting from his palm-patterned shirt, tried to pass her a drink. Arrogantly, they washed by, tipping rowing boats this way and that.

"*One* day," added Rod. "When I'm rich."

"Did you put your pocket money in the boat box?" Maggie reached out after a vivid brimstone butterfly.

"No he didn't. He bought a horror comic."

"*You . . .!*" Rod turned on his brother.

"Well, you did."

"I didn't spend all of it. I put the rest in the box. Well . . . I will, when I get home."

Low overhead flew an approaching jumbo, its roar following behind it as if attempting to catch up. Maggie put her hands over her ears while the boys stared, fascinated.

"*Bugger you!*" Maggie shouted to the pilot.

They were now opposite the place where Wellington Gardens came down to the river and the sight of both home (though strictly, only their chimneys were visible) and the massive jet, too bulky to be sensibly airborne, made Rod shout, "Suppose it crashed?"

"The odds are, one will."

"*Here?*" His voice was high.

"Just about."

"Honestly?" Now Peter was worried.

"Pardon?"

"*Honestly?*"

"Yes." Maggie nodded.

"But we might be killed."

"We might be." Something caught her attention and she bent down to pick a small pink flower. "Know what this is . . .?"

They shook their heads dumbly.

"Campion. No point," she cried, seeing their mingled expressions, "fretting about it. The jets."

"We ought to move somewhere safer!" Rod was truly agitated, his face so terribly pleated, the sight of it made Maggie smile. "We *have* moved somewhere safer," she replied teasingly.

"But . . ."

"There's safe and safe," she said. "Or rather, there's nowhere safe."

The inside of Peter's stomach shrank and crumpled like a tired balloon. His mother could make the world sound such a dangerous place. Sometimes he liked her to do it, sometimes not. He wanted the feeling taken out of everyday shapes and sounds and put into a story. In a story it became different, like a tiger, behind bars. "Tell us about the man who threw a body out of a plane," he urged quickly.

"*Bits* of a body," she replied, "into the river."

"*This* river?" He was startled, half-sorry he'd started her off. She laughed. "No, it's all right, not this river. Into the marshes somewhere, Essex I think. Or that's where it was washed up. One bit of it."

"Which bit?" They drew closer to her, Rod threading his arm through hers.

"The torso. With the arms on. The arms had been left on."

"Who did it?"

"This man. Hume. He was brought up in a Dorset village you know."

"He *wasn't!*"

"Yes he was."

96

"*Not* Sigvales!"

"I can't be sure."

Their skins puckered.

"And this man he chopped up . . ."

"Setty."

"Setty, yes . . . why did he chop him up?"

"Well, it's very difficult to dispose of a body . . . in a way it can't be recognised."

"How did they know who it was without a head?"

"Fingerprints. He'd left the arms on you see, careless clot."

"Ugh!"

They walked on silently for a while, the grasses brushing their bare legs.

"And why did he do it? Why did he chop him up in the first place?"

"Oh, he said he'd seen Setty kick his dog once."

Rod didn't raise his eyes. Horror created a standstill in his head. For once he could think of nothing to say. Then, in a self-comforting rush, he burst out aloud, "But people don't murder their own family, do they?"

"Nearly always actually," she said. "Most murders are family entertainments."

Swiftly, to drive the terrible thickening shadows out of his head, to establish a safe, luminous place for himself and his own family, he said (almost scornfully), "But *you*'ve never been nearly murdered, have you?"

Understanding the course of his imagining, Maggie threw her head back and laughed out aloud, her shouting laugh. "I thought you *liked* horror stories."

"*Have* you though?" His insistence had to be requited. There was a circle of territory to be declared secure, a circle from which wolves shrank back into their forests. "*Have* you?"

She looked down at him briefly. He felt the warmth of her amusement, a warmth that did not wholly envelop him, *could* not until he had the guarantee of her reply.

"Yes," he heard her answer. "Yes I have been, might easily have been, nearly murdered once."

And when he dared to gaze up at her, it struck him that her eyes looked curiously bruised, like imperfect enlargements of themselves, quite at odds with the smile on her lips.

"When?" Peter was demanding throatily as if strange juices had erupted from his stomach.

And she told them about Castel di Principe.

It was all flatly disappointing.

As they walked back along the bank, a long, blue-canopied pleasure boat passed them, a line of life-belts as new and white as peppermints decorating its side. Watching it, Peter felt deflated by his mother's story. Perhaps she hadn't told it as well as usual, but he couldn't see anything very frightening in a crowd of boys. Not frightening to *her*. It was all rather tame.

And when they reached home and she rooted about in the drawers to find the one hurried picture Kit had snatched from the car as they'd left, *that* seemed tame too. A crowd of urchin children grinning and waving. *Very* tame.

The wolves retreated behind their dark pines and the boys switched on Dr. Who.

9

"KEITH'S JUST DOING his bees . . . Please come in, won't you!"

"Doing his bees?" Maggie echoed with surprise as if struck by a quite new, more agreeable, aspect of Keith Ferguson. And then, as a further thought occurred, "Oh dear, does that mean we're too early?"

"Not at all. *We're* rather late. Please come through."

And Sally Ferguson, pinkly made up, leaking gardenia scents like gases, wearing spotless beige and white co-ordinates, led them in to a beige and white sitting room where inhospitable cut-glass bowls of peanuts and crisps sat in their own highly polished reflections.

She waved her arms around vaguely as if displaying her furniture which was both expensive and dull, square but not extravagantly so. The chairs awaited occupants with an air of tension.

Belinda, standing in the small conservatory which, like their own, led from the sitting room into the garden, remained with her back to them, attention fixed upon a robotic figure on the lawn.

"Say hello, darling."

"Hello." She turned and gave them a short, but ravishing smile. "Look at Daddy," she ordered with pride.

The Makins — Maggie, principally — had several times watched a gathering of Dorset beekeepers and were not perhaps as impressed as they ought to have been. But there *was* something engaging and odd about the large, bulbously suited figure in a square space hat — a box blanked out with fine black mesh — standing amongst suburban rock plants and red brick walls. The entire garden, considerably larger than their own, seemed meshed and protected. A cage was erected over a small patch of raspberries, green netting suggested strawberries, streaks of tinfoil fluttered above less distinct foliage and three young saplings on the lawn were wrapped in wire netting. Even the bird table had barbed wire wound round it.

A massive glove was raised in monumental salute as their faces pressed close to the glass.

"He has to go through the frames at this time of year," fussed Sally, her charm bracelet jangling. "Let me do the honours. Sweet or dry?"

"Sweet or dry what?" Maggie glanced round and spotted two decanters on a silver tray.

"Will sherry be all right?" The anxiety within the question was neutralised by Sally's swift and covert assessment of Maggie's loosely worn shirt and jeans.

"Lovely, yes. Dry, please."

"And Mr. Makin? *Kit?*"

"Yes, dry, thank you."

"I'm afraid it's just me with a taste for the sweet." Sally seemed driven by a perpetual need to apologise.

The figure from outer space moved jerkily towards them and presented itself close to the other side of the glass. "Thought you'd be interested to see this business," came a raised voice from behind the black mesh square. "I've . . ."

"Sorry?" Kit turned his ear to the glass.

". . . Got a set of clothes for you if you like." He waggled a gloved hand to indicate they should open the door for him.

"Hello, hello, hello!" He stepped inside, forcing them back into Sally's tray.

"Whoopsy!" she cried.

"Being country people," he said, "I *thought* you'd be interested."

"Yes indeed. Aren't we?" Kit turned to Maggie, whose cheeks were sucked in as though she were biting the inside of them.

"Yes," she replied steadily. "Our neighbour kept bees. They used to swarm in our orchard."

"Good," exclaimed Keith. "Fascinating creatures!" He removed his asbestos gloves revealing the central stump on his left hand which magnetised Rod's attention.

"Knock that back and slip these togs on." They became aware of a pile of blue, weatherproof clothing and another square bee hat on the conservatory shelf.

"What *happened* to your finger?"

"*Rod!*" Maggie tried to hush him.

"Bitten off," explained Keith, holding out his right arm like a policeman until his wife hurried to put a small glass of sherry into the large hand.

"What?" said Peter.

"Bitten off in a rugger match. Damn fool. These things happen. Chap had his ear torn off in the same game."

"Some game," said Maggie in a strangled voice, sipping frantically. The Makin family dared not look at one another.

"You two interested in rugger?"

"We've never played it." Rod, acting as spokesman, answered politely, the weight of his mother's foot overlaying his sandal.

"You will." Keith Ferguson made it sound like a threat. "O.K.?" he drained his glass. "Clamber in."

Kit fumbled his way into a vast pair of waterproof trousers and hauled them up. The elasticated waist came halfway up his chest. Maggie gave a little snort.

"Doesn't matter what you look like," said Keith sternly. "It's the protection that counts. Now the veil . . . *Fine* . . ." It was secured over a little straw hat that must have been Sally's once. Keith helped fasten the drawstrings under Kit's armpits. ". . . And the anorak. *Terrific!*"

Kit's glasses began to slide down his nose but as they were impossible to retrieve behind his mask, he held his head unnaturally high to prevent their falling off altogether. "Fancy me?" he asked his wife.

"Fit? Take your gloves . . . you can handle the smoker if you would . . . here you are. Off we go!" Keith was ready, eager to start.

"Into the dragon's jaws," remarked Maggie closing the doors behind them.

"Such a lovely day again," offered Sally. "I do hope it's going to be a fine summer."

"How much honey did you get last year?"

"None at all to be honest. I think it was the weather."

"And the year before?"

"Oh, that was the first year — the bees hadn't settled in. This year we're really hoping for something."

"You must be," said Maggie drily.

"Can I have some crisps?"

"Rod is it? Or Peter?" Sally tapped her forehead in light query.

"Can I?" repeated Rod patiently.

"Belinda, hand them round, there's a good girl."

"Oh-h-h . . . I want to watch Daddy."

"Well, perhaps the boys would like to help themselves!"

Quickly the boys went and sat down on the putty-coloured carpet beside the low table on which the cut-glass bowls were symmetrically arranged. With a resolute air, they began eating.

"Of course, I have nothing to do with them." Sally edged a little closer to Maggie.

"Oh, you should . . . they're rather rewarding creatures, bees." Maggie watched Kit light the roll of corrugated paper inside the smoker. "They're the women's libbers of the insect world," she said.

"Oh dear." Sally laughed uncertainly.

"No, I like them," Maggie repeated as if she wished to be taken perfectly seriously. "The women do all the work."

"*Ah!*" Sally allowed her upper arm to brush Maggie's as though some agreement had been tacitly established.

"And run the business side as well. The whole show."

"I do hope they'll be careful." Anxiously, Sally's attention slid to the men for a moment, and then, as if by association, she cried, "All right, boys?"

"*And* it's only the females who sting."

"Is that so? Goodness, what a lot you know!"

Keith was removing the lid from the hive — it was a boxy, modern design, like a series of small crates, a form of tower block for bees — and began lifting out the top sections one by one, pointing out items of interest to Kit who puffed his bellows at arm's length. One frame Keith threw on the ground.

"Do look, boys," said Sally. "It's awfully interesting."

"I'm doing a project on bees at school," said Belinda superciliously.

"We do projects too." A little sullenly, still clutching the bowl of crisps, Rod joined her. Peter slumped behind.

"What's yours on?"

"Dinosaurs," said Rod.

"Tanks," said Peter.

"Keith does get stung rather often," Sally quavered, little creases shaping themselves round her mouth.

"And they have this system," Maggie went on, oblivious of the others, "of shoving the drones out in the autumn."

"The drones?" said Rod.

"The *males*," said Belinda scornfully.

"Who does?" asked Peter.

"Who does what?"

"Who shoves them out?"

"The worker bees," Maggie answered him, watching the men.

"But he doesn't seem to mind," concluded Sally limply.

Kit appeared to be standing too far back to be very helpful. Even from here, the onlookers could see an angry black streamer of bees spiral out of the hive. Holding one of the frames up carefully, a dark cloud of bees encircling his head, Keith lumbered over the lawn towards them. They pressed their faces to the window to see what he was trying to indicate with a thick, gloved finger.

"Can you see?" Maggie moved to allow Peter in front of her. "They've built brood chambers on the honey frame."

The brownish comb, irregularly built up to different thicknesses, was crawling with bees still trying to feed the young grubs in their cells.

"What does that mean?"

"They've got their functions muddled up . . . they should have laid their eggs in the deeper frames below."

"What's he doing?" Peter pressed his ear to the window and Keith bent down to shout. "He says they'll have to be destroyed," he interpreted for the others.

"He's breaking off the queen cells . . ." Maggie watched Keith snap off the longer, protruberant cells containing young queen grubs.

Kit, head tilted back as far as the axis of his neck would allow, puffed vaguely at the frame and peered at Keith's finger tracing the movement of a bee with a dab of silver paint on its back.

"That's the queen," said Belinda.

"Why's it silver?"

"So you can see it, of course," sighed Belinda.

"Look at her," said Maggie wonderingly, "surrounded by all her attendants." The marked bee moved through the others, an adoring, or defending, retinue protecting her space.

"I expect you'd like some lemon squash, children . . .?" Sally gave them her flickering attention.

"Not just *now*," answered Rod, interested at last by the intense activity of the bees.

"Thank you," said Maggie.

"Thank you," he echoed.

"Oh well . . ." Sally fingered a charm on her bracelet and looked purposelessly about, "later perhaps." Then, in what

Peter thought was a false kind of voice, she continued, "*There* now . . . isn't it all wonderful? And why is it, Maggie — I *can* call you Maggie, can't I — why do the drones have to go in the autumn? Where do they go?" Her tone was stiff with politeness.

"They don't *go* anywhere," grinned Maggie, her eyes following the movement of the queen. "They die." She looked up laughingly, "They're only sex objects you see. Once they've done their job they're worse than useless — literally. When they mate with the queen she tears their sex organs out . . ."

"*What!*" A horrified cry from Sally, who glanced quickly at the children to see if they'd heard this shocking piece of information.

". . . if they were allowed to hang around they'd eat up all the winter store of honey, so they have to go. Crudely simple."

"So they're killed off . . .?" Sally still sounded faint with shock.

"No, just evicted, but they're so feeble and useless without the women to look after them they fade away."

"Dear me."

Peter thought Mrs. Ferguson sounded as though she felt a society for the protection of drones ought to be formed.

Keith, bridesmaided by Kit and his bellows, had returned to the hive. An angry face appeared over the neighbouring wall and disappeared, swiftly.

"There's Mrs. Sinclair."

"I expect she's going to complain," Belinda observed.

The colony was clearly furious. Kit performed slow foot movements like a Greek dancer as the insects wreathed themselves around him. Each step, even when apparently executed sideways, took him further and further away from the hive. Without turning to look at his assistant, Keith beckoned Kit towards him. Some sort of conversation was exchanged between them and Keith's box-like head made a nodding indication in the direction of the house.

Walking very stiffly and carefully, head erect, Kit's blue and alien figure came towards them.

"Mind out!" said Belinda, retreating.

"Don't let him in!" squeaked Rod and dived after her.

Kit was being pursued by bees. Behind him, Keith patiently continued his examination of the hive. Maggie crushed her forehead to the glass.

"What?" she yelled. Through the dark square of mesh she noticed Kit's glasses had slipped and swung from one ear.

"I think I'm being stung." Faintly.

"What?" she shouted.

"I seem to have a bee up my nose."

"He seems to have a bee up his nose." Maggie turned to Sally for permission to let her husband in. The children left the room and clustered behind the door.

"Oh dear!" cried Sally, lost.

Kit's voice was raised but supremely controlled. "Keith recommends I go into a darkened room!"

"The potting shed!" mouthed Sally, pointing. "Try the potting shed!"

In processional and stately fashion, Kit with a single salute of thanks, turned and walked towards the potting shed, which adjoined the house at a right angle to it. Once inside, and clearly thinking nobody could see him, the dignity evaporated. Maggie glimpsed flailing legs and arms, a frantic tearing off of the veil, before the door mercifully closed on his discomfiture.

"Oh, I've had thirty or forty stings in one day!" beamed Keith later, crushing a third small sherry in his large hand. "Never came to any harm."

"No? Good."

Peter looked at his father whose jaw was now joined to his neck in a single, unangled column: the swelling had obliterated all normal outline. His nose and upper lip were thickened as though George Foreman rather than a dozen bees had attacked him. He thought his father had been tremendously brave and restrained. If it had happened to me, he thought with horror, I'd have screamed. Even the *idea* of bees trapped around his ears, nose and scalp made him want to scream — but he *did* think about it because he was so bored and there was nothing else to do. They couldn't play in Belinda's room because Belinda seemed to enjoy filling glasses and listening to the conversation about redundancies and bankruptcies that had been going on for ages and ages. She sat with her knuckles pressed to her mouth, eyes ardently shining at each speaking face in turn, while carefully pinning her legs at the knee so she was decent.

Beginning a yawn, and stifling it, he wondered what had happened to the man who'd chopped up bodies and dropped them from a plane.

Rod, carefully pulling hairs out of the goatskin rug on which he lay, kept a closer ear upon the talk in case anything — however distantly familiar — provided him with a launching pad for one of his own opinions. He tugged at Belinda's skirt and hissed, "What's the definition of a Stone Age bra?" But she turned away from him, back to her father's current of computer sounding words. "An over-the-shoulder-boulder-holder," Rod muttered. And then something quite extraordinary happened. Just in the middle of a remark about excessive capital outflow, Mr. Ferguson fell absolutely silent, staring in front of him as if he were in a trance.

Looking from him to Belinda, from Belinda to her mother, Rod noticed that they were all afflicted by the same dreadful complaint. They gazed at Mr. Ferguson, small, politely eager smiles fixed to their faces as if they were frozen in time. Alarmed, he glanced at his own parents. They were less rigidly affected — Kit was re-crossing his legs and Maggie pushed at the skin around her nails — but they, too, made no effort to speak.

Then he noticed that the china ornaments were shaking on their shelves and he became conscious of Maggie scowling upwards and he was awakened to the coarse presence of an aeroplane over the house. The windows rattled violently, then, more discreetly, and gradually the sustained roar of the engines began to recede.

"Yes, capital outflow . . ." Keith Ferguson resumed, waking from his trance.

"In the summer," Sally Ferguson confided unilaterally, to Maggie, "we can't hear ourselves speak in the garden at all. Still . . ."

She was prevented from listing any of the compensations by Maggie's forcefully expressed conviction that they were keeping the Fergusons from their lunch. She rose to her feet.

". . . see how these statutory wage controls will bite . . ." continued Keith Ferguson, apprehending her only vaguely as though she were a cat scratching to be let out of the room, a job someone else could deal with.

"We must go." Maggie addressed him firmly.

". . . and a far more careful distribution of aid into the weakened industries . . . Yes, well . . ." He seemed to grasp at last that Maggie was determined to remove her husband. "Very interesting *indeed*," he said heavily, gripping Kit's knee. "Must discuss it again sometime. Soon."

"Delighted," Kit responded, "though as you see, I'm

106

basically at variance with you on the handling of controls. Any tighter and they become politically explosive."

"Psychologically explosive," said Maggie.

"What?" Keith rose, his gaze weaving blankly. "Oh, yes. Mm. I suppose."

"Boys!"

"Sorry about the bees. They'll cure your rheumatism if you have any."

"No," bowed Kit, "I haven't actually. But I'll bear it in mind."

There was a small orchestrated phase of squeezing and little expressions of gratitude while Peter yawned more openly and Rod walked out into the hall.

"I'll come and play with you this afternoon if you like," Belinda said.

"What?"

"About half past two."

Peter stared at her slittily, unable to think of a reply. "I don't know," he said and he pulled at the tail of his mother's shirt.

"What happened to that man who chopped up bodies?" he asked her as they crossed the road to go back home.

"Why? Do you want some advice on slicing up small girls with blue eyes?" said Maggie.

"What happened to him? Was he executed?"

"No. He went to Switzerland and killed three more people. He's due to be released soon."

"*Released!*" whistled Peter, seeing a man with a cleaver in Wellington Gardens just as plainly as he saw the dipping plane trees and a child's yellow rubber ball in the gutter.

"What man's this?" Kit lifted the latch on the gate and let them through.

"Set *free*?" persisted Peter.

And when they entered the front door and were met by the smell of roasting lamb and potatoes, he was certain that the rival, ineradicably rotting smell of number 43, came from something awful stored deep inside the house. The head that had never been found perhaps, bricked behind the attic wall. Or was that part of another story his mother had once told . . .? The story of . . . Christie, was it? Christie, yes. The man whose own head, Maggie had whispered, lowering her face and sliding her gaze to each of them in turn . . . the man whose own head was "the shape of a stinkhorn".

10

"But it's a *good* house for hide and seek," insisted Belinda.

Peter didn't want to play hide and seek. He didn't want to stay indoors at all. He wanted to hire a rowing boat or, better still, if he could persuade his father to give him enough money, one of the little motor boats available further upriver at Hammond. If he *had* to stay indoors then he preferred to get on with glueing his model aircraft carrier.

"In fact," reflected Belinda, gazing critically round at the boys' grubby and cluttered bedroom, "that's the best thing about it."

"O.K.," said Rod, "you hide." He put down his copy of *Gunflash* and rolled off his unmade bed.

"You've got to count to a hundred," said Belinda sternly.

"O.K." Rod was quite content to accept her rules.

She went out on to the landing. They heard her swear Maggie and Kit (who were stripping the staircase wall) to secrecy, and then heard her tiptoeing along the uncarpeted landing.

"You're meant to be counting," Peter reminded his brother.

"So are you."

"I'm not playing."

"Yes you are. Why not?"

Peter made a desultory attempt to pencil over one of the World War One action transfers lying on the top of his toy chest beside him. It was a booted and helmeted German advancing with a bayonet. "I'm busy," he said.

"Piddle," retorted Rod, leaning over him to see how many transfers were left to do. "Why have you done all the Germans first?"

Peter had put them inside the trench drawn on the card

that accompanied the transfers. It was sandbagged and protected by three lines of wire. He'd put the Germans in a defensive position.

"Until I've done them, I don't know where to put the English."

Rod looked for a while. "Let me do one," he demanded.

"No. They're mine."

"Actually," Rod remarked, "you *have* to put the Germans in the trench being attacked. They're all facing that way." It was true. The manufacturers had organised the balance of the battle.

"I know that, stupid."

"Do you think she's ready?"

"I don't know. Start from eighty."

"Eighty-one . . . Eighty-two . . . Eighty-three."

"She'll 've gone in the attics."

"Of course . . . Eighty-seven . . ."

They set off.

"Will you tell us if we're warm?" Rod called to Kit.

"No," he said. He was sweating with exertion, his hair clinging damply to his scalp. You could see how thin it was becoming. His face was so swollen his chin made no protrusion at all.

"Oh-*oh*!"

"No," he repeated mercilessly. "It wouldn't be fair."

"Anyway, she'll have gone to the attics."

Together they clattered up the small, narrow staircase, the low ceiling overhead bulging as though weighed down by dead birds gathered in the roof.

She was easy to find. Belinda, accustomed to white painted walls and crisply printed curtains, had been more apprehensive than she'd expected finding herself on the strange, uppermost floor of number 43. It was quite unlike the other houses in Wellington Gardens, all of which, despite minor, orderly conversions by their various owners, were laid according to an identical pattern. But the others were smaller, semi-detached. Number 43, on its island site, bereft of matching neighbours, had its own crazy pattern.

"It's weird," she said, when they found her. "It's like a brain."

"What do you mean?"

She shrugged and swivelled round on her heels. But they understood dimly. The five small interconnecting rooms with their tiny doorways — only two with porthole windows, the others without windows at all — were like a network of cells. It was a place for midgets.

"It's awfully dark in there," she said, pointing to the bit she hadn't felt like exploring. Gloomy lumps of abandoned furniture stood there stored under grey dustsheets.

"Now it's your turn," she instructed Rod, who had been, marginally, the first to find her. Cunningly, she remained where she was to count, so that he couldn't come and hide on the top floor. Then she counted aloud every single number between one and a hundred. Peter did noughts and crosses with himself on the grimy panes of the round window while she plodded gamely on, eyes closed.

"Ready!" she cried, and leapt off downstairs, her pony tail swinging. Slowly he followed her.

"Did he go past you?" She was asking Maggie.

"Couldn't say."

"Oh, go on."

"Didn't see a thing."

"Humph!"

"What?" said Peter as he groped past his parents, clinging to the brown stair rail.

"Warm."

"Oh, good," he said, and quickened his step.

Rod had cheated. He had gone into the first of the three kitchens and closed the door which they, of course, couldn't open from the hall side because the knob had dropped off. When they went outside, round to the back door, and entered from that end of the house, Rod opened the first kitchen door and let himself out into the hall, scampering back upstairs.

Peter and Belinda bumped into Maggie who'd forestalled Rod and caught the kitchen door before it had closed on her again. "He's diddled you," she said, "I'm just going to make us some tea."

Peter was furious. "He *always* cheats!" he yelped plaintively. "I'll bash him for this!"

"Please don't." Kit's bulk intervened between hunter and hunted on the staircase as he came down for tea. "Somewhere beginning with L," he hissed.

"*I* know!"

"Where? Where?" Belinda hurtled after him two stairs at a time. The stairs were ankle deep with musty ochre wallpaper.

"The lavatory of course!"

It was she who exclaimed indignantly, "He's locked himself in!" as Peter rattled the handle and kicked the door.

"We've found you, you rotten cheat! Come out of there!"

"I'm *occupied*." There was an extravagant rustling of paper.

"Is he telling the truth?" Belinda wound one foot behind the calf of her other leg and scratched at something with the toe of her sandal.

"Of course he's not."

"He might be," she hesitated.

"You don't know him!" exclaimed Peter, kicking the door again. "He never plays fair!"

"Oh," she said sternly, as though he would have to be punished for this.

But that wasn't her attitude at all when, after several determined attempts, the chain flushed and Rod came out holding *Gunflash*.

"You are funny!" cried Belinda, and took his arm in a thoroughly friendly way.

Peter's anger altered. He felt a real change in its degree, as though moved into top gear. "You didn't have to go in!" he screamed. "You didn't! You didn't!"

"I did," answered Rod calmly.

"You didn't! You didn't! It doesn't even smell!"

"It's only you that smells," said Rod, walking away, Belinda's arm threaded through his.

"Anyway," added Belinda disloyally, "this house smells all over."

"I hate you! I *hate* you!"

"Don't get in a bait, silly, it's your turn now."

Just to get away from them, he succumbed. I'll go somewhere they'll never think of, he vowed hotly.

He crept into Kit's bedroom. As in theirs, the single bed was unmade, the sheets twisted and hurled all ways, muddled on the floor with papers, muddy shoes, books and odd things from abroad, foreign currency, strangely packed sugar cubes, undeveloped films. Kit's tribal carvings, small, naked figures collected from all over the world, were heaped against one wall, awaiting suburban display. They stood beside his guns . . . two shotguns, an air rifle and a heavy nineteenth-century 12-bore with fine silver chasings.

He had meant to creep into the capacious wardrobe, a huge mahogany cave of Aunt Carrie's, but the doors wouldn't close because so many things were wrapped up in bundles and stuffed inside. It smelt of Kit in the morning, warm and thick, as though the body leaked moisture in its sleep.

Unable to wedge the door against himself, he panicked and dived for the bed, anywhere, before they stopped counting.

He struggled under the concealing tumble of sheets and blankets. The springs creaked complainingly at his intrusion and showered him with dust. It was cramped under the narrow bed. He had to wriggle this way and that. There was a large suitcase of Kit's there, several more pairs of shoes, a pile of magazines and a full ashtray. The crushed, blackened tobacco stank. He tried to get comfortable and waited.

They took a long time. He could hear them calling to one another, feet thumping all over the house, making the boards shake. Once they opened the bedroom door, but clearly, taking a look round at all the gaping furniture, abandoned any suspicion he might be there. They were too easily convinced he would have crept back to the attic. Their movements overhead betrayed them.

Bored, he pulled magazines towards him. They were old pin-up magazines, *Playboy*, *King* and *Penthouse*. They were terribly rude. It made his skin tight and hot looking at them.

The girls mystified him. Why did they do what they did? Why did they want to stick out their huge great bosoms like that? Or finger their triangles? And poke their bottoms in the air? He felt peculiarly, but not unpleasantly, sick. He knew what men did to women. He knew women had an extra hole and men put their thing in it, but that knowledge and these pictures didn't quite seem to go together.

The house began to tremble, deeply, as if from its foundations. Even before he heard it, he knew it was a plane, the shudder was now so familiar to him. The dull, intermittent throb increased, passed slowly overhead and made its ponderous departure.

A sheet of lined paper lay between the slippery pages of the magazine. Drawn on it in thick pencil, the outlines emphasised as if the artist had gone over them several times, was a row of bare women, all bending over showing their bottoms and behind them, just looking, stood an ugly little man. He was very muscular, covered with thick strokes of hair and held, in one hand, his own enormous willy. It was absolutely huge, nearly half his total height, and stiff. It was helmeted like a soldier and softly shaded-in to suggest a difference in colour from the rest of the squat little body.

Peter found his mouth was dry . . . with horror or, perhaps, excitement; he simply couldn't tell. His feelings were so foreign, so confused there was no means of isolating and naming them. He was simply conscious of a kind of bonfire in his chest, a smouldering, leaping, guttering sensation. The burning heat of it spread throughout his body as if he were blushing in every vestige of himself and yet he was not blushing, not really. Apart from an intensity of heat at the edges of his face, he was not blushing in a fashion he understood as blushing at all.

Amidst this confusion of feeling were mingled streaks of shame and bewilderment. Who had drawn this thing? Not his father, surely? . . . It was not a grown up's drawing.

Grown ups don't draw pictures like this, he thought.

The *style* of the drawing was rather crude and childish— except for the carefully, lovingly defined willy which could almost have been drawn by a separate hand. But why was the man so small and ugly? Why were the women so many and so arranged?

He had no means of answering his own questions. In a way he didn't even want to. He had a nasty feeling that the answers might be as unwelcome and grotesque as the drawing itself if he guessed at them. He half-hated the whole thing.

The door opened.

He seized the drawing wishing to hide it, then realised it must remain where it was, between the pages and he pushed it back.

The weight on the floorboards, the depth of their sinking, told him that the person in the room was not Belinda, not Rod, but Kit. Peter closed his eyes and screwed his fists together and lay very quietly.

Two drawers were opened, rummaged, then shut. First one, then the other. Kit found whatever he was searching for quickly and, to Peter's relief, left again, shouting up to the floor above as he did so . . . "Tea? Anybody want tea?" And then, without awaiting any answer, he limped slowly downstairs.

They came running down the attic stairs whispering and giggling together. "We didn't have a *proper* look in here!"

They came in and paused.

"What a mess!" Belinda remarked. "Doesn't your mother do *any* housework?"

"This isn't her room."

"So?"

No reply was forthcoming from Rod. He was attacking the wardrobe.

"Ugh, it's full of dirty clothes . . . Do they have a room *each*?" She sounded reluctantly impressed.

"Daddy couldn't sleep properly with his leg."

"Ugh!" she said again, discovering something else that offended her.

"And he had terrible nightmares . . ."

Peter began to feel ashamed of his parents' untidiness, ashamed that Belinda should be so observant of it. Until he'd overheard her petulant comments, he hadn't really been terribly aware of it. And worse, he was ashamed of lying here in the fluff and dust beneath the bed with these horrible magazines. He felt contaminated by them. He wanted to be found. He kicked against the bed leg and made the springs whine.

"There!"

They dived for him and scooped up thick armfuls of bedding like little dogs.

"Phoo!"

"Come on. Got you!"

"It took you ages."

"We were playing upstairs. We were playing castaways."

Again he felt the sudden, uncontrollable anger and recognised some part of it as the stabbing anger of jealousy. He was jealous but didn't quite know why. The pain pierced him so savagely he wanted to say he'd had a better time than them. He'd had a far more *interesting* time. He hadn't missed them at all.

"Look what I found," he said, pushing the pile of magazines towards them.

"Ho-ho! Rudeys!" exclaimed Rod, reaching under the bed and sliding the pile free.

"Ooh!" Peter heard Belinda squeal. Then giggle. He rolled out from under the bed and found them both on their knees, bent over a girl who lay full length on a fur rug, knees apart. A python wound itself round one uplifted arm, then across her hips, its wicked head held aloft in her other hand.

"'Pat-sy's Pet'," Rod read out carefully. He still left little gaps between the syllables, having been taught to read that way. Peter despised it. "'Pat-sy is a great an-i-mal lov-er. She has man-y an-i-mals but her big-gest play-mate is Perc-y the Py-thon' . . . Percy the *Python*!" he hooted, looking up. "What a dippy name! . . . 'Most peo-ple are a-fraid of snakes, says Pat-sy, but Per-cy is love-ly. He has a won-der-ful smooth skin'," he read.

"Let me have a look!" Peter snatched it away. (Rod seemed untroubled by any stilling shock of feeling.) He glanced uncomfortably at Belinda whose warm face bore an unusually naughty, arch expression. It startled him for a moment. She caught his glance and tittered, her mouth wide open, her tongue protruding slightly.

"They're calling us!" Rod scrambled hurriedly off his knees. Peter heard nothing.

Belinda was already on her feet. "Quick!" she gasped and giggled again, "we'll have another look later."

He pushed the magazines back under the bed with his foot alongside the magazine containing the drawing. He was glad they hadn't seen that.

Maggie had made an Instant Sponge. It smelt eggy and sweet. The kitchen was warm with it.

"There!" she said. "It looks just like the real thing. Milk or orange?"

They were all very quiet and polite, hardly daring to look at one another.

"What's wrong with you all?" mused Kit, preoccupied as he looked upwards.

Another plane approached. "Bloody thing!" he roared at it.

"You get used to them," Belinda soothed, biting delicately into a chocolate biscuit. She viewed the cake with suspicion.

"Like factory workers I suppose," remarked Maggie sourly, "who say they're used to the noise and have actually gone deaf but don't know it."

"I haven't gone deaf," said Belinda.

"How do you know?" Rod spoke from the mouth of his glass.

"Well of course I know."

"You can't know. Can she?"

"What?" said Peter.

Rod laughed, "There you are, you see."

"I wasn't listening to what you were *saying* . . ." Peter had discovered this device years ago, but Rod didn't pursue the topic. Instead, he winked at Belinda.

"There's a definite pattern to it . . ." Maggie was saying. And Kit was scoffing, "You're wrong you know, trying to fit things into patterns. You do it all the time. Over-analyse, get stuck, find a mess and design a pattern for it. That's what primitives do." He showed his appreciation of the Instant

Sponge by cutting another slice. "Do you suppose this thing is full of anabolic steroids and bird droppings?" he said.

"No, truly," Maggie persisted. "Like the deafness, it's a way of surviving, isn't it? Of coping with the stress . . . everybody's got a way of coping with their particular stresses."

"Like what?" Kit spoke with his mouth full, rudely.

"Sometimes passive, sometimes aggressive . . . it's like the noise. Some people go deaf. Others just shout louder and louder. Something happens to our senses. They can't function naturally. The more pressure there is . . ." She tried to think of an example but failed and went on, ". . . the less well they function. Heigh-ho! In the end we'll take leave of our senses altogether I expect."

Peter slipped a biscuit off the plate thankful for once that the grown ups talked on oblivious of the children. He didn't want anyone to speak to him. All the same his interest picked up when he heard his mother saying *that* was why she hadn't wanted them to have a telly. "You can do without your ears altogether watching telly," she said. "Don't have to listen at all. But your *eyes* . . . oh God."

"You're getting at me again," rebuked Kit with unfelt heartiness. "Getting at my business. There's such a thing as information. Did you know what *your* children know when you were their age?"

"Information!" snorted Maggie. "*Inflammation.* Inflammation of the sensory organs. Facts, facts, *farts.* True stories except they're not true at all since they don't tell people the truth about themselves, *that's* what stories are for. Who wants novels? Who wants plays? Hearing about *other* people, oh, that's all right. Ah, poor things, you can say until you get bored with saying it. Isn't it *awful*? Like a cup of cocoa? . . . Has it ever struck you . . . ?" she began, but Kit interrupted her.

"To be quite frank," he was saying, "I always thought you were downright mean not letting them have a telly while I was away. They could have seen what I was doing. You might even have seen *me*."

"And everything else as well. Bodies, blood, severed legs, the whole picnic. What's the corpse count today?" she asked Peter.

"What? Pardon?"

"How many bodies have you seen today? This week? Any idea?"

"What?" he repeated, blushing.

But she returned her attention to Kit. "Has it ever struck you," she repeated, "that your children, everybody's children — in this country — have seen more corpses than any other kids at any other time in history? Not in the home, oh no. Keep death out of the home, *real* death. But split, splat, how about that, another number bites the dust! Right there! On the little ornament in the corner of the lou-ow-nge. Next to the brass fender and the hearth brush, right underneath the wedding photograph of Auntie Lil and Uncle Eric. Not that it matters. Blink. Blink of the eye and it's gone! What does that do to the senses, for God's sake?"

"It makes a lot of people very angry," answered Kit severely, "and in the best sense. You *could* argue that Vietnam was brought to an end because of television, though not through any effort of yours since you so assiduously avoided soiling your vision."

Peter heard real enmity in his father's voice. He recognised it. It corresponded to things he felt within himself at times, towards Rod, towards the world.

A silence had fallen over the tea table.

Then, lightly, Maggie commented, "Oh well, we're all in a muddle . . ." She brushed crumbs into the palm of her hand. "That's what comes of our brave new world and its freedoms, its wonderfully extended limits." She sounded sarcastic. "It's exciting for a while then things get muddled."

He didn't know what she meant. But he felt muddle in his own chest. He looked at his father. Kit was irritably attempting — and failing — to strike a match. "They've got mean with the sandpaper," he said.

"I'm a coward basically I suppose," Maggie said and took a cigarette from Kit's pack. "When things get really confused, really mixed up, I want out. At least, I want to revert to stereotype. Feels safer you see."

"*Stereotype?*" echoed Kit drily. "You? Like hell. If you had a decent acting job you wouldn't feel half so jaundiced about the world."

"No, you're wrong," she said doubtfully.

"You want to be like . . ." he paused and smiled at Belinda, "like Sally Ferguson?"

"In a way, yes."

"Bilge," said Kit still smiling stiffly at Belinda. "You could no more be like Sally Ferguson than you could steer a rocket to the moon."

"Ah well," Maggie gave a self-deprecating smile, "that just shows how muddled I am."

"Right," said Kit heavily.

"We can't afford to smoke like this you know."

"Right," he said again and drew deeply on his cigarette, eyes on hers.

"*Why* couldn't you be like my mother?" Belinda was curious.

"Because my wife is both ambitious and a slut. Neither of which, my dear, your mother is."

"I'm *not* ambitious." Maggie sounded hurt.

"She's not a slut," said Rod.

"Ah," smiled Kit, expelling smoke, "that just shows how muddled I am then doesn't it?"

"You're not being fair."

"No. But then, as the man said, there's nothing fair in love *or* war."

"Stop it!" Peter jumped up. Anxiety tore at him.

"Yes," said Kit, "I think we should. How we all miss Hymie."

"What do you mean?" cried Peter.

But his father just smiled and Peter realised that Hymie, detecting an ambiguous snarling in the air, would have barked.

Part Two

All the great dangers threatening humanity with extinction are direct consequences of conceptual thought and verbal speech. They drove man out of the paradise in which he could follow his instincts with impunity and do or not do whatever he pleased. There is much truth in the parable of the tree of knowledge and its fruit, though I want to make an addition to it to make it fit into my own picture of Adam: that apple was thoroughly unripe! Knowledge springing from conceptual thought robbed man of the security provided by his well-adapted instincts long, long before it was sufficient to provide him with an equally safe adaptation. Man is, as Arnold Gehlen has so truly said, by nature a jeopardised creature.

On Aggression by Konrad Lorenz

11

"And where's *yours*, Makin?"

"Mine?" Peter swallowed.

"Where's *your* maths prep?" Mr. Oliver, his form master, pressed the curiously raised wave of his lips together until they, like his nostrils, formed a white relief.

"I . . ."

"Yes?" In the effort to restrain himself, Mr. Oliver rapped Peter's desk with his ruler. He had freckles, pale splotches running into one another, on the back of his hands.

"I didn't know we had any . . . *sir*."

"But I *told* you . . . I told you quite clearly. Twelve boys in this class managed to hear me quite clearly. Why were you unable to do so?"

"I forgot, sir."

He often said he'd forgotten instead of confessing he hadn't heard. Forgetting seemed more curable, less definite, less of a lifetime's sentence than not hearing.

Mr. Oliver checked himself. The skin of his pale forehead eased so visibly, the sandy cap of his hair slid backwards. "Ah!" he cried softly. "Were you wearing your aid?"

"I don't know."

"You don't *know*!" The exasperation returned. It seemed not feasible.

Peter's head hung. He concentrated on reading the names inscribed on his desk lid. Mr. Oliver's voice receded.

"I'll give you one more chance . . ."

Petals of thankfulness opened in his chest.

"Thank you, sir."

"Very well. One more chance. I know you have your

difficulties but you've got to learn to cope with them. Organise yourself a little better . . . Yes?"

"Yes, sir. Thank you, sir."

"All right, Makin. You'll stay in at break and do it then."

Gratefully he slipped out of Mr. Oliver's angry orbit. He couldn't bear any more shouting. His mother had shouted at him as she'd flown off for a last week of non-stick pans. She'd loosed an artillery of orders. "Feed your bloody rabbits this morning!" she'd yelled. And . . . "Make sure you've got your bloody bus fare . . ." And . . . "Clean your revolting shoes for God's sake!" And . . . "Get *yourself* a drink can't you, the waitress has gone off duty!"

The after-effects of her hysterical voice were with him still. A residue, an inflammation unable to be relieved by scratching. His father had seemed to be on her side. At least, he'd made no attempt to quieten her as he sometimes did. But these days, thought Peter, soothing seems to make her worse. Salt stinging the wound.

Anyway, she'd shouted at Kit too. "Fix this sodding handle would you!" she'd bawled, thundering on the door with both fists.

He picked up his pen. Thinking of her frightened him. Something had happened. Changed. When they'd lived in London before, years and years ago, she hadn't been like this. Not really. She'd always been short-tempered but that was part of her energy, he knew that, something that couldn't be taken away without taking away all her inventiveness and gaiety. You put up with it, for the sake of the other things. And anyway, her explosions were short things, little explosions of fury followed by laughing self-rebuke and apology. All over. All done with. Small black clouds followed by sunbursts.

But now . . . carefully, using the edge of his textbook, he drew a thick black line across the page, burying his upper teeth against his lip to steady himself . . . At Sigvales, she'd been peaceful. Also, he perceived in a blurred sort of way, lonely. She'd turned to them for company, talking, talking, sharing jokes, telling stories. And then Dad had come home and though it made no kind of sense, the homecoming had seemed to make her lonelier than ever. She'd spoken less and had gone about her tasks, scything and milking and digging, with a silent intensity that frightened them off. He and Rod had preferred to be with Dad, he reflected, writing the date in the margin.

But now . . . now the anger was constantly there. You couldn't ignore it any longer knowing it would blow again. A dandelion clock. Puff. Gone. There was always the worry of it being there, growing.

"What?"

"For God's sake, Makin, wake up!"

He couldn't think what Mr. Oliver wanted. "I'm sorry?" His mind flew into fragments.

"*Sir.*"

"I'm sorry, sir."

"You haven't *started* yet!"

He dare not say, "Started what, sir?" and lowered his eyes to the neat page.

A broad white finger came down on the textbook, jabbing at Exercise Eleven. "*Do* it," breathed Mr. Oliver's voice, trembling a little. "*Do* it."

"Sir."

He moved on, his brown and white check sports jacket seeming to bristle. Cotley-Smith looked at Peter scornfully. Although, thought Peter, he is more stupid than me.

He was glad when the bell went and the others ran out of the classroom leaving him alone with his prep. The work itself he didn't find difficult. Only remembering to do it. Or discovering that he should do it. That was the difficulty. At the school in Chewton Caundle, they'd never had prep.

If my mother goes to work to pay for the school fees, he thought, I wish she wouldn't bother. And then, more cheerfully, he remembered there was only one week to go until half-term.

His misery dissipated altogether after break. Mr. Scholfield took them for History and he liked that. He knew a lot about Roman Britain because the countryside surrounding Sigvales had been strewn with Roman remains, Roman villas and, at Badley Hill, part of a mosaic floor with dolphins and lion-like creatures adorning its border. Once, Maggie had taken them to another high place, high on Knattersbury Hill, to help excavate a Roman temple. With trowels and a little wire brush they'd worked all day among the cleared trees, exposing the corner stone of some small building that might, someone had said, might have been a priest's house. And as they'd scraped carefully round the foundations, Rod had unearthed two coins, two greenish brown discs with worn edges and the head of an

Emperor still faintly discernible on them. *That* had been exciting. Not quite as exciting, though, as the skeleton somebody else had found, the bones so arranged you could tell the corpse had been curled up on its side like a baby.

The class liked hearing about that. He was invited to stand up and tell them of his finds and as he talked, he had felt himself back there, among the sighing trees with the sheep bleating in the meadow below and the wheat standing yellow in the far bowl of the valley.

"Today," announced Mr. Scholfield, beginning to write on the blackboard, "we shall start to look at the Dark Ages . . ."

The Dark Ages . . . the wonderful heading made Peter quiver and he turned to a new page to copy it down.

As he wrote, Mr. Scholfield began to talk of King Arthur, his sword Excalibur, his twelve knights, and most magical of all, their search for the Holy Grail . . .

"What did the waiter say when the man complained there was a fly in his soup?"

"Don't worry sir, there's no extra charge."

"You should be so lucky, the last customer had a hedgehog in his!"

"Would you keep your voice down sir, or everyone might want one!"

Peter lay on the grass listening. The patch of turf behind the school was dry and prickly after mowing.

The boarders went on giving silly answers, some of which made him laugh. He didn't know any answers himself and struggled to think one up. All the day boys were silent.

"What does a cannibal call a missionary on a bicycle?" challenged Rod, trying at the same time to stand on his head.

"Meals on wheels, I know that one," sneered Collins, Rod's mentor. But a few of the others laughed.

"Can't you stand on your head, Makin Two? It's easy."

"I can," said Peter.

"Go on then. Show us."

Grimly, he made a cup with his hands and placed his head against them, giving a little spring with his legs when he felt secure. Mercifully, it worked. His legs went up, and, wavering a bit, remained in the air. Blood poured into his head as he stayed there, listening to the grudging sounds of admiration.

"That's nothing," said Cotley-Smith when he came down. "Have you got a second hand on your watch? Time me."

A steady, inverted shape, he remained poised for forty-six seconds.

"Do it together," said Rod. "See who can do it longest."

But Cotley-Smith sat, legs bent and apart, his face gently purple. "Just a sec," he gulped.

"Let's have a competition," someone else suggested. "Two teams."

They looked around at one another trying to discover a principle by which the teams could be divided. A click of ball on bat came from the nets.

"Boarders v. day boys."

Peter's heart sank. He hated the unfairness of the separation. It was one of those boundaries there was no crossing. It was no good his mother saying boarders pretended they were superior because they were jealous of those who went home at the end of every day to a decent tea and television and a late bedtime. Peter didn't, at that moment, feel such things to be advantages at all.

For a start there were more boarders. They began running about all over the lawn recruiting good head-standers. He looked at his own side who seemed to have lost interest in the competition and were either gazing at the cricket practice or sucking grass or pretending to be asleep in the sun.

"Who can do it?" he asked.

"Sometimes I can," volunteered Townson who was tiny and had an elderly expression that gave him a freakish air.

"Go and find somebody!" Peter pushed his brother, but Rod just screwed his mouth up and made a rude noise. Outside the intense relationship with his brother, his sense of competition was liable to lapses. Peter had a faint, betrayed feeling as though Rod *wanted* him to lose. "Go on, you beast. It was your idea!"

"Knickers," said Rod. "It's too hot," and he flung himself backwards on the grass, splayed in sun-worship.

In the end it was Peter against the boarders, one of them, Allan, a senior boy, which seemed unfair. Patel offered to be referee.

He couldn't always do it. Now he felt *certain* he wouldn't be able to do it and part of him retreated from the uneven contest. But then, as he cupped his hands and realised he was the sole representative of his side, a further, more pitiless part of himself dully insisted that he had, at least, to try. All the same, if the bell for afternoon school had at that moment rung, he would have abandoned the dutiful impulse quite shamelessly.

"Go!" Patel pretended to fire a pistol.

He pushed first one leg, then the other, up. They met, stayed together and straightened. Good, he was nicely balanced. Some of them, he could see out of the upside down corner of his eye, were a bit slow getting up. He hoped points would be deducted for that.

Feeling his own well-balanced body, a confidence gathered within him that in its own inexplicable fashion, seemed to consolidate his control. One pair of legs to his left, came down.

"Twenty-five seconds. Rotten."

"Thirty."

Another figure keeled over backwards. Only four of them remained in position. There was a definite cheering from the day boys. He knew it was the day boys because he could hear Rod's voice. The sound surprised him.

"Forty . . . forty-five . . ."

He felt as if he could stay up for ever.

"Fifty . . ."

Two boys collapsed together. He couldn't see who his remaining rival was, but he heard the others shouting . . . "Makin! . . . Cotley-Smith! . . . Makin! . . . Makin!"

By an effort of will, he forced the weight of blood gathering in his skull back upwards.

"*Sixty!*"

One whole minute! The cheering became quite frenzied. By moving his neck slightly, as if it were a hinge, he was able to exercise perfect control over his legs.

"Cotley-Smith! Cotley-Smith!"

And louder still: "Makin! Makin! Makin!" He was conscious of more legs, a thickening of legs, a crowd gathering. Then, quite suddenly, taking him wholly by surprise, his hips bent and his whole body, taken unawares, caved in. He fell flat on his back. But the wail of disappointment that rose from the crowd was so deafening, so exclusively for him, that his own personal disappointment was washed away by it. For a split second, before his supporters ran round him, he saw Cotley-Smith, straight as a blade, suddenly wobble and crash. Another cheer went up, but not, he thought, as loud as the one that had greeted him.

"One minute seventeen seconds. And Makin, one minute fourteen seconds. Jolly good." Patel shook him by the shoulder. He glowed.

The bell clanged and the gathering broke up. Peter went to

afternoon school with a new lightness of spirit. He had glimpsed the real possibility of victory. It *could* be his, not always somebody else's.

One day I *shall* win, he thought. One day. And all afternoon — throughout the games period and even in prep when he worked on his tank project — the refrain whispered round his head.

One day I *shall* win.

"For God's sake woman!"

Kit raised his hand as if to strike his wife, then paused. "Get a hold of yourself you silly bitch . . . anyone would think . . ."

Would think what?

Rod and Peter sat over the half-eaten beans Kit had warmed up for them, forks halted.

"You're going to pieces."

"How *dare* she!" screamed Maggie, straight into Kit's face as though daring him to complete the blow.

"She's only being kind. In her way."

"*Kind!*"

"Yes. You don't imagine she's . . ."

They watched their father. Watched the slow lightening of his face as some thought came to him, a thought that promised to be comic. The two adults stood face to face, movements frozen.

"You don't imagine she's *after* me!" His big head went back on the swollen neck. Hinges moved and released laughter, excoriating swathes of merriment. "Not *me*! Not Sally Ferguson!"

Rod began to eat.

Maggie flung the enamel dish still crusted with Sally Ferguson's neatly crimped pastry into the sink.

"She feels sorry for me, that's all." Kit pushed up his glasses and rubbed his eyes with the back of his hand as if mirth had made them water. "She thinks I'll starve if there isn't a woman around to push pap down my throat."

"Is *that* all you think it is?" Maggie was cold.

"It was very sweet of her. And it was an exceptionally good steak and kidney pie — I haven't had one in ages."

"It's an attack on *me*!"

"Oh." Kit reconsidered. "Is *that* what you think it is? What a shame, I thought you imagined she'd come to seduce me."

"Me! Me! *Me!*" Maggie crushed a hand to her mouth to silence herself.

"Well, I should exploit it if I were you." Kit turned away. "She was just being neighbourly."

He had dismissed his wife.

"And you'll let her . . . *You'll* exploit it. Pretending you can't do a thing for yourself."

"I'm busy that's all. Busy slaving over a hot house all day long."

"Pretending you can't even go out and shop for yourself!"

"There's a lot to be done."

Kit sat down opposite the boys and picked up the newspaper folded back at the small ads. "Get on with your tea," he said calmly.

"*Pretending . . . !*"

"I finished the hall wall today," he said, reading.

"Pretending you can't bloody . . ."

"I rang Colin today too. About the *Ask Uncle* page."

"You didn't!" Maggie's attack evaporated. "You can't do that."

"No, I can't. Someone else is doing it."

"Thank God for that."

He looked up at her quizzically for a second. "What *do* you want?" he asked briefly and returned to the newspaper.

"Can I have the sauce?" said Rod.

Kit passed it to him, adding, "Anyway, I've fixed up an interview for myself tomorrow."

"Doing what?" Abstractedly Maggie began preparing their own supper.

"Selling advertising space."

"You can't . . . !"

"What *can* I do, for Christ's sake? Half the time I don't think you ever want me to do anything again and half the time you're on the point of cracking up trying to do it all yourself. I can't stand much more of it . . . I just won't have you organising my life *and* ruining your own."

"Do shut up, Daddy," said Rod, scattering gouts of H.P. over his remaining beans. "I hate it when you argue."

I hate it too, thought Peter, but he couldn't have said so. His feelings were too blown about and strewn to say so clearly. Oh, *Hymie*, he thought, achingly.

"Advertising space . . ." repeated Maggie slowly, her face as vacant as if it *had* been struck. "I'm sorry, Kit. I don't mean to get so . . ." She sat down, biting her lip. "I *can* manage," she insisted. "Honestly."

Kit looked at her in such an odd, fierce way, Peter felt something rebound sharply against his rib cage. But his father's expression dissolved, replaced by a grudging tenderness. "It can't go on though," Kit murmured, "not like this . . ."

"It shouldn't *be* like this." Sliding a thumb nail between her teeth, Maggie shook her head, distraught. "I despise myself," she said, "for being like this. I must try harder." And she passed her hand up, over her face and through her hair.

Kit reached out a hand but did not touch her. "No," he said simply.

"Peter nearly won a headstand championship today!"

They turned from one another and looked at Rod.

"Did he?"

"Did you?"

And he told them, trying to resurrect his own excitement, trying to spread it over their agitations. Their eyes smiled, their approval a distant, manufactured thing, a poor veil for sorrow.

As he spoke, he began, for the first time, to fear that their antagonism was something that might accumulate, something that would swell and cluster until it acquired an unbearable weight. Before, these quarrels had been short skirmishes, things that ended as neutrally as they had begun.

The dread stayed with him, sucking away his earlier rapture. It almost spoiled Star Trek, but perhaps that was because it was a repeat of an episode he'd seen before and it didn't hold his attention as undividedly as usual.

When he was in his bath, his mother, who was passing by on the landing, called something out to him.

"What?"

"*Have* you fed those rabbits?" Her head appeared round the door.

"I was going to."

"Huh." She thought better of what she was about to say and remarked instead, "Daddy's promised to build them a run." She paused, eyes blanking for a second, then mentioned that she had to do the washing tonight, so would he please put on a clean pair of pyjamas.

He did as she asked and took the dirty pair downstairs for her, dropping them on top of the pile of dirty clothes she'd dumped on the scullery floor.

His eye was caught by bloodstains.

He bent down, a hand slowly reaching out. Sharply, he withdrew it. His mother's nightdress was covered in old brown blood. He stared, wondering what fearful wound could have caused such bleeding as this. It was too profuse for a domestic cut.

For the second time in successive days, his mind veered curiously towards his father and then recoiled in horror.

Hearing Rod running downstairs with his armful of washing, Peter hurriedly pulled one of Kit's shirts over the incriminating, frivolous garment. Then he replaced his own pyjamas on top of the pile and ran from the scullery knocking Rod against the edge of the kitchen table in his haste to escape both the sight of those stained white frills and the perplexity of feeling that spun around his heart.

12

HE ROSE VERY early to feed his rabbits.

So determined had he been to remember, he'd barely slept but tossed wakefully, trying to recall what it was he simply must not forget and then—remembering each time that he had to concentrate upon *rabbits*—had fallen asleep for a further uneasy interval.

When he went outside in his dressing gown he found dew on their pitiful stretch of glass. It was very quiet. The background rumble of traffic had not yet stirred itself and the air was given back to birdsong.

He wanted to see how the river looked at this hour, but reluctant to be seen in the street with his dressing gown on, dragged an orange box to the wall and climbed up, surprised to notice that the brown, withered stems which had knotted themselves between the bricks now possessed delicate green leaves and starry white flowers. He peered over the top of the wall and saw a light mist rising off the river, making the trees on the Sweetings bank appear to float in a still and pearly tide. A swan slid by.

He felt happy.

Hovering against the wire mesh on their hind legs, noses quivering, the rabbits greeted him. Both were a pale mushroom colour with clear white bands around their chests. Chrysanthemum had a white nose as well and Poppy, white paws. He detached the front of their hutch to stretch for their water bowl and saw that their bedding was bile-coloured and wet. It smelt sour. He hadn't cleaned them out for ten days or so and the sight of brownish-yellow smears on Poppy's lower chest made guilt turn like a key in his stomach. All the same he didn't feel like cleaning them out just now. There was nowhere to put them while he scraped the hutch clean, he told himself. And then, with an even more comfortable sense of justification, he decided they'd grown so large he couldn't do the job on his own anyway. Holding them required an adult. When they kicked with their powerful back legs, they left wicked scratches on your arm.

He heard a clock strike the half-hour and was surprised because he'd never heard the clock before and wondered if it was the one on the church next to the Scout Hut which must be fully a quarter of a mile away. It couldn't be seen from here.

After filling the water bowl at the scullery tap, he went into the kitchen to fetch some bread from the bin in the cupboard that now served as his pantry. As he opened the door four or five small black darts leapt out and flew, in a scuttery blur, across the red tiles and under the rickety yellow wooden doors below the sink.

He found himself pressed back against the wall beside the pantry, his heart lurching nauseously. Amongst the ancient, mingled smells of this house then, was the smell of mice. That horrible dull, biscuity odour of droppings that must now (he thought, aghast) be scattered amidst their own food.

He released the press of his shoulder blades against the wall a little, wondering why the presence of mice should upset him so. Mice didn't usually alarm him. At Sigvales the cats had brought them into the house quite regularly, laying the small brown bodies in those places they'd selected as altars. Rats too.

Once, he thought, his brain still tight, once I found a dormouse in the larder. He'd tried to keep it alive for two days. And on another occasion, Sam Price, their neighbouring farmer, had opened his palm and shown him a harvest mouse he'd discovered while scything down the long grasses in the hedgerow. An exquisite little creature, tiny, with very black eyes and a pointed nose, it had just curled up in Sam's palm and died. "From fright," Sam had said, taking it gently with his other hand and tucking it back into the dim covert of hawthorn roots.

Those creatures hadn't sickened him. (He still remained tense against the wall, trying to convince himself he wasn't a baby.) They were simply animals with a perfect right to life. He hadn't wanted to trap or poison them. Sometimes he'd even shouted angrily at the cats as they'd padded proudly by, ears flattened, eyes enlarged, their prey still squeaking between their teeth. But that, he thought, had been different.

Why it was different, he couldn't tell. But he *had* been repelled by the skinny black darts he'd caught thieving. For a while longer, he remained motionless, then he forced himself to turn and look into the cupboard, picking up packets and jars gingerly, each movement of the hand preceded by a cautious sweep of the eye. He found fine black pellets strewn on the newspaper Maggie had used to line the shelves. With effort, he removed all the things he thought they would need for breakfast, then he took the bread to his rabbits.

Kit was the next one down. He looked odd in his suit.

"You're early," remarked Peter, who had dressed and sat behind the cereal and sugar and jam not feeling like eating anything. "You look peculiar."

"Of course I do," said Kit, "I can't do this damned shirt up with my neck the size it is."

Yes, that was it. The tie trapped the shirt collar only approximately in place. But his father bulged everywhere, not just at the neck. The buttons of his double-breasted suit — so smart, five years ago — strained desperately to contain him.

"You're getting fat," said Peter.

"Damn! *Damn!*" Kit stopped struggling with his shirt collar and looked more generally, more despondently about his person. "Lack of exercise," he observed gloomily. "Just not fit enough." He minded about that. Peter could tell from the dismal planes of his father's face. Early as it was, Kit's face shone with sweat.

"I've got a button missing," he clicked to himself and went off in search of the sewing basket.

"Are you coming with *me*?" Maggie's voice rang down from the landing.

"Yes, O.K.?" Kit could be heard answering.

"If you're ready in time."

"I'm just doing some mending."

Peter tried to persuade himself to eat some cereal. Would a mouse nibble its way in from the corner or could it climb up the side and crawl in from the top?

"Fed your rabbits?" Maggie appeared, smeary-faced.

"*Ages* ago."

"Oh, good boy!" She paused, genuinely pleased, then muttering further approvals, hunted other things out of the evil cupboard.

"We've got mice," he said.

"Hell. I thought so. I thought I could smell them." Then,

jamming the kitchen door open with the radio, she switched it on and yelled, "Kit, put rat poison on your shopping list would you?"

There was an indistinct response.

"Can I have egg and bacon?" Rod trailed in, his head an explosion of curls.

"No." Maggie was kneeling, adjusting the volume. It was *Thought For The Day*.

"There's no bacon and even less time."

"Oh-*oh* . . ."

"Sorry."

Rod slumped at the table. "What did the waiter say to the man who complained there was a fly in his soup?"

" 'Don't . . .' " Peter began but Rod told him to shut up. "I'm asking Mummy," he said.

" 'Don't worry, there's no extra charge,' " said Maggie. She began spinning plates across the table as though she were playing shove ha'penny.

"No. 'Don't worry, sir, the spider on your bread will deal with it.' "

She laughed. "Any more like that?"

Kit came back in his shirtsleeves, a thread of white cotton gripped between his teeth.

"What did the waiter say to the man who complained there was a fly in his soup?" Rod demanded of him.

"Uh-hu . . ." Kit shook his head.

" 'Don't worry . . .' " Peter began.

"Shut up!" screamed Rod. "*Dad?*"

But Kit shook his head again.

" 'What do you expect in a restaurant like this?' "

"What did the waiter say to the man who complained there was a fly in his soup?" Peter burst in, wanting a turn.

" 'Never mind'," suggested Kit, removing the cotton from his mouth and threading it, " 'we'll soon have it rescued.' "

"Oh, you *know* it!" He was bitterly disappointed.

"I *thought*," said Maggie, cutting slices of bread an inch thick, "that instead of white in the hall, we might make a virtue of its darkness and have red."

"*Red!* It's like the inside of a whale's belly as it is."

"Well exactly. White woodwork, red walls."

"Blimey," said Kit morosely, stretching.

Peter thought of his mother's wounds and looked down at his plate. Then, "What?" he asked, aware of attention beamed towards him.

"Toast?"

"Yes, please. No, thank you," he said.

"Make your mind up."

"No, thank you."

"Why ever not?"

"I don't want any."

"You've got to eat *something*," his mother insisted. "Go on, I'll make you some . . . Rod?"

"Bugger!" roared Kit as a knot appeared in his thread, a tangle of strands looping from it.

"Haven't you got another shirt?"

"No."

"Why not?" demanded Maggie, preoccupied by her toast-making.

"Because somebody hasn't ironed one."

"*Who*, do you suppose?" she countered sarcastically.

"Well, not the fairy queen for one. Nor even the Queen of England. Not Raquel Welch, not Lulu . . ."

"I should take it off if I were you," Maggie rattled things. "You can't sew a button on while you're wearing it."

"I'm demonstrating that such a feat is, entirely, possible."

"Ten to rotten eight," said Maggie as the Bach chorale faded. "How do you feel?"

"Feel?" Kit looked up. "About what? . . . The colour of the walls? The domestic responsibilities of this house? Or the state of the economy?"

She grinned, briefly. "Your interview, dafty."

"Oh, brimful of confidence. I shall cut quite a dash in my out of date, under-sized suit and beer-stained tie, wouldn't you say? Oh Christ! I hate being poor."

"Are we poor?" asked Rod anxiously, taking his toast and submitting it to critical scrutiny.

"Not *really* . . ." said Maggie.

"A bloody sight poorer than we were."

"It'll be all right once we've sold the cottage," said Maggie brusquely.

"*Once* we have, yes . . ."

"Well, it will," she persisted. "Here, Peter. Get it eaten."

"Who in fuck's name wants to live there any longer? It's so far away from work *or* pleasure it takes a lifetime's savings to travel in search of either."

Half-listening, Peter scraped disconsolately at the black bit of his toast.

"Lots of people," snapped Maggie. And then, "I don't know why you don't try renting it out."

"I've told you why."

"Because," she concluded automatically, in a mimicking voice, "it won't pay the bills."

"Right."

"We needn't go to Hill House," said Peter.

"Oh yes you do need," his mother replied. "It's worth every penny."

"The coffee's boiling over," observed Kit.

"Oh screw it!" Maggie seized the pan and held it over the sink wailing, "I'm not dressed yet!"

"What the devil's *that*?"

They all looked up and paused at Kit's exclamation. A drill, or rather several drills, had started up in the distance, accompanied by crashing sounds. As they listened, the sound was augmented, then drowned by the noise of an approaching plane. Maggie turned the radio up louder. "Eight o'clock, nearly!" she panicked, slopping coffee into cups.

Kit bit the thread, stuck the needle in his tie and fastened his shirt cuff. "That's better!" he said admiringly of his handiwork.

My father is *nervous*, Peter thought incredulously, as he noted the lines running beneath the surface self-congratulation. *Nervous!*

The pips went and Kit checked his watch. "I don't have to be there till ten-thirty," he said.

"Well, *don't* come with me then!" Maggie seemed to think he was criticising.

"I'd rather."

"You'll be exhausted if you have to walk far," she muttered, squashing a lump of frozen butter on her own piece of toast. Peter looked again at his slice and quelled a surge of nausea.

"What *are* they doing?" Kit questioned irritably, fiddling with his other cuff.

"Knocking something down," suggested Rod.

"Wellington Gardens probably," his mother observed.

"*What!*" he squawked.

"Believe me," remarked Kit, "if the average council tenant could see the damp and squalor in which we live, they'd tear the place down out of political compassion. It floods, you know. That's why it smells so awful."

"Aunt Carrie never said so."

"Sally Ferguson did."

"Oh *yes*," leered Maggie, adding, "what's for lunch then today? Did she say?"

"I told her," Kit replied with dignity, "that I should be out for lunch today. I hate to say this, darling, but you and your younger son are going to be late."

"Hurry! Hurry!" gobbled Rod. "Clean my shoes for me, will you Pete?"

"Why should I?"

"Go on."

"Yes, would you, darling?" pleaded Maggie.

It was so *unfair*. Specially when he'd made the effort to get up so early and do all his own things in time. With bad grace, Peter scraped back his chair and did as he was asked. They were announcing the latest unemployment figures on the news.

"Is your head all right?" Maggie was asking, worried.

"Fine."

"*Sure?*"

"*Fine!*" his father repeated angrily.

"You haven't eaten your toast, Peter," his mother said.

When they got home after school, Kit was pasting lining paper on the wall with such fixity, he scarcely greeted them. He still, Peter noticed, had the needle stuck through his tie. It showed above the apron. But he dared not tell him so, something in his father's face prevented him.

Quickly, he unfastened his briefcase and took out the books he needed to do a little work on his tank project. It was too hot and damp to play outside. The air was thick with hopping things.

"They're demolishing those shops on the corner," said Rod, sitting on the stairs at his father's feet.

"I noticed."

"Well . . . They were empty anyway." Rod unwrapped his lollipop. The two shops had had Closing Down Sale and Slashing Reduction notices pasted on their vacant, dusty glass ever since the Makins had come to Wellington Gardens.

Kit seemed disinclined to talk. "Mind out of the way, would you?" was all he said to Rod who shifted himself to one side a little, amid the curling tongues of paper.

Maggie arrived home about a quarter to six. She burst in. "I've got something special for supper!" she cried and paused.

There was a sullen air in the hall. Gently, she closed the door behind her.

"What is it?" asked Rod, who was sitting on the lower stairs reading his comic. Above him, Kit raced a brush expertly upwards.

"Chopped herring . . ."

"Ugh!"

". . . and a few strawberries."

"Oh *goody!*"

"Well?" she pleaded, standing still and gazing upwards.

Kit looked down over his shoulder. "I'm considering a future in p. and d.," he said.

"P. and d.?" she repeated, "Or a Ph.D.?"

"Painting and decorating," he said.

"Oh."

"Oh," he mimicked.

"No good?"

"They feel that a man of my experience and talent would be wasted on them."

"Oh, darling . . ." Her voice faded upward.

"Never mind," he said, flattening a wrinkle. "My compensation money will see us through another five days' high living."

"You keep discounting *my* earnings . . ." began Maggie desperately, but her voice trailed. "I *am* sorry," she said.

"Don't be sorry. I'd've hated it." He finished the edges of the paper and leaned back against the bannister. "I *don't* discount yours, but it gets deducted from mine. Anyway, in the end it isn't yours, it isn't mine. It's ours."

Rod looked up. "We're not going to starve, are we?"

"No," smiled Maggie, with difficulty. "You mustn't worry about the money. It's not the money that's important."

But Rod thought it was. Hoping for reassurance, he followed his mother into the kitchen where Peter sat, working at the table. "Hello," he mumbled without raising his head.

"Hello, darling . . ." She stooped to kiss him and stood thoughtfully for a moment.

"Strawberries," said Rod.

"*Strawberries!* Where?" And Peter leant over the table to sniff at the shopping basket. He smelt summer, warm earth, sunshine on green leaves.

"Daddy hasn't got it has he?" Fingers creeping slyly into the basket, Rod was questioning his mother.

"Not this time."

"I don't like it," he said, not quite sure what he meant. But it made him feel apprehensive when he saw the dullness of defeat in his father. Kit had looked bruised, almost. Like a boxer. (In the last fight Rod had watched on television, the holder of the title, losing, had appeared blank-eyed behind the violet swellings, crazed, lashing out at an opponent who'd already left the space where the blow landed. He didn't like it.)

"What shall we do to cheer Daddy up?" said Maggie.

"Take him to the pub?" suggested Peter.

"Why not, yes. After supper, shall we?" She smiled at him. "See if there's some change left from the shopping, Rod?"

She meant on top of the fridge where Kit always left her whatever change there was from the day's purchases. Pushing a ball of string and a tankard full of dead lilac out of the way, Rod shovelled the money that was there, towards himself. "Lots!" he said. It seemed a lot to him since it was all in silver. Two of the ten pee pieces he slipped in his trousers pocket to put towards the boat.

Maggie bent over Peter, glancing at his work as she reached beyond him for her basket. "Tanks, still," she said.

"It'll take a term nearly, to do."

"Why tanks?" she asked.

"I like them."

For a moment she hung over the book he was using to copy a drawing of the British Mark V. And then, taking the blood-stained bag of fruit, she sat down beside him, plucking stalks from the plump, bright strawberries.

"*What* a funny looking object!"

"What, this . . . ?" He pointed to a box-like contraption, a coffin-shape on tracks. He was pleased by her interest.

"Yes."

Rod bounded over, head pushed between them. "That's Little Willie," he said before Peter could name it.

"Little Willie?"

"Yes."

Maggie screeched with laughter. "I don't believe it!" she cried. "How *could* they?"

"It wasn't ever really used . . ." Peter began authoritatively.

"Shut up! I'm telling her!"

"It's *my* project! *Yours*," Peter said contemptuously, "is about dinosaurs."

"Little Willie," put in Maggie, laughing still, "*looks* like a dinosaur."

"Well, it wasn't used. They used Big Willie."

This remark of Rod's provoked wilder laughter from Maggie. She popped a strawberry in her mouth to silence herself and laughed around it, deliciously.

"Shut *up*, will you! Anyway, you're wrong." Peter was beside himself with frustration.

"No, I'm not." Rod pushed his nose in the air and waggled it then said, "Can I have one?" to his mother and helped himself to a strawberry.

"The first tank to be used *properly*," sighed Peter with the crushing confidence of the factually knowledgeable, was Mother."

"It wasn't!" Maggie sounded appalled.

"Yes it was. Look." And he turned the pages of his book to show her the picture. Mother was a weird rhomboid with a wheel on a shaft sticking out of the back.

"I'm not sure I like that," his own mother said.

"Well, it didn't work very well." Peter mistook her drift but she didn't bother to correct him. She had fallen quite silent, mechanically hulling the fruit, eyes fixed on a picture which showed old-fashioned cavalrymen dismounted, holding their horses and staring at the tank in disbelief.

"It must have been awful," Peter added thoughtfully, chewing his pencil, "trying to fight in it. They couldn't see anything. Couldn't see where they were going."

"They couldn't hear anything either," observed Rod, leaning heavily on Peter's shoulder.

"Push off, will you?"

"Why *tanks* though," persisted Maggie, only half-attending to their argument. "Why not elephants or sticklebacks or frogs?"

"What do you mean?"

"Why do *tanks*?"

He couldn't really penetrate what lay behind her question, but he tried. He pondered for a moment. "They're *winners*," he said at length.

"*Winners?*" She was puzzled.

"I got the rat poison." Kit came in.

"*Winners?*" she repeated.

Peter tried again, thinking she was unsatisfied with his first answer. "All-powerful," he said. But her interest seemed to be extinguished. She wasn't laughing any more.

"Oh thanks." She addressed herself to Kit who took a strawberry from the colander. "Hands off," she reproved, tapping his wrist.

"We're going to take you to the pub after supper!"

Rod ran round the table to his father and, holding him about the waist, jumped up and down as a signal that he should be lifted. But Kit ignored it, simply holding Rod's upper arms. "Splendid," he murmured vaguely, as the violence of Rod's bouncing made his glasses slip.

"Can we have a Coke there?"

"Sure."

"Can we *really* afford it?" Rod was beseechingly anxious to know.

"Most certainly we can afford it!" cried Kit and lifted him suddenly.

Maggie counted out exactly seven strawberries in each of the boys' bowls. Kit had ten. She had five.

13

THE MIDGES WERE busy in the thick, evening air. Kit swatted at them irritably as they sat overlooking the river on the high, prow-like balcony of The Swan. "Bloody things!" he complained, picking one out of his beer and trapping another on his wrist. "Who d'you suppose *sent* these buggers to get me?"

"Lord, you're paranoic." Maggie was drinking cider. "It's because of the swallows," she said. "The swallows haven't come back."

"Who says so?" He felt argumentative.

"I haven't seen any. Have you?"

"Now I come to think of it, no. But then I don't go around looking for swallows much."

"Thousands of them must have died last winter."

"No, they just heard how things were in this country and decided not to bother," yawned Kit.

Maggie laughed sourly, picking a blown strand of hair from her mouth.

The boys asked if they could play on the lawn on the far side of the narrow road below the pub. It went down to the river withdrawn a little by the tide, leaving the pub's landing stage protruding from the mud. A group of mallards quacked and dived in the shallow water.

It was agreeably dangerous climbing up the wooden supports of the landing stage. They were smeared with violent green weed that made the boys' sandals slip. They played on them for some time.

Tiring of it eventually they went and threw stones in the water. They heard Maggie's voice behind them.

"Don't frighten the ducks," she called faintly. But it was fun making the ducks scurry, their yellow feet beating beneath the water.

"Watch mine jump!" Rod tried skimming his stone obliquely But it disappeared with a single, baleful plop.

"He-er-erh . . ." Peter made a sneering sound and tried himself. He fared no better.

"You need a *flat* stone," he said. Searching carefully, he found one, threw it at a perfect angle and made it leap three times.

"I'll show you . . ." Kit and Maggie joined them, Kit still clutching a half-full mug. With a grunt, he bent, selected his stone and sent it spinning, leaping more times than they were able to count: a lovely display.

"*You* try." Peter looked at his mother.

She spent a long time finding her pebble, rejecting all those with any irregularity. Then she crouched low and with a sideways cut of her arm, sent it skimming, bouncing half-way across the river.

"Oh," said Peter, peculiarly disappointed. "How do you do it?"

"You must make the stone actually spin as it leaves your hand," she said. "Even in the palm of your hand it must be spinning already. Don't just throw it."

She watched them try for a little longer. Small growls issued from Kit who was being consumed by insects. "I'm going inside," he said. "It's a slow death out here."

She half turned to go with him, then paused. "Do you mind if I go for a walk?"

"Oh you and your bloody walks!"

"Do you mind?"

"Do what you like. I'll take the boys home in a minute."

But the boys wanted to go with her. There was something smothering about Kit's canopy of dejection. Besides their mother was in a good mood and that usually meant she could be milked for a story.

She took them on a circular route. She wanted to see the gardens, she said, so they wandered down the walled road towards the boatyard and the church. Alongside *Up the Sheds* and *Cunt* someone had now painted FUCK LIBERTY EQUALITY AND FRATERNITY in very neat white letters. It was passed by unheeding people walking their dogs or couples cradling one another's shoulders as they whispered other things.

They went through the embankment gardens, stopping to gaze across the water at a rusting hulk in the boatyard where, even now, banging repairs were being done although

143

the westerly sky was pinkening in a strained, blurred fashion, as if it had a headache. And they stopped to giggle at the naked ladies playing netball over the still, thick pads of yellow water-lilies. Then they hurried, giggles tucked away, through the ladies' own, enclosed garden, a cloth of turf surrounded by shaped battlements of yew, and then up, over the little bridge into Lion House Gardens. Azaleas swarmed and blazed in the tawny sunlight.

"Wait for me!" cried Maggie, hanging over the edge of the bridge to look.

"They're all wrong," she commented when Peter returned to her.

"What?" he said.

"All wrong."

"Wrong?"

"Too bright. Too fierce."

He tried to see what she meant. He quite liked the Japanese garden himself. He liked the tiny shrubs and trees, the rustic bridge and stepping stones. No, he didn't really understand what she meant. The azaleas were pink and gold and purple and crimson. They were nice.

"They smell of nothing," she said and turned away, leaning back against the concrete. "Just look at *those* colours . . . !" And she pointed at the immaculate municipal borders below them. Scarlet and pink tulips, arranged in rows behind savage yellow antirrhinums, defended a clean-shaven stretch of grass upon which the public were requested not to walk. "Lined up for battle," she grinned. "If you *do* step on the grass," she said, "the flowers lean over and bite you."

"They *don't*," he said, as though she were stupid. They looked all right to him. Sort of gay. Mostly, though, they bored him. His gaze slid away from them. People were playing bad tennis on the pink courts. The sight of them, their caged clumsiness, reminded him of two things together — of the Fergusons' garden, a luxury of meshes . . . and the mice he'd seen that morning, so swift by contrast. These people had flat, lumping feet and graceless wrists. "Will you put the poison down tonight?" he asked.

"I suppose so." She sounded tired. Perhaps though, he thought, looking at her, she was just reluctant. She had no relish for killing things. The cottage at Sigvales had been full of cobwebs and moths. Spiders were allowed free range of the bath and a chrysalis, a fine, delicate green thing, had been left for a year on the lavatory well in the hope it would turn into something. Perhaps, he thought wistfully for a moment, it did. One day it wasn't there any longer, anyway . . .

"I hope you do," he made himself say darkly, "or they'll eat all our food." In a way, he wanted to be horrible.

"What will? What will?" Rod returned from a race with himself.

"The mice."

"Will they die in the pantry?" There was a squeamish expression on Rod's face.

"No. They'll go very discreetly behind the skirting board and die in agony there."

"Agony?" repeated Rod with some appetite.

"Rupture their guts."

"Yukky!" But he didn't really care as long as they were dead.

"Can we have a go on the ferry?" Peter tried to give his mother a beguiling look.

"It's a bit late now," she observed, but quickened her step nonetheless. "We'll see." And when they were nearly home she walked right past the bottom of Wellington Gardens towards Queen's Lodge Park.

"*Are* we going to the ferry?"

"We'll see."

The pinkness of the sky smudged and ran through a haze. "I think it may storm tonight . . ." Maggie looked up. There was a strong fragrance of flowering currant from one of the high, overhanging gardens they passed, as though the scent were a sweat squeezed out of the leaves by heat.

"Women don't kill ever, do they?" Peter asked suddenly.

The confusion of things in his imagination abruptly fashioned themselves into this unexpected question. Even he was surprised to hear himself. But in an odd way, it embraced a number of troubling, undefined curiosities that had brushed against the underside of his skull.

"Sometimes they do," argued Rod. "I think." And he tried, silently, to think of an instance.

"*Do* they?"

"Sometimes," said Maggie.

"When? Who?" The tongues of relish started to stir.

"Sometimes they kill the men they love."

"Well *that's* pretty stupid!" It confirmed a lot of what Rod felt about women, judgments he'd absorbed from his powerfully transmitting world.

"If the men betray them in some way," Maggie explained. "Leave them for another woman, usually."

"Oh I see." Yes, he understood that. A little better, anyway.

"They're not strong enough," said Peter, kicking a paper cup along the ground, "to kill men."

As Maggie turned to answer him, a plane droned overhead, coming closer.

"What?" he said.

". . . strong in here. *Here!*" Maggie was tapping her chest.

"That's useless," he muttered, not knowing what she was trying to indicate. The cup stuck on his toe.

"Well then," Rod was sneering, "*how?* How do they do it then?"

"You don't *have* to be strong to shoot somebody!" Maggie seemed amused, she flung her hair back over her shoulder. "That's why evolution's gone crazy."

"Why has it?" Rod knew all about evolution. He had a book about it.

"Because the strongest are no longer the fittest," she said, "once you've got guns. In fact it's the other way round, rather."

"What?"

"When you've got guns. There's bound to be hooligan rule. Bound to be." Now she was looking away from them, speaking to herself. "The strongest are those without scruple, without inhibition," then she laughed, a short, hollow laugh, her eyes coming back to them. They were hypnotised by her. "A bit like you," she said.

"What do you *mean?* What do you *mean?*" Peter demanded, a slight panic alerted in him.

But the plane was flying above them and she climbed up the step into the park with a sidelong look of amusement. She seemed for a moment to be absorbed by the long, blue shadows of the horse chestnuts. For a few strides she walked silently and then, with a small sigh of self-rebuke, she brought herself back to Peter's original question. She smiled widely down at him. "Anyway," she said, "most women murderers use poison, not guns."

Although the fading engines were still laying their carpet of sound overhead, Peter heard her quite distinctly. "Poison!" he cried aghast and turned to look at Rod, to whom the conjunction of things was equally clear. Both experienced a delicious trembling sensation.

"*Rat* poison . . .?"

"Ye-e-e-es!" Maggie turned on Rod, crouching, leering, encircling the hazel iris of her eyes with white.

"Eek!" He scurried backwards. "Don't! DON'T!"

"Hah! Hah! Hah! Hah! *Hah!*" She advanced on him, arms curved outward like wings, fingers drooping from loose wrists, to the evident surprise of two old ladies who shambled arm in arm down the path towards them, moving their feet fearfully and singly forward as though they walked on marsh or ice.

"*No!*" Rod fled, squeaking.

"No! No! Yah!" Peter danced in front of his witchy mother, drawing her attention to him so that he, too, would be pursued.

"HAH!" she pounced, then stopped, breathless. "Too hot," she gasped, "for running." And clasping her ribs, she told him instead the true story of Mary Elizabeth Wilson who had poisoned four men, two of them her husbands, and Rod crept back to listen.

A new, impatient noise fretted at the sky and in the distance, downriver, a helicopter appeared, like a bee, enlarging as it drew closer, its low flight following the course of the river. It passed them, blades whirling.

"Just listen!" Maggie stopped and put her head to one side as it puttered angrily away. "How many noises?"

And obediently they listened hard, surprised to find the peace of the parkland blurred by rumbles and thuds they'd pushed to the edge of their hearing. A bus, a plane, motor mowers, powered boats, a slow-moving lorry, several dogs barking and the feeble pip of birds.

"Hear everything?" Maggie asked, urgently, her own attention pressed to the world.

It was like . . . like pressing your ear against the chest of a sleeping person, thought Peter. And finding it full of private machinery in motion. Sleep lay merely on the surface, a sleekness, a stillness and under it all, crashing, gurgling components working ceaselessly on. "Half the time nobody listens," said Maggie.

There was nobody at the ferry.

"He must have closed." Disappointed, Maggie looked at her watch. "It's nearly eight." She gazed towards the white blossomed bank where thick, creamy clusters of elderflower were beginning to show. "Ah well . . ." she sighed.

"Let's go to the playground."

And before she could answer, the boys had started to race back in the direction they'd just come from, towards the swings and roundabouts, mercifully free of mewing and tottering infants at this hour.

They raced hard, sticking their chins out to have the edge over one another. Then Rod, trailing a little, heard Maggie cry out: "He *is* here!" But Peter, who had not heard, was heading fast towards the swings and Rod, ignoring his mother, galloped in grim pursuit.

When, some twenty minutes or so later, they returned, pink-faced and hot, Maggie was still deep in conversation with the tall, white-haired man. She stood on the floating planks, one hand on the rope rail, rising and falling a little in the wake of a solitary racing skiff which, crewed by nine men curved like slaves, sped down the centre of the river. Their coach, megaphone in one hand, cycled along the towpath towards them, not looking where he was going. They had to skip out of his way."

"Let's see those puddles, Four!" he boomed.

They giggled.

Maggie waved. "Mr. Turville closes at eight in the summer," she called, adding as they joined her, "so you just missed a ride."

They groaned extravagantly.

"Never mind," she said, "we talked instead." And she went on talking to the pale-eyed man who leant against a punt pole and spread his espadrilled feet on the planks to balance himself.

It struck Peter that in spite of his white hair, the man was no more than . . . oh, forty-five or so. But he had an odd, removed look. Peter hung about, mildly interested.

"*We're* going to have a boat," he volunteered, in the middle of their conversation. Maggie was talking about Sigvales. She broke off and laughed excitedly.

"Are you so?" said the tall man gravely. "What kind of boat?"

"What?" (The man's voice had been very low.)

"What kind of boat?" It was an educated voice.

"Um . . ." Peter looked about.

"*That* kind," said Rod, pointing to a small white launch with a scarlet canvas top that was moored a few yards beyond the Ark.

"Ah . . ." mused the man and, smiling slowly, returned his attention to Maggie.

Rod jumped back on the towpath and threw sticks for a black and white dog with a corkscrew tail that seemed to be without an owner. Peter stayed near his mother, bouncing lightly up and down to the water's slow motion.

She was describing things. The smell of a horse's hoof as metal burned into the horn. The sparks of the smithy. The way to shear a sheep from the belly outwards, holding the animal this way or that (she moved her body and her arms to demonstrate). Rolling the fleece, clean side outwards, starting from the tail end and knotting it with a twist of neck wool so that the shoulder fleece, the best quality, was the part that showed in the finished bundle. "I once saw a man shear a ewe's nipples right off," the ferryman said and she gave a small cry of horror before continuing in her trance-like fashion to tell of this matter and that. Of the sounds the chick made inside the egg, answered by the broody, imprinting her note on the hatching infant. Of the brown caul that had to be torn from the calf. Of the man whose arm was broken inside a mare when he tried to deliver a foal. Of the separate wines to be made from elder — its berries, its flowers. Of the speckled cockerel that attacked her, of woodpeckers and sorrel and cheese.

The man's eyes followed her carefully, silently, smiling. Every now and then he nodded and showed a pale surprise. The hairless skin of his chest, exposed by the V of his faded denim shirt, was deep, deep brown.

Peter listened, seeing things in a new way. This was the ordinary detail of the life he had recently lived. Living it, doing it, being it, it had seemed nothing. Now, seeing it transposed, seeing pictures, the quality of the detail was altered. He understood something of his mother's loss and pain.

"Come on!" called Rod. "It's getting jolly late."

The dog had gone its independent way.

The sky was crimson at its base, piling upward to a toneless mauve.

"Come *on*!" he yelled again. "We'll be missing Jacques Cousteau!"

"I'm sorry, yes. Heavens. *Daddy*," enumerated Maggie, shocked by herself. "Goodbye then, how nice it's been . . ."

And they left, a ragged, irregular trio, only gathering together at the road's edge.

"He had a nervous breakdown," said Maggie, looking cautiously to left and right.

"Who did?"

"Mr. Turville, the ferryman. He used to be an aeronautical engineer, working for the same company as Belinda's daddy."

"*What* happened?"

"He broke down. Gave it all up. Now he just does the boats."

They thought about it, briefly. It seemed, on reflection, an odd thing for a man to do, just crossing the river from one bank to the other day after day.

"He can't be very rich," decided Rod.

"No, I don't suppose he can be."

Kit was watching Jacques Cousteau. He looked up sulkily, a beer can in his hand. "Oh he*llo*," he said sarcastically. "I'm very grateful for the time you allowed me to be alone with my thoughts."

"Oh Kit!" She flew to him, arms out, then enclosing. "I know. I'm sorry."

"Will you be in for the rest of the evening?"

"It's those two," she murmured. "Better for them. *You've* got me now." And she laid her head on his chest while the boys' faces blanked off all but the image the screen lazily offered them.

14

"Oh-oh-oh . . .!" yawned Peter and put his comic down.
". . . What shall we do?"

Rod, squinting to try and see what was on television beneath
the milky distortions of bright afternoon sun shining across the
screen, merely grunted in private exasperation.

"I hate the day before my birthday," sighed Peter. "It's the
worst day of the year." Everything fell quiet and slowed down,
he thought. The grown ups retreated into themselves as if
saving up their energy for the following day when they would
be full of a ferocious gaiety that you had to share in or be
shouted at. He groaned again quietly.

There were other things contributing to the boredom.
Half-term. The heat.

Apart from the one night, a week before (the night they'd
visited The Swan with their parents) when thunder had rolled
like slow lead balls across the sky and sudden sheets of lightning
had made all the trees and houses look both quaint and
alarming like a nasty moment in a Disney film, the weather had
continued unrelentingly fine. Even the rain which had fallen
that night, slashing vertical poles of it, had done little more than
flatten any garden plant daring to stand upright. The lawns
were turning a prematurely tired, dry brown, people went
about their business with fewer and fewer clothes on during
the day, and in the evenings they sat outside the pubs with their
drinks under blue and orange umbrellas. On the corner, the
men who were demolishing the shops, had backs the colour of
sweet chestnuts.

Inside the house it was cool. But there was nothing to do.

Kit, the radio crackling beside him, was making steady,
crimson progress up the stairwell. His arms looked like a

butcher's. Maggie was out, egg-promoting. Already she'd put in for another chicken-costume. The satin stank of sweat she said. She looked awful when she came home, her hair flat and lank.

"Only *one* more day . . ." sighed Peter again, looking up at the yellow ceiling. Small flies were clustering around the light fixture.

Rod changed channels and watched the cricket for a few seconds before changing back again. "Oh *no* . . .!" he moaned as he caught sight of his mother caressing a packet of cereal. She looked as bright as an ox-eye daisy.

("They *know* what's good for them!")

"Hoo! Hoo!" snorted Rod, about to change back to cricket, but a Cagney film was trailed and he hesitated.

"Well, not even one day really . . . nine hours . . ." Peter calculated more cheerfully.

"It's not fair," growled Rod out of the corner of his mouth. "You being in the under-elevens."

This was a recent quarrel. It had started when Rod discovered that the age of entrants for Sports Day competitions was determined by whatever age they were on the closing day for applications, June 1st. Since Peter was eleven on June 5th, this meant he qualified as under-eleven and would compete against Rod in the same races (if, by any chance, both were chosen for the same event). Rod had overlooked the unlikelihood of their qualifying for anything, though Maggie persistently drew attention to it to try and de-fuse the issue. "In the *swimming* . . ." he argued, as if half-wanting a tussle. But swimming didn't start until after half-term as his mother pointed out, so they couldn't know how strong the competition was. The problem might never arise.

But Rod festered. He had never overcome the injustice of his brother continuing to be older than him. Nor, since his own birthday fell one week and one day after Peter's, that it sometimes fell on *Friday* the thirteenth, which seemed the height of meanness. Nor, because stupid people tended to give them both the same present, that he always knew what half his presents were going to be eight days in advance. His fury gave Peter a certain pleasure.

"Hard cheese," said Peter. It was an expression of indifference he'd learnt at Hill House, and liked.

The door opened, admitting Kit, his brush carefully upturned to catch the dribbles on his wrist. "What on earth are you two *doing* indoors on a day like this?"

"It's too hot out," remarked Rod, adding, "Hey, this is a gangster film, *great*!"

"Why don't you get on with these project things that have to be finished before exams begin?" Kit's gaze drifted.

"Cagney," said Peter.

"Oh. *Cagney*," Kit echoed and he paused before adding, "I was going to do your rabbit run today, but the ground's too hard to drive the stakes in. When it rains again, I'll do it. O.K.? . . . I remember this film . . . *Angels With Dirty Faces*, isn't it . . .?" He went away and put his brush down somewhere before returning.

"One of the advantages of being a housewife," he remarked to no-one in particular. "Gangster movies in the afternoon. *And* drinking all day if you feel like it."

"Have you got our presents yet?" Rod propped his chin on his hands.

"Never you mind."

"Have you though?"

"Shut up, toad, I'm listening."

"Only eight more hours and fifty more minutes . . ." tormented Peter.

"Belt up, you." Rod placed the grippy hands of his Action Man more firmly around his carbine and hoped he might get a new uniform for him or better still, a new Action Man. An Action Man sailor, the kind with a beard. "I wonder if the new Action Man's got a scar on his face like the others," he mused. "If he's got a beard, he might not have."

"Oh, *shut up*!" the others chorused.

"I've done the kitchen door," Kit announced proudly when Maggie came home. "Had a good day in the battery box?"

"Oh thanks!" she cried, dumping the limp yellow slither on the banisters. "Phew! B.O. A new problem among hens."

She tried the kitchen door knob gingerly, opening the door as if it were made of paper. "Terrific!" she flattered. "It works!"

"Of course it works!"

"And the hall?" she looked about admiringly. "That works too, don't you think?"

"I'll know better when I've finished. It feels like being in an elephant's womb at the moment."

"Fool," she laughed, "I like it."

She went into the kitchen, handling the door delicately, and heaped her heavier belongings on the table. "I'll buy a cake tomorrow," she hissed at Kit, indicating with her head that he should close the door after him.

"No, I'm going to do *everything* . . ." he insisted, failing to exclude Rod who crept under his arm.

"Are you doing the tea?" piped Rod.

"Oh hello, Big Ears."

"Have you got our presents?"

"Oh Lord, I forgot all about presents."

"You *didn't* . . ." He laughed disbelievingly. "I know you didn't. Can I have the tea on *my* birthday next year?"

"Of course. It'll be your turn." Maggie rolled up the sleeves of her pink cotton dress and said apologetically, "You'll have to have your presents together tomorrow."

"That means I've got the same as *him*!" He gave a small, petulant stamp.

"You'll see." She smiled and suddenly looked very pretty in spite of her squashed hair and shiny face.

"Bugger," said Rod.

"*Now!*"

"*Well.*"

"Hey! Look!" Something distracted Maggie's attention and she leaned over the sink to see out of the window better. The leaves of the plane tree in the road outside hung over their wall and dropped above the dustbins, pressing their greenery against the glass. "Look!" she repeated, twisting her neck to peer upwards.

"What is it?"

"Keith's bees have swarmed."

They crowded to the sink and peered up through the foliage. Suspended from the arching branch was a black sack which seemed, Peter thought, as he wriggled himself further forward, to be moving. The dark glimmering mass hung perfectly still in itself but it was surfaced by a glinting skin of wing as the bees pressed themselves more closely to their own centre.

"We'd better tell him," said Maggie, anxiously.

"I think I hear the factory hooter calling." Kit picked up bucket and brushes and eased away from the sink. Maggie giggled. "They won't sting now," she said. "They're full of honey. Haven't you heard of the gorge before the swarm?"

"Sorry." Kit bowed politely and edged backwards through the door, a civil smile varnishing his face. "Ever so, terribly, pressingly BUSY. He can chase his own bloody bees."

"Go and tell him, Peter darling," pleaded Maggie, fascinated by the living black sack, dark and heavy among the translucent leaves.

Five minutes later Peter returned, trailing behind Keith, the urban spaceman. Keith wore a sparkling white boiler suit. Muslin was swathed around his neck beneath the square, black, obliterating helmet. Behind them, running a little, came Belinda holding a spiral notebook and sharp pencil.

"I'm taking notes," she declared when Maggie opened the door, "for my project." And she gave Rod, whose head protruded from behind Maggie's waist, a withering look.

"You'll get stung," he said to her nastily.

"No she won't," intervened Keith, unaware that his appearance belied his assurance. "Awfully sorry about all this," he said from behind his black panel. "Have to tackle it from your side of the wall I fancy. Not a lot of space . . ." He hummed quietly to himself. "Got a pair of step-ladders, have you?" he concluded, having assessed the situation.

"Of course. They're right here." They were in the back scullery.

"Splendid. How many kitchens *have* you?" The black screen scanned round.

"Three. Of a kind. Here you are." Maggie dragged the ladder from the wall.

"Excellent. *Now.*" He looked about him. "Children indoors, I think. At the window."

"Oh . . ." protested Belinda, "But . . ."

"You'll see better from there and you'll hear us talking perfectly well."

"You mean . . .?" Maggie began.

"You're a capable creature and you know a bit about it."

"I've never taken a swarm," she said faintly.

"Just stand back with the smoker, that's all you need do."

"I think," said Maggie firmly, "I'll stand on the draining board and poke it through the little window at the top."

"As you wish." He was, inevitably, expressionless. Lifting the ladder outside, he erected it and tested the lower rung carefully.

Indoors, Maggie tested the draining board. "I think it'll hold," she muttered.

"Now!" and she tentatively squeezed the bellows.

"You've got to light the stuff inside," Belinda pointed out, licking her pencil in readiness. Rod passed the matches.

"Quite a swarm!" came Keith's voice. His startling body

was caressed by leaves. The black square turned towards them. "Twenty thousand or so I'd say. Little devils, I thought I'd prevented them from swarming by cutting out those cells with Kit . . . It *says* remove queen cells and drone cells . . ." His voice faded.

"The queen wants to fly," called Maggie, sticking her bellows through the window and puffing. "It's freedom she's after. You can't blame the old girl."

"I like your father's overalls," said Peter to Belinda. "He looks just like an astronaut."

"Yes," she said. "He wears white specially. Navy blue maddens them you know. Bees will attack anyone in navy blue."

"How do they know it's navy blue?" asked Rod.

"That's why they stung Daddy then." Peter looked up at his mother and intercepted a quizzical glance from Maggie. "How long have you known that?" his mother enquired of Belinda.

"Oh, I've *always* known. What's happening? I can't see. I'm going to stand on your kitchen table. May I?"

"Interesting business, eh!" Maggie turned at the shout and yelled back, "Yes! Very!" Her voice sounded full of smothered laughter.

The figure outside parted the leaves a little with his great white paws. The box-head nodded. "This is the only time the drones ever leave the hive," he called, whether for Maggie's benefit or Belinda's was unclear. Delicately, he began cutting away the leaves round the top of the swarm.

"They're not drones," said Maggie soothingly. She gave the bellows a boisterous puff. "Drones don't go out at all—except for sex!"

"They don't do anything much," Belinda informed the boys, "except sit around."

"They can't even *feed* themselves, can they?" Maggie added to the contumely.

"I'm not sure." Belinda made a doubtful squiggle.

Raising her voice to reach the perching figure outside, Maggie yelled, "Somebody told me they haven't got the right shaped jaws for feeding themselves."

"Not sure about that . . ." came the answer, "I'd need to look that up." As he clipped, he revealed more of himself. He looked like a mythical owl, roosting. "I know the workers feed them while they're young though."

"The workers feed them all the bloody time," laughed Maggie, releasing a jet of smoke. "Don't they?"

Looking up, Peter could see up his mother's pink cotton dress. Small, crusty blue veins rose inside her thighs. "*Why* do the drones come out?" he asked quickly to stop the horrible, fierce note in her voice. He hadn't heard first time.

"For *sex*, silly!"

"For sex?" he repeated wanly.

"The queen goes on her mating flight," Belinda supplied in an exaggeratedly sensible manner, then pushed her fist against a sudden impudence of her mouth. She folded her lips tightly over this small lapse.

"Oh, yeah?" grinned Rod, seizing on it. "How do they do it then?"

"In mid-air," said Belinda, which made Rod choke with hilarity.

"Oh, shut up," complained Peter, wondering when the bees would break from their sack and start attacking.

An authoritative "Now!" came from the other side of the glass. But Keith's fully revealed figure looked curiously purposeless.

"You want the skep on the ground!" shouted Maggie.

"Could you — er — would you — er — *hold* it?"

Maggie muttered something venomous. "Hang on!" she called out loud.

"What would happen if he just left them?" Peter asked her.

"They'd revert to the wild." She jumped. "I expect they've prepared a home for themselves somewhere nearby."

"So why is he catching them if they've made a home for themselves."

"To make more honey." Maggie tugged at the door. "And plenty of money," she carolled, going outside.

"Do you like honey?" Peter enquired of Belinda.

"No," she said, "I hate it."

"Does your father?"

"No. Nor does Mummy."

"Oh," he said, bewildered by all the trouble that was being taken.

Maggie positioned herself with the skep.

Keith Ferguson gave the branch an apprehensive shake. Nothing happened. The seething bag remained undisturbed. He shook again, more boldly. Then, peevishly, almost. One, two.

Like a huge, ripe fruit, the swarm dropped. Peter saw his mother's arms sink with the shock but she hung on, her face fissured with alarm as stray bees spiralled after the main swarm.

Awkwardly, the boiler suit descended and Keith relieved Maggie (whose head swung frantically from left to right) of her zithering burden.

"The big chopping board!" yelled Maggie through the window.

The children looked at one another nervously.

"You," said Rod.

"No, you," said Peter.

"Oh!" Belinda made an impatient cry. "Where is it, you babies?" She put her notebook down and spun a competent look round the kitchen. The board was under the sink.

Peter bent to retrieve it and saw an oaty scattering of rat poison. "Here," he said, "you take it."

And Belinda did.

"This," she declared, making an aristocratic exit, "is an extremely valuable experience for me."

They came indoors very pleased with themselves, the three of them. The skep was to be left where it was until Keith had prepared a hive in the cooler, late evening.

"Very obliged to you," he bowed, taking his leave. And opening the kitchen door with a flourish, staggered, as the knob came away in his hand. The knob on the far side of the door fell to the ground. A dull roar was heard from Kit.

"Oh, good heavens! Oh dear! So *sorry!*" The spaceman swayed feebly.

"It's all right," assured Maggie. "It was broken anyway. I should go out the back door."

After they'd left on an oil slick of apology, she examined her arms. "Not a sting," she murmured wonderingly. "Not one. Did you ask Belinda to your birthday tea tomorrow?"

"No," said Peter firmly.

"Oh well, never mind. I did."

15

Peter woke early.

He closed his eyes then opened them again, gradually, to take in all the newness of being eleven. It sounded substantially older than ten. At his other school, boys and girls left when they were eleven, passing some magic divide, thereafter establishing themselves in a bigger, more serious world.

But he felt no different really.

He lay still and turned his head to see if there were any parcels on the floor . . . There were none.

His heart revolved violently. He sat up. Searched. Nothing. Quickly, but quietly, he rose and tiptoed to the door. Nothing outside.

He hurtled downstairs two steps at a time, the red speckles dry on the wood beneath his feet. The kitchen door had been jammed open with a bucket. He flew into the room.

Nothing.

She really *had* forgotten. A briny black feeling boiled up inside him. Hot and salt, a distillation of tears and hurt and hate, it raced up and overflowed the tight container of his feelings.

She *had* forgotten.

Overhead a door clicked gently but he heard nothing until his mother crept into the kitchen behind him. "Happy birthday!" she cried. And he turned on her, driving his fists into her stale softness, the alien softness of a newly dead bird. "You've forgotten . . . !" he screamed, hating her for being too busy to remember him. And then he stopped. Vaguely, he realised she had wished him a happy birthday. She could not have forgotten after all.

Maggie hugged him to her, deep into the acrid stuff of her nightdress.

"Poor Peter," she murmured. "Of course I haven't . . ." And they hung together for a moment before, his mood changing, he pulled away and squeaked: "Where is it? What is it?" He hopped in anguished excitement.

"First," she said mysteriously, "you must get your clothes on. And you'll have to stir Rod, too."

"Why? Why wake *him*?"

She put a finger to her smiling lips.

The feeling — subtly altered, yellower — threatened to return.

He knew what it was. But he said nothing, all the excitement expelled by the need to share.

He pinched his brother awake. "Get up," he said grumpily.

Rod woke like a light bulb going on. "Where is it? What is it?" he shrieked. "Oh! Happy Birthday!" And he dug under his pillow for a screwed up package with a nest of Sellotape woven round it. "Open it!" he said. "Go on. Hurry!"

Rod waited impatiently for a moment while Peter tore at the resolute packaging. "Go on! Go on! It's something you'll like." And before Peter could fight his way through the paper to it, "It's a catapult," he said.

"Oh." And then, as he found it, tightly swaddled in tissue, "Oh, it's a *good* catapult."

They both knew what it was though each held on to his disbelief in case it wasn't. But it was.

Moored at the end of Wellington Gardens where the river lapped thinly up to the edge of the road, was a little black and red rowing boat. A new pair of oars stuck out of it like upturned chicken legs. Behind, opaque ribbons of mist made birthday streamers.

"Oh . . ." breathed Peter. And then again . . . "Oh!"

"Mummy! Mummy! Mummy! And *Daddy*!" Rod leapt up and down unrestrainedly then threw himself at Kit who'd come out in his dressing gown. "It's super! Fantastic! Fantabulous!" He was stuck for words, and danced.

"Is it really ours?" Peter stared.

"You must think of a name for it."

"*Big-Wig*," said Rod, thinking of *Watership Down*.

"No, silly. It's got to be a girl's name. Boats are girls."

"Why? Ours is for boys. It's a boy. *Big-Wig*."

"It's *not*!" screamed Peter, the incipient rage breaking through.

"Come on now," cautioned Maggie. "There's something else for you at home."

They reined themselves in and allowed her to shuffle them back home where two lifejackets, one orange, one yellow, awaited them. They'd been kept in paper bags in the conservatory and Peter thought he must have passed them thousands of times when he'd fed the rabbits. Then he remembered he hadn't fed his rabbits yet and the number of things he had to remember seethed together like a ring of flies around his skull.

"Eggs and bacon for breakfast?"

"No, thanks," he said.

"I thought you *loved* eggs and bacon?"

"I've gone off eggs," he said desperately.

"Bacon then?"

"All right."

"Cheer up," she said. "It's your birthday." And her insistence that he should be happy hung on him like a heavy gold collar.

Fastidiously he cut away all the rind she'd left on; then removed all the little bluish ovals of bone.

"The post will be here soon," she said vivaciously, watching him. And then she switched on the radio so everyone had to shout to be heard.

Turning both taps on hard she cried, "I must rush," and smiled hotly at him. But she paused long enough to pour out two glasses of fresh orange juice, a special treat, holding both glasses up to the light to ensure that each contained precisely the same amount as the other.

After she'd left, limbs like propellers, Kit cleared up, fastened them into their lifejackets and took them down to the boat. Peter, who had allowed himself to be secured inside the orange lifejacket without protest, felt more and more hostile about its terrible luminosity. He wanted the yellow one and stared at Rod's back with a very set expression.

The boys sat either end and Kit rowed them out into the middle of the river, cutting its fine brown skin cleanly with the oars.

When it was their turn they found it more difficult than they had expected. Each used one oar at a time while Kit handled the other. The little red boat constantly swivelled round to Kit's pull because his was so much the stronger. Rod laughed wildly at the splashing he caused but Peter felt thoroughly disheartened by the whole performance.

"Practice, that's all," calmed his father. "It'll make your arms ache at first." It did. It amazed Peter how stubbornly the water resisted him, making his oar skid and slip upwards without effecting any noticeable movement. "I wish it was a canoe," he said bitterly. Canoes looked easier. He'd seen boys his own age (even smaller) dart through the water like young Indians.

"You'll get the hang of it," Kit promised. "Take both oars." And he wobbled to the end of the boat leaving Peter to cope.

His arms just wouldn't work together. One oar dug in, the other lurched upwards. He tried again. This time the left oar almost escaped him. It seemed drawn so longingly away by the current he was tempted to let it go rather than be dragged after it.

"Steady on!" called Kit seeing a motor boat approach on a cleavage of water.

Peter pulled both oars in and sat very still as the motor boat chugged level and dispersed its rubbery waves towards them. They rose and fell deliciously.

"Now me!" said Rod.

"Not yet."

"It's my turn!"

"Not *yet*!" And again Peter tried to break beyond the limited circle of movement. But the fury that had been feeding all morning, now dyspeptic and assaulting, broke out of his mouth in a howl. The boat swung round meanly.

"Oh, for crying out loud!" Kit's massive arms, reddened by the sun, folded, as if each restrained the other from something worse. "You'll learn," he shouted impatiently. Then, more gently, "I promise you."

"Rod's *rocking* it!"

"I'm not." Rod, sitting behind him, sounded full of feigned indignation.

"You are! You are!" He daren't let go of his trailing oars.

"Let Rod have a go."

Peter pulled the oars in on their locks and ill-temperedly rose, clutching at air as the boat tipped first one way and then the other.

"You'll have to do it together. Change over together, balancing."

They managed it, matching each movement carefully. Peter sat down full of loathing for the orange lifejacket.

"That's fine. Good. Now let's try again."

The sun was warming already, sweeping away the mist with its bright brooms. Pigeons warbled in the gardens all along the bank.

"I'm doing it!" shrieked Rod. "I'm *doing* it!" They moved one messy yard downriver.

"That's it, *good*. Remember your right arm is stronger than your left. Allow for that."

An oar jolted out of its lock and they circled to a standstill.

"Hah! Hah!" jeered Peter.

"Shut up or I'll smash you with this!" Rod bawled over his shoulder at his brother.

"You *can't* do it."

"Oh belt up, the pair of you." Kit was looking bored.

"I *will* do it." Again Rod tried, bringing the handles of the oars up so high and close to his face that he nearly fell backwards. "I thought we were going to have a motor boat," he bleated.

"Let's go in." Kit spoke sharply. He manoeuvred himself into the rowing position and Rod crawled sulkily to the far end. "Take us for a proper row then," he said.

"All right," sighed Kit, "I'll take you up to Mr. Turville's, that's where the boat has to be kept."

With short, jerky movements (because the oars were too small for him) he rowed them upriver towards Queen's Lodge ferry, his breath coming in brief stabs from his nostrils. Mr. Turville, standing at his tiller, was crossing the river, bringing a single passenger from the Sweetings bank, a man in a bowler with a briefcase perched on his knees. As if he were a tall, blue, distant carving — a Viking shape — the ferryman saluted them.

"You'll get the hang of it eventually," Kit repeated, clambering out of the boat and securing it.

"Pleased, are you?" Mr. Turville watched and nodded.

"Yes, thanks," they mumbled, their arms hurting.

Kit sent them to the fish and chip shop to buy lunch for all of them. He was too busy preparing tea, he said, to cook lunch. Plates and bowls were strewn around the kitchen. The sink spewed pans. Here and there a cookery book was propped up against something, open and splattered.

When they returned, the warm, stomach-melting bundles of newspaper clutched to their T-shirts, they found Mrs. Ferguson waiting on the doorstep, a froth of tissue paper in her arms.

"Ah!" she cried as Kit opened the door, "I do hope you won't mind, won't think it impertinent . . ."

"What is it?" asked Rod, standing on tiptoe to peer.

"Only I thought you might, perhaps, be glad of a cake for the boys' tea . . .?"

"Oh, Daddy's . . ." Peter began, but hearing his father's vigorous cries of "How *kind*!" and "How splendid!" and "Just the thing!", he refrained from telling her about the cake Kit was making.

"Well I won't keep you." She retreated, one eye on their newspaper parcels. "I just thought your wife would be so very *pressed* . . ." And she ran with little steps down the path, face tilted towards them over one shoulder . . . "Many happy returns then!"

"Why did you . . .?" Peter began again, puzzled. "Why . . .?"

"*Ravenous!*" Kit inhaled the deep-fried odours and swung his sons indoors with a cradling arm. "Let's get unwrapped as fast as we can!"

His own cake was being creamed in a big, butter-coloured bowl, the one that Maggie never, ever used, even at Christmas. She said it made her think of female slavery. Women just didn't have forearms like that any longer. Kit put down Mrs. Ferguson's cake and, picking a wooden spoon out of the bowl, licked his own thoughtfully. "Mmm," he ruminated, "pretty professional."

Rod poked the paper petals of Mrs. Ferguson's cake apart. "Errk," he said, "it's a fruit cake. I hate raisins."

"*Mine*," said Kit, "is a chocolate cake. And you may lick the bowl later."

"Hurrah!" they cried.

They started tea before Maggie came home.

Belinda had arrived in party dress. A blue dress, with a white frilled pinafore over it, white knee socks and blue, button-over shoes with heels that raised her above Peter's head. With her she had brought an oblong parcel, exquisitely wrapped in pink and silver flowered paper. It was a box of modelling clay.

"Thank you very much," Peter had said politely, happier now that the afternoon post had brought a gift token from his grandmother.

As they sat down, an ambulance whing-whanged down Wellington Gardens and stopped about halfway, its siren continuing to flap and wail.

"Did *you* make all this?" Belinda looked over the feast as though playing a game in which she had to memorise each item and list as many as possible afterwards.

"Yes," said Kit proudly, giving a little bow. His chocolate cake had risen beautifully. He'd smothered it with thick, brown butter icing, trailed a fork through it to make furrows, scattered it with silver balls he'd found in a phial that had moved house with them several times and staked it out with eleven white candles. It sat in the middle of the table, surrounded by their favourite foods . . . cold chicken, sausages, salad, Scotch eggs, crisps, Twiglets and sandwiches filled with peanut butter, Marmite, sardine paste and shrimp-flavoured cream cheese out of a tube. Mrs. Ferguson's cake looked very shop-like. It had toasted almonds scattered thickly on top of it.

"It's quite good," said Belinda. "Have you got any jelly?"

"We don't like jelly."

"I'm going to make pancakes if you have room for them," said Kit.

"Scrummy," agreed Belinda and refused all the sandwiches because she didn't care for the fillings. "I'll have a cold sausage," she decided and it lay on her plate, a solitary, pinkish finger with one fatty edge. "Will you take me out in your boat, Peter?" she smiled, and his face burned.

"If you like," he shrugged.

"It's not his, it's ours," said Rod.

But today she had decided to devote herself to Peter. "I should like that *very* much," she replied and Rod's mouth was too full to say anything further.

"What?" Peter lifted his head.

"What are you going to call it?"

"Haven't decided," he mumbled.

While Kit's back was turned she brought her mouth very close to Peter's ear and whispered, "After tea, shall we look at those pic-*tures* . . .?"

"I can hear you," lied Rod.

A key was heard turning in the front door, then, more oppressively as the door opened, the dull whine of the ambulance.

"Hello, darlings!"

Maggie, burdened as usual, carried a white cardboard box sacredly above all her other belongings. "Crikey!" she exclaimed and stopped. "What a spread! Kit, you *have* been marvellous!" Her eyes alighted on the chocolate cake, its unlit candles ranged like palings around its perimeter. "Crikey!" she exclaimed again. And laughed.

Kit relieved her of her packages. "A cake, I imagine," he grinned, taking the cardboard box.

"Yes."

It was a small white cake with blue scallops and whorls and Happy Birthday in wavy blue lettering that peered out from beneath a scanty piece of fern. "I never thought you'd manage it," she confessed and gave a one-sided smile that emphasised her tiredness. Her hazel eyes had a gravelly look to them, as they moved over the table. "What? *Two* cakes, Kit! That's pure exhibitionism!"

"Mummy made *that* one for the boys."

"*Did* she?" Maggie gazed levelly at Belinda. "How very thoughtful of her."

"She said you wouldn't have time to make one."

"Well she was right. I must thank her."

The dread began its thin coiling in Peter's stomach. It came with his mother, he couldn't think why. Once he'd felt it in the presence of certain teachers, the dry, disguised kind who said one thing and meant another. They watched you, people like that, watched to see which way you'd jump in response to them, having a trap ready whichever course you chose. He kept his head down, picking at breadcrumbs.

"What?"

"Have you had a nice day?"

"Yes, thanks."

"Did you go out in the boat?"

"Yes."

"Was it fun?"

"Quite."

There was an awkward little pause, then his mother asked, "Have you thought of a name yet?"

"No."

She gave up. Peter felt himself relax. "You've done wonderfully," she sighed, sinking down and addressing herself to Kit. A web seemed to close over her. "Better than I could have done."

"Dad knows what we like," said Rod.

"I bought Peter a lovely present," volunteered Belinda. "It cost two pounds sixty."

"That's most generous of you." Maggie sounded as though she had ashes in her mouth.

"*I* think they should call it the *Pollyanna*."

But nobody answered Belinda, and after a few frustrated moments of listening to their exchanges, she was driven to tell them everything she'd received for her birthday last month.

"Yes, I'm quite pleased with myself." Kit scratched himself and gazed round at the nibbled feast.

"Just as well I came home in time for the washing up," Maggie mused.

(There it was again, the pricking of needles.) Then: "I'd like to see you in your boat," said Maggie.

"Can I have the yellow lifejacket? It is *my* birthday!"

It was better next time.

I can nearly do it, Peter thought, as the oars pulled forward together and the boat slipped backwards through the water. A moorhen dived suddenly nearby.

"I like it." Belinda smiled at him from her bench. "It's lovely. Will you teach me how to row?"

"I might," he said gruffly, looking away. Pride drove him to make a wonderful sweep with his oars. Later they looked at the pictures.

"I'm *perfectly* capable," he heard his mother saying as the dishes clattered.

"You can't take the strain. I can see it in your face, you can't really cope."

"I can *manage*," he heard her insisting, her voice close to a wail.

"I love you," his father said, but so sadly (Peter thought) it sounded as though he'd lost something very precious to him.

"It's *got* to work. I've got to make it."

"I love you," his father said again. Softly.

16

On Friday, Kit sent them to Cubs on their own. Maggie was late coming home.

They were to meet that evening, not at the Scout Hut, but a couple of hundred yards further down the Embankment road, at the outdoor swimming pool. The pack was practising for the Cubs and Scouts Swimming Gala. Rod and Peter danced along the road swinging the bag with all their swimming things in it, between them.

"What *is* the definition of strain then?" gasped Rod, leaping, as always, to touch the lilac, now bending brown on its stem.

"Stop tipping the basket," complained Peter and hurried to keep up as they hopped and bounded past the graffiti and on, towards the church.

"*What's* the definition of strain?" persisted Rod, tugging.

As they emerged from the marquee of leaves, they felt a cool speckling of the intermittent rain on their faces. The weather was changing.

"Go on. Shall I tell you?"

"I've got a secret," said Peter, changing the subject.

"Yeah?" Reluctantly interested, Rod slowed.

"I *have*."

"What then?"

"In here." Peter nodded at the deep straw bag.

"In here?" Now Rod stopped and buried his arm between the towels. "What is it?" His fingers touched a round piece of metal and something made of wood. "What've you got?"

"Put it back! It's a *secret*!"

"But what's it for?"

Peter told him. They giggled.

As soon as they could, they left the pool. They'd done well. Akela had said they would both be in the team. For a moment, they stopped to gaze at the poster announcing the Gala, pasted outside the swimming pool next to another that advertised the forthcoming visit of the Prime Minister to the Hammond and Popesvale Conservative Association. It made them feel rather grand.

It had been warm in the water. The cold rain pricking lightly at the surface had made it feel like a bath. Now, hair damp beneath their Cub caps, the warmth was newly stoked by excitement. They ran alongside the river, away from the other boys who hung about fighting mildly on the pool steps. The clouds, full of dark, unreleased weather, made the evening seem far later than it really was. The boatyard buildings had merged into a single, black monumental shape.

"Anyone looking?"

They glanced covertly about them. But the threat of heavier rain to come had kept the dog walkers and couples indoors this evening. Nobody sat outside the pub although it was obvious from the babble and the blaring sound of a juke box that came out of its yellow doorway and windows, that it was enjoying the usual Friday custom. They loitered while a solitary cyclist passed them and then they scuttled up the steps of the Embankment Gardens, leapt across the concrete pools and, darting between the shrubs and trees that crowded the little path, slipped into the ladies' garden with its yew parapets. The air was dark under the low branches.

"You can climb up behind, I think," said Peter.

They found they could. Under the statuary was concealed a generator or something of the kind. A label stuck to the door had a lightning flash on it and the words, DANGER KEEP OUT. It was a bit ominous but neither of them said anything. Instead, they hauled themselves upwards over the rocks, climbing until they emerged behind the queen of the company, the lady who rode two winged horses rearing above massive oyster shells. She had her back to them, a broad back set upon grand buttocks. Her hair flew, her arms were bent and rising. There was a strong smell of algae and dank water. Below them (and it was weird to see them from this position), flinging themselves upward in worshipping abandon, were the rest of the naked team, lips parted, breasts solid, thighs sporty. The boys stood for a moment, hidden by shadow, gazing downwards. They could, Peter thought, his eyes moving slowly from one grey figure to the next, be either angry or . . . (and he searched for a word that would work) . . . or . . . *beseeching*. The word came at him out of nowhere (school hymns perhaps). It was only the sluggish, dripping sound of water that made them seem pitiful. He tried to imagine looking at them like this with some angry music playing instead, and just as he thought it, the pub's juke box changed its faint tune to a sudden snort of rock that was almost instantly lowered. Probably, the door had been closed.

Alerted to a movement on the path that reached away from the pool, the boys shrank back. A middle-aged woman in a long raincoat hurried towards them without looking up, her head too busily directed in searching sweeps of the bushes, "Ching! Ching!" she called. The silliness of it, their own apprehension, made the boys nearly explode with mirth. A Peke, breathing stertorously, waddled across the grass. Its owner waited impatiently for a moment and then they disappeared together.

"I can see bats," whispered Rod. They both looked up. Black darts cut across the air so swiftly, they couldn't be sure they'd seen them.

"Come on, then!"

They climbed out from behind the rear screen of rocks and slithered down as far as the nearest vast shell. Leaves and cigarette packets floated on its ditchy water. Peter found a place to put the basket down and burrowed inside for the brush and tin of paint.

"There's not much left in," he hissed disappointedly as he prised off the lid. It was the remainder of the hall paint, a lovely purplish red which looked nearly black in this half-light. He was going to paint bikinis on the ladies, he'd dreamt about doing it two nights ago and it had seemed, in his dream, a wonderful idea. He'd woken, full of an intense, inexplicable happiness.

Peter pushed the brush down, squashing the bristles so that as much of the half-inch of paint as possible would adhere to them. Rod snatched it from him and scrambled down to the ledge below where an innocent lady knelt. His head bobbed, a small cartwheel of green and gold. He made a stupid lunge which effected nothing but made him giggle in a squeaky way.

"Give it to me! Give it to me!" Peter lowered himself beside Rod. "You're just messing about. I want to put swim-suits on them." He took the brush from Rod's weak grasp.

"You watch, right?" Rod gave a subdued wail of protest, nothing serious, and taking the basket climbed up higher again to be in a good guarding position.

Moving his feet carefully, Peter tried to approach the stone figure face on. From a crack in her crutch, a leaf of hound's tongue fern had grown. It made him want to screech with laughter, and pushing his brush at the comic pudenda he was suddenly too feeble to do much more than flick. Dark crimson beads sprang across her belly. Her expression of bleached rapture remained unaltered. He sighed crossly. It was difficult to get close enough to be accurate and because the stone he stood on felt slimy he gave up any attempt to reach her breasts. The one below might be easier.

He lowered himself to the next ledge and found himself almost embraced by a crazy looking woman on her knees. She was a much simpler proposition. Carefully, but without wasting precious time (the gates, he knew, were closed at half-past nine), he painted a bra across her molehills. The emulsion ran slowly down to her belly button as though she bled from the heart. More aggressively, he thrust the brush between her thighs, painting quickly, not in strokes, but in a general swizzle of colour. Above him, Rod was limp with laughter.

"Watch *out*!" Peter ordered in a whisper, his hand moving wildly. The adornment was becoming violent. (The roof of his stomach had risen, sucked upwards by fear and excitement and something stranger than either of those things.)

A sudden gust of wind caused a susurrous of movement among the leaves and brought a sweep of rain that felt icy on his hot cheeks. Slowly, awkwardly, he moved closer to the centre of the pool — a more exposed position — where another gymnast sat, arms and legs splayed open as though about to unbalance and topple over into the water. The sound of a car passing in the road alongside him, made Peter hasten his movements. He became careless. A thick red sensation bloomed inside him as if he himself were a bag of paint, splashing, sploshing, spilling as he went. His mouth was dry.

"Let me have a turn! It's my go!"

He ignored Rod's hissing and crept teeteringly along the narrow rim of the lower pool, brush and tin carried outwards, one in either hand to maintain his balance. A grey girl with bobbed hair reached for her leader. Wobbling towards her, he secured his footing and slapped the brush at her buttocks, two round, receiving fossil apples. But the paint was running out now and he had to screw the bristles round and round inside the tin to coat them much at all. Robbed of a nice liquid slap of paint, he just wiped first one side of his brush and then the other again and again on her grainy, pomegranate bottom, smearing it hopelessly. The movement, the ruthless slap of the wrist, the harshness with which he used his brush, drove great wedges of satisfaction into him. He was aware of soft, panicky cries from Rod above him in the darkening garden but he went on until not one scrape of paint was left.

"Come on! Come on!"

A slow, creaking bicycle passed in the road, the chain grinding. Guessing at the time, he thought there must be half an hour to go until the gates were locked. He looked up and saw the pale, apprehensive disc of Rod's face. It was like an old sixpence. A large bird, disturbed, flapped heavily in the trees.

It was done. About to fling the empty tin in the bushes, an instinctive cunning stopped him. He must cover all traces. A swift glance at his hands showed they were stained by a colour far darker in this fading light than it ought to be. With a calmness that belied the glutinous surges of his heart he washed the brush in the pungent black water of the pool and then rinsed his hands, wiping them on a lily pad he ripped off its stalk.

Anxiety was stealing up behind the triumphant feeling, destroying the edges of it like the black curling of burning paper. It became ragged. He cleaned obsessively praying his hearing would not fail him now. The happiness that had so strongly illuminated his dream, receded.

Then, at a further suppressed cry from Rod, he ran quietly away, waiting for his brother to join him in the bushes. Rod came tumbling down, humping the basket. Hurriedly, Peter put his brush and tin inside, ramming the towels on top.

"There's someone coming!"

But it was only an abrupt rush of rain on the leaves, hurling them downward.

"They'll know! They'll know who did it! There'll be marks on the towels!" Rod was close to tears. His face looked a funny, putty colour beneath the little peaked cap.

"No they won't stupid." Peter sounded very authoritative. "This stuff's soluble. As long as the brush is put back they'll never notice anything. Not even the towels." He rubbed his palms over the royal blue towelling. He knew the chaotic housekeeping of his home only too well. If his mother *did* notice, she'd simply assume his father had made the mess. "As long as *you* keep your trap shut," he added rudely, and then, with a brave toss of the head, "It's only a joke anyway."

His brother's babyishness made Peter knife-sharp as he led the way out of the deserted gardens. Pausing before crossing the exposed concrete area, he felt briefly glad they wore dark-green jerseys. They were a perfect camouflage. As they waited, a car drew up outside the pub. The engine and then the headlights were switched off and somebody shouted a greeting. Opposite, the yews waved morosely in the churchyard. "O.K.?" he muttered, "Now!" And they ran across the pale concrete slabs to the steps, skidding down them into the road, cave-like under its vault of leaves. "Walk normally!" he hissed, slowing his own pace.

"Let me see your hands," whimpered Rod, but Peter wouldn't show them until they'd gone some way. Under the light of a street lamp he held them out for inspection. They looked ordinary enough since they were generally discoloured with something. The sight of them seemed to soothe Rod. When he asked whether they would go to prison if they were found out, he sounded quite matter-of-fact. But it required effort. He didn't want to appear soppy. Nor did he wish to be outdone in the matter of jokes. "What's the definition of strain?" he tried again.

Peter made an irritable gesture as if he were above that childish kind of joke, but when Rod shouted, "Teeth marks on the bog wall!" he gave an hysterical shriek of laughter.

Overhead, above the leaves, the broody clouds trapped a jet inside their black feathers.

"Nice day?" their mother called as they slithered past her through the kitchen.

"Yes."

"What have you been doing?" She began to follow, but seeing them unwilling to stop for her, faltered and returned to her scrubbing of their school shirts.

A wedge of honeycomb, looted, leaking its gold, sat in a saucer on the kitchen table. Beside it lay Kit's folder of photographs.

"How did you get on?" Kit had started to paint the bannisters white. He was on the top landing.

"Fine."

"We're in the team."

"In the team?" Maggie's echo floated upwards, a bright bubble. They went into their bedroom and stuffed the tin beneath Peter's bed. His hands weren't badly stained. With a touch of inspiration, he opened the box of modelling clay Belinda had given him and rolled the surgical smelling stuff between his hands. It made his palms pale.

"In the *team*, did you say?" The bubble rose.

"Go on down," said Peter tersely.

Obediently, Rod walked out of the door and hung over the stair rail, "Yes," he cried. "Both of us."

"Well done!" shouted Maggie from below.

"Terrific!" shouted Kit from above. And they laughed at one another through the stair well, peering comically.

"I thought you disapproved," Kit called down to his wife.

"Disapproved? Of what?"

"Competition. Competitive sports."

"I do."

Rod's head went up and down, vaguely following. His mother dried her hands on her apron and turned away. "But what's *that* got to do with it?" she added ironically over her shoulder. "It's your world, not mine."

"Eh?" Kit paused. "What you say?"

"She says it's your world," supplied Rod, loosening his necker.

Kit made a deprecating noise. "Ours, she means," he called down sardonically to his son. And he thrust a victor's thumb through the bannisters.

"It's after half past nine." Maggie stood at the door of the sitting room. The boys ignored her, watching the programme.

"*Later* than that," she looked at her watch. "Ten to ten. Did you go out in the boat today?"

There was an exchange of gunfire on the screen. A coloured boy weaved down the street taking cover in an alley.

"*Did* you?"

(He crouched, his face oily with sweat.)

"I'm *talking* to you!"

"What?"

"*Did* you go out in the boat today?"

"Yes."

"Well?"

"Well, what?" Peter's face was glued to the screen.

"Did you *enjoy* it?" she screamed.

He turned and saw her split face. He made himself look into the cracked eyes. "Yes," he said steadily, then found his attention race thankfully away from her.

The door slammed.

She came back with two glasses of milk, two pieces of Sally Ferguson's fruit cake and two apples. The tray clanged on the table.

"*Supper!*" she shouted, cupping both hands to her mouth as if she were calling from a cliff top. Idly, Rod reached for his drink, eyes lapping the screen.

"FIRE!" she yelled.

"What?" Peter's head revolved for a second.

"Oh, never mind," she sighed and left them in peace.

There was little to worry about, Peter told himself as he slid down into his rumpled bed. She never looked at their hands or ears or the backs of their necks like Granny did.

But when Maggie came in and knelt beside him to tuck the bedclothes in, the bed seemed to rise on an expanding paint tin. "You were late tonight," she murmured absently, and he pretended to be very sleepy.

Kit came in rubbing a rag between his fingers. He smelt of turps. "Sleep well," he bade them.

"Tell us a story!" Rod lifted his head from the pillow and tried to look charming.

"It's ten frigging fifteen."

"About Vietnam?"

"No."

"Were there any women soldiers there?"

"Among the North Vietnamese, yes. Why do you ask?"

"Crumbs," said Rod thoughtfully. "Oh, I saw a picture."

"Women *soldiers*?" queried Peter disbelievingly. "I thought you *said* . . ." he challenged his mother scornfully, "that women didn't do things like that. That women didn't *make* wars and things." He felt aggrieved that all the blame should be heaped on his sex.

"*Some* women . . ." she murmured, and bent to kiss him. Her hair irritated his cheek.

"Are there women soldiers in this country?"

"Some," she said again.

"Of a kind," put in Kit.

"No, nowadays, there are real ones," Maggie sighed, her

strained gaze on Peter's face. Her eyes were like crushed fruit. He moved a little so that his own gaze went past her to his father. "What kind?"

"In all the Services . . . secretaries in uniform. Marching nurses, that kind of thing."

"No, *real* ones," said Maggie. "Bridget Rose, and Bernadette . . ." she reminded him.

"And . . ."

"Oh *them*," Kit said. "They're psychotic."

"Who are they?" Peter demanded, a queer slippery beat starting up in his throat.

"Twenty past ten," said Kit.

"Girls," said Maggie. "Angry girls. I don't know if they're crazy or not. They're *angry*."

"What do they do?" Rod wondered apprehensively. "Do they kill people too?"

"I don't know." Maggie rose abruptly, staggering a little as though her bones failed her. "Goodnight, darlings."

But she left a disturbed scent behind that troubled them both. In the darkness guilts and anxieties were stirred by it.

"Do you think we'll be found out?" whispered Rod fearfully.

"No."

"We might be."

"It doesn't matter. Mummy would laugh."

(That's what he *had* thought, at first. It was she who'd found the women so funny. She who'd laughed openly. That was the spirit in which he'd thought of daubing them.)

Peter turned over on his side, his back towards Rod, and pushed his knuckles against his teeth. Something had gone wrong. It had become a bad thing.

As his hand had worked, something bad had taken over. But it had been nice to do.

The merging of good and bad bewildered him. But still, even now, behind the bewilderment, there glowed a sense of pleasure.

17

"IT WAS AN unwinnable war. The defeat of the big battalions. Funny . . . in the end, that was the most shocking thing about it — if I'm to be unattractively honest. None of us thought the Americans had any right to be there, but in the *end* . . ." Kit's voice wavered, and then, with some acerbity, he said, "One was so often taken to *be* American."

Keith Ferguson was making sympathetic noises. The photographs lay between the two men on the kitchen table.

Peter burst in on them. "*Daddy!*" he screamed. His eyes bolted out of a white face.

Kit hardly moved. "What is it?"

"*Quickly!*" He pulled at his father's shirt. "Quickly! Please come *quickly*!" Dragging with all his weight he hauled at his father's immovable mass, desperate that he should come. He felt the mass shift slowly as if barely able to support itself. "My *rabbits!*" he screamed.

They went out then, through the hall, through the conservatory, all three of them.

Crushed behind the wire of the hutch Chrysanthemum stared at them, her jaws working rapidly over a naked, pink thing. There was a faint squeaking. Her white nose was streaked red.

"Dear God!" Kit lurched unevenly forward, his thick fingers fumbling with the latch. Tearing the front of the hutch away and flinging it on the yellow grass, he plunged his arm after the rabbit who darted into the inaccessible half of the hutch, the other side of the partition. Behind her in the scarlet straw, she left the mutilated hindquarters of a baby rabbit. Poppy, seizing the opportunity, jumped out on the lawn and bounded to the far corner of the garden.

"Open the top!" pleaded, shouted Peter, hysteria scraping his voice.

There was an alternative opening, a lid, which exposed both chambers. Beneath it, Chrysanthemum had bunched her taupe body over the last of her blind offspring. It was too late.

Bile broke upward through Peter's chest. Falling down on his knees, he was sick on the lawn, wave after merciless wave of mess spouting foully out of him until only a dribble escaped the corner of his mouth despite his stomach's rough attempts to force out more of its own disgust.

He was aware of running movements, cursing. A big, hard hand on his back. It was Mr. Ferguson's.

"Here!" (He heard the voice above him.) "You look after Peter, I'll deal with the rabbit."

Kit was limping across the lawn. The two men changed positions and Peter began to cry quietly.

"I'm sorry, Peter, I'm *so* sorry," his father was muttering, falling clumsily beside him.

But he couldn't think, through his dazed horror, why his father should be apologising — for it *was* apology, not pity, he could hear. It was his *own* fault. Forgetting to feed them, he thought numbly at first, the sourness of his mouth appalling him. He had forgotten again.

(Keith had Poppy by her ears. Its legs threshing, the rabbit swivelled in his grasp.)

And then he thought, it is a punishment for the thing I did last night. And he doubled over as a fresh spasm wrenched him.

A handkerchief was smothered to his mouth. The smell of turpentine provoked a further rictus, a dreadful gurgle. His fists seemed smothered in slime.

"I'm sorry! I'm so sorry . . . !" his father kept repeating. And he hauled Peter to his feet, a boneless tube.

They stumbled away together. Water was splashed in his face as he hung over the sink. He heard Rod's voice squeaking, "What is it?"

"It's my fault," moaned Kit, "I never gave them the space they needed."

But it made no sense.

I did it. Me, thought Peter, the water running off his chin. He didn't want them cuddling him when he was so wicked.

Rod ran outside and then, quickly, returned, full of wonder. "I thought they were both female," he was saying blankly as Peter dried his face on a tea towel.

178

"We all did." Kit ran a glass of water. "That's why I didn't think it would matter. Oh Peter, I'm so ashamed." And he offered him the glass to drink from.

"I've shut them in," Keith Ferguson came awkwardly into the kitchen, his big hands swinging. There were several gashes on them. "They just need a bit of cleaning out." And he stood there, staring around him.

"Why did she do that?" gaped Rod, but nobody answered him. Kit and Peter were bound together with silent guilts.

"Well, you've still got two jolly good rabbits," Keith Ferguson attempted cheerfully, then, hearing his own insensitivity, fell quiet.

A few minutes later Maggie came home with her Saturday shopping and finding them all in different, inert states of shock, took charge. She washed and dried Peter's face properly, fetched him a clean shirt, toothpaste and a tooth brush, then turned her attention to Keith's scratches which she bathed, then dabbed with iodine. After she'd prepared some coffee she said firmly, "I'll go and clean the hutch — I suggest the boys go out in their boat."

They stirred. The housewife was at her business. The dispiriting lethargy was being swept out of them like dust. Keith turned one of the photographs towards him, the one of a woman running at the camera, a small bound corpse in her outstretched arms, behind her, a long blurred wake of people fleeing, the trail reaching back to the flat horizon. "When you've got a moment . . ." he murmured, and then looked up, meeting eyes again, ". . . when you've got a moment, I should like to talk . . ." He pushed himself up from the table, leaning over orange-stained hands and tried to find some small courtesy with which to steady himself. "How's the book coming along?" he tried gaily.

"Oh . . ." Kit turned even further away, twisting as if from the intolerable image of the photograph. "*Well* . . ." he concluded with a shrug. Then realising this wasn't adequate, added mockingly, "It takes all a fellow's time to run a house in this condition."

Keith Ferguson mistook him. "And how *is* the leg?" he enquired concernedly.

"Oh, the *leg's* fine . . ."

"Would you *like* to go in the boat?" Maggie leaned towards the children.

They mumbled consentingly.

The two men moved themselves.

"Will you forgive me?" Kit asked his elder son.

But Peter didn't comprehend him. "Yes," he said, for convenience' sake. His father's concern hovered, a mere irritant at the edges of his own. He was very frightened at the thought of what his mother might have to say to him when the other grown ups had left the room and he hoped they could all go out together, now, so that she shouldn't have the opportunity to turn on him.

Keith Ferguson — and his father — let him down. The one backed out of the kitchen, his face puckered by a form of sympathetic kindness that simply didn't fit while the other muttered something about changing and went upstairs.

Peter waited. He sat, arms folded around the battered void of himself, watching Rod flick through the photographs. They were beginning to lose their flatness and smoothness. One had a ring of coffee on its back. He waited for his mother to pick her time. She prowled round, moving things.

"It's a shame," she said gently. "I'm sorry you had to see it. Another quarter of an hour and there'd have been nothing, nothing at all to see."

She minds for *me*, he thought, with surprise, and a weakening swept through him.

"Who knows," she was saying, "it might have happened before. You can't sex rabbits easily."

Sex, again.

Her hand lay lightly on his shoulders.

"*Why* did it happen?" tried Rod, hoping for a sensible answer at last.

But she spoke to Peter. "I think you'll get your run now," she promised softly and she slipped her hand over his hair.

"But *why* . . .?" wailed Rod, obsessed by the shock of a mother gorging her infants.

"She knew there wasn't room for them to grow up in. Something told her, better this way."

"Better . . .?" He was not placated. Although Rod had seen nothing more evil than a little soiled straw, the enlarged, imagined image of the rabbit, chomping, remained with him a long time.

Perhaps it was linked with his fear of being found out. The two things wavered, coalesced, in his mind, as if pleased to have found one another and delighted to have him to torment. He was unnaturally polite and amenable all day, in the effort to avoid undue attention. The penalty he paid was boredom. The outing on the river struck him as dull. As dull as the pre-cast slab of sky overhead.

In Peter's mind, the rabbits and the statues became of identical size, identical chiselled greyness. In one swift vision, the rabbits were enormous stone objects, terrible toys. In another, the women stretched out their heavy arms in a mixture of pleading and triumph, a ghastly prelude to hugging. One wore a little ruby pendant of blood in the pleat of her lips.

He sat very tight and quiet in the boat doing everything as his father suggested he should. As a result, without his being aware of it, his rowing improved.

This, in the perverse balance of things, cheered Kit immeasurably. "You may be capable of rowing yourselves to school yet," he applauded.

They'd almost forgotten this had been their original ambition. The scale of it appalled them. The idea of travelling half a mile upriver, viewed in the light of their present ability, created a challenge neither felt in the least like meeting. They looked dolefully at one another, sharing the bleak suspicion that their father would hold them to the challenge.

"Three more days to my birthday," said Rod glumly. "And I've *had* my present."

"Tell us about the war, Dad," urged Peter as they moored the boat and began the walk home. Anything to make colour crackle in front of the obliterating grey. If he could talk to Keith Ferguson about it, he could talk to them.

And Kit, to please his children, to please his *penares*, to seduce himself, talked all the way to Wellington Gardens and all the way through lunch until he became aware of Maggie's crenellated silence. After that, he completed his atonement by constructing a rabbit run into which Poppy and Chrysanthemum, unperturbed by their morning's experiences, delightedly hopped, their noses trembling with pleasure.

Rod saw it first.

Because his birthday fell on a Thursday, the same day as the local paper was delivered, he saw it when he went downstairs to collect the post.

It wasn't a very good picture. It was pale and grainy. Anyone who didn't know might easily have thought the defacement of the statuary was no more than a common smudge of printer's ink. But it was enough to make his head revolve like an electric fan. VANDALS DISFIGURE SCULPTURE, it read.

Vandals.

He shrank from the description. Furiously his eyes skipped through the prose, leaping over the long words and coming to a cold halt at the line "police have been trying to discover . . ."

His mother came downstairs yawning, her birthday greetings distorted by a stretched jaw. Quickly, he placed the post on top of the newspaper.

"What's up? You don't look very festive." She grinned, turning down the hall towards the kitchen.

"Well," he invented quickly (although the words lay uncannily close to hand), "I haven't got a proper present to come."

"You miserable little . . ." she began lightly, then broke off to cry, "*Sod* it . . .!" The kitchen door had stuck again. "We'll have to get a man in," she muttered hunting among the paint pots for a chisel she knew was somewhere there. By wriggling it round you could turn the lock.

"Let me!" Rod rushed to help her. Her fiddling was too blind and impatient to be effective.

"*Thank* you, darling," she succumbed, surprised. Then, as he made the chisel connect, "Bravo! A homunculus handyman."

He laughed nervously. She *couldn't* be cross with him today. Today was his armistice.

She lifted a parcel off the top pantry shelf and gave a little jerk with her body as though avoiding an unwelcome touch. "There is *something* you see," she smiled. "And I expect," she went on, with one eye on the handwriting of the day's letters, "that Granny's sent you a gift token."

"She sent Peter one."

"Exactly."

She began to prepare the eggs and bacon and the fresh orange juice. "Only two more days on the chicken run!" she sang out jubilantly to herself.

"And then what'll you do?" enquired Rod politely, sliding the papers on a stool beneath the table.

"God knows," she said, "I'm sure I don't. Come on, open up!"

As he ripped off the brown paper to reveal a German staff officer's uniform for his Action Man, Peter tumbled in cross-faced with sleep. His hair, washed the night before, looked like a derelict thatch. Rod's curls merely looked cloudier than usual.

"Ooh! You lucky pig!"

"Say Happy Birthday, darling."

"Happy Birthday." Peter banged his own gift down on the table.

"Hey, thanks! This is super, Mum, just what I wanted!" Rod peeled the Cellophane off the uniform. "I thought you hated me having these things."

"I've decided I'm powerless to change you. I might just as well scrub stripes off zebras."

"Why didn't I have one?" demanded Peter.

"What? An Action Man uniform?"

"Yes."

"Well Rod had to share his present with you last week. Horrible to have nothing at all today." She grinned at him. "Don't worry," she said, and reached up to the top shelf.

"Oh, *thanks*." It was a penknife. He really wanted one.

"O.K.?" She hugged him. "I should do your rabbits now before you forget."

He waited until Rod had unwrapped the model Spitfire he'd bought for him. Then he said, "Can I have a go with your new uniform?"

"Maybe."

Peter stamped a little and sneezed.

"Go *on*," said Maggie.

He went, but he still felt thorny and cross.

When he sloped back into the kitchen Maggie was saying, "Why don't you really try to row to school just once, before term ends?" (The bacon smelt good.) "Make it an aim for yourselves."

Rod gave an indistinct response.

"Well that was the whole aim of the thing I thought." She broke an egg in the pan. "And it *is* possible, I've worked it out. They'll let you moor it at the Hammond Boat Club, then all you have to do is go through the tunnel under the road there and up the gardens on the hill. Easy."

"I know that," said Rod, face in the fridge. "You said so before."

"Well?"

"Well what?" demanded Kit boisterously, appearing already dressed. "Happy Birthday, Rod."

"About the boat . . ." prompted Maggie.

"Ah yes. Well, I'm expecting you to make the journey at

least once before the end of term. That gives you three and a half weeks. Plenty of time . . ."

"Oh, why bother?" Bitterly, Maggie flicked fat at the eggs and they ballooned as if hurt.

The boys glanced at one another. Rod pulled a face. Peter felt indescribably heavy. It was just one more thing in the bundle on his back . . . exams and sports and catching the bus on time and rabbits and rowing . . . prep . . . finishing his project . . . I can't bear it, he thought. I hate it.

"It was *your* idea, remember," Kit was saying. "*You* wanted the boat . . ." And then, restraining himself, "You'll get a lot of fun out of it in the end . . . It's just practice, just mastering the art. It's always fiendish to start with."

"You'll have to help them." Maggie arranged food on the plates.

"I do." He was opening the post.

"I've got a gift token!" shouted Rod, waving it.

"How much for?" Peter looked. "Same as me," he said, satisfied. "I'm going to buy an Action Man uniform with mine."

"Oh, for Christ's sake!" said Maggie sharply, putting a plate in front of him. "Why do you have to be so jealous all the time? Fight, fight. *Argue.*"

"I'm not arguing. I don't *like* egg," he said, exasperated.

Maggie uttered a suppressed scream and shoved the egg off his plate and on to Kit's, leaving a speckled trail of fat.

The drills started down the road. "A quarter to eight!" she cawed.

"Hey!" Kit looked up, face alight. "Someone's interested in the cottage."

"No!"

"*Yes!*"

"Oh." The quick flame died on Maggie's features. She turned away, busy, her lips seamed whitely together.

"Aren't you *pleased*?" pressed Kit.

"Of course."

"*Lots* of people have been interested," observed Rod.

"All the same. There's been nothing for weeks." Kit was unusually excited. His face shone.

"I'll have to go down there," Maggie remarked. "The grass must be head high."

"I'd go, but I need to be here." As if to emphasise the need, Kit looked round for the papers to make his daily trudge of the small ads.

"They're here," said Peter who was sitting on them.

"What can you make but not see?" gasped Rod.

"A noise," said Maggie pointedly.

"No. A smell."

"A *smell*!" quarrelled Peter. "You *can* see a smell."

"You can't."

"You can see onions. And smoke from a fire."

"But you can't see the *smell*. You can't see the smell in this house for instance, can you?"

"Oh do shut up. You ought to be dressed, Peter."

"What?"

"Dressed!"

"I know a better one," he said. "What did the policeman say to his stomach?"

"You're under a vest," retorted Rod, one eye on his father. "I saw that one in the *Cracker*."

"What special thing would you like me to bring home for your tea, Rod?" Maggie, who had not stopped to eat herself, was poised over their plates, already anxious to clear away.

"Aren't these the statues you were telling me about?" Kit passed her the local paper, folded over. "The Maenads or whatever they're meant to be. Some funny old man's fancy."

"Little buggers," she said slowly, reading. But she hadn't time to finish the item and put the paper down while she hurried to scrape things off the plates into the bin.

Peter, whose lungs had suddenly ceased to fit at all well inside his rib cage, watched her, mouth furring.

"Get dressed," she said, not even looking at him. Her mind was on something else.

He stole a cautious look at Rod who was examining his staff officer's uniform with myopic attention and a scarlet face. "All right." He hurtled from the kitchen to fetch his clothes, his legs so watery, he tripped on the stairs.

As he picked himself up, he heard his father's rumbling laugh. "They rather invite it," he was saying. But there was no sound from his mother.

By the time he came down, searching for his tie, she appeared more concerned about the cottage. Frowning deeply she was reading the agent's letter and muttering, "You still haven't told me if there's something special you'd like for tea."

Rod was speechless. She waved a hand at him absently. "I'll find something," she said.

And that was that. It should have been simple then to forget the whole thing. Just to let the incident fade. He wasn't worried by mention of the police, oddly. He was so certain they could never be found. And yet it didn't go away. It lodged with all the other lead pieces on Peter's back.

When he sat at his desk, he slid his new penknife into the palm of his hand, lifted the lid of his desk and carved his initials thereon. It was forbidden to do such a thing, but he felt the keenest possible need to do it.

18

"GOSH, HAVEN'T YOU finished your project yet? I've finished mine."

Belinda, in a sunsuit, with straps over her shoulders, sat on the bed hanging over him. She never, reflected Peter, wore the same thing twice.

It was Sunday and the last day he had left before exams began in which to finish his project. He felt a bit desperate about it — as though the tanks themselves were advancing inexorably on him.

"I've been busy," he replied, carefully outlining the gun turret of a Sherman Firefly.

"I drew a honey extractor. Daddy bought one the other day. He's going to let me use it." Between each sentence she delicately kicked him in the small of the back as he knelt on the floor using the top of his toy chest as a table. "How long will it be before your house is finished?"

"Finished?" He was labouring hard. It's not quite right, he thought, sitting back on his heels to study the drawing. "I don't know," he shrugged, preoccupied.

"Will the smell have gone then?"

He didn't answer. She was annoying him.

"Mummy says it's your drains."

Silence.

She tried again. "Shall we go out in your boat this afternoon?"

"What?"

Wearily, she repeated herself.

"If I've finished."

"Oh, you are *slow*. Well, I'll get Rod to take me."

"Perhaps I will. This is the last drawing, but I've still got some writing to do. And the cover."

"Why don't you just cut out a picture from that magazine you're copying from and stick it on the front?"

She was full of suggestions. She vexed him.

"It'd spoil the magazine." He gripped the edge of it defensively.

"Oh, well." She flounced off the bed and crossed to the window sill which was littered with toy cars and trucks. "You've got nothing proper to play with," she complained.

"I've got lots of things." He turned the paper round the other way to do the shading.

"Nothing *I* want to play with."

Why do you come then, he wanted to say.

Now she had found her way to the cupboard, a warehouse of plastic train tracks, Lego pieces, broken models, jigsaw shapes, Dinky cars and guns of every description. "What do you play with dolls for?" she asked contemptuously, waving his old Action Man at him. One hand and a leg was missing.

"He's not a *doll*!"

"They *are* dolls."

She took off the jacket which was easy since it had lost all its fasteners.

"They're real uniforms," he insisted without lifting his concentration from the Sherman Firefly. "They're real soldiers."

She fell silent for a moment. Outside lay the comparative peace of Sunday. The drills had stopped but the pigeons warbled lubriciously as they watched the ripening of soft fruit in the rows of gift-packed gardens.

"He's not a *real* soldier!"

He didn't bother to reply.

"He's *not*!"

Spinning round to the challenge in her tone, he saw that she'd taken all Action Man's clothes off. She thrust the pink, feebly bent and jointed figure out in front of her and waggled it at him. One handless arm was raised in a self-protecting gesture.

"He hasn't got a dicky!" she screeched.

"Leave him alone!"

Furiously, Peter scrambled to his feet but she danced back from him as he tried to snatch his toy from her taunting grasp. She held it higher, jumping.

"Hasn't got a dick-y!" she sang, then, losing interest, "Silly doll!" And she flung it on the lino-covered floor.

"Stop that!" And Peter ran to his wounded soldier, picking him up, cradling him.

"It's only broken anyway. All your things are broken."

But he loved him. And clasped him tightly. The amputated figure bled into him. "Why do you come here? Go away!" he shouted, his vision filming.

"I *was* going. I only came to give your silly mother a message." But she showed no signs of going. She stood on a single tiptoe, swivelling round like a ballerina.

"It's an invitation to meet the Prime Minister. *I'm* going. Mummy said she'd take me. She said it would be *an*" (she emphasised the correctness of the word), "an historic occasion."

"I don't care," he said, and he didn't really, but he felt jealous all the same. Action Man's face was pressed close to his chest. Belinda raised one leg out behind her and stretched her arms forward while keeping her mouth ungracefully open. For a moment she looked like one of the statues in the Embankment Gardens.

"She wondered whether *your* mother would like to go, which," concluded Belinda, swinging her leg back to the ground and doing some toe pointing, hands on hips, "is very nice of her considering how rude your mother is."

"She's not rude." But she was. Often. He knew that.

"*And* your father's a fraud."

"What do you mean? He's not. He's *not*!" He crossed his arms in hard diagonals across his chest, holding his own shoulders, protecting both himself and his toy. A smell of stew filtered upstairs into the bedroom. "What do you *mean*?" he repeated angry and tearful.

"Daddy says he must have been stupid to get shot like that. He must have run away."

"Of course he didn't run away. Well," he corrected himself, struggling to picture the situation in his head, "he had to run. You have to run if you're ambushed like that, but he wasn't running *away*."

My father is not a coward, he wanted her to understand, but the words, lodged in a dam of unreleased weeping, eluded him.

"You don't. You lie low, Daddy said."

He couldn't bear the idea of her father talking about his father in this loose and horrible fashion. He imagined the big, thick-limbed man talking to his womenfolk . . . it struck him as an act of treachery. "Your father can't know, he wasn't there. He's never been in a war."

"Yes he has," she pouted victoriously, "he was in Malaya."

He daren't argue with that. If it were true, he was the more afraid. "I . . .," he began, "I wish you'd . . ."

"All right, darlings?" Maggie's head appeared round the door. "Rod's all on his own in the garden, why don't you come down and play together?"

"I've brought you a message," cried Belinda, delivering it. And then she said she could stay and play until her lunch was ready at half past one. Maggie, nodding amiably, told Peter to put his project away for now.

It was important to show Belinda the real things of war.

He took her into the scrapyard of his father's bedroom and showed her the bullets, the National Service dress uniform, with its navy peaked cap, the Sam Browne, the two 4.10s and the air rifle, the gaiters and the little canvas bag for hard rations. "*See!*" he cried.

But she seemed unimpressed.

"Daddy lets us borrow these to play in. To fight in," he went on anxiously, and reaching his fingers along the top of the wardrobe he found Kit's tin helmet which he put on together with a khaki shirt that had been used for painting and was much too large. He tucked it into his trousers. "Look," he pleaded, resplendent.

"Can *I* have a hat?" she asked.

He let her wear the officer's cap rather reluctantly — but only after Rod had burst in saying he wanted to play too, and let his hand stray longingly towards the cap. "That's Belinda's," Peter had said then.

They took care with their dressing. Belinda gave herself a black fibre-tip moustache, then Peter used the pen to draw a swastika on a clean handkerchief of his father's which he asked her to bind round his arm. Putting his hand up the small, iron-hooded grate in their bedroom, Rod found enough soot to smear on his face. "There *are* women in the North Vietnamese army . . ." he said doubtfully, looking at Belinda who'd put her cap on at a jaunty angle. She grinned, exposing a tooth she'd blacked-out. She wasn't taking it seriously. "You're not allowed to hit girls," she said in advance of the game.

"Why not?"

"You can hurt their . . . *things*," she explained mysteriously.

"Well, whose side are you going to be on?" Peter didn't

want her on his but was offended when she said she'd be on Rod's side. He became aware that below them, there rumbled the terse exchanges of another battle, short matching sentences with no clear definition which were being pitched back and forth.

"If I'm an officer, I can give orders," declared Belinda, and promptly decided that the boys' bedroom was the British camp and Peter had to go while she and Rod built fortifications.

Out on the landing the sound of the argument below blossomed more rosily. It was about who should do what, or seemed to be. An oven door slammed.

Hurt, deeply troubled by Belinda's calumnies about his father, Peter wanted to go away and hide. He wanted to be beyond earshot of those bitten-off stumps of sound. He climbed up the narrow dusty staircase and hid in the darkest of the attics. As his eyes became accustomed to the gloom and he was able to discern the heavy lumps of hooded furniture better, he began pushing them together to form a barricade.

It isn't true, he thought hotly. It isn't true. He made his camp and tucking himself down in the furthest corner, waited for the others.

He had to wait a full quarter of an hour because they were happily occupied with their own efforts at least as long as that, but he didn't care. It was nice in the dark. At length he heard them come out of the bedroom calling. They mounted the narrow stairs. Far below them, Maggie's wailing rose to a steady, painful pricking. It was nothing more to Peter than a signal on his radar screen. Bleep, bleep, bleep, it winked on the furthest circle of his consciousness.

"Where are you?"

He dug himself into his corner, sub-machine gun clasped between thighs and chest.

Their prowling was hesitant. They knocked against things. He narrowed his eyes.

Suddenly a silence fell and he could hear their wary breathing. "He's behind there," Belinda whispered. His fingers tightened round the trigger as they sprang against the squat chair he'd pushed in front of him.

"Tut-tut-tut-tut-tut-tut!" He aimed.

"Got you!"

"Tut-tut-tut-tut!"

"I've got a laser gun. You're dead!"

"Tut-tut-tut-tut!"

"You're *dead*! You're captured!"

Maddened by the impotence of his fire, Peter fought hand to hand in the dark, lashing out against arms, legs, rifle butts. "*You're* dead," he shouted, "I shot first!"

"I'm bullet-proof!"

"I'm from outer space!"

Belinda would not obey the rules. He knew it was her leg he held in his hands. She was above him, straddling the chair. He pulled, then tightening his grip on the coarse fabric of her ankle sock, viciously twisted the leg back from the knee as she fell.

"Ow-w-w-w-w!"

It was a dreadful scream. It swung the attic round after it. Dimly, another voice, further away, yelled.

"You're for it," hissed Rod in the jumble of darkness. Belinda was making loud roars beside him.

"Shut *up*!" Peter ordered her, trying to clamp one hand across her mouth. She bit him.

It was his turn to yelp.

"Come out of there!" It was Maggie's voice from the landing below. "Come *out*, I tell you!" Her footsteps tumbled up the wooden stairs as she drew closer. "What *are* you doing to Belinda?"

"Nothing."

"Come *out*!" She was right outside the low doorway.

"They're hurting me!"

"You little bastards, come out when I tell you!"

"She says . . .!" Peter began in a high-pitched voice, but he choked on his own muddled grief.

"Peter's trying to break my leg!"

"She . . .!"

Maggie had them. One in each hand, dragging, banging, bruising. She hauled them away into the light, Belinda crawling pitifully after them. Then she began hitting them.

"No!" Peter moaned as his mother's arm came crashing blindly down across his shoulders. He glimpsed the ragged linen of her face.

"What are you doing! What are you doing!" she kept insanely screaming. Peter covered his head with his arms and then, after a second's terrifying pause, felt himself seized again by the arm. "What's *this*!" She tore at him, her fingers, unable in their frenzy, to separate flesh from material. His skin was cruelly pinched as she ripped the insignia from his arm. He thought she was angered by his taking a clean handkerchief. "I'm sorry," he bleated as she shook him, so violently, his teeth cracked against one another. "*This!*" she repeated, and, dropped from her grasp, he rolled over on the floor, feeling splinters of wood against his face. "It's Daddy's hanky," he wept, dust gritting his lips, "I'm sorry . . ."

When he said that, she burst into tears — crazy, turbulent shudders of noise that made him ashamed for her. He swayed uncertainly to his feet and saw her leaning, face against the sepia wall, her back a hook of pain.

The children's own whimpering ceased as Maggie's grew. They shuffled their feet. Belinda's moustache had run where her tears had flowed through it.

Vainly, Peter attempted once more to prosecute . . . "She said . . ." But he couldn't say what Belinda had said. It wasn't true. "I'm sorry," he whispered, woebegone.

Maggie's form stilled against the wall. Her shoulders stood out like thin axes. "Don't *you* be sorry," she said fiercely into her fists. "It's me. I don't know what's wrong with me." She didn't move.

Belinda spoke up faintly. "I think it's time for my lunch," she said.

"*All right up there?*"

Kit's voice looped up the stairwell.

"Come along." Maggie turned, inexplicably calm. "I'll clean you up." The handkerchief dangled from her fingers. She was fungus-white. "It's me," she said again, her jaw hard, "I make it worse."

And she took Belinda gently by the arm. "Let me tidy you up."

They trooped mutedly downstairs to the bathroom and let her attend to them. Peter's back throbbed where she had struck it. She hates me, he thought stiffly, that's what's wrong with her. She hates me. And the littered confusions of his head resolved themselves with this perception.

I understand, he thought. And the burden of what he understood sealed itself coldly within his heart. He did not weep.

She was very delicate and quiet with them, dabbing at their soilings with a gentle concentration. The others submitted to it gladly as though it pardoned and erased all that had gone before.

But Peter, who had been shamed in front of the others, held

himself rigid, his eyes frozen on the blank surface of the mirror above her head, his whole body a glacier of resistance. I am safe behind this, he thought, feeling the separation of the ice.

"I make it worse," Maggie said again at lunch. (But he didn't care what she said any more. His heart was closed against her.) "It's the fighting . . . the continual fighting. Where will it all end?"

"You're tired," his father said and he put another potato on her plate.

After the meal was over, Peter returned to his project, writing the last page in a fine italic script he had learned at Hill House School. He was very proud of it. Proud of the whole book. There were twelve pages in all, half of them drawings, well and accurately executed. All the spellings were correct, he'd checked them. (He thought with scorn of Rod's messy dinosaurs and fractured spelling. Rod had completed his four-page project a fortnight ago. He hadn't cared.)

Now, there was just the cover to do. With Mr. Scholfield's help he'd worked out the design. He was going to draw a chariot at the top and the latest American tank at the bottom to indicate the historical development of mobile warfare. The title would go in between and then he would stick it on the cover of his blue folder.

But Belinda came round again, with her father this time. To complain, Peter thought. But nothing like that happened. She was as arch and buoyant as ever, making faces and swinging from her father's arm. He might have imagined the whole episode he thought, looking at her. If only his back didn't ache so.

Peter, she declared, had promised to take her out in the boat this afternoon and Maggie said that if he had made a promise, he must keep it and she would come to watch them.

Only partially consoled by snatching the yellow lifejacket before Rod could get hold of it, he grumpily put away his project for the second time, a worm of worry beginning to turn in his chest. Got to finish it. Got to finish it, he determined, and stumped downstairs.

They were further delayed by Keith's description of the second-hand extractor he'd bought and a gleeful account of the pigeon he'd trapped in his green plastic netting.

"You ought to shoot them," Kit said.

"I have *thought* about it," murmured Keith wistfully.

"You could borrow my gun."

"It's a built-up area, you see." Keith was plainly longing to shoot.

"Go over on the other bank and have an orgy. Some of the buggers are bound to nest there."

"Could we, Daddy? Could we?" Rod looked up.

"Only when you can row that far. Then, I promise you."

"Oh *no!*" Maggie cried.

"Why ever not? They're an absolute menace, even you admit that. You can't feel soppy about pigeons, surely?"

"It's not *that*," she said savagely.

"What then?"

She simply delivered herself of a long, corrosive look and gathered the children together.

"It's *my* bank," she muttered vehemently to herself as Peter, dipping one painful oar after another, struggled towards Sweetings, determined to prove that he *could* row that far.

They struck across the common, away from the crowds that had gathered round the croaking ice-cream van.

Among the moons of elder blossom and the deep grasses, creamed with clover, Maggie's spirits rose. "Doctor! Doctor!" she sang, "A bee's just stung my nose . . . Should I put cream on it?" She paused deliciously, and looked round at them, eyebrows raised. But nobody had the rejoinder. "No!" she concluded, answering herself. "It'll be miles away by now!" And she shared in the hoots of laughter.

"Doctor! Doctor . . .!" Rod took up the refrain, "I've only got fifty-nine seconds to live . . ." He giggled. "Just a minute!" he ended, exploding. They scorned the nettles, brushing past them. Belinda made a garland of ox-eye daisies and wore it on her head. Far away, yacht sails glimmered.

"Tell us a story!" danced Rod, leaping. "Tell us the truest, most horrible story you know! Tell us . . ." And he jumped over a tiny inlet of water, both feet together, ". . . a story *so* lovely and horrible, it frightens even you!"

And trailing a hand through the flowering grass heads, fescue and sorrel and rye, she told them, marginally censored, the story of Myra Hindley and Ian Brady.

Peter was having terrible trouble with the chariot. It was the last thing. He was very close to tears as he rubbed it out yet again.

"Time for bed." Kit lowered the Sunday paper and looked at his watch.

"But I've *got* to do it!" Peter wailed, "Mr. Scholfield said."

Kit looked. Under the figure of a statuesque woman, arms upraised, the paper was wearing thin from rubbing.

"Boadicaea?" he queried, "what's wrong with her?"

"It's the *chariot* . . ."

"Never mind, son." He cupped Peter's chin with his calloused hand and turned the cracked face towards him. "You're worn out. Why don't you climb into your bath and let me do it for you? I've got a book somewhere I expect. I can copy it."

"Would you?"

"Of course I will."

"Poor Peter," murmured Maggie from her circle of lamplight, "I was horrible to you today."

He went gladly, joining Rod in the bath. "You've got a bruise on your back," Rod said when Peter lowered himself in front of him.

"Is it big?"

"Not *very*. Oh, and by the way, if you *don't* let me borrow your penknife . . . I'll tell on you. About you know what."

Kit was hunched over the page, glasses slipping down his nose, tongue thrust into one cheek, making it bulge. "I've nearly finished," he said. "Do you like it?"

Peter, warmed by his bath, looked over his father's shoulder. "Well?" Kit turned his head to him and brushed Peter's cheek comfortingly. "Do you?"

"Yes," he answered faintly. "Who's he?" And he pointed to a curious, dwarf-like figure with thick hair on his chest who had appeared beside Boadicaea and was leering up at his queen.

"Oh, him? He's just a bit of fun," said Kit, squeezing Peter's sore shoulders.

Part Three

None of us stands outside humanity's black collective shadow. Whether the crime occurred many generations back or happens today, it remains the symptom of a disposition that is always and everywhere present — and one would therefore do well to possess some 'imagination for evil', for only the fool can permanently disregard the conditions of his own nature. In fact, this negligence is the best means of making him an instrument of evil . . . What is even worse, our lack of insight deprives us of *the capacity to deal with evil*. Here of course we come up against one of the main prejudices of the Christian tradition, and one that is a great stumbling block to our policies. We should, so we are told, eschew evil and if possible neither touch nor mention it . . . This apotropaic attitude towards evil and the apparent circumventing of it, flatter the primitive tendency in us to shut our eyes to evil and drive it over some frontier or other like the Old Testament scapegoat, which was supposed to carry the evil into the wilderness.

Civilisation in Transition by C. G. Jung

19

"WA-VELL! WA-VELL!"

"Haig! Haig! Haig!"

The little boys reached the end of the short pool, touched and swung round, the water streaming over their backs. The three leaders, neck and neck, were followed by one dawdler. Their bodies worked through the water like small engines, their breast stroke perfect diagrams of movement.

"Haig! Haig!"

The shouting rose as a child in black and yellow striped trunks nosed ahead. The pumping became furious. The cheer-leaders ran from one end of the pool to the other, poking their heads between parents' shoulders to shout their encouragement. Nobody from Auchinleck was in this race, which — so Rod had explained — gave the others a chance. Nor, he had added, was there anyone from Percy. Of *course*. His derision had made Maggie laugh. She sat now, beside Kit, her pink cotton dress spattered with water.

Kit had found one of his headaches coming on at the prospect of the school sports, but he had come nonetheless. Looking round, he was surprised to see so many fathers were here. Either business was very good or business was very bad. He joined in the applause as the tiny contestant from Haig grasped the end of the pool and breathlessly turned to see how far behind his rivals were.

A whistle blew.

"It's their turn now," Maggie hissed, agonised.

"No, it's not. It's the nine-and-under crawl. Then it's us." Kit consulted his mimeographed sheet. "Are you nervous?"

"Of course. Aren't you?"

"A bit."

"It matters so much to them."

A master in a track suit was marshalling the under-nines. Behind them, in readiness, towels slung around their shoulders, hopped Rod and Peter. Rod waved. He'd said he could win this. But Maggie knew Peter was confident he could do better than his brother. Although the afternoon was warm under its swaddling of cloud, some of the competing boys shivered.

"I'm so glad I could come," whispered Maggie who was currently out of work. "Altogether, it's quite a day." Later on, she was going with Sally Ferguson to hear the Prime Minister speak. She hoped her one good dress wouldn't be too drenched by then.

"All right? On your marks!" The master, whose navy track suit had a double white line running the length of it, raised his arm.

They were off, five lean brown darts.

Indulgently, the headmaster smiled and turned to speak to a parent beside him without taking his eyes off the swimmers. On his other, right-hand side, stood a table of trophies.

Too sick with anticipation to pay much attention to the under-nines, Maggie allowed her gaze to drift towards her sons who hovered slowly from one foot to the other. They were outside the circle of cheering and looked very cold.

All too swiftly, their turn came. There were four in their race. The Makins, One and Two, were ranged at the farthest end from the master who lifted his whistle close to his mouth as he issued instructions. Overhead, a plane oozed lazily through the cloud.

"On your marks!"

They bent, arms back like chick wings, eyes focused on the water.

Maggie gripped her husband's hand.

"Ready! Set! . . ."

"Peter's looking at the teacher!" she cried.

The whistle pierced the air.

The three nearest boys plunged at its shrilling. Peter, switching his gaze to the pool, dived after them.

"Silly chump," said Kit amiably.

"He couldn't hear," Maggie said, distraught. "He was watching the whistle." And she peered through the spray. The three leading boys were together, arms beating the water like paddles. Peter was a few critical seconds behind, his head flung desperately from side to side.

"He's got himself in a state," cried Maggie, sharing his panic.

"Wa-vell! Wa-vell! Wa-vell!"

"Auk! Auk! Auk!"

And louder still, as the end of the pool was reached for the first time: "Gor-don! Gor-don! Gor-don!"

"Rod's holding his own." Rod, a largely unrecognisable splashing, was a head behind the leader, levelling for second place. Peter, still trailing, threw up water like a harpooned whale.

"*C'mon!* Peter! Peter!"

"Shh!" Kit drew her back into her seat. "*Wavell*," he said.

"Wa-vell! Wa-vell!" She was out of her seat again. There was half a length yet to go. "*Wa-vell! Wa-vell!*"

The din was terrific as a battle was fought out for first place, boys leaping and rushing around the pool. The headmaster clasped a hand to his forehead, whether in real or mock tension, Kit wasn't sure. Rod was tiring.

Six feet, five, four . . .

"*Oh!*" Maggie sat back, disappointed.

One after the other second and third seized the lip of the pool. Peter ploughed in after them.

"Never mind," said Kit.

"It's only a competition," said Maggie with dull self-mockery.

A few minutes later Rod pushed his wet body through the parents who stood behind his. "Rats!" he grimaced, but he wasn't depressed, "I beat Peter," he said and bared his teeth in triumph.

"I wasn't really trying." Peter's head appeared, hair plastered over his eyes, his mouth disconsolate. "I didn't care about winning, so I didn't try."

"Don't say *that!*" Maggie hissed, fearful that other parents might overhear and think her son unsporting, although he was only voicing her own attitude aloud. "Anyway, it isn't true."

"It is. It is." He nodded his dripping, scowling head up and down.

"*No* . . ." she said and she explained what she'd seen when the whistle went.

It was so, he realised. With being conscious of his mistake, he *had* watched Mr. Bell. The disappointment was bitter.

"You *could* have won," Kit was whispering but the wounds of anger and self-pity were too raw to be soothed. He had failed in front of everybody. *They* wouldn't know why. Humiliation made him sink back inside.

"It makes me so angry . . ." His mother took his hand and burrowed for his eyes with hers. He tried, discreetly, to pull his hand free. ". . . they ought to know. Fancy putting you furthest away from the referee. How stupid can they be!"

Please don't, he ached to say. Please, don't fuss. It only makes things worse.

"Doesn't it make *you* furious, Kit?"

Be quiet, be quiet.

"I've got to get changed," he said flatly and tugged himself free, sliding between the warm, dry clothes of spectators.

"All right, all right," Kit conceded later. "Fine. Just don't say you didn't *try*, that's all. It sounds frightful. You've got to try, whatever you're doing."

"Dad?"

"Yes?"

"Can I be a boarder next term?"

"Why, son? Why should you want that?"

"I just do."

"But why?"

"I'd like it better."

"Is it *better* to be a boarder? Are they the top dogs?"

"I suppose so."

"Oh, Peter . . ."

He was pressed against the nice tyres of his father. The rough chin scraped against his forehead. There was a good, dry scent of sweat in the cotton shirt.

"I want to," he mumbled.

"It's very difficult," Kit sighed. "*Very* . . ."

"If I went away," said Peter suddenly, safe in the warm nest of arms and chest, "Mummy might like me better."

"*Peter!*"

Kit held him away, his hands tight on his son's arms, and stared at him. Peter's head drooped. "But she loves you!"

He said nothing.

"She *loves* you!"

The arms went round him again, thick and beautiful and strong. They were locked tightly together, father and son.

"She loves you, Peter . . ."

He could hear the resonance of the words in his father's chest, but he didn't believe them.

"It's hard for her. Try to understand."

It was so nice to be held. He let his body go limp, pushing all the perplexities of dreams and dwarfs and defeat from his mind.

"I've let her down, in a way . . ." his father was saying, "it's nobody's fault. But, just for the moment, we're all dependent on her and . . . Try to understand."

Let her down? Fear tightened itself around Peter's throat. What did his father mean? That he *was* a coward? No . . . *no!* You are *not,* he cried inwardly, you are not a coward. You have not let her down.

"Can you see that?" asked Kit softly.

And then it broke out of him, a slow wail as though some limb were being twisted. "I painted the ladies, Dad, *I* did . . ." And he pushed his head against his father as hard as he could to staunch the weeping.

"You painted the ladies?" His father sounded puzzled. And then, more slowly, "You painted the ladies . . . *you* . . . ?"

Dumbly, Peter nodded. A shuddering passed through him.

"So *you* painted the ladies . . . !"

Through the wall of his father's chest, Peter felt a rumble, like the heavy tumbling of water. He felt the fleshy jolting of underlying muscle and diaphragm, a warbling union of sound and movement. His father was laughing. "*You* . . . !"

"Don't tell her!" It was she who had laughed first but she wouldn't laugh now, he knew that. She would tower with rage, a wild barbed tree.

The arms clasped him, holding him firmly against the motion of laughter until he too, relaxing his fears, was carried by it, up and down, a passenger aboard their private dipper of mirth.

"Try to *understand*," his father urged him again later. "Try to help her. To please her."

And so, when Maggie said she could fit one of them on her lap if either of them wished to see the Prime Minister, he dutifully said that he would like to go although he didn't really care one way or the other. The idea of sitting on her lap frankly horrified him.

If it pleases her, he thought grimly, I shall go.

As he washed his hands and face carefully, and sought to discover a parting in his hair to make himself look older, an uninvited image came to him of the man who had once conducted them round his ghost-ridden house, his aid turned up so far howlback prevented his hearing their chattering remarks and questions. There was no reason for it. The memory simply fell across his inner landscape within a shaft of sunlight, a lazy fragment of lost summer, framed by distant and approving laughter.

Sally Ferguson jogged along on her little heels. She seemed to need twice as many steps as Maggie. "It's so *exciting*!" she kept on panting. "Such a wonderful opportunity!"

Even Maggie seemed cheerful although Peter had heard her protesting to Kit that she didn't really have any desire to go to the meeting. "I can't see the political objection when we've got a coalition government," Kit had argued and she'd then complained it wasn't a political objection she had, it was just the idea of all those Tory women gathered together under one roof. "Oh *do* go," Kit had said. There'd been a lot of talk about the Prime Minister's private state of mind and he was curious.

So here she was, gay and breathless, saying "I'm so glad you asked me!" in response to Sally's small explosions of joy. Peter couldn't understand his mother's many aspects. It was hard to tell which bits really belonged to her, he thought, resisting Belinda's attempt to take his arm.

Outside the hall they signed a petition presented by a crowd of constituents pointing out the dangers of low-flying aircraft to the locality and demanding that they be re-routed.

"It's a waste of time," observed Maggie, "but never mind." And she added a dashing signature before elbowing through the bystanders.

"I do hope they don't jeer," quavered Sally, dragging Maggie after her. She was well known to people inside the hall and kept flapping a wrist from the mast of her arm while uttering squeaks of recognition. She took a long time to sit down but subsided eventually amidst the municipal flowering of hats.

"Can you see?" whispered Maggie. Peter peered through the nodding heads and saw a platform empty of people. An enormous Union Jack was draped across the back behind a table and three Bentwood chairs. At the front of the stage were self-conscious heaps of spotlit carnations. The whole place smelt like a greenhouse.

They waited for ages while the hustling and the rustle of conversation went on undiminished. Sally and Maggie were a sibilant part of it. They were discussing food prices and agreeing vehemently with one another.

"I got a star for my project," said Belinda, "what did you get for yours?"

But he'd heard no more of it. Life had been full of exams exerting their own obsessive strain over the past two weeks and he shook his head in an obstinate refusal to speak. He wished he'd brought a comic and he wished he wasn't sitting on his mother's lap.

Suddenly shushing cries swept through the hall, each woman hushing each neighbour in turn. A man was smiling on stage clutching his notes and moving his head from side to side with a quick, jerky motion.

"Ladies!" He jerked again, harassed beneath his smiling, " . . . and *gentlemen*!"

A little titter.

It was all rather like a talent contest he'd once watched on a pier, thought Peter. The expectancy, the flowers, even sitting on his mother's lap. It must have been years and years ago.

The man took a step backwards, raised his arm like a railway signal, and rapturous applause burst forth drowning his words of introduction. Some of the women rose in their seats. Sally clapped with her hands above her head.

The leader of Her Majesty's Government, the Right Honourable Mrs. Helen de Winter, stepped from the wings acknowledging her wild ovation. A gloved hand performed slow wheels.

"Isn't she *tiny*!" thrilled Sally Ferguson and Peter heard his mother's indrawn snort of amusement. The clapping seemed to last for five minutes. Eventually Mrs. de Winter raised both hands for silence and reluctantly the applause died away. She *was* very small. And very . . . *smart*, in a way. She wore a plumey hat of emerald feathers, and a navy silk coat over a navy, white and emerald dress.

But once she started speaking in a high, finely modulated voice, Peter found his attention wandering. She spoke of the country's economic situation and the words slid through him without trace like a very bland, invalid meal . . . something white and steamed. Instead he thought of the stone women and the way his father had laughed and the promise he'd given never, ever to tell Maggie. The relief of having told was so sweet he barely minded Mrs. de Winter's neutered address. But he must have fidgeted for his mother surreptitiously unwrapped a boiled sweet and stuck it in his mouth. It had a sharp, green flavour. "But we, as women . . ." The voice entered a more forceful register. The tendrils of her hat, lifting, swinging as she leaned forward, Mrs. de Winter brought an immaculate, white-gloved fist down so hard on the table, the water jug bounced. ". . . represent a force for peace. However . . ." She cast her piercing gaze over the audience and waited for the pause to take effect. ". . . we must be more than merely *rep-re-sent-at-ive* . . ." The word became as long as a goods train.

"Hear! Hear!" A faint mumbling from the hall.

". . . More than mere *emblems* . . ."

"Hear! *Hear!*"

"More than mere *symbols* of peace . . ."

The approving murmur swelled and became an equivocal growling sound.

". . . We must actively demonstrate our power for peace. The nation — no, not just the nation . . ." Her head was flung bravely back. The eyes radiated beams as though she wore contact lenses. ". . . the world *itself* has need of us!"

Applause halted her progress. In front of Peter's stomach, Maggie's hands slowly banged together and stopped. The Prime Minister waited, the scarlet line of her lips trembling slightly, her eyes now fixed on a single point at the side of the hall. With laconic interest, Peter followed the line of her vision and decided she must be holding herself steady on the Stone Age wall chart suspended at the source of her gaze, a systematic array of flints and axe-heads.

The applause died away. There was a very long pause.

"We have . . ." Mrs. de Winter began again, her expression unaltered, "we have a responsibility in these troubled times . . ."

Everybody waited.

". . . A responsibility in these times," she said again. A tangible sense of unease communicated itself to Peter. He stared hard at the speaker who seemed to have lost her thread. There was a slight dart of pink across the scarlet lips. ". . . to express the qualities . . ."

Perhaps, Peter thought with interest, she is reading the words off the wall. But when he looked again he saw only the arrowheads and axes.

The man sitting beside Mrs. de Winter poured a glass of water and tactfully pushed it within her reach but she appeared not to notice.

"We have in these times . . ." she began again, and some of the women started coughing quietly, holding their programmes to their mouths.

"Oh Lord," he heard his mother whisper, as she shifted her thighs under him. "How embarrassing."

Tears were silently rolling down Mrs. de Winter's face, thin mercury channels gleaming in the spotlight. ". . . A *duty* . . ." The thin voice strained for control.

Sally Ferguson's profile was tensely aghast.

". . . As the wives and mothers . . ."

He felt the whole audience unite in an effort of will. He crunched his sweet abstractedly.

"Shut up," whispered Belinda, scowling at him.

". . . of this nation . . ."

Onward, the audience silently urged. A fresh thread of tears lowered itself over one of Mrs. de Winter's cheeks. ". . . to demonstrate that . . ." And quite suddenly, her pose altered. Her gaze flew away from the wall, back to her notes. The voice took on new purpose. ". . . that an attitude of uncomplaining self-sacrifice, habitual selflessness, a readiness to go without ourselves in order that others might, in the long term, prosper — that such an attitude is as positive a contribution in restoring health to our nation and our strength in the world as any adherence to political dogma . . ."

And she had recovered, won through the dreadful moment of collapse — only the merest acceleration of her delivery and a high insistence of pitch betrayed her.

"Oh dear," lamented Maggie lightly ten minutes later when the whole thing was over, "perhaps she *is* cracking up. Kit's forever saying so."

"Not at all," replied Sally firmly, lifting Belinda's plaits. "She just lost her place briefly. It must be awfully difficult. I couldn't begin to do it."

"Kit says it's the menopause."

"Men always say stupid things like that."

"Yes," said Maggie ruefully, "I suppose they do." And she seemed content to leave it at that as they shuffled out of the hall amidst a crowd of people who equally seemed to have overlooked the lapse. They chattered brightly as if nothing whatever had happened, though to Peter the hesitation felt as though it had occupied the major part of the evening. But then that was the only bit he'd bothered to listen to.

"She dried up," he said scornfully to Belinda. "Well, not dried up exactly, she was leaking blubber all over the place." He giggled feebly at his own joke.

"No, she was not," retorted Belinda sharply as they wound their way home under the dark trees. Where the trees parted, the sky was still unreally light in the blue, midsummer dusk. "You're just saying that. Making it up," she said and tossed her plaits.

Peter's mouth dropped open with incredulity. He was shocked. He stood quite still and then had to run to catch up with Belinda before she joined the older women.

"Hey!" he protested, his voice low. "I *saw* her."

"You must have very good eyesight."

"What are you two squabbling about?" Sally Ferguson rounded on them and Peter, sensing the pale lurking of a lioness, dropped back a step or two, away from the street lamp. He saw Belinda's shoulders rise and fall dismissively. "*He* says she was no good."

"Oh?" There was a combined tutting in the shadows.

"You couldn't have been listening properly," said Sally.

"She's all right," said Maggie. "She's all we've got, poor cow."

"Poor cow?" echoed Sally in a challenging sort of voice, then she and Maggie resumed their own private exchanges.

He told Kit that Mrs. de Winter had forgotten her words, and howled and been embarrassing for ages and ages.

"Told you!" his father cried over his head to Maggie.

"Rubbish!" she said, peering at her own reflection in the hall mirror. "For a couple of seconds she faltered a bit. That's all. He," she grinned, ruffling Peter's hair and destroying his parting, "was asleep most of the time so I don't know how he can judge. No. She was fine." She smiled it off, adding, so as not to antagonise, "She's not much of a speaker, let's face it. Competent probably, eloquent, no."

"Competent, my arse," grumbled Kit, and limped off to watch the news. He was still bickering mildly when he and Maggie came upstairs to kiss the boys goodnight. "Nothing to do with her being a woman," he was arguing. "It's her *ability* I'm questioning. She's just been chosen as a figurehead, an illusion of peace and unity. Bollocks."

"Shall you be fixing the knob tomorrow or shall I just order a new door?" murmured Maggie, banging Peter's pillow.

"I'm going to start painting in there tomorrow," he said.

"You haven't answered my question," she said sweetly.

"What?"

"Forget it," she said.

"I warn you," threatened Rod in the blue gloom of their bedroom (a stripe of gold was still visible in the darkening roof of the sky outside), "I really mean it, I warn you . . . if you don't let me *keep* that penknife I'll tell."

"Too late." Peter smiled into the sheets. He'd already removed his penknife from Rod's trouser pocket.

"What do you mean, too late?"

"It's too *late*. I've told."

"You've *told* . . .?" There was a long, wondering silence. Rod, momentarily, was stunned.

20

BUT NOT, OF COURSE, for long.

Early the following morning, waking to a babble of song in the leaves outside the window, Rod rose, dressed quietly, and rowed himself across the river to the far side.

"You didn't!" Peter denied him. "You did *not*!" He lay in bed and kicked his bedclothes into a knot.

But Rod simply whistled tunelessly and re-did the laces of his plimsolls one by one.

"What's it to you?" he ventured coolly at length while Peter turned, face down, and struck his pillow several times. "We'll both go shooting."

For some reason his remark increased Peter's acrimony. "I don't believe you," he blared into the chocolate-stained pillow, recalling other, earlier deceits of Rod's.

"Don't then," replied Rod, "I don't care." And he pulled his swimming trunks off the window sill to see if they were dry. His imperturbability suggested he was not lying. Or that he was very, very good indeed at lying. "You're a liar," said Peter wearily, without any real conviction.

"Oh, fiddle." His brother shrugged and went off to find a towel.

Up the road the drills began and the rest of the household flew from its beds as though a siren had sounded. Boards thumped, springs whanged, chains were flushed and doors slammed. Peter went downstairs, tried to pour himself a glass of orange from a gallon flagon, spilt some and, bending to search for a floorcloth under the sink, discovered a dead rat, neatly hooped, its tail a most elegant pinkish hook. Involuntarily, he leapt backwards and then, very cautiously stretching out his right thumb and forefinger, pulled it a little by its stiff tail, remembering that once, when he'd caught a live mouse by its tail, the tail had come away in his hand.

The corpse moved easily in one piece. The sharky mouth revealed small, sharp teeth, the whiskers were spruce as a new toothbrush. He picked it up and put it on Rod's chair.

Rod took for ever to sit down. "Must we have Wheatinuts all the time?" he complained, looking in the larder.

"It's GOOD for you," cooed Maggie, less hurried this morning. "Anyway, the new packets have got jokes in."

"So it has," he said, examining the box. "Good-o."

"It's my turn for the thing inside."

"I fetched it."

"Share it, for God's sake. Or shall I just tear the bloody thing in half?" snapped Maggie.

"Ah-h—ee-ee-ee!"

"*Christ!*"

Kit pelted downstairs one foot heavier than the other.

"Get it *out* of here!" Maggie had pointlessly, but classically, leapt on to a chair.

"What the hell . . .?" peered Kit. ". . . Oh, my God!"

"*He* put it there! *He* did!" Rod bawled furiously, and as he bent to pick up the rat, Kit seized his arm. "Don't you dare throw it," he yelled.

"I wasn't going to. I was going to pick it up. Mummy said."

"You were going to throw it," asserted Peter, seizing his opportunity.

"Oh, get the bloody thing out. What did you have to do that for?" Maggie descended from her chair.

Peter said nothing but tried, and failed, to snatch the cereal packet first.

"*Why?*"

"Why what?"

"You heard?"

"He's jealous."

"Jealous? Why?" demanded Maggie. "What for?"

"I'm not."

"He is."

"Shut UP!" Kit carried the rat outside the back door at arm's length. As he opened the door the sounds of the drills bellied in at them as though a large wild animal were crouching out there behind the dustbins.

"Why are you jealous this time?"

"What?" said Peter.

"I rowed across the river on my own," Rod explained.

"Did you?" Kit, returning, was impressed. "Did you honestly?"

"*Honestly.*"

"Well done, Rod," said Kit, gripping his younger son's shoulder in congratulation.

"They've got the same amount in. It's just the glasses are different sizes." Maggie put the boys' milk down on the table.

"I suppose I'll *have* to take you shooting now."

"Oh *no*!"

"I promised." Kit regarded his wife mildly. Hair fell over her harassed face.

"Yes *please*," said Rod, opening the jokes book.

"Oh bugger, bugger, bugger." Maggie sat down hard and buried her forehead in her hands. "There's quite enough fighting and sniping already. Why encourage it?"

"We're not fighting. It's a very disciplined sport."

"Can I have the rifle, Dad?"

"I *hate* it."

"Oh, don't be so wet. Much better for them to learn to handle the real thing. They won't be so casual and slaphappy about guns then."

"When can we go?" asked Peter nervously, avoiding his mother's eye.

"I *hate* it!" she shrieked louder than ever.

"Why did the man throw a clock through the window?" said Rod.

"Why did he?" responded Kit happily.

"He wanted to see time fly."

"And now *rats* . . .!" moaned Maggie from between clenched fists.

"I tell you what, you can eat whatever we shoot, that should make you feel a whole lot better."

"Who always sleeps with their shoes on?"

"A tramp," suggested Peter.

"No, stupid," Rod gave his brother a shrivelling look.

"Let me have it next."

"Go on, who goes to bed with their shoes on?"

"I don't know. Let *me* have it."

"A horse you dumb-dumb." And Rod wheeled his body away lifting the book beyond Peter's grasp.

"I shall move in here today." Kit gazed round at the yellowed kitchen. "Can you cook in the other kitchen?"

"I can cook, but we can't eat in there. I'll have to carry all our food into the sitting room," said Maggie resignedly.

"What does a seven foot butcher weigh?"

"Oh, shut up."

"Go on, guess."

"I don't know," fulminated Peter, impotent with rage.

"Meat, dafty."

"Well, it won't be for long," soothed Kit above the uproar. "We could clear it out together this morning."

"You can clear it out. I'm clearing out."

"Where are you going?" Kit asked of his wife as she barged out of the room. The door swung to behind her and she had to knock to be let back in. She seized her coffee mug, her features marble hard. "I wish we'd never bought you that damned boat," she said, not looking at anybody, "it just multiplies the occasion for argument by a factor of ten." She reached the door for the second time. "*And* you haven't even thought of a name for the sodding thing yet."

"We'll have to call it after you," Kit called to her retreating back. "Mad Maggie."

She was waiting for them outside school in the old Morris.

"There's Mummy!" cried Rod, pleased and ran across the road waving. Peter trailed after him, his mouth elaborately expressing nothing.

She was happy and mysterious, like a corked vessel. Something was making her gay again. "I'm going to the cottage tomorrow," she said, and Peter thought that must be the cause of her pleasure. Rod was so busy talking, he didn't have a chance to tell her his good news.

"Cheer up," she said to him, aside, listening to Rod's chatter.

Belinda was helping Kit sandpaper the kitchen walls.

"Daddy says," she informed them, rubbing vigorously, "that you can't have any honey yet . . ."

Kit, seeing his wife's luminosity, stopped.

". . . he took out the combs in a frame, put it down for ten minutes in the potting shed, and . . ." Belinda, oblivious, carried on.

"What is it?" asked Kit softly, his own face alert and light.

". . . the bees came and stole it all back again."

"*Did* they?" hooted Rod. "They look just like burglars in their striped sweaters."

"Good news!" said Maggie, almost laughing with relish.

"Yes? Tell me yours first."

"You too?"

"Yes." And then she did laugh out loud. They embraced happily.

"I've been offered a part. A proper one. Well, a small one. It's only . . . what's the matter?"

"Go on," he nodded.

She searched his face.

"How did they . . . ?" began Peter but Belinda shushed him. She was watching the adults.

A small curling of doubt had begun to work on Maggie's mouth. She spoke in a more ordinary tone. ". . . only a little travelling, mostly in the London area . . . to schools, pubs, clubs, that sort of thing. The Actor's Bus Company . . . they have a reputation." Her sentences had become lame. "Aren't you pleased?" she ended.

Peter, looking for the breadbin which had been moved into the adjoining scullery, found it, took out a loose crust and saw, beyond his father's broad, still back, Maggie's draining eyes.

"How ironic," Kit was saying. "That doubles the size of the celebration we must have."

"You?"

"Yes!" And flinging his arms around his wife, Kit hugged her, lifting her briefly from the floor. "Chief sub-editor . . ."

"Afternoon and evening shifts?"

"Yes."

"Have you got a job?" enquired Belinda.

"That's right."

"Oh." She thought about it with interest but said nothing. The boys wanted to know exactly what the job was, where he would have to go, how often and what he would be paid.

"Will we be rich again?" asked Rod.

"Rich no. But the bank manager might be more polite. All we need now is to sell that cottage somehow." He turned again to Maggie, his delight obliterating the blank moon of her face.

"Oh Kit," she murmured, flowing into him. "I'm so glad for you, so *glad* . . ." Her voice ended on a broken, upward breath.

"And *you*!" he reciprocated, "I'm glad for you too."

"Oh well," she shrugged and turning away from him, began to unload her shopping.

"What do you mean, 'oh well'?"

"Oh *well.*"

"You don't think . . ."

"Out of the question," she said. "The timings would clash."

"No . . ."

"Impossible," she declared without emphasis.

"Will we be able to have another car?" Peter asked, wrestling the stale crust between his teeth, but his parents were absorbed in one another, each trying to overcome an agonised inability to stare the other in the face.

"We could have a mother's help or something," Kit tried, hands not quite touching his wife's now busily moving form. "An au pair."

"In this house? In this state? Who'd come?"

"I've got the time to put it right. The job doesn't start till September."

"Neither does mine," she mused ironically, adding, "No, if we were both nine to five, or just one of us was, it would be different."

"Why make difficulties? We could afford some help . . . *will* be able to? People are desperate for jobs now, they don't judge a job by its decor. Truly, Mags, we *could* afford it."

"With our debts?"

"I don't want a mother's help," interrupted Rod and Belinda grimaced sympathetically.

"Ugh! A horrible *nanny,*" she said. "Rice pudding and smacked bottoms."

"Nonsense," Kit persisted without conviction.

"The children come first," said Maggie, putting things away in the cupboard.

"They're not babies," Kit said.

"No, we're not babies," confirmed Rod. "And I don't want a nanny, thank you."

Kit tried again, more desperately. "What makes you think that you're best for them? Or that I am?"

Maggie didn't answer. She was tying her painting apron on.

"On the whole they might have a nicer time with someone else."

"Meaning I'm awful at it?" she said.

"Not just you. Me too. We've become very short-tempered recently. They don't get much out of us."

Peter shrank from the conversation. I can't bear them talking like this about us, he thought, the bread turning sticky in his mouth. He couldn't swallow it.

"It might be the best possible thing for them," Kit was saying.

"I *know* I'm awful!" Maggie's tense control cracked. She reached for and clung to Kit. "But I want to try. I want them to be able to cope with the world as it is. I want them secure and complete and I *know* I'm making a broken egg of it, I *know* that . . .!" Her nails dug into Kit's arm as she clutched him and wept. Peter watched her coldly, the safety of ice asserting itself. She was gabbling.

". . . But I want, oh, I want . . . I *must* try. And sometimes I bring the world indoors, it sticks to me . . . I just make it worse . . .!"

She was getting silly and hysterical. "Shall we go and play in your house?" Peter said to Belinda, but she shook her head, too consumed by interest to leave.

Suddenly Rod grabbed at his mother. "You're a lovely mummy!" he protested. "You're the best!"

Peter was nauseated by his brother's flattery, though he too would have liked to stem the terrible weeping. . . . I don't know how, he thought. I don't know what to do. Rod was drawn into the tangle of figures, they clung together in weak, mutual solace.

"We're going to go shooting later," Peter informed Belinda whose pale eyebrows met in a continuous blonde track above her frowning eyes. "But you can't come," he added quickly, "there aren't enough guns."

"I wouldn't want to."

"This won't do," Kit was saying, easing himself away from the splintered stack of love and hurt. "The boys."

Maggie stepped away from him, head lowered to conceal her grief. "I'll make your tea," she whispered.

"Can we have chips?" said Rod.

"Yes, darling."

"Can we have it in front of the telly? It *is Tomorrow's World*." As though the seriousness of the programme justified his request.

"Yes, darling."

"Will you take us shooting after?" It was Peter's turn to press the advantage. His mother crushed a howl down beneath the heel of her hand.

"We'll see," said Kit looking at his wife anxiously.

"You *promised*."

"We'll see," conceded Kit, guiltily.

He took them. But they shot at nothing. "There are too many people around still," he explained. "We'll have to come very early in the morning."

"How early?"

"About four."

"Will you get up at four tomorrow?"

"Oh Lord," Kit said, "I don't know about that."

Peter was about to grumble but, wading through the silvery-lilac feathering of the grasses, he suddenly remembered his own good news. "My project," he said proudly, "was the best."

"Now that *is* good news!" Adjusting his rifle to the other shoulder, Kit joyfully folded his right arm around his son. "I thought it was good," he said, "I'm glad they did too."

Peter glowed. It was nice being out here in this pink, sinking evening with his father. Even the unused shotgun felt good to hold. The pigeons, unaware of their escape, bumbled noisily in the branches of the few elm trees that still lived. Those which were diseased and dying stood like skeletons of winter in the rounded, summer landscape.

Kit rowed them back across the brown river. The boys sat either end, dreaming and happy.

"You *will* have to think of a name," urged Kit, looking behind him to make sure his crossing was clear.

"Will you tell us about the war, Daddy?" Rod caught at his father's amiability. A flock of gulls coming inland, settled on the Sweetings bank. Kit smiled ruefully.

"I don't much want to," he said.

"Why not? I want to know."

So did Peter. He wanted to know the truth. An old sore of anxiety troubled him suddenly.

"It's a funny thing," murmured Kit, "but my father wouldn't talk about the war either. He was a prisoner in Changi."

"What's that got to do with it?" asked Rod petulantly.

Kit rested his oars for a moment and watched the water dripping from them. "The ones who say they had a good war," he said thoughtfully, "they're the ones to ask. They don't mind talking about it."

"But *why*?" Rod wouldn't let go. Peter, who sat facing Kit's back, saw its sad and drooping aspect. Slowly his father's arms resumed their movement, and the thick folds, which had sunk above his waist during this past inactive year revealed themselves as relics of defeat. "Once you've seen the real thing . . ." Kit was saying.

"Like those photographs?"

"*Like* those photographs, yes. But not so well composed."

"I can't stand it!"

The mug crashed against the television screen and broke. Coffee dregs dribbled over the intact image of drawn faces, clamouring hands. A woman tore at her long, black hair, maddened by grief.

Maggie was on her feet, screaming. "I can't *stand* it!" One hand gripped her forehead as though it contained a wicked pain. "Sitting here, sitting, watching . . .!"

"Take it easy." Kit rose and went to switch the news off just as the commercial break started. A serene and pearly Maggie turned to face him on the screen. Runnels of coffee trickled over the smiling image.

"Oh Jesus!" Maggie flung herself into the depths of the armchair, her sobbing made wild by laughter. "The conjunction of things!"

The children sighed. She was at it again.

"I'm mad and bad and dangerous!" she screeched, curled small in the chair as though by making herself smaller and smaller, she could escape something.

"If you want to make a catalogue of sin," remarked Kit testily, staring down at her, "you might add that you're guilty of exaggeration."

His demeanour was reassuring to the boys. She *was* being ridiculous, and Rod at least felt no compunction about continuing to watch television. Peter tried to share his absorption but couldn't help being aware of his parents. There seemed to be an invisible obstruction between them.

"Maggie darling . . ." Kit was trying to scoop her out of the chair, but the small sharp rocks of her spine, visible through the clinging brown fabric of her dress, tightened against him.

He left her until she was quite exhausted and then he tried to gather the boys up for bed. Crossly, Rod detached himself from the television. As Peter passed his mother, she muttered into a cushion, that she would come up in a moment. She had gone very limp as though someone had knocked her senseless.

When she came into their bedroom, she was calm. Only the heaviness and the swelling of her eyes betrayed her. Kneeling beside Peter, she cupped his face in her hands and kissed the tip of his nose. "So your project was best? Why didn't you tell me?"

He couldn't think what to say.

"You worked hard at it. It's right that it should be the best." For a few seconds she remained looking down at him in a vague, preoccupied fashion. It made Peter wriggle a little having her staring like that.

"Forgive me," she said at length and grinned wearily, "if you can. I do get angry, I don't mean to. I don't want to. All I want is for you to be happy." Her eyes welled up alarmingly, but she controlled herself and shifted her weight on to the other knee. "I'd like to take away all the things that make you unhappy," she said. "Just wipe all the obstacles out of the way. But it's hard." And with a crooked smile, she kissed him again, more lingeringly, on the cheek.

Still he felt himself unable to say anything. Her unhappiness entered him like the water that flooded the lock. *Try to please her*, his father had said. *Try to understand*. He couldn't understand, but he wanted to relieve her of the ache she suffered for them.

"I love you," she murmured in his ear and he knew then that it was true. That behind all the thorns, the tangle of stems, the weird black fruits, there was love of a kind it was hard to reach out and touch. His arms tightened around her neck, dragging her down to him fiercely.

They clung together, their inexpressible passion hard. "It's all *right*, Mum," came Rod's laconic voice, "you don't have to worry."

And she sprang, released, out of Peter's grip, a painful laughter confusing her face. "Thank you, my darlings, thank you for . . . for being . . ." And she stood uncertainly, gathering herself. "Tomorrow," she said suddenly, "I'm going to the cottage. I'm going to sort it all out." And then turning, one hand on the light switch, she gave them a last, blown kiss. "Forgive me," she said, mortified. "Forgive me."

21

SHE WAS AWAY for two days.

The house eased. Kit whistled ceaselessly as he sandpapered the yellow kitchen to a lighter, pinkish shade that took away the pallor of decay.

On the morning after she'd left, he had risen at half past four and had taken them shooting, having cleaned the guns himself the night before. The air had been cold and fresh. Fine sheets of gossamer were still drawn over grass and hedgerow, the river lay still beneath the yellow webs of willow. Stealthily they had prowled alongside the hedges, starting up the birds. Kit had shot a brace of pigeons, the boys nothing, but they hadn't minded. Their trousers soaked with icy dew, they had felt warm and exhilarated inside, excited by the sharp crack of the rifle in the still air, by the sudden flap and tumble of wings, by the shocked silence of birds.

They were together; there was no argument.

"Why did you laugh at that old man in the haunted house?" Peter had asked his father as they'd rowed back home. He'd held the pigeons, dangling by their legs.

"Old man . . .? Haunted house . . .?" Kit had struggled to remember.

"*You* know . . ." And Peter had explained. The old man, not unlike a large, ginger pigeon himself, with his pouting figure and skinny legs . . . "*You* remember . . ."

"Oh, yes . . .!" And his father, thinking of him, had laughed again.

"Why did you?"

"I admired him. He'd overcome his disability so royally. He'd become just like everyone else."

"What do you mean?"

"He'd acquired the means of hearing just like anyone else and then behaved just like anyone else, by refusing to listen. But he did it with . . . *majesty*."

"I don't really understand!"

"You will," Kit had grinned, pulling strongly on the oars.

She was there when they came home from school on the second day.

(She had seen them from the massy bay windows of the front sitting room where she'd gone to wait for a glimpse of them, pretending to clean the windows until they made their running, punching, wrestling approach down Wellington Gardens.)

From as far away as the front gate Peter noticed that her face was altered. She stood in the porch waiting, her face as sweet and still as a woodland pool.

"Darlings!" She hugged each of them. She smelt faintly of newly-cut hay.

"Were they haymaking?" asked Peter, surprised by the picture he suddenly had of the village, of the farmers, each man out on his hillside, a small buzzing insect turning the green to gold.

"They were, yes." She thrust one arm through his, the other through Rod's, and bore them indoors. "I have something for you," she smiled and led them into the other sitting room, the one with the tiny conservatory opening off it.

Something swooped in their chests.

"*What?*"

"What is it?"

Smiling still, her closed lips barely able to contain her delight, she opened the conservatory door. "Hymie!" she called.

"*Oh!*"

A clumsy, feathery, wet-nosed, corn-coloured object hurtled at them uttering ecstatic, disbelieving yelps.

"Hymie!"

"Oh, *Hymie!*"

He bounded all over them. He knocked them to the floor, then licked their faces desperately, frenzied by his inability to lick them both at once. The magnificent blond plume of his tail beat back and forth scattering papers and plastic soldiers about the room while his joy was expressed in short, breathless yaps.

In between his hurried rediscoveries of their faces, he turned to look up at Maggie as if, both grateful and unsure his bliss would last, he needed to check with her that all was well.

"Can he stay?"

"He must. He's been pining, Sam said." (The dog had visited the cottage every day and lain in the wild, neglected garden until they'd called him for his dinner, Sam had said.)

When the dog had come racing towards her, body flattened by his speed, tail still awkwardly bent a little to one side, his delight had made tears sheet her face.

"Oh thank you, thank you!" sobbed Rod, unable to stop his own happy weeping. And Peter, silently, clasped the dog, burying his face in the barnyard smell of his coat.

"You're the *perfect* dog!" cried Rod.

Hymie *was* the perfect dog. He possessed perfect love. A curling, spuming cross between collie and labrador, he was one of the dogs of childhood. Best of all, he loved Maggie. He was protective of her, obedient to Kit and playful with the children. His love was so consuming, he sometimes suffered terrible divisions of loyalty when the different members of the family asserted themselves as individuals. If the boys ran from the house to play, he would creep after them, slinking back guiltily if Maggie called him. If she were to raise her voice at the children, he would snarl uncertainly. But though he would snap at whichever of the boys he felt had started a squabble, he never let his teeth so much as graze an arm, because worse, far worse, than a squabble was his fear of being excluded from their game.

"Don't get him too worked up," Maggie warned now, as the dog, half-leaping, hesitated and bared his teeth with anxiety. Although they no longer teased him, he hadn't lost that ancient trace of bewilderment he displayed whenever he found it hard to distinguish between fight and play.

"Oh, Hymie! Hymie!" wailed Rod, in love, his arms around the dog's neck.

Kit, coming in to discover what all the noise was about, found a seething muddle of creatures on the floor and, seeing their rapture, smiled.

"Pleased?" Maggie murmured to the boys, her own pleasure as bright as a lamp.

"*Pleased?* I'm, I'm . . . *exaltipated!*"

"Of course I'm pleased . . ." cried Peter.

"We can train him to be our gun dog," said Rod.

When Keith Ferguson knocked and put his head around the back door, Hymie barked deep and furiously. The head wavered, then, with challenging boldness, remained exactly where it was. "Yours?"

"Yes." Maggie held the dog by his collar. She explained.

"He's certainly decided the place is his!" cried Keith with serrated jocularity.

"Yes."

Hymie had spent half an hour padding around the house, sniffing perplexedly, unable to define the precise change in atmosphere. He scented and considered, returning his nose more than once to particular corners, particular objects. There was, his detection suggested, a difference, although after careful examination, he came to a conclusion of tenancy. A tenancy he clearly believed he shared.

"There's a nice fellow," said Keith. "All right if I pick off the swarm?"

"Have they done it again?"

"Afraid so."

And she went to the window to glimpse the small clustering of bees. They shimmered, dull bronze among the thirsty leaves. She marvelled aloud at the way bees returned to the same spot.

Keith had not, this time, bothered with any protective clothing. His shaking was firm and swift, his collection casual. The task completed, he broke off his salute of thanks to rub at his left wrist. Maggie opened the window and called out, "Can I put anything on it for you?"

"Good Lord no. No, it's nothing at all." He was mildly disconcerted that she'd noticed. "I'll have that honey for you soon, I promise. Perhaps you'd like to see the extractor at work, when it's ready?"

"Of course," Maggie cried, giving Peter, who stood beside her, a secretive, sidelong smile. "Love to."

"Can we take Hymie for a walk?" interrupted Peter.

Maggie waved in a leavetaking fashion through the window and said, "Yes, let's. There are lots of things I should like to tell Mr. Turville." And when Kit, who was sandpapering the far wall, gave her a comically enlarged look of suspicion, she tossed her hair and grinned. "We two mad old drop-outs can gas away for hours."

"Drop-out?" he echoed, in a querying tone as though he expected her to explain herself better.

But she just edged past him, laughing breathlessly.

Hymie wouldn't let them fight. When they rolled on the prickly brown grass, kicking, he pounced on them, trampling them apart under his rough, dry pads.

Mr. Turville thought him a fine dog. He gave him the fat off his ham and talked at length of a spaniel he'd once had that had been run over. "You want to take care," he advised in his soft voice. And, asking them to wait a minute, disappeared into his Ark returning with a lead that had been hanging on a hook for five years. "There," he said, his sky-pale eyes very still. "You don't want to lose him."

They took Hymie in the boat and he stood, uncertainly at first, his tongue hanging out as he watched the wilful curling of currents. Then, satisfied, he lay down quietly in the bottom of the boat, head resting on his paws, eyes fixed on Maggie.

They threw sticks for him and he bounded eagerly through thistle and nettle to fetch them. Then they threw a stick a little way out in the water and he plunged in, swimming to it, grasping it, turning slowly, his head held stiffly out of the water. Only when the stick was safely delivered did he shake himself violently, soaking the boys and making them squeal.

I'm so happy, thought Peter, hugging the wet beloved animal, who now smelt of algae. "Can he sleep outside our room?" he asked, thinking that all the granite shadows would be sucked out of the night by Hymie's warm, solid presence.

"He'll never make a gun dog!"

Kit gasped with mirth and leant back against a tree trunk, studying the dark, crushed path Hymie had made through the grasses as he'd raced ahead of them pursuing pigeons. The upwards flutterings he caused delighted him.

"We'll *train* him," persisted Rod. And gruffly lowering his voice, he shouted, "Here boy, here! *Stay*, dog." Hymie, lifting his head at the sound, laughed and wagged his tail more furiously than ever.

His happiness irradiated all their succeeding days.

Maggie was leaving to do a new commercial. "Another perfect wife and mother part," she grinned, when Rod asked her what it was for. "Detergent this time. *God*, how I digest my principles!" It was the first day in over a week she'd had to rush off early. Kit stopped her flight to take her in his arms and gathered her to him in a long, close embrace until Hymie yelped and whined, pushing his head between their legs. They were compelled to break off their own loving and caress him instead. "Silly creature," Maggie said fondly.

"Only one more day of term!" sang Rod eating round the

melty centre of his toast. "Whoopee!" And the moment his mother left the room, he began reading a comic at the table which had, for the time being, been brought into the sitting room.

"You shouldn't do that," rebuked Peter without real reproach.

"Why not? *He* does." Rod nodded at his father. "Old behind-the-Times."

Peter said nothing more. He didn't really feel cross. Term was ending, Hymie was here, his project had been entered for a national competition. Even having breakfast in here had helped loosen the knot in his stomach because he didn't worry so much about mouse droppings in the food. As he thought about it, he realised that something else had happened, some change, some lightness in the house, and his mind moved wonderingly over all the changes searching out the key alteration. I can row well, he thought. And the exams are over.

But that wasn't it.

Perhaps it was the cheerful whistling that filled the house as his father worked. Or his willingness to go out with them when they demanded he should, instead of making excuses to stay indoors. That's it, he thought. My father is better. And he looked at him. Or what could be seen of him behind the newspaper.

"Crikey!" Peter deciphered the headlines on the page that faced him. "The Prime Minister's been murdered!"

"*What!*" Noisily Kit rustled back to the relevant page to see what he'd missed. Then he gave a shout of amusement. "Not exactly," he said. Under a large picture of Mrs. de Winter, speaking, one arm upraised in that curious ambiguity of aggression and defence, it read: 'NIGHT OF THE LONG KNIVES.'

"It was a pretty shrewd remark though," his father acknowledged, pushing his glasses up his nose. "We'll certainly have to see what happens next . . ." And he embarked on a helpful account of the political scene which interested neither of the boys and was cut abruptly short when Kit noticed the time.

"Quick!" he urged. "Or you'll miss that bus."

The scraping of his chair, the crackling of newspaper, the agitated barking of the dog momentarily alerted all the other little panics. Peter forcibly removed his tie from Rod's neck and hurriedly stuffed his books in his briefcase. Will he make us row to school tomorrow, he wondered, full of worry. It *was* the last day. Will Dad make us? And he slipped out of the house as fast as he could before the idea occurred to Kit.

But halfway along Wellington Gardens, Peter had to turn round and go home again with Hymie who had wriggled out of the front window and chased them up the street. Rod and Peter quarrelled over who should take the dog back, but when Rod said, "It doesn't matter, no-one's going to give you a black mark on nearly the last day," Peter sulkily gave in.

As he slammed the front door behind him for the last time, he heard the dog whining in the hall.

22

THE BEST THING about Hymie was that he frightened Belinda. When he'd jumped up at her in welcome she had screamed, bunching up against the wall, arms beating him down. Her terror had amazed the boys.

"He's only a dog," Rod had said scornfully. But she, seeing teeth, a wet tongue and large abrasive paws on her dress, had continued screaming quite hysterically. She had stopped coming round to play.

It quite compensated for the rain that assiduously poured down throughout the first week of the holidays. The boys didn't mind. They fought in a pleasant, dilatory fashion, a threesome tangle that included the dog. He made them giggle. And apart from the one day when Kit took them out to the Air Museum and they clambered into the cockpit of a bomber aeroplane examining the controls, they were left unbothered to watch as much television as they liked. Their father, Rod observed, was only too glad for them to leave him in peace as he busied himself cheerfully with the decorating. His whistling, an erratic medley of Fifties' musicals, trickled through the house, stopping only for the news bulletins which he noted with an almost religious observance. "Got to get myself clued up again," he said earnestly.

There was a kind of peace. Even the rain, streaming steadily across the glass while they played Monopoly or stuck their models together, seemed to contribute to it. Maggie, when she came home, was subdued, but pleasant. Almost, thought Peter, searching for the right word . . . almost *polite*. As if she had surrendered. Peter thought it was something to do with Hymie's being there. She loved the dog deeply. Every evening, after tea, she took him out on her own in the rain, trudging through the wet, deserted park beside a swollen and putty coloured river, calling occasionally on Mr. Turville, who made, she claimed, the best coffee she'd ever tasted. His Ark, she said, was full of small bright songbirds that flew freely about. He had an invalid wife who lay, white, in a cot bed all day.

She came back soaking, filled with a sweet lassitude, a dreaming form of tiredness that seemed to exclude any acerbic outbursts. All that disturbed her was the dank burgeoning of the house's odour which was worsened by the heavy rainfall. That made her hunt round the house, sniffing out its source. "It must be the drains," she muttered, going from one plug hole to the next. But until there was a substantial sum of money to spare, nothing could be done.

"When it stops raining . . ." Kit murmured, applying the white, satin-finish paint.

"When it stops raining," said Rod, "we can go shooting again. I haven't shot anything yet."

They woke one Wednesday morning to a blaze of heat, to a boiled and glaring light that made Peter feel, when he opened his bedroom window, as though steam were rising out of the earth and pavements. He smelt a warm, strong fragrance of honeysuckle from the climbing plant that smothered the Fergusons' façade across the road.

All the leaves were polished green again. They glistened. Weeds had rioted in front gardens the length of Wellington Gardens.

"It's stopped!" he cried to Rod, who blinked sleepily from his bed. "We can take Hymie exploring."

Maggie was downstairs in the sitting room, looking out with pleasure at the bright morning. She flung open the conservatory doors to let the sunshine in. "Perhaps the smell will go now," she said, breathing in deeply.

"It's all mixed up with the paint smell now," said Rod.

Hymie tore past them into the garden, cannoning into Maggie's legs. "Good Lord!" she cried, alerted by his eagerness. "Your rabbits have made a burrow under the wire!"

"What?" shrieked Peter, and he ran outside in his pyjamas. He found Chrysanthemum immediately. Her white scut protruded from beneath the fall of pampas grass. Trying to grab her, he cut his hand on the sharp leaves, but bravely he hung on. Hymie, straining against Maggie's grip, barked with excitement. Poppy was nowhere to be seen.

"Hymie will find her. *Him*," said Maggie. "Let him out when you've had your breakfast."

"It'll be too late," he wailed. "Hymie'll eat my rabbit."

"No it won't. No he won't. She won't have gone far. *He* won't. He'll be eating his head off somewhere."

She was so confident, he succumbed, glancing anxiously through the open doors as he ate.

"I'll fill the hole they've made with stones," offered Kit.

"Pardon?" (A plane cruised overhead.)

Kit repeated himself.

Maggie, raising her voice, said, "They'll only try again now they've got the idea. The run's a wash-out really. Anyway, Hymie needs the space."

"Perhaps they'd *like* to be freed," said Rod. "We could take them over to the other bank and release them."

"Or shoot them," remarked Maggie with a touch of derision.

"No!" exclaimed Peter, though the idea of releasing them had some appeal. He wouldn't have to feed them any more and the truth was, his rabbits bored him rather. They were a bit of a nuisance.

"Why not?" Rod demurred, but the topic was stifled by an exclamation from his father.

"They've put in an offer!" he cried, eyes hastily scanning a letter. "Not bad. We only lose about a third of what we paid, and these days . . ." He looked up, delighted. "Give us a smile!" he exhorted, seeing Maggie's sealed expression. "They won't be sending me to Newgate."

She said nothing, reaching out for the rest of the post, seeing what was for her.

"It's something *definite*," Kit tried again, determined to have a positive response from his wife. "It means you won't have to worry about your part in keeping up the family finance."

"I don't," she answered shortly.

"Of course you do," he claimed, his voice teasing. She tore open a long brown envelope and began reading.

"We'll get rid of the pong," said Rod. "Thank goodness. I can smell it all day. All mixed with paint. I can taste it, it puts me off eating, it smells like . . ."

"Don't feed the dog at the table," rebuked Kit as Peter gave his crust to Hymie.

Maggie, looking up, waving the report, cried, "Peter's got a Beta Plus!" She stretched for his hand and squeezed it exuberantly. "You've got a Beta *Plus* darling! Oh, you must have

229

tried so hard, that's *terrific* . . ." She released his hand, ran round the table and smothered him to her. There was a smear of marmalade on her cheek. Although he could think of nothing to say, he was very proud. He smiled against her warm body. It was a good grade. (They didn't give form places at Hill House but he knew that there would be furtive comparisons next term until each boy knew roughly what his positioning was.

Maggie broke away from him and began reading out the various teachers' remarks.

"What about me?" said Rod. Kit took the other fold of paper and looked on his behalf. The bill was discreetly tucked inside. "Ah!" Kit rubbed it between his fingers.

"Yours or mine?"

"I'll take it." Maggie held out a hand and carried on reading. "Latin. Has tried really hard in first term's work on this subject . . . English. An excellent effort."

"What about *me*?"

"History." Maggie continued. "Is probably the best pupil in his class."

Peter's heart expanded. It felt as warm and round as a teapot.

"Rod's got an Alpha Minus," said Kit expressionlessly.

"Have I? *Really?* Let's look."

"That's very good, Rod." Maggie sounded grave.

The swelling of pleasure in Peter's chest broke suddenly. "Oh well, it's easy stuff in his class," he said. "Baby stuff."

"It's not. That's not true. I've got the same maths book as you!" Rod's face was a challenging scarlet.

"It's been harder for Peter. A Beta Plus for him is the same as an Alpha Minus for you."

Rod rounded on his mother indignantly. "It's *not*!" He was was not to be robbed of his honour.

"You've *both* done very well," Kit intervened, "I'm extremely pleased with *both* of you."

"An Alpha Minus!" marvelled Rod.

"Anyway," insisted Maggie, "it isn't the mark that's important. It's the effort you've put into it over the term that counts. That's what I'm so delighted about."

"You *used* to say," Peter remarked bitterly, "that it didn't matter what we got as long as we were happy at school."

"An *Alpha Minus* . . .!"

"Oh shut up!" screamed Peter. "And I'm *not* happy at school, I'm *not*!"

"I think you both deserve something."

Rod's attention turned. "Oh *good*," he said, "I'd like a camera."

"Well, *something* . . ." Kit qualified.

"Another Action Man outfit?"

"Perhaps."

"Oh, *don't* cry, Peter!"

It was so cruel. He let himself again be pressed to his mother's nightdress, to the loose breasts beneath. It isn't fair, he wept silently, it isn't fair. It is always like this. Always *him*.

"Come on now . . ." And she cuddled him gently.

"You should be very pleased with yourself Peter," he heard his father say. And he had been but he couldn't be now. It was spoilt.

"It's horrible being an older brother," comforted Maggie.

"How do *you* know!" He leant his head back, away from her, eyes tight closed and howled: "*You* don't know what it's like! *You* don't understand!"

She gathered him to her more tightly, but he resisted, trying to struggle free. A jet made a sudden ripping sound in the sky outside, as though it had come down vertically, a blade tearing through the fabric of the atmosphere.

"I want you to be *happy*!" she was saying dimly, and he wondered at the constant, feeble repetition of her desire, wondered whether his father had ever told her what he'd said about wanting to be a boarder. And he felt a heavy longing to hurt her. "*You* don't understand," he said again cruelly. "What did you send us there for in the first place?" It had been her idea, he knew that.

"I wanted you to be . . ."

Don't say it again, he shrieked inwardly and covered his ears. "It's a horrible school! I hate it!"

She let him go at last. She was looking forlornly at Kit.

"You don't really hate it," said Kit quietly. "I know the work's harder but it's not a horrible school. Your mother," he ended lamely, "was only trying to do the best thing for you."

A fresh burst of frustrated weeping assailed Peter.

Kit, as if realising his last remark had been a subtle little treachery, tried to recover himself by commenting, "And I think she's been proved right. You've both come on a good deal."

"There's no competition between the two of you anyway," Maggie put in. "That's not what they're judging. It's you in relation to the other boys in your class."

"All the same," smiled Rod, wiggling his eyebrows, "*Alpha Minus*."

"Oh shut up, you complacent little worm." Maggie's restraint ended. "Stop gloating. Go away and gloat somewhere else."

"No," said Rod, his natural confidence reinforced. He knew they couldn't send an Alpha Minus out of the room.

"Go and start looking for Peter's rabbit."

"It's his, not mine." He was aggrieved too.

"Get out! Get out! Get out!"

She was on her feet now, her face laterised by fury.

"Keep your hair on," murmured Rod, going.

"That's hardly fair . . ." remarked Kit to his wife.

"*You?* You bastard . . .!"

"Me?" He was genuinely puzzled. He couldn't think what he'd done and Maggie was in no state to tell him. She fought with her own wild anger, standing white and clenched over the table, silently bidding her demons down.

Rod came back into the room. "I hadn't finished my breakfast," he pointed out with some injury. His mother remained as she was, eyes closed over an apparent pain.

"Get on with it quietly," whispered Kit. "And I tell you what, tomorrow morning I'll take you shooting until you bag something. O.K.?"

"Great!" Rod attacked his mush of cereal with relish.

"Will you?" Peter's suffering retreated from the centre. "Will you *really*?" And he raised locked hands over his head with delight.

Control visibly regained, Maggie gave a taut, blenched smile. "Well done, Dad," she said.

"Excuse me," said Peter. "Have you seen my rabbit?" He wasn't expecting to find Keith Ferguson at home and he looked awkwardly down at the massive brown shoes, polished like wardrobes. The man's huge proportions overwhelmed him.

"No I haven't. Has it escaped? I hope to God it hasn't found its way into my lettuces." He said this rather violently as the possibility struck him. He was as obsessive about his small patch of vegetables as he was about his beekeeping. "I'll wring its neck if it has."

"Oh." Peter dug his hands in his trouser pockets, gripping his penknife for comfort. "Well, if you see it . . ."

"Yes, yes of course. I'll go and check round for it."

It seemed to be a dismissal. Peter mumbled his thanks and went down the path. A thin, windy whistle alerted him. He looked round, seeing no-one. The whistle, a single, amateur note, was repeated.

When he glanced up he saw a pair of bare legs hanging like stamens out of the plane tree.

"Up here!" hissed Belinda. There was a faint giggling. She was with her friend Kathy.

"What is it?" he said gruffly.

"*I've* got your rabbit," she said in a loud whisper. "Hang on." And she descended the trunk slowly, searching for toe-holds, showing her knickers. "You're not supposed to look," she smiled sweetly as she touched the ground.

An uncomfortable, snorting sort of breath escaped him.

"I've got it. I've put it in our garage."

There were a number of garages built where the coach-houses of a nobler era once stood behind Wellington Gardens. She, followed by a secretive looking Kathy, took Peter to the Fergusons' garage, rolling up the grey metal door easily.

Poppy was inside a cardboard box with a seedling tray placed over the top to let air through.

"She was simple to catch," said Belinda, scratching the rabbit between its ears. Peter was rather annoyed Poppy should let someone else handle her/him so readily.

"He," said Peter. The garage smelt strongly of peat and petrol. He looked enviously at Belinda's expensive chrome and scarlet bicycle.

"I want to keep him."

"You can't."

"Why not?"

He hesitated. "Your father wouldn't let you."

"Oh yes he would." She was utterly confident. "I'll tell him you wanted me to have the rabbit."

"But I . . ."

"If you don't," Belinda enunciated slowly, poking a withered piece of parsley at the rabbit, "I'll tell your mother about the painted ladies."

He stared at her, his ears burning. She looked up at him steadily, her pale eyebrows slightly raised. Kathy tittered and stood on one leg.

"What do you mean?" he stuttered at length.

"Rod told me," she said. "What you did." She made it sound as though he alone were responsible. In a sense, this was so, but his easily inflamed sense of injustice made him feel extravagantly angry with his brother.

"Rod's a stinking liar," he told her, but she remained impassively crouching, her thighs outspread in a V shape, her eyes on his.

He made a swift, inward reversal. All right, he thought. All right. ". . . You can have them both if you like," he offered. She sprang up. To his astonishment she flung both arms around him and kissed him passionately.

He felt himself blushing a slow, dull red, as an unfamiliar sensation bolted through him.

A soft, indrawn squeak from Kathy made him collect himself. He scowled and brusquely wiped his mouth with the back of his hand. "You don't have to do that," he said loftily.

"Oh thank you, thank you! You're *fabulous*!" Belinda clasped her hands together and he felt weak.

"Stupid," he said, and shook her off when she tried to touch him.

"You'll have to get it," Belinda said. "I'm not going near that pong-y dog of yours. You could let me have the hutch too."

"I'll have to ask," he warned, suddenly afraid of his mother's temper.

"They won't mind."

He didn't ask. Only his father was at home (and he wouldn't care particularly). Peter could hear the radio playing in the kitchen and was able to creep into the back garden and drag the hutch across the lawn without being seen. Chrysanthemum thumped about a bit inside.

The two girls were playing hopscotch on the pavement outside the Makins' back gate but willingly broke off to help carry the hutch between them. The rabbit pressed one fearful eye to the wire as she was tipped back and forth, then scuttled into her darker compartment.

"I'll put it into the garage for now," Belinda obliquely ordered her friend. She had a little negotiating of her own to do. Peter wanted no part of it.

"See you!" he gasped and slipped away, his insides still feeling oddly swollen by the impact of Belinda's kiss.

"About these rabbits . . ."

Maggie stood on the Fergusons' front door step and addressed Sally Ferguson.

"Come in, won't you?"

"About these rabbits . . ." repeated Maggie following.

"Yes, are you absolutely sure you want to get rid of them?"

Peter, sulkily trailing after his mother, observed a tremor of surprise in her shoulders. She hesitated in the hall. "Get *rid* of them?" she echoed.

"You *are* sure?" repeated Sally. "I realise, now you have the dog, but still . . . I was thinking of Peter . . ."

Belinda had been very adept. Maggie's tone and demeanour perceptibly altered. "If Belinda *really* wants them," she said. "*More* important . . . if you're prepared to let her have them . . .' She sounded lost.

Peter relaxed. He'd been terrified she would insist on the rabbits' being returned . . . and *then* what? The possible consequences appalled him.

". . . it's just that I thought Keith would . . ." she was suggesting vaguely.

"Oh, he'd do anything for Belinda. *Anything*."

Sally's face was as vapid as ever, though her tone suggested feeling. Perhaps, thought Peter, Belinda has ways of blackmailing her father too. As he thought it, Keith appeared. He didn't look like a man under threat.

"Oh, there we are!" he cried. "Just the person I wanted to see!"

"I rather thought you might," said Maggie. "Are you sure it's O.K.? I don't know what these children have been fixing amongst themselves."

"Ah." He paused doubtfully, but all the adults were now pinioned by their children's stratagems. "Well, if *you're* sure," he said.

And they all laughed together in a hearty way. "Little monkeys," cried Keith affectionately. "I can fix up a run in no time."

More wire, more netting, thought Peter looking out of the Fergusons' lounge window at their trap-set garden.

"A drink . . .?"

"That's very kind."

"Keith said . . ."

"Yes, I said I should get round to that honey I promised you. *August*, already . . ." He unstoppered the decanter. "I expect you'd like to look in the hive?"

"Well, I . . ."

"Keith's so thrilled somebody's interested in his bees. I keep well clear of them." Sally made a little face. Belinda clattered into the room. "Oh, hello," she cried. "Daddy says I can have the rabbits."

"Have you said thank you, dear?"

"Thank you," Belinda repeated demurely. Maggie wavered mildly, then smiled.

Already Keith was busying himself assembling boiler suits and bee masks. While the women chattered, Belinda winked at Peter and he looked stiffly away. He didn't want to be involved with her at all. Interrupting his mother, he asked if he could go and look at the hive with her.

"Of course. Delighted." It was Keith Ferguson who answered him. He slapped Peter's back with a palm like a mat. "You can wear my stuff. They shouldn't be too troublesome at this time of evening."

"Oh I don't know . . ." murmured Maggie doubtfully, but thought better of what she'd been tempted to say. She fastened the ties of the cotton breast-piece that hung from the mask, under her arms. "Do I look funny?" she laughed.

"You do now," said Peter a minute later when she zipped herself up in Keith's boiler suit. "You look like something from Mars." And he giggled happily, sensing her mood.

They went outside. Peter was pleased that Belinda should watch him doing this even if he did look peculiar in a borrowed raincoat. It was quite hard to see properly behind the fine, black wire mesh of his veil.

Maggie chattered to Keith as they trooped across the grass. "You must know Mr. Turville . . ." she was saying as she avoided spray from the sprinkler (which, Peter reflected, was a little unnecessary after the preceding week's rain).

"What, the crackpot boatman? I do indeed. Used to hold down a very good job." Keith, whose only concessions had been a sou'wester and a pair of gauntleted gloves, began to ease the top off the hive. "What about him? Do you know him?"

"Oh, nothing," she said, "I just wondered."

"Gently does it . . . stand a bit closer Pete, old chap."

The top was removed exposing vertical sections that almost touched one another where the golden hexagonal cells had been unevenly built up by the bees. A violent communal buzzing greeted them, a mechanical sound, like something powered by electricity. There was a light fragrance of honey.

"Ugh!" Peter recoiled as the insects thudded against his cage. It felt as though they were going to fly straight into his eyes and nose.

"Christ! Oh Christ! Look out!"

Keith, viewed through a fine criss-cross of bars, had leapt back from his lowered inspection of the hive and was beating insects away from his face with unmistakable terror. Maggie, better protected, looked at him with consternation, then peered inside the hive herself.

"Good Lord!" she gasped, her features invisible. "Come here Peter . . ." And she beckoned him with a big glove.

The buzzing rose to a berserk pitch.

"Ouch! Damn! Get off! Oh bugger!" Behind them, Keith retreated, arms scything the air.

"What's happened?" Nervously, Peter steeled himself to put his head down inside the roar. The creatures were crawling thickly over the comb, concealing it from sight here and there by the density of their bodies.

"Wasps!" said Maggie. "Look . . .! They've killed all the bees." She lifted a frame out and underneath were littered small, curled corpses. "*And* they've eaten all the honey."

A few sticky traces of clear-coloured honey oozed free of the comb, but very little. The wasps sucked and buzzed and bored their way through the hive.

"Hooligans," muttered Maggie, watching them. It had been a terrible and merciless invasion.

Overhead, a jumbo jet groaned against the air.

Kit had turned up the volume to hear the commentary better. He was watching the British Heavyweight Championship.

"God Almighty," he groaned, hands to his head. "Dunn's fighting like a kipper fillet."

"It must be his bad time of the month," mused Maggie, entering. She was longing to tell what had happened but neither Rod's nor Kit's head revolved her way. Peter joined them like a flash. "I've been *missing* it!" was all he said.

"I'm sorry about the rabbits," he mumbled later, in bed, not meeting his mother's eye.

"Sorry?" said Maggie. "You're not really sorry."

He was silent. As soon as she turns the lights off, he vowed inwardly, I'll *mangle* my brother for telling Belinda. (He'd been longing to do it all day.) I'll *pulp* him.

"Still," his mother went on, absently, "I daresay Belinda will remember to feed them." She stood, looking dry and

237

withdrawn for a moment. "I'll call round there later when I see their car come back. Poor Keith . . ." Keith, at his own insistence, had been driven to the Casualty Department of the West Middlesex Hospital. He'd thrown Sally's bicarbonate of soda mixture into the sink. Maggie gave a wry smile and put her hand over her mouth.

It was signal enough for Rod. "Tell us a story, Mum . . ." He tilted his head beguilingly. Maggie checked a small shadow of exasperation. "I'll read one," she said, "I'm too tired to make one up."

And she ran a finger over the higgledy-piggledy rows of books until she found the one she wanted. Then she sat on the end of Peter's bed, making his sheets stretch pleasantly tight over him and read an Orkney tale by George Mackay Brown, a tale of the time King Hogni led his warriors against those of King Hedinn thinking that the rival chieftain had stolen his daughter Hildr from him, unable to believe Hildr had gone out of love for the lord. They fought on the island of Hoy, a battle that Hildr attempted to stop. But unable to persuade her father of the foolishness of the battle, she crept over the slain men at night turning them all to boulders of stone — only to have them rise again at dawn and continue the merciless slaughter until every man was slain, every soldier was stone.

"What happened to the enchantress Hildr?" read Maggie, her face rosy in the shell-pink pool of light. "Nobody knows, but perhaps on a spring night the wind that keens through the Trowieglen is the voice of Hildr, uttering the eternal protest of women that love is more important than war — that when the face of love appears the world is quickened with blossom and fruitfulness and seed and springs rise up, and time is renewed; but the face of war turns everything it looks upon to stone."

The boys lay silent.

"Is is true?" asked Peter wonderingly. "That you can hear her voice in the wind?"

"For those who have the ears to hear, maybe," his mother replied gently. "But," and she was caught, as if by a sudden turn of a knife below her ribs which made her dip her head sharply towards her chest. "Perhaps Hildr doesn't exist any more."

"What's happened to her?" questioned Rod anxiously, pulling his sheets up to his nose.

"Perhaps she, too, has been turned to stone," Maggie answered at length.

23

IT WAS A pearly morning.

Peter gazed at the quiet, milky world, its only tints the palest pink and grey, and thought: this must be what heaven looks like. It seemed all river. The trees swam. Even the pigeons whose colours were worn by the morning had become fabulous water fowl, rising out of thin, moving mists which streamed from their wings. Involuntarily, all of them (even Rod), kept their voices very low.

Peter, brushing through the dew behind his father and Rod, had two pocketsful of cartridges. They made his anorak weigh heavily, down to his knees. He didn't mind. It was good, this hunting feeling. Rod, he thought, as his brother turned and gave a silly, exaggerated grin of excitement, didn't understand the feeling at all. Each boy carried a 4.10.

Today, I *will* shoot something. I *will*. Peter changed his gun over to the left hand taking the greatest care to keep the barrel pointing downwards. His teeth were clenched together with tension and determination but it wasn't an unpleasant tension.

They crept low and slowly alongside the scrub and trees. Birds, singly, took off from one shadowy branch and settled wraith-like in another. It didn't seem real.

Swiftly, without a word, Kit raised his air rifle, looked down the sights, took aim and fired. The crack made the boys rock as it bellied off into the mist. It was a perfect shot. The pigeon, with a last uprising of wings, flapped, then thudded softly to the ground. The trees trembled.

"Shall I get it?" Peter whispered.

"Just a minute!" Rod was taking hurried aim at the same tree. Kit's hand, urging patience on him, was ignored. There was a lighter crack and a struggle of wings crashing against leaves.

"Good God!" whistled Kit in surprise. "You've got a quick eye."

A pigeon dropped a little from its branch, squalling and straining to regain height. For five seconds or so it seemed to remain in one position trying to hold itself up on the air, then it managed, awkwardly, to rise, battering its way back into the foliage . . . It gave two long hooting sounds of distress and fell silent.

"I got it!" Rod was jubilant.

"Hang on," Kit ordered softly, "it hasn't fallen yet."

"I'm going to fetch it."

"Well . . . all right." Kit sounded doubtful.

Damn you, damn you cried Peter inwardly as his brother went plunging through ribbons of mist to the foot of the elm and stood there, looking curiously upward, his shoulders cloaked in the soft, pearly stuff.

He waved to them to join him.

As they approached, he muttered, craning his head upwards, that he thought the bird was still hidden up there in the leaves.

"Hell." Clicking his tongue in exasperation, Kit sighed. "It's probably wounded." He stepped back to assess the tree. "You'd better climb up and get it," he said.

"What *rescue* it?" Rod couldn't comprehend that.

"I'll have to break its neck."

Neither boy let any repugnance show on his face. They both knew it was the kindest thing to do. Rod leant his gun carefully against the trunk and wandered round it, finding the best ascent. Then he jumped, hands gripping ivy-covered knobs, feet slithering and kicking until he found a secure foothold.

He was a good climber. He disappeared swiftly among the leaves, his limbs mere agents of movement above them.

"O.K.?" Kit called.

There was a pause.

"It's halfway along this branch."

They peered. They saw the branch he meant. They saw a fragment of Rod's face.

"Can you do it?"

"Yep."

In the tight silence that closed about them they saw the branch shudder and heard a terrified squawking from the bird. Rod, astride his branch, his legs now dangling visibly above them, shuffled himself along, eyes fixed on his prey.

The round ruby eyes swivelled, staring at him out of the

bird's profile. Its beak was open and blood glistened stickily on its soft grey breast. As he drew closer, screeches of fear tore out of the bird, the sounds increasing until they became a single note. The branch sank a little beneath his weight.

"I can't do it," he called, his own voice high. He was about eighteen inches away from the pigeon.

"Can't reach it?"

"Can't do it," he gulped, throat dry. He clung rigidly to the rough wood.

"Knock it down," Kit suggested and waited as the cries swelled more terribly. Every bird in the district would have flown by now. "Push it!" he advised in a low, urgent voice. "To me."

Rod seemed to be transfixed. All he could see was the small scarlet cave of the pigeon's beak and the blood that smeared its once immaculate breast.

"Can't do it!" he whimpered. The little jewelled eye was filming over.

"Oh, for God's sake!" Kit was desperate to put an end to the frightful sound.

With a sudden lunge, swaying horribly, Rod struck out. There was a succession of panic-stricken squawks, all running bleatingly into one another, and then the pigeon cartwheeled through the air.

"Well done!" Kit pounced. Peter saw his father seize the bird and then, half-stooping towards him as if in demonstration, close one hand over the bird's head, smothering it, the other over its feebly protesting wings. He brought his left knee up to give himself a means of tension, and pulled. The struggling ceased. The wings sank. The head lolled loose.

"There!" Slightly breathless, Kit eased his body straight. "O.K. now?" he called upwards.

There was a silence and then, from high among the swagged leaves, came a small, suppressed sobbing.

"Come on down." Kit's voice was kind.

Revulsion had welled up in Peter at the breaking of the pigeon's neck, but now, hearing his brother's babyish weeping, a new sensation took over. He felt strong and contemptuous. As a sign to his father that he didn't occupy the same weak territory as Rod, he uttered a long, bored sigh of despair.

"He'll be all right once he's down," confided Kit. "I expect he's a bit frightened of the climb." Raising his voice he cried, "Don't look down, just feel with your feet!"

Rod's legs felt like strings. When he reached the ground, he had stopped his mewing. The descent had demanded all his concentration. But he looked crumpled and beaten.

"It's all over," said Kit, squeezing his son's shoulders.

"Now it's my turn." Peter picked up his shotgun and gave Rod a derisive look.

"I want to go home," muttered Rod.

"All right, son," his father said and halted Peter with an upward palm. "They'll all have flown," he murmured.

They rowed home in silence, Rod stunned by his experience, Peter speechless with the white rage of the unjustly treated.

"He's a baby!"

"Now, Peter . . ."

"He's absolutely wet!"

Seeing his mother cradle Rod with such sweet pleasure, his jealousy became many-faceted, flashing and confusing him. "He spoilt my go!"

"You'll have another chance I expect," said Maggie wearily, her younger son clasped to her breast. His face was swollen and discoloured with the weeping that had rushed out of him when they'd reached home and found Maggie beating eggs in the scullery.

"I never, ever want to go again," whimpered Rod. "It's horrible. I hate it."

"He's stared death in the face," Maggie remarked over Rod's head, "and he didn't care much for the real thing."

Kit gave a short laugh. "Perhaps it was a salutary experience," he said.

"It certainly *was*," Maggie replied, and rocked her son comfortingly.

My mother, Peter thought, is *pleased*. Her expression was glowing, peaceful.

As she rocked, Rod wriggled deeper into her embrace.

"It's for the best," she murmured to him, stroking the hair from his forehead. "Now you *know*."

"I hate killing," Rod said again later as he watched the whitening of the kitchen. It was turning into a different realm, a pure cell. "It's *horrible*," he repeated fervently and then, as a dreadful thought struck him, "Will there ever be another war, Dad?"

Kit ran his brush carefully along the line between wall and

ceiling. "There's always a war somewhere," he said. "More than ever now." And he listed the little wars. Looking down at the boys over his shoulder, he smiled shamefacedly and told them how excited he'd been when the fighting had started in Ulster. "It was new," he confessed. "A chance to get out of the office. To see some action." But then, (he went on returning to his careful painting), the sickening had set in. An endless, brutish string of wars had smouldered into being. "Or perhaps we just took more notice than before . . ." He dipped the brush and wiped it carefully on the edge of the tin before extending the whiteness. Each war, he said, with its pernicious stream of dispossessed . . . Protestants, Catholics, Bengalis, Biafrans, Vietnamese, Eritreans, Cambodians, Arabs, Kurds . . . The world was at war with itself, he said, painting over the freshly prepared surface.

They listened willingly.

"But Dad," said Peter, after he'd finished and there'd been a little time to think. "*If* there was another one, a big one, a *Russian* one perhaps, wouldn't you want to go? Russia and China say, or Russia and *America*. What about that?"

Kit gave him an amused look. "I wouldn't want to leave you again," he said. "Or Mummy. It isn't fair on you."

"But *you*." Rod took up the questioning. "Wouldn't you want to go, just to see?"

"I've seen enough."

"Truthfully though," Peter persisted. "If you were completely bullet proof, wouldn't you want to then?"

"Ah well, *then* . . . completely bullet proof, eh? I might, yes."

Maggie ceased pushing her clumsy needle through the torn shorts. "What?" she said, looking up, her face half shadowed by the angled fall of lamplight. A deep incision of weariness opened darkly beneath her left eye. "What?" she repeated faintly.

"Why don't we go again tomorrow?" Rod said for the second time.

"Go . . .? Shooting, you mean?"

"Why not?"

She stared at him, absently tugging at the needle now stubbornly lodged in the thick corduroy. "I *thought* . . ." she began, but faltered, her gaze wandering away from him and back to her awkward handiwork.

"Oh not *again*." Kit looked up from his book on lay-out. "I'm knackered," he said, "by all this early rising."

"Oh, *Dad* . . ."

"We could go a *bit* later," Peter suggested, not in the least surprised by his brother's recovery. Rod never stayed down for long.

"No. I'm pooped."

"You're not *limping* any more," said Rod.

His father looked up, a slow tide of amazement stealing over his face.

"Do you know something," he said. "You're right. Did you hear that, Mags?"

"What?"

"I'm not limping any more."

"No," she responded dully, then giving him her full attention briefly, "No, it's good."

"Let me do that." Kit rose, pushing the book and papers off his knees and sank down on the sofa beside her. "Come on, fish fingers," he grinned, and took the mending from her limp hands. "Well, well . . ." he mused. "Things *are* on the up."

"Oh, go on, Dad. Just *once* more."

"Oh, for God's sake!" Maggie pressed her hands to the sides of her head.

"You can't, my darling, *change* human nature . . ." Gently Kit nibbled the thread and severing it, brought his mouth to her stiff knuckles. She didn't move.

"It's something in me, isn't it?" she muttered. "Something in me makes you want to do these things? A sort of rivalry?"

"What are you talking about, Mags?"

"You know what it does to me."

"I don't know what you're talking about," Kit said candidly.

"I'm so full of anger. I don't know why. I don't know how it got in me." She spoke rapidly but steadily in a low monotone. "The world's leaked into me. Perhaps. I don't know what it is. All I know is, the more of it there is in me, the more you manufacture in yourself. A kind of competition between us. A silent, unstated argument. Violence of a very tidy kind. And you're trying to transmit it to *them*!"

"I'm not trying to do anything of the kind," said Kit wearily, his hand still closed over hers. "We are as we are and that's that."

"Why does it have to be guns?" she went on bitterly, gazing at knuckles so white at their surface they looked like a small alpine range. "Why all the things I hate most? What are you trying to do to my children?"

244

"My darling girl, I'm trying to amuse them . . . teach them a skill. A *sport!*"

"Sport! Ha! You men and your sports. Keith with his cannibalistic rugger, you and your sporting slaughter . . ."

"They're *interested*. They can't help that."

"Look where it got you."

"You can't change human nature," he repeated softly. "It's perfectly natural."

"Human nature *has* changed," she said violently. "It *is* changing. That's what frightens me. It's becoming unnatural. Things are turning in on themselves. Against themselves."

"Nonsense."

"And it's in me too. The change. Why can't people admit it? Can't they hear it in themselves? In their voices? The things they say? The way they say them?"

"You're taking everything far too seriously," Kit said kindly. "And it's *so* sad, now's the time you could be easing up. We'll have some money soon, there's my job . . ."

But she burst out savagely, "It's not money, or shortages, or jobs that frighten me for the future. It's people! It's what's in their heads. Or what isn't . . ."

He laughed very gently, holding her to him like a baby. "What do you imagine's got into them?" he asked her tenderly, "Solid lead? Clouds of cadmium? Or a double dose of the fiendish Y chromosome . . .?"

She wouldn't be comforted. "You're not to go," she said.

"Darling Mags, *I* don't want to go. I want nothing better than to lie peacefully in my little pit at four-thirty tomorrow morning."

She was shut in, fighting her own battle.

"We could go on our own," said Peter, hoping somehow to relieve the conflict between his mother and his father.

"Of course you can't!" Maggie snapped from within her cave.

"Oh, I think they could, they're sensible enough. Today taught them something, you know," said Kit thoughtfully.

"What?"

"Care, patience . . ."

"Can we then?" Peter was excited at the prospect.

"Just because *I* shot one this morning!" jeered Rod, but not too seriously because he too wanted them to go on their own and if they argued now they might not be allowed. His instinct was shared by Peter who restricted himself to a baleful look and repeated that they *were* sensible. They *would* take care.

245

I will shoot *two*, he promised himself silently. I won't come home until I have two.

His mother opened her smudged eyes and looked at him distantly. Meeting her gaze, he was shocked by the expression they held. He saw a bleak isolation that he'd only ever before glimpsed in the very old or very ill. She made him uncomfortable with her staring but he didn't flinch.

"All right," she decided heavily. She seemed to swallow something and a small weak light was kindled in her face. "If you promise me *faithfully* you'll take care."

"They understand all the dangers." Kit was very confident about his sons. Peter was proud.

"Dad's taught us everything," he said. "Honestly."

"Yes, *honestly*," confirmed Rod.

"You must wear lifejackets if you're going to cross the river on your own . . ." She'd never insisted on it when Kit was with them, she knew how much Peter loathed his, and it seemed better not to have sulking. But now she was full of precautions they must take, from the kind of knot they must use to moor the boat, to pointing their barrels down and taking the dog.

"Why Hymie?" grumbled Rod. "He'll just frighten all the birds away." But she seemed to think Hymie afforded extra protection and, fearful that she might refuse to let them go without the dog, he gave in ungracefully.

(At *least* two, Peter was thinking. Maybe three.)

"Done!" Kit put the trousers down. "Anything else?" he enquired, anxious to make peace.

"There's a pair of socks . . ." She rummaged for them half-heartedly.

"Come on, Rod." Peter spoke with a new maturity, his voice pitched lower in his throat. "We'd better clean our guns and get things ready."

"O.K." They became companionable, serious.

"What?" said Peter as his mother spoke.

"I'll leave a picnic or something out for you," she said with a hollow attempt at cheerfulness.

"Yes, that would be good. Thanks." He sounded manly and courteous. Kit smiled to himself and made a fist inside the heel of the sock.

"It's the only way they'll learn . . ." he was saying as they went out of the room, ". . . you shouldn't really try and stop them when they're ready to take things on."

24

PETER WOKE, THINKING he was still in the cottage at Sigvales. In his half-dreaming state he'd been listening to the night sounds that travelled through the low window of his old bedroom, the active chatter and screeching of animals in their night kingdom. So many of them, it sometimes sounded as though the hills and fields teemed with animals openly rejoicing at their freedom to speak and run and stretch while the exiled animal, the king of the predators, slept. In the still and moonlit valleys, their cries were huge, uninhibited, defiant almost, although that impression was merely a trick of the night. In the day time the same cries would have been thrust under the carpet of human activity.

His eye moved over the otherness of this window and he realised he was not in the cottage but that the sound he could hear which had brought all the other echoes in its wake, was the sound of Hymie whining and scratching at the door.

He looked at the clock.

"We've slept through the alarm!"

Rod sat bolt upright. Peter shook the clock as though it were to blame.

It was ten to five. Still time enough.

(*Three*, Peter vowed to himself silently. At least.)

Rod let Hymie in and patted him. "Good dog," he said. "I expect he wanted our sandwiches."

Maggie had left two plastic boxes outside on the landing, packed with sandwiches, biscuits and apples.

"I'm hungry," said Rod, eyeing his.

"We haven't time now. We must be off."

Hurriedly, gathering up their belongings, they dressed and sped downstairs led by the yelping dog.

"Shush!" Peter hissed at him, wrestling with the kitchen door. But it was jammed. Without a pause they ran to the front door and let themselves out. The air smelt startlingly fresh and sharp outside in Wellington Gardens as though the trees had laboured peacefully all night, sucking city dust and odours into their veins. Now they rested, their cleansing done.

Curtains were drawn at all the sleeping windows. The only intimation of human life was the distant sound of a train dragging trucks along the track. It was exciting and special to be up alone at this hour. Even the dog was making extra-plaintive noises as though he felt custom were being breached and he hung back hesitantly until Rod whistled him along.

Once in the park, he bounded happily along beside them. Invisible strands of web caught at Peter's face as he ran ahead between the trees to the ferry. But while he was untying the boat Rod jumped into it followed by Hymie. "I'll row," he said. "You can do it coming back."

"Can I wear the yellow one then?" Peter pleaded, hand reaching out towards Rod's lifejacket.

"It's mine," said Rod and struggled into it, balancing expertly, feet wide apart. "Hey," he called, "do you know what Dad said when I asked why boats were girls?"

"What?" said Peter huffily, thinking, I won't argue. I don't want things spoilt. This is perfect.

"They're for having fun in!" And he tittered without really understanding the joke.

"Huh," grunted Peter, unable to think of an answer, and clambering in. He was determined to be self-restrained.

Because they were later than they had been the previous morning, the thin, pale light of early dawn had been warmed by a haze-obscured, but rising sun. Now, all was gold. Through a mist the colour of haloes, leaves glittered, tipped by the coming light. Even the water was a dark, thick gold — like Saxon plate, veined and tooled by hidden currents. Topaz slipped and fell quietly from the blades of their oars. Their jackets made crude, hard-edged abstractions against the gilded background.

Too dazzled and full of his own shimmering anticipation to speak, Peter sat behind Rod, one hand on Hymie's collar, and gazed about him. On either side of them, circles of water spread outward, discreet ripples that told of fish.

From the Sweetings bank swelled a fury of birdsong.

With Hymie obediently to heel, but uttering fretful little whimpers as though this submission vexed him, they followed much the same course as they'd followed yesterday, moving westwards along the bank until they came to the common land strewn with veiled and glowing shapes. The mist played curious tricks, revealing only half a tree or bush, making rootless growths drift above the ground. They chose a base beneath a flickering ash tree and put down what they could. Peter shared out the thick orange-bodied cartridges and they loaded them into the guns, closing the barrel with a satisfying snap. It all felt quite different without their father there.

"O.K.?" whispered Peter.

"Sure." Without even noticing it, they'd pared their language down to the minimum of a true partnership.

There wasn't long to wait. They stalked quietly. Even Hymie shared in the spirit of the thing for the moment. Together they came to a gliding halt as a number of birds rose. Then as their eyes fixed mutually on a single bird, the same thought struck each of them.

"Who shoots first?" It was Rod who asked. With a sudden access of generosity, he went on, "You have first go. I shot one yesterday, after all."

Peter, brutally torn between waves of gratitude and indignation, gaped, "You . . . you *didn't*," he stuttered. "Daddy killed it. That doesn't count."

"Of course it counts."

"It *doesn't* count."

Hymie whimpered anxiously and sat down.

Rod simply lifted his shoulders slightly and gave a long-suffering smirk. "As you like," he said, enjoying the phrase. But it was easy to see that in his heart he believed he was one pigeon ahead.

Peter held his quarrels back. He could almost feel them pressing against the bars of his chest. And then, attention deflected by the soaring of pigeons from the elm Rod had climbed yesterday, his whole demeanour acquired a fresh, hunting attention. His eyes narrowed. "Yes," he whispered to himself, "*now*."

A little raggedly, they fired together. And missed. The double crack died away. The birds flew into another tree, disappearing within shapely clusters of ormulu leaves.

"Blast it!" Dejectedly, Rod left his arms fall to his sides. Without waiting for his brother to collect himself, Peter snapped open his gun, shook out the empty cartridge and, blowing away the sharp whiff of smoke, re-loaded and raised the gun to his shoulder, swinging in a more north-westerly direction, the sun behind him. Shrouded as it was, he found the shifting brilliance of the light deceiving.

A few birds, disturbed by the crack of gunfire, were still stupidly fluttering up from their ethereal hiding places. A little wildly, Peter squeezed the trigger and felt the heavy recoil against his collar bone. Luck, not skill, guided him. As if nailed against the sky for a split second, a bird hung still, then dropped, a black kite-shape, to the ground. "I got it! I got it!" he cried gleefully, jumping from one foot to the other. He plunged off through the sparkling grasses to find it, followed by Hymie who started to bark at Peter's jubilance. Behind him, he heard Rod cry, "One all."

It was a rook. Hymie found it but was very reluctant to pick it up. He just stood over it shamefacedly. When Peter saw the bird he was surprised since he'd been looking for a soft grey shape. It lay on its back with its head twisted sideways, a big bird with a wonderful petrol sheen on its plumage. He picked it up. It felt heavy and warm. He didn't much care for the feel of it in his hands, for the slumping weight of the body and the fine vein of bone within the wing, but he had to take it to show Rod. The warmth and softness and stale feeling reminded him of something he couldn't quite remember.

"Look!" he cried, his face flushed. His approach disturbed Rod's firing position.

"One all," Rod repeated over his shoulder and vainly squeezed his trigger.

"Huh!" snorted Peter, as the echo died away. "You were just firing into space."

"So were you. One all."

All right, Peter thought. All right. One all. Now I'll shoot another.

He believed luck was favouring him. He must act quickly before the magic faded.

The sun climbed more strongly in the sky making the mist shine and he turned his back on it, facing the slinking royal snake of the river where gulls were beginning their slow swoop and circle. Paper shapes.

"What?"

"Anyway," Rod was saying, "it's got to be *pigeons*. That's the whole point of the thing."

Peter pressed his lips grimly together and said nothing. Luck, he thought. *Luck*. Be with me.

But after half an hour they'd used all but two of their cartridges and had hit nothing. The air was warming. Hymie, bored, seemed to have gone off hunting on his own account. They could hear him barking and making birds fly somewhere in the distance.

Near them, there were no birds to be seen at all. They'd fallen totally silent and the boys daren't go further inland in case they went illegally near a public highway. Maggie had been very adamant about that.

"We've been too noisy," said Peter. "Let's sit very quietly for a moment."

"We could eat our breakfast."

"All right."

They sat down, the wet grass soaking their jeans and making the fabric cling icily to their legs. Rod held a peanut butter sandwich between his teeth and re-loaded his gun with his last cartridge as Peter tore his bread in hungry rags.

"There!" Catching his brother off-guard, Rod swivelled and with a speed and elegance Peter briefly, involuntarily, admired, took aim. There was a shuddering and clattering of metallic leaves and a dark coloured pigeon flopped to the ground. Without a word, Rod removed his sandwich from between his teeth and finished eating it. Then he rose to his feet and went in search of his prize. "Two one," he declared.

Frenziedly, Peter searched the air for birds, forgetting his breakfast, but Rod's shouting and bounding (which attracted Hymie, leaping over the grass like a gazelle, his belly hair soaking) ruined any further chances.

Hymie leapt up to him wagging his whole body, licking Peter's face as he tried, clumsily, to slip the orange cartridge into the barrel. "Go away!" he cried, his voice thick with suppressed tearfulness, and Hymie hung back, his tongue lolling pinkly.

Swinging his pigeon by the legs, Rod returned. "It's getting late," he said, putting the lid back on his picnic box.

"What are you doing?" Peter was suspicious.

"Going home of course."

"You can't go home yet!"

"Why not? I can. I've used all my ammo." He continued to assemble his belongings purposefully.

"Because I've got to shoot one more," cried Peter inwardly. Aloud he said, "You can't because *I'm* rowing back. You said so." He stood there, victorious.

"I can row myself," said Rod calmly. "You can't stop me."

"That's not *fair*!" stormed Peter. "It's just not fair. You know why you're going really! You're a cheat!"

"It's getting late," Rod repeated wearily. Peter looked at his watch. It was ten past six, just after.

"There'll be people about soon," continued Rod. "And Dad said it's dangerous then."

Peter was incapable of uttering any sound. Rod might be right, but he was using the time as an excuse, to make himself appear to be the winner. "That one yesterday doesn't count!" he screamed suddenly, struggling not to cry. And furiously gathering up his clothes, shotgun and boxes, he began running towards the river. Rod, whistling the dog to heel, followed indolently.

When Rod reached the boat, Peter was already in his life-jacket. He turned his head away from Rod while he fiddled with the straps. Rod flung his pigeon in the boat and Hymie, in a single leap, bounced in after it, making the boat rock violently. The dog stood guard over the bird.

"Why are you in such a stew?" queried Rod. Peter, refusing to speak to him, jumped in hesitantly and clambered into the rowing position. The air seemed suddenly full of birds. Even a family of ducks, the ducklings now a dull colour, slid out from the bank upstream.

"Hurry up, will you!"

But Rod took his time, unloosing the rope and jumping in with a studiedly casual air. His impact, when he landed, made one oar slip out of its lock. Peter cursed inaudibly, then, "What?" he said, his head turned away as he began to pull.

"You'd better throw that rook out," repeated Rod.

"Why? Why should I?" Peter faced his brother indignantly.

"They'll be cross if they see that. You're not supposed to shoot rooks."

"I can if I want."

"Shall I throw it out for you?"

Peter, his hands full, screamed, "Put it down, you pig! Put it down!"

But Rod, seizing the black, feathered body, made a pretence of dropping it overboard. "Shall I? Shall I?"

"*Stop it!*" Peter sobbed, frustration overwhelming him. An oar slipped upwards and he fought to regain his balance. "Leave my bird alone!"

Hymie, who lay between them, raised his head nervously,

watching the bird itself as if he understood the matter of the argument. He seemed to be waiting for it to fly up.

"Dooby-dooby-doo-day! Let's throw the rook away!"

Rod, half-rising from his seat, bird swinging from his grasp, was suddenly knocked sideways as Hymie, wanting to be involved in what was either a dispute or a game, leapt for the dangling bird and hurled his full weight against Rod.

The boat rocked fearfully. With extreme, painfully stretched slowness, Rod, like a bulky yellow parcel, veered to one side, clutched fruitlessly at the air and toppled over the edge, exuberantly followed by the dog, who yelped with excitement as he flopped into the water.

Peter up-ended his oars and laughed. It was wonderful to be able to laugh. It wound out of him like a release of poison. Rod, his mouth full of water, floundered, gasping, fighting off the dog's boisterous attempts to lick his face. He uttered a gurgling yell as Peter pulled away from him. When he tried to shout again, Hymie half-leapt upon him in the water, putting his paws heavily on Rod's shoulders, momentarily sinking both of them. He seemed to be encouraged by Peter's laughter for he turned his yellow head and appeared, himself, to laugh. His jaws were wide open as once again he pushed his face in Rod's, submerging him a little below water.

Rhythmically, Peter dipped and pulled, the water streaming after him in a dull gold arrowhead. Rod can swim, he thought at first, almost humming aloud with amusement. He's got his lifejacket, he thought. And then he thought, Rod never gets hurt. And then, more slowly, he thought, the dog will rescue him.

And then, a curious deafness settled on him, a vast extension of his disability, a deafness that streamed from his ears silencing everything but the soft dip and drip of water from his blades. A deafness that was his own to control as he wished. After one long, strenuous pull, he paused briefly, resting his oars against his chest. Feeling around in his pocket, he found his last cartridge. He took it out of his pocket and threw it overboard. He heard no splash. He heard nothing. He withdrew silently from the gilded picture, from the soft, bright morning, from the little drawing of boy and dog soundlessly splashing in the water. He saw an arm upraised and spray sheeting, a glittering sheaf of water. He saw moorhens paddling.

And then, in the wide ocean of unhearing, inward voices spoke. The voice of his father speaking of the old man, speaking while he rowed, just as he, Peter, rowed now. Of the old man who, able to hear, behaved like everybody else *by refusing to listen . . . with majesty.*

One picture overlapped another in his head in dissolving focus . . . the old man, striding across the lawn, shears in one hand, a faint whine accompanying him — and the picture of smooth flowing water pierced by the small upturned dart of a dog's head.

A lightness overwhelmed him. A great happiness as though he were part of the refulgent golden light that surrounded him.

This beautiful suspension stayed with him as he completed the crossing, reached the mooring place and stepped out. There was no wobbling, no uncertainty, only a gliding ease of movement as though his wrists and heels were lightly oiled. His jacket slipped from him. The rope knotted itself silkily. He saw as he secured the boat (or thought he saw, for the pictures slipped like film through a viewing machine) the pale, blue-shirted figure of the ferryman who stood beside the door of his Ark smiling and saluting, a rope coiled round one shoulder. But he couldn't be sure, the landscape had become illusory, a series of veils he could pass through, brush aside.

He ran home on soundless feet, through the dappled avenue of chestnut trees, the river glinting beside him. He had left his possessions, all but the air gun, behind in the boat, but that didn't matter. It had all worked out. His heart sang.

A logic, a finely stitched embroidery, was being pieced together in his head. She will be glad, it spelled in shining letters, she will be pleased at an end to all the fighting. She will love me only now. We shall all be happy.

And he ran, past the silent houses, lightness making his pace easy, all the way home.

The click of the gate made him realise that the sweet anaesthesia was dissolving, but he noted the fact serenely as though observing something of somebody else. He let himself in through the front door.

The smell struck him most foully, the force of it shocking his senses back on the alert. It was the old sub-oceanic staling, fishy traces, yellow crystalline salts of the sea gathered on seaweed. But worse. It streamed into his throat and nostrils. It was a worse, a more immediate gas.

He ran to the kitchen door, shaking it in vain. Then, a new cold horror climbing into his mouth, he ran out of the house and round to the back door, but that too, was locked. The step-ladder Keith Ferguson had used to capture his swarm was still resting against the wall beside the back door. Clumsily thrusting the steps against the brickwork beside the kitchen window, he clambered up, clasping his gun fiercely under one arm.

The kitchen walls blazed white. Everything was white. The sheeted furniture, the enamel cooker, the naked body of his mother.

She lay crouched, curled up, back pressed against the door, staring at him.

He stared back.

A weight fell over him, enabling his mind to move only one slow step at a time. He took in the marble pallor of her face, the half-open mouth, the sudden upward slide of the iris, the crescent of white. He could not look at her naked body.

As if to hide herself from him, she feebly raised her arms to cross them over her face and he noted the scarlet streamers binding her wrists.

He understood directly and simply what it was she had done.
All I want is for you to be happy.
His mind worked very slowly. He was unable to move.
Just wipe all the obstacles out of the way.
Her eyes forced themselves again on his face. She was trying to speak but he could not hear through the glass. Weakly, she fell forward on her brightly bandaged arms and attempted to crawl across the floor, her face held up, her lips moving.

It came to him out of nowhere, the voice of Townson, his elderly, wizened-looking schoolfellow, saying that the bleeding of women was called the curse.

It was unreal.

He took in the unreality, the air like fog in his mouth.

Somehow she got to her feet, raising herself on the edge of the dust-sheeted table. As if conscious of her nakedness, her arms were half-raised across her breast exposing the unlovely lacerations of her wrists. Briefly, she stood in the posture of the statue.

Pushing the gun across his body into his left hand he thrust the butt against the glass. At the second attempt, the pane shattered. The tinkling of glass made sharp fragments of sound in his ears. Her lips moved.

"Help me," she mouthed, leaning her whole body towards him but not daring to leave hold of the table.

Keeping his eyes on her face to avoid the terrible whiteness of her body, he pushed the gun through the jagged aperture in the glass, breaking more fragments beneath it and, leaning as far as he could without falling, extended it over the draining board towards her.

In one wild movement she let go of the table and lunged for the barrel, holding it with both hands. Her sudden weight on the end of it nearly dragged him over the fangs of glass.

Neither could move without failing the other.

A kind of sickness rose in him.

All the weight and horror of the event rolled towards him, a dark cumulus gleaming at the edges as though a sun was eclipsing behind it.

Peter screamed. He could not move. He could not even shift his eyes from his mother's fainting gaze.

"Daddy! Daddy! Daddy!"

At first, Kit, dimly hearing the routine clangour of the house at some depth below him, stirred and turned in the luxury of dream. And then he heard, not the words, but the note of the cry that rose and entered the half-open window of his room.